- 西方語言融合東方思維 -

絕對考上 導遊+領隊

/ 英語篇 /

Tour Leader & Tour Guide

For English License

考生必讀

題型分析 v.s. 本書特色

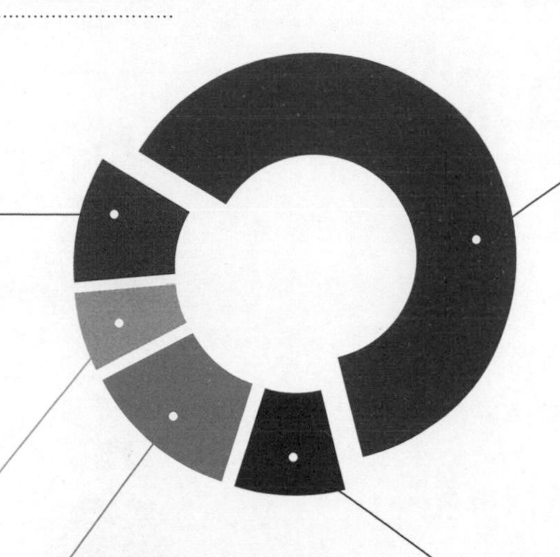

單字題型

- 單字題型占比約65~70%
- 本書根據近年測驗題型，整理分析領隊及導遊考試最常出現的1000個單字及相關字詞，幫助考生快速累積單字量，預測命題範圍

對話題型

- 領隊每年約5~10題；導遊約10~15題
- 題型涵蓋觀光旅遊、景點、交通、在地飲食文化、地理常識及自然生態等。本書根據題型收錄模擬情境對話及片語的應用

片語題型

- 領隊、導遊每年約考3~5題
- 包含情境式對話、機上緊急應變與安全處置、旅遊行程規劃等。本書特別收錄常考片語整理

閱讀測驗

- 領隊、導遊每年考10題
- 閱讀測驗命題方向，涵蓋景點介紹、行程安排、歷史文化、時事新聞及觀光政策等。文章中常會出現較艱深的單字語彙，本書並加強收錄同義詞及反義詞

文法句型

- 領隊每年約3~5題；導遊約5~8題
- 本書將近千種文法句型，分析常考題型範圍，歸納出90個重點文法規則，由淺至深，並結合考題搭配練習。考生只要加強練習解題規則，就能輕鬆拿下文法題型

計分方式

	考試日	測驗方式	考試科目	計分方式
外語領隊	3月	筆試 (占總分100%)	執業實務 執業法規 觀光資源概要 英語	▪ 執業實務、法規及觀光資源各科50題，每題2分 ▪ 英語單科80題，每題1.25分 ▪ 英語不得低於50分，筆試四科總分須達240分 ▪ 持華語資格報考單科英語，筆試不得低於60分
外語導遊	3月	第一試 筆試 (占總分75%)	執業實務 執業法規 觀光資源概要 英語	▪ 執業實務、法規及觀光資源各科50題，每題2分 ▪ 英語單科80題，每題1.25分 ▪ 英語不得低於50分，筆試四科總分須達240分 ▪ 持華語資格報考單科英語，筆試不得低於60分
	5月	第二試 口試 (占總分25%)	口試	▪ 口試60分及格

考試加分小工具

本書讀者每年創下 "全國榜首" 記錄
選對一套好的書籍，你還可以善用我們提供的各項資源
掃描QR CODE，立即享有讀者專屬服務

www.magee.tw/istudy

用聽的也能考上

本書首創「**老師語音導讀**」有聲書！即使開車或走路，用聽的也能準備。許多文字不易表達的概念，透過老師提點快速掌握必考，提升學習效果。

書籍即時修正

領隊導遊考試隨著政府政策的改變，考生須隨時更新考試資料。馬跡中心官網貼心提供最新修正與讀者交流，考生可即時更新時事、法條勘誤修正。

線上實力檢測

考生實力測驗，註冊即可免費獲得200點「**線上歷屆題庫測驗**」：

1. 註冊會員 https://www.magee.tw
2. 登入 exam.magee.tw 立即體驗。

考試經驗分享

加入「**馬跡中心**」粉絲團，取得即時考情資訊。馬跡團隊非常樂意分享我們的考試方法及帶團技巧，歡迎學校、機構課程合作 (02)2733-8118。

如馬前卒、凡是走在前、想在前
作為開路先鋒、不斷開拓、創新
穩健與踏實的足跡、一步一腳印

馬跡領隊導遊訓練中心

MAGEECUBE COMPANY

關係企業

達跡旅行社

提供領隊、導遊帶團資源及工作機會協助.業務涵蓋國內外旅遊、公司團體旅遊、畢業旅行等.

Mac. Ma 現任達跡旅行社董事長、投入旅遊市場20年以上資歷、同時為國際線專業領隊、導遊.目前擔任馬跡訓練中心班主任、致力於培養旅遊業之菁英人才.

Company Profile

我們不斷在思考的是、
如何將商品及服務做得更好、更完美
如何讓遊客都能擁有美好回憶的旅程。

我們深深知道
領隊導遊是旅行團體的靈魂
所以我們從領隊導遊訓練開始

這是一個需要專業、傳承的領域
提升旅遊業、領隊及導遊的品質與價值
是我們傳承的目標、也是一直堅持的理念

2008年 馬跡品牌創立
延續我們對於觀光產業的尊敬及發展潛力
經過多年與學員的共同努力之下
現在經常看到馬跡學員活躍於旅遊市場上
表示這個理念正被傳播著
這是讓我們最感動的地方

Mageecube

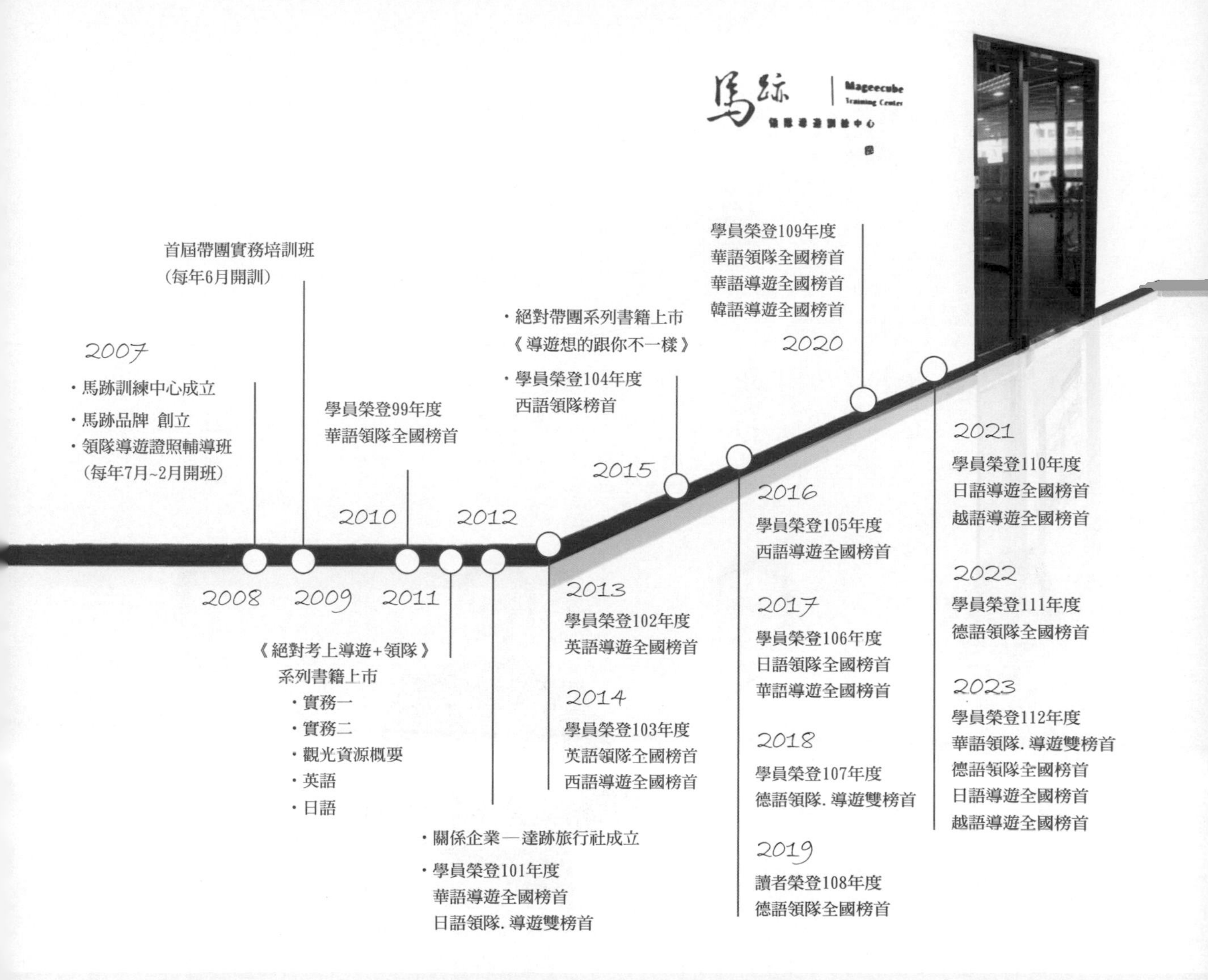

序

《絕對考上系列》書籍，集合專業訓練團隊與旅遊業資深國際領隊、導遊及旅遊從業人員，分享我們二十年來的專業，以創新思維突破傳統教學模式，藉由本書寫下我們多年考證及輔導教學的經驗，希望透過正確理念的傳達，能大幅提升領隊及導遊的質與量，打造高品質旅遊職場。

十多年來，馬跡中心成功協助數萬名考生順利考取領隊、導遊執照，更幫助無數的新手圓夢帶團！我們提供完整領隊導遊訓練(證照輔導課程、帶團人員訓練、海外帶團研習等)，並於馬跡官網 WWW.MAGEE.TW 即時更新考情資訊、法規修正、線上測驗等，以點、線、面提供全方位訓練服務。

我們衷心希望，所有有心想成為領隊、導遊的朋友，都能夢想成真！

目錄 | Contents

Unit 01

情境篇

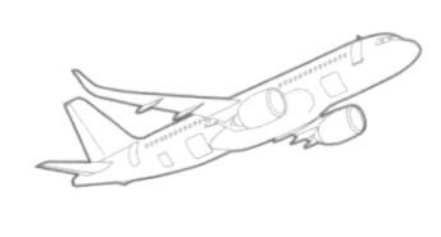

Chapter. 01

常見旅遊會話用語

Unit 02

文法篇

Chapter. 01

動詞

目錄 Contents

Unit

04

測驗篇

掃描 QR code或登入網址
www.magee.tw/istudy
用聽的也能背單字！

目錄 | Contents

Unit 05

口試篇

Chapter. 01

外語導遊第二試

Chapter. 02

文章範例

老師語音線上導讀

用聽的快速記得1000個領隊、導遊重要單字

Unit .

01.

情境篇

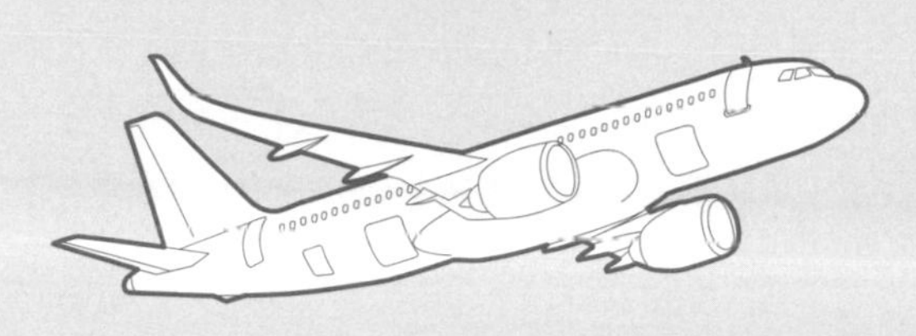

英語領隊導遊考試高分關鍵，
在於你能認得多少單字。
本單元以旅遊情境結合觀光用語，
讓考生能更熟悉命題情境，提升作答速度。
本書另歸納歷年常考1000個單字，
收錄於測驗篇單元。

Chapter. 01 | 情境 | 常見旅遊會話用語

熟悉題型情境及用語，加快解題速度！

| 英語領隊導遊考些什麼？ |

領隊導遊不完全考旅遊英語

領隊、導遊考試在英語單科的命題方向，以單字、片語、文法、對話及閱讀測驗等題型為主，試題為單選題，共80題，每題1.25分，滿分為100分。

本科目在題型設計上，常以觀光旅遊等情境命題，而在文法、片語及單字方面，實際上就和升學考程度類似。藉由本單元的實境模擬，幫助在閱讀時更快看懂題意，有效學習旅遊專有名詞之應用。根據近年考試分析，單字占比有明顯增加的趨勢，為強化考生解題速度，建議除了解基本文法句型外，更要熟悉相關字詞用法，隨時補充單字量【請參見 Unit 04.測驗篇】。

【標示下底線的情境用語，可自由替換相關字詞】

情境01 辦理登機手續 Check-in for a Flight

領隊 請問華航的報到櫃台在哪裡？
Excuse me. Where is the Check-in Counter[1] for China Airline[2] ?

【註❶】Check-in Counter 報到櫃台、boarding gate 登機門、transfer desk 轉機櫃台
【註❷】China Airline 中華航空(CI)、Eva Airways 長榮航空(BR)、Mandarin Airlines 華信航空(AE)

地勤 請問你的目的地在哪？你可以借我看你的機票嗎？
Where is your destination? Could you please show me your flight ticket?

噢，你是飛往加拿大的班機，是在第二航站；這裡是第一航站。
Oh, you're flying to Canada. It's in Terminal 2. This is Terminal 1.

右轉，順著指標走，你就會看到機場接駁電車，搭乘接駁電車就會抵達第二航廈。
Turn right[1] and follow the signs, you will see the airport skytrain. Take the airport skytrain to terminal 2.

【註❶】turn right 向右轉、turn left 向左轉、go straight 直走

領隊 我是旅遊團領隊，有30位團員，請問何時開始辦理登機？
I'm a tour leader, guiding 30 people in the group. What time can we check in ?

請問貴航空公司是團體報到或是個別報到劃位？
Excuse me, should we check-in in a group or individually ?

地勤 本航空採個別報到劃位唷！
We take individual check-in.

領隊 可以盡量將我們的座位安排在一塊嗎？
Could you please arrange our seats as close as possible ?

地勤 請讓我看一下機票和護照好嗎？
May I see the tickets and passports[1] ?

【註❶】passports 護照、identification 身分證明文件(護照、旅行證明文件等)

領隊 這是我們的護照。我們用的是電子機票，但我有帶電腦印出的影本。
Here you are. We are flying with e-tickets, but I have a printout.

地勤 由於機位超賣，我們會將您們的座位升等成商務艙。好了，這是你們的登機證。登機門是B4，請在7:30前抵達登機門。
Due to the overbooking, we'll upgrade you to business class. Okay, here are your boarding passes. The boarding gate is B4, please arrive there before 7:30.

▶ 1-4

情境 02 辦理行李託運 Bag Drop

旅客 這是我的託運行李。
This is my check-in baggage.

地勤 託運行李前，請先閱讀航空公司的託運規定與守則，請問裡面有沒有任何違禁品，例如髮品噴霧或剪刀？
Please check with the airline regulations and look at the restricted articles guidelines before checking in your lugguages. Are there any banned items in your lugguage such as hairspray or seissors?

旅客 沒有。
No.

地勤 請把它 / 它們放在磅秤上。
Please put it / them on the scale.

旅客 有超過重量限制嗎？ 行李超重須加收錢嗎？
Is it over the baggage allowance? How much do you charge for excess baggage / the overweight ?

地勤 如果你的行李超過免費行李額度，超重的部分就需要付費。
If your baggage exceeds the free checked piece and weight allowance, excess baggage charges will be applied.

你的行李超重兩公斤，你可能丟掉部份物品或將一些東西放在隨身行李中。
Your suitcase exceeds the weight limit by two kilograms. You might want to give up some items or put them away in your carry-on bag.

旅客 我有一個旅行袋。這件可以當隨身行李嗎？
I have this duffel bag. Can I take this as carry-on ?

地勤 那個袋子符合尺寸，所以可以當隨身行李。
That bag complies the dimensions, so it can take as carry-on luggage.

這是你的行李收據，請在登機前確認你的行李通過 X 光檢測機。
Here are your baggage claim receipts. Please make sure your baggage passes through the X-ray machine before you board the plane.

▶ 1-5

情境 03 通過安檢 Security Check

安檢　當通過安檢時，請把所有的手提行李放上輸送帶。
When going through the security check, you need to put all carry on luggage on the conveyor/carousel.

請清空口袋、脫下鞋子及皮帶。
Please empty your pockets and remove your shoes and belt.

請取下您的手錶，再通過一次金屬探測器。
Please remove your watch and pass through the metal detector again.

旅客　我的照相機裡有底片，我不希望底片受損。
I have a film in my camera, and I don't want to damage it.

安檢　X光機不會傷到你的底片，但如果你要的話，我們可以拿在手上檢查。
The x-ray machine won't harm your film, but we can inspect it by hand if you like.

旅客　那沒關係，就讓它直接通過機器吧。
That's OK. Go ahead and run it through the machine.

情境 04 尋找登機門 Finding the Boarding Gate

旅客　我們的班機將在20分鐘後起飛，所以我們最好快點到登機門。打擾一下，你能夠指出我們的登機門在哪嗎？
Our plane will take off in twenty minutes, so we'd better hurry to the departure gate. Excuse me, could you show us which way to our boarding gate ?

▸ 1-6

地勤 讓我看一下您的機票。嗯，您的班機在第20號登機門登機。
Let me see your ticket. OK, your flight is boarding at Gate 20.

旅客 請問如何前往第20號登機門？
Excuse me, how could I get to the Gate 20 ❶ ?

【註 ❶】Gate 20 第20號登機門、the information desk 詢問台、the transfer desk (connecting flights counter) 轉機櫃台、lounge 候機室、Ladies' room (restroom / toilet) 洗手間、currency exchange 貨幣兌換處、duty free shop 免稅店、VIP lounge 貴賓室、left luggage 行李存放處

地勤 走電扶梯下去，左轉，順著指標走到你的登機門。
Just go down ❶ the escalator ❷ , turn left and follow the signs to your gate.

【註 ❶】go down 向下(樓)、go up 向上(樓)

【註 ❷】escalator 電扶梯、lift 電梯、stairs 樓梯

情境 05 機上作業 On Board

空服員 請把行李放到上面的置物櫃。
Please place your luggage on the overhead compartment.

旅客 請幫我把包包放上去好嗎？
Would you please put the bag up there for me？

空服員 這裡的置物櫃看起來已經滿了，我們再幫您找一個新的空間。
The overhead compartment here seems to be full; we need to see if there is any space in another one.

機長 各位乘客們，午安。歡迎搭乘星宇航空118航班由紐約飛往台北的航班，我是機長Mac Ma。我們目前正以每小時400公哩的速度飛行在高度3300英呎的高空上，若您在飛行時有任何問題，歡迎隨時告訴我們的空服員，機組人員將會立即為您服務！
Good afternoon, passengers. Welcome on board. This is your captain Mac Ma speaking. First, I'd like to welcome everyone on Starlux Airlines 118. We are currently cruising at an altitude of 3,300 feet at an airspeed of 400 miles per hour. Should you have any questions, please contact our flight attendants. The cabinet crew will serve you to your satisfaction during this flight from New york to Taipei.

筆記型電腦和其他電子產品在起飛15分鐘後，以及安全帶指示燈熄滅才能使用。
Laptop computers and other electronic devices cannot be used until 15 minutes after take-off, or after the seat belt sign has been turned on prior to landing.

空服員 星宇航空很榮幸在降落前能提供小島風味給您品嚐，賓客們可以享受一系列免費的特調飲品。請問您想喝點什麼飲料？
Starlux Airlines is proud to offer you a taste of the islands even before you land! You'll enjoy a wide variety of complimentary drinks to make your flight as enjoyable as possible. What would you like to drink？

旅客 請給我一杯湛藍星空和一杯去冰的現榨柳橙汁。
I would like a glass of Sci-Fi Cosmos 2.0. and a cup of freshly squeezed orange juice[❶] without ice.

【註❶】orange juice 橘子汁、water 水、hot water 熱開水、tonic water 奎寧水、coffee 咖啡、coke 可樂、diet coke 無糖可樂、sprite 雪碧、apple juice 蘋果汁

空服員 您想要吃什麼？牛肉或是魚肉？
What would you like for dinner / lunch, beef or fish[❶] ?

【註❶】beef 牛肉、fish 魚、chicken 雞肉、pork 豬肉、rice 米飯、noodle 麵條、mashed potato 馬鈴薯泥
特殊餐食（BBML 嬰兒餐、CHML 兒童餐、VLML 蛋奶素食、VGML 嚴格素食、AVML 印度素食餐、DBML 糖尿病餐、LSML 低鹽餐、LFML 低脂肪餐）

旅客 牛肉，謝謝。
Beef, please.

▶ 1-8

不好意思，請問可以幫我整理桌子嗎？我剛吃飽。

Excuse me, could you please clean the table for me? I just finished the meal.

空服員 沒問題。

No problem.

旅客 請再給我一條毯子好嗎？ 對了，你能順便教我如何使用這個機上娛樂系統嗎？

Would you please give me an extra blanket [1]? BTW, could you show me how to operate this in-flight entertainment?

【註 ❶】blanket 毯子、pillow 枕頭、earphones 耳機

空服員 好的。你可以用觸控的方式打開螢幕。這個包含音樂、電影、新聞、資訊、電玩、電動等。你也可以在螢幕上更改語言。

Sure. You can start by touching the screen. It covers music, movies, news, information, video games, TV shows, and radio programs. You can also switch languages on the screen.

旅客 不好意思，我好像暈機了，請給我一個嘔吐袋好嗎？

Excuse me, I feel like I'm getting airsick/vomiting. May I have an airsickness bag [1]?

【註 ❶】airsickness bag 嘔吐袋、any chinese newspapers 中文報紙、magazines 雜誌

空服員 好，請您先深呼吸、放鬆身體。我幫您將座椅放倒。

Okay, please take a deep breath and relax your body. I'll help you recline the seat.

情境 06 機上換位 Change Seats on Flight

領隊 不好意思，我是○○旅遊的領隊。50A 及 50B 的客人有帶小孩，可換到更前面的座位嗎？

Excuse me, I am the tour leader from ○○ Travel. The guests in 50A and 50B are traveling with children. Is it possible to move their seats closer to the front?

空服員 我去確認一下，請稍等。

Let me check for you, please wait for a moment.

領隊 好的，謝謝您的協助。

Alright, thank you for your assistance.

空服員 讓您久等了，這兩位客人可以換到 20D 與 20E。
I apologize for the wait. These two guests can be moved to seats 20D and 20E.

領隊 謝謝你的幫忙。
Thank you for your help.

機上相關需求

- 不好意思，您介意跟我換位子嗎？
  Excuse me. Would you mind changing seats with me？
- 這個行李袋我可以掛在衣櫥裡嗎？
  Could I hang this bag in the closet？
- 請教我怎麼啟動這個 (機艙娛樂設施) 好嗎？
  Would you show me how to use this (in-flight entertainment)？
- 不好意思，我座位上方的燈開關在哪裡？
  Excuse me. Where is the switch of the light / reading light over my seat？
- 不好意思，可以麻煩您倒杯水給我？
  Excuse me. Could you bring me a cup of water？
- 麻煩請清理桌面。
  Clear the table, please.
- 不好意思，請問廁所在哪裡？
  Excuse me. Where is toilet ❶ ？

  【註 ❶】toilet 廁所；occupied 廁所有人在使用；vacant 廁所無人使用
- 我什麼時候可以買一些免稅品？
  When can I buy some duty-free goods？
- 我是否可將座位向後傾倒？
  May I recline my seat？
- 這個班機會準時抵達嗎？
  Will this flight get there on time？
- 幾點會到台北？
  What time will we arrive in Taipei？

▶ 1-10

情境 07 過境 / 轉機 Connecting Flight

旅客 我有一個轉機航班到墨爾本，但我們的抵達班機延誤了。請問我要怎麼到國內航線 / 國際航線的航站？
I had a connecting flight to Melbourne, but our arriving flight was late. How can I get to the domestic/international terminal?

抱歉，這裡是辦理過境的櫃台嗎？
Excuse me. Is this the transit counter？

地勤 別擔心，我們會協助您尋找替代方案。
Don't worries. We'll help you make alternative plans.

旅客 您可以提供給我航空公司的電話號碼讓我能打電話嗎？
Can you give me the number of the airline so that I can call?

地勤 當班機延誤時，通常航空公司會派人在抵達處協助您，今晚我們可以協助您。
The airlines always have ground crew at the arrival gate to help you when a flight is late. We can help you tonight here.

旅客 我記得當我們預定這個航班時，這個班機是今天唯一的轉機航班。
I remember that when we booked this flight, our connecting flight was the only one on this day.

地勤 通常轉機航班之間都是連接好的，如果我們今天無法提供您轉機航班，我們會查詢其他航空公司是否有空位可以讓您搭乘。
Usually the ticket is connected with other airlines. If we cannot accommodate you, perhaps another airline has some open seats to your destination.

旅客 如果我趕不上今晚的班機，我可以待在哪裡？
Where can I stay if I can't get the flight tonight?

地勤 因為我相信早上六點半就會有班機可以給您搭乘，您可以考慮住在機場附近。
Since I believe there is a flight out at 6:30 in the morning, you may consider just staying nearby the airport.

旅客 我需要自己負擔房費嗎？
Do I have to pay for the hotel?

地勤 航空公司會支付百分之五十的房費。
The airline company will pay 50% of the price.

情境 08 錯過班機 Missing a Flight

旅客 我們原本應該搭乘四點四十分的班機去紐約，但我們找不到登機門，錯過班機了。
We were supposed to be on the 4 : 40 flight to New York, but we couldn't find the gate and missed the flight.

地勤 別擔心。如果有位子，我們會安排你們搭乘下一班飛機。
Don't worry. We'll put you on the next flight if seats are available.

旅客 萬一班機客滿呢？
What happen if that flight is full ?

地勤 要是那樣，我們會將你們的名字放進候補名單的最上面，你們取得座位應該不成問題。
In that case, we'll put your names at the top of the standby list. You shouldn't have trouble getting some seats.

旅客 我們的行李怎麼辦？我們要如何提領？
What about our baggage ? How will we get them ?

地勤 你們抵達紐約後，須前往我們的行李招領處。你們的行李會在那邊。
You'll need to go to our baggage claim office when you arrive in New York. They'll be holding your baggage.

▸ 1-12

情境 09 填寫入境卡 Disembarkation Card

空服員 請填寫入境卡及行李申報單。
Please fill in the disembarkation card[1] and the Baggage Declaration Form.

請您在到移民關前，先填好這張表格。
Please fill out this form before you show yourself at the immigration.

【註 ❶】E/D card 入出境申報表(移民關通關用)、Baggage Declaration Form 行李申報單，又稱 Customs Declaration Form 海關申報單。

領隊 不好意思，我是〇〇旅遊的領隊，我姓林。我們這次團體共有 30 人，只要身上別有這款黃色牌子，都是我負責的旅客，是否可讓他們排在一起呢？
Excuse me, I'm the tour leader from 〇〇Travel. My last name is Lin. We have a total of 30 people in our group. Anyone with this yellow sign is one of my assigned passengers. Is it possible to have them all grouped together?

服務員 當然，那麼請各位排在 1 到 3 號櫃檯的隊伍後方。可否先讓我確認每位旅客的入境卡是否沒有問題？
Sure, then please have everyone line up behind counters 1 to 3. May I first verify each passenger's immigration card to see if there are any issues？

領隊 好的，我知道了，謝謝。
Okay, I understand. Thank you.

情境 10 入境審查 Entry Immigration Inspection

移民關 歡迎來到巴黎。 我可以看一下您的護照嗎？
Welcome to Paris. May I see your passport please？

領隊 這是我的護照，這是入境申請表。
Here is my passport. And this is the E/D card.

移民關 你這次旅行的目的是什麼？
What is the purpose of this trip？

領隊 觀光。
Sightseeing.

移民關 你們從哪裡來？
Where do you come from？

領隊 臺灣，台北。
Taipei, Taiwan.

移民關 你打算停留多久？
How long do you intend to stay？

領隊 我是領隊，我們會在這裡停留8天。
I'm a tour leader, and we are going to stay here for 8 days.

移民關 你的簽證期限是兩個星期，你打算待更久嗎？
This visa is good for two weeks. Do you intend to stay longer than that？

領隊 我們只是過境貴國。
We are only passing through the country.

移民關 你打算住在哪裡？
Where are you going to stay？

領隊 今晚我們會住在BigBank旅館。
We will stay at the BigBank Hotel tonight.

移民關 好的。請看著攝影鏡頭，並按下按鈕留下你的指紋。一旦您獲得批准並允許入境，機場出入境區的官員將會在您的護照上蓋章。
Okay. Please look at the camera and press the buttons to leave your fingerprints. Once you are approved and granted an admission, the official of the immigration area of the airport will stamp your passport.

情境 11 提領行李 Baggage Re-claim

旅客 我在何處可取得行李呢？
Where can I get my baggage？

地勤 下載Reclaim on Demand，它是專為未來行李提取而設計的自動化系統。可以讓乘客清楚知道他們的行李出現的時間和地點。從APP顯示，你們班機的行李會從12號輸送帶出來。
Download the app: Reclaim on Demand. It is an automated system designed for the future of baggage claim. It gives passengers the visibility regarding when and where their bag will appear. It shows that the baggages from your flight will come out on carousel number twelve.

▶ 1-14

旅客 哪裡有行李推車？
Where can I get a (luggage) cart？

地勤 在靠近門口的地方。
Near the entrance.

情境 12 失物招領處 Lost and Found

旅客 不好意思，我想通報一件行李遺失的情況。我剛剛乘坐 118 航班從東京抵達。
Excuse me, I would like to report a missing suitcase. I just arrive on flight 118 from Tokyo.

地勤 您總共遺失了幾件行李？可以請你描述一下袋子的樣式嗎？
How many pieces of baggage did you lost？ Could you describe what your bag looks like?

旅客 它是一個有黃色條紋的黑色旅行袋。
It's a black duffle bag with a yellow strap.

地勤 我可以看一下行李條嗎？
Can I see your baggage claim tag？

旅客 這是我的行李條。
Here is my claim tag.

地勤 請填寫此表格。我們將向您發放 100 美元，以便您購買所需要的東西。我們將盡可能盡快找到您的行李箱。
Please fill out this form. We will issue you up to US$100 so that you could buy the things you need. We wil try our best to locate your suitcase as quickly as possible.

旅客 找到之後可以送到飯店給我嗎？
Could you deliver it to my hotel as soon as you find it？

情境 13 海關審查 Customs Inspection

海關 您已被選中進行隨機行李搜查。請打開您的行李。您有東西要申報嗎？請將行李放在櫃台上。
You have been selected for a random luggage search. Please ope your luggage. Do you have anything to declare？ Please put your bags on the counter.

旅客 我沒有東西要申報。
I have nothing to declare.

我身上有新台幣十萬元現金。這是我們的海關申報單。
Yes, I have NT$100,000 in cash with me. This is our customs declaration.

海關 關稅是按照海關進口關稅對進出口貨物徵收的稅款。
Customs Duty is a tax imposd on import and export goods in accordance with the Customs Import Tariff.

您可以離開了。
You are free to go!

情境 14 兌換貨幣 Currency Exchange

旅客 我們想換些錢。請問匯率是多少？
We would like to change some money. What is the exchange rate？

你們有收取國際匯兌手續費嗎？
Do you charge handling fee for foreign exchange?

兌幣處 是的，我們每筆交易收取新台幣一百元。請告訴我您需要換多少。
Yes, we do. We charge NT$100 per transaction. Please tell me how much you want to change.

旅客 我要換五百元美金。
I'd like to change US$500.

兌幣處 請在兌換單上簽字，寫上你的姓名和地址，好嗎？
Would you kindly sign in the exchange form, fill in your name and address？

您要怎麼換呢？(你要什麼面額的鈔票？)
How would you like to change？

▶ 1-16

旅客 請給我六張五十元面額的、五張二十元面額以及十張十元面額的。
Please give me six fifties, five twenties, and ten tens.

兌幣處 事實上，你可以在網上購買外幣，且得到最佳的匯率。
In fact, you can order your foreign currency online and get the very best rates on your money exchange.

★ 出入境 DEPARTURE / ARRIVAL

單字	中文	單字	中文
Hand baggage	手提行李	Airport terminal	機場航廈
Accompanied Baggage	隨身行李	Airport Service Charge	機場服務費
Unaccompanied Baggage	後送行李	E/D (Embarkation / Disembarkation) Card	入出境登記卡
checked luggage	託運行李	Boarding Gate Number	登機門號碼
Excess Baggage	超重行李	Boarding Pass	登機證
In Bond Baggage	存關行李	Customs Declaration	海關申報單
Luggage tag	行李牌	Luggage claim	行李領取處
Red Line (Goods to Declare)	紅線檯 (應報稅櫃檯)	Green Line (Nothing to Declare)	綠線檯 (免報稅櫃檯)
International airport	國際機場	Identification Card	身分證明
Domestic airport	國內機場	Surname	姓
Transit	過境	First (given) name	名
Transfer	中轉	Date issue	簽發日期
Departure lounge	候機室	Expiry date	失效日期
International Vaccination Certificate	國際預防接種證明書	Yellow Book	黃皮書 (國際預防接種證明書)
Duty-fee shop	免稅店	Currency Allowance	貨幣攜帶限額
Taxi pick-up point	計程車乘車點	Life Belt	救生帶

Shuttle Bus	定時往返巴士	Disposal Bag	嘔吐袋
Rent-A-Car	租車	Oxygen Mask	氧氣面罩
Captain	機長	Loading bridge	候機室至飛機的連接通路(空橋)
Pilot	飛行員	Scheduled flight	定期班機
Flight Attendant	空服員	Non-scheduled flight	加班班機
Storage room	行李艙	Connecting flight	銜接航班
Aisle seat	走道位子	Non-stop flight	直飛航班
Center seat	中央位子	Turbulence	亂流
Window seat	靠窗位子	Airsick	暈機
Lavatory occupied	廁所有人	Jet lag	時差失調
Lavatory vacant	廁所無人	Hijack	劫機
Emergency exits	緊急出口	Crash	墜機、空難
Escape slide	救生滑梯	Hostage	人質
Ramp	扶梯	Smooth flight	平穩的飛行
Landing field	停機坪	Bumpy flight	不穩定的飛行
Control tower	控制檯	Life raft	救生艇
Boarding check	登機牌	Life vest	救生衣

▶ 1-18

情境 15 電話訂房 Phone Reservation

領隊 您好，我是○○旅遊的領隊。這次想為團體旅客訂房，麻煩替我確認空房狀況。
Hello, this is tour leader from ○○ Travel. I would like to make reservations for a group of tourists. Could you please check the availability for me？

服務員 好的，請問要預定何時呢？
Sure, may I ask when would you like to make the reservation？

領隊 10 月 15 日星期日。
Sunday, October 15th.

服務員 好的，總共需要幾間房呢？
Okay, how many rooms in total do you need？

領隊 我們總共 30 人，因此需要 15 間房。可以的話，請安排 10 間雙人床的房型，以及 5 間雙床房。
We have a total of 30 people, so we need 15 rooms. If possible, please arrange 10 rooms with double beds and 5 rooms with twin beds.

服務員 10 月 15 日可提供房間，全部房間都是禁菸房可以嗎？
Rooms are available for October 15th. By the way, all rooms are non-smoking rooms.

領隊 當然可以。順帶一提，您能告訴我有關貴飯店的設施嗎？
Sure. Could you tell me your hotel facilities？

服務員 我們有一個酒吧、健身房、游泳池、網球場和一個自助餐廳。
There are a bar, a gym, a swimming pool, tennis courts and a buffet restaurant.

領隊 太好了。謝謝您的資訊。請問飯店有提供無線網路使用嗎？
Great. Thanks for the information. Is Wi-Fi available at the hotel?

服務員 整間飯店都可使用無線網路。
A wireless internet connection is available throughout the hotel.

領隊 是否有為殘障人士提供無障礙設施，例如可調節床、淋浴座椅和無障礙通道？
Do you provide facilities for disabled people, such as adjustable beds, shower chairs, and barrier-free paths?

服務員 當然！為提供無障礙住宿環境，飯店提供輪椅客人入住的客房特色包含較低的掛衣桿、可調整的床、淋浴椅和可升高的馬桶座。對了，請問住宿當天要搭什麼交通工具過來呢？
Sure! To provide a disabled-friendly lodging environment, the features of a guest room for people in a wheelchair include lower cloth rails, an adjustable bed, a shower chair, and a raised toilet. Oh, may I know what transportation will you take on the day of check-in？

領隊 當天會包車前往，請問有停車場嗎？
We will be there by a charter vehicle. Is there a parking lot available？

服務員 有的，在您抵達時，大廳的工作人員也會協助您搬運行李，請放心。
Yes, there is. When you arrive, the staff in the lobby will assist you with luggage. Don't worry.

領隊 我知道了。可以麻煩您以 mail 寄送訂房內容確認嗎？我的 mail 是 _____，可用 mail 或電話聯繫，電話則是 886-000-000-000。
I see. Can you please send the confirmation letter via email？My email address is _____. You can also reach me by email or phone. The phone number is +886-000-000-000.

服務員 好的。之後會寄送過去。此外還有任何需特別要求的部分嗎？
Okay. I will send it over later. Is there anything else you need or any special requests？

領隊 請問能協助我們預訂歌劇票和當地導覽嗎？
Is it possible to book an opera ticket and a local tour for us？

▶ 1-20

服務員 當然可以。我們飯店的禮賓服務可以協助。
Sure. The concierge service in our hotel can help.

情境 16 訂房確認 Room Reservation Confirmation

領隊 您好，我是○○旅遊的領隊。我們現在正從機場前往飯店途中，想先與您確認今日的房間。
Hello, I'm tour leader from ○○ Travel. We are currently on our way from the airport to your hotel and would like to confirm our room arrangements with you.

服務員 您總共預約了 15 間房，其中有 10 間雙人房，5 間雙床房對嗎？
You have a total of 15 rooms reserved, including 10 double rooms and 5 twin rooms, is that correct？

領隊 是的，沒錯。現在是否能提供我們所有旅客的房間號碼呢？
Yes, that's right. Is it possible to provide the room numbers of all our guests now?

服務員 好的，我確認一下，請稍等。
Alright, let me confirm that for you. Please wait a moment.

讓您久等了。房間已經為您準備好了。
Sorry for the waiting. The rooms are ready for you.

領隊 好的，我知道了。謝謝您。我們大概再 30 分鐘會抵達，可以麻煩您先準備房間的鑰匙及早餐券嗎？
Alright, I got it. Thank you. We will arrive in about 30 minutes. Could you please prepare the room keys and breakfast vouchers in advance？

服務員 沒問題。
No problem.

情境 17 辦理入住 Check In

領隊 我有事先預約，團體名為「○○旅遊」，麻煩協助 check in。
I have made a reservation in advance, and the group is called "○○ Travel." Can you please help me with the check in？

服務員 好的，請給我所有人的護照。
Sure, please give me the passports of all the individuals.

領隊 在這邊。
Here you are.

服務員 請稍候。
Please wait a moment.

讓您久等了，這邊是所有旅客的房間鑰匙及早餐券。早餐在一樓餐廳用餐。
Thank you for your patience. Here are the room keys and breakfast vouchers for all the guests. Breakfast is served at the restaurant on the ground floor.

領隊 早餐幾點開始呢？
What time does breakfast start？

服務員 我們從六點供應至十點。
It starts from 6:00 a.m. to 10:00 a.m.

領隊 你們的餐廳提供歐陸式早餐嗎？
Does your restaurant supply a continental breakfast？

服務員 是的，我們有提供，而且是自助餐。
Yes, we do, and it's served in a buffet style.

情境 18 房間相關問題 Room-Related Questions

旅客 房間內可以使用 Wi-Fi 嗎？
Can I use Wi-Fi in the room？

服務員 可以的，密碼就是房間的號碼。
Yes, the password is the room number.

旅客 房間與房間互打內線電話時，要如何撥打呢？
How to make an intercom call between rooms?

服務員 請在房號前加 0 就能撥打了。
Please dial 0 before the room number to make an intercom call.

旅客 如果需要洗衣服務呢？
What if I need dry-cleaning service？

▶ 1-22

服務員 如您需要乾洗服務，請將您的衣物置於洗衣袋中，並填寫房間裡的表單。
If you need dry-cleaning service, please leave your clothing items in the laundry bag and fill out the form located in your room.

情境 19 客房物品賠償問題 Compensation Issues

服務員 您好，我是 ABC 飯店的大衛，請問是○○旅遊的林小姐嗎？
Hello, this is David from ABC Hotel. Is this Miss Lin from ○○ Travel？

領隊 是的，請問有什麼事？
Yes, what can I help you with？

服務員 事實上，10 月 15 日入住的房間，其中有一間房有些問題。
Actually, there is an issue with one of the rooms for the stay on October 15th.

領隊 具體情況為何？
What's the specific situation？

服務員 6010 房的冰箱壞掉，棉被也有破損。我們判斷應是人為破壞，可以請您與貴公司的旅客確認嗎？
The refrigerator❶ in Room 6010 is broken, and the blanket is also torn. We suspect it was caused by deliberate damage. Could you please verify with your company's guests？

【註 ❶】refrigerator 冰箱、blanket 被子、toilet 馬桶、light 燈、desk lamp 檯燈、bedsheet 床單、curtain 窗簾

領隊 我知道了，可以提供給我現場的照片嗎？
I understand. Can you provide me with on-site photos？

服務員 好的，現在立即傳送過去給您，麻煩您確認。
Sure, I'll send them to you right away. Please have a look and confirm.

領隊 我知道了，一旦確認後會再與您聯繫，再見。
Okay. Once I have confirmed, I will contact you again. Goodbye.

服務員 再見。
Goodbye.

領隊 您好，我是○○旅遊的領隊。請問大衛先生在嗎？
Hello. I'm the tour leader from ○○ Travel. Is Mr. David available？

服務員 您好，我是大衛。
Hello. David speaking.

領隊 我看到稍早提供的照片了。現在正前往下一個景點的途中，我已與旅客確認了，的確是我們的客人不小心弄壞的，造成不便，非常抱歉。
I've seen the photos you mentioned just now. We are currently on our way to the next destination, and I have already confirmed with the guests that it was indeed our guest who accidentally damaged it. I apologize sincerely for the inconvenience caused.

服務員 不會，能夠確認真是太好了。然而，關於維修費用，我們必須向您們要求賠償。
That's great that you helped us confirm it. However, regarding the repair cost, we still have to request for the compensation from you.

領隊 當然。賠償的部分可以請您以 mail 寄送報價單嗎？
Sure. Can you please send me the quotation for compensation by email？

服務員 可以，我們一旦確認金額將會寄送給您。
Certainly, we will send it to you as soon as we determine the amount.

領隊 感謝您的協助。
I appreciate your assistance.

情境 20 客訴問題 Customer Complaint issue

領隊 您好，我是○○旅遊的領隊。其中一位入住這裡兩晚的旅客對房間有點意見。
Hello. I'm the tour leader from ○○ Travel. One of the travelers who stayed here for two nights had a problem with the room.

服務員 請問是哪一間房呢？
Which room is it, please？

領隊 3118 號房。房間內的水龍頭一直在漏水，我們 2 小時前打電話聯繫過櫃台，櫃台回覆會前往房間確認，但我們剛剛回到房間後問題依然存在。
It's room 3118. The faucet [❶] in the room is dripping, and we contacted the front desk by phone two hours ago. They assured us that they would send someone to check, but when we returned after dinner, the issue still exist.

【註 ❶】 air conditioner 空調、washing machine 洗衣機、light 電燈

▶ 1-24

服務員 請稍等一下。
Please wait a moment.

很抱歉房間裡的水龍頭漏水所造成的不便，剛才我們的員工已前往 3118 號房確認，但看起來是短時間內無法修好的問題。
Sorry for the inconvenience of the tap dripping in the room; our staff did go to room 3118 to check, and it seems to be a problem that cannot be fixed in a short time.

領隊 請問可以更換房間嗎？
Can we change this room ?

服務員 很抱歉，今天很不巧地房間已額滿，要更換的話...
I'm sorry, but unfortunately, all the rooms are fully booked today, so if you want to change...

領隊 無論任何房型皆可，請先幫我們換到至少電燈會亮的房間。如果是比現在更小的房間，我會和客人交換房間，麻煩你們了。
Any room type will do. Please just move us to a room where at least the lights work. If it's a smaller room than what we have now, I'm willing to swap rooms with the guest. Please assist us with this.

服務員 讓您久等了。今天的話還有一間小型雙人床的房間，是否可請客人移動到林小姐的房間，林小姐再換到這一間呢？
Sorry for the waiting. We have one small double bed room available. Is it possible to move the guest to Ms. Lin's room and then move Ms. Lin to that room?

領隊 好的，麻煩了。客人的行李也麻煩你們移動。
Alright, I understand. Please proceed with moving guest's lugguages as well.

服務員 我們現在將會前往客人的房間，麻煩您告知客人。
We will head to guest's room now. Please let the guest know.

領隊 好的，麻煩您盡速處理，謝謝。
Alright, please handle it as soon as possible. Thank you.

服務員 很抱歉造成不便。
Sorry for the inconvenience.

情境 21 辦理退房 Check Out

旅客 早安，我想要提前一天離開。我的房號是 608，這是房間鑰匙，我可以現在結帳嗎？
Good morning. I'd like to leave one day earlier. My room number is 608 and here is my room key. Can I settle my bill now?

服務員 早安，我會處理付款程序。您先前有支付押金以確保預定，包含稅金和 15% 服務費，帳單金額總共 800 元，請問您要如何付款？
Good morning. I will process the payment. You pay a deposit in advance to secure the reservation. Including taxes and 15% sevice charge, your bill is $800 in total. How would you like to pay?

旅客 刷卡。
By card.

服務員 順帶一提，還有其他需要我協助的嗎？
By the way, is there anything else I can assist with you ?

旅客 飛機是今晚才要飛，行李可以先寄放這邊嗎？
My flight is leaving tonight. Can I store my luggage here temporarily ?

服務員 好的，為您保管至下午五點止。
Alright. We will keep your luggage until 5:00 PM.

★ 膳宿 ACCOMMODATION

單字	中文	單字	中文
AP (American Plan)	美式計價 (房價包括三餐)	EP (European Plan)	歐洲式計價 (房價不含餐費)
MAP (Modified American Plan)	修正美式計價 (房價包括二餐)	CP (Continental Plan)	歐陸式計價 (房價含歐式早餐)
BP (Bermuda Plan)	百慕達計價 (房價含美式早餐)	SWB (Single with Bath)	單人房
DWB (Double with Bath)	雙人一大床房	TWB (Twin with Bath)	雙人兩床房
TPL (Triple Room)	三人房	Quad Room	四人房

▶ 1-26

單字	中文	單字	中文
extra bed	加床	twin bed	兩張單人床
Connecting Room	兩房相連，房內有門互通的房間	Adjoining Room	兩房相連，房內無門互通的房間
Complimentary Room	給予免費的房間	Presidential Suite	總統套房
Courtesy Room	貴賓室	Junior Suite	標準套房
Deluxe Suite	高級套房	Rate sheets	房價表
Advance deposit	訂金	Safe Deposit Box	保險箱
air conditioner	冷氣機	hair dryer	吹風機
shampoo	洗髮精	soap	肥皂、香皂
hairspray	噴霧髮膠	comb	梳子
razor	刮鬍刀	faucet	水龍頭
toothbrush	牙刷	toothpaste	牙膏
toilet	馬桶	bidet	淨身器
toilet paper	衛生紙	bathtub / tub	浴缸
shower	蓮蓬頭	drain	排水孔
Banquet Room	宴會廳	Buffet Service	自助餐
Cocktail (Before Drink)	雞尾酒 (餐前酒)	Table Wine	佐餐酒
Liqueur (After Drink)	餐後酒	Chef	主廚
Front Office Manager	櫃檯經理	Porter	行李員
HouseKeeper	女管家	Butler	男管家
elevator	電梯	lobby	大廳
parking lot	停車場	balcony	陽臺

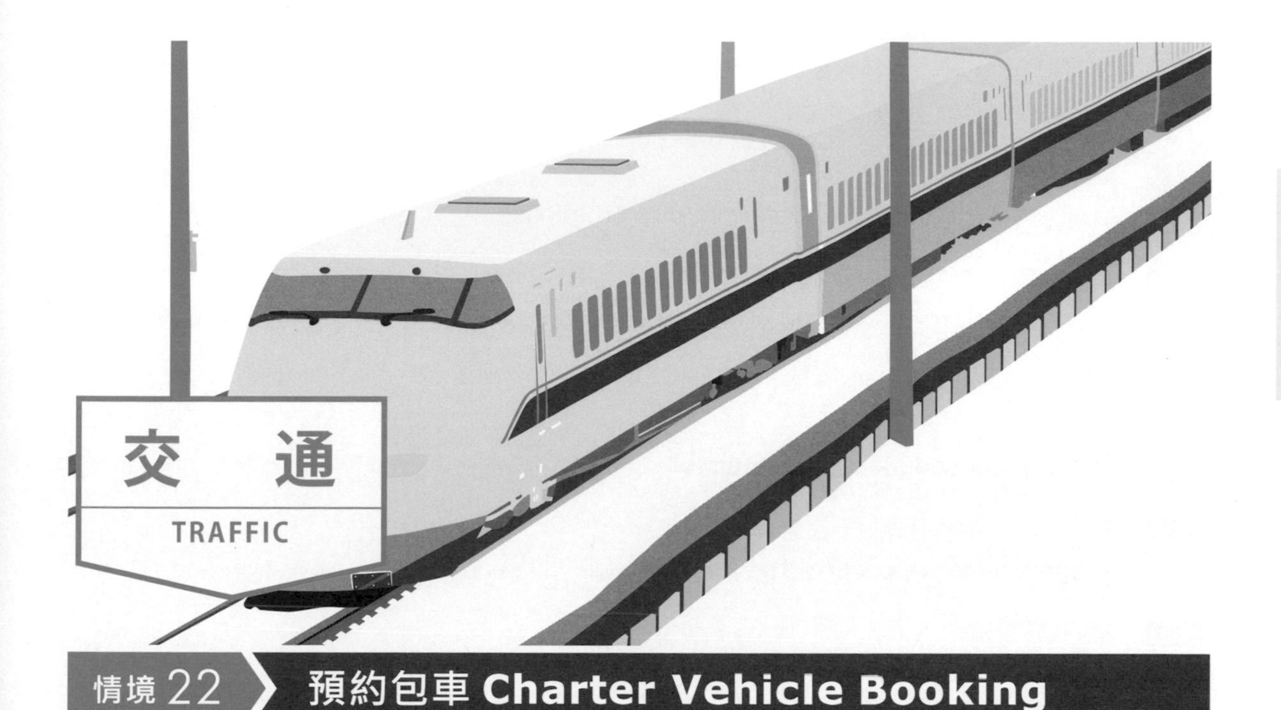

情境 22 預約包車 Charter Vehicle Booking

領隊 早安，我是○○旅遊的領隊。我們想預約包車。
Good morning. I'm the tour leader from ○○ Travel. We would like to make a reservation for a charter vehicle.

服務員 請問想要租借的日期？
May I know the date you would like to rent the vehicle？

領隊 從 10 月 15 日到 10 月 19 日，共五天。
From October 15th to October 19th, a total of five days.

服務員 人數大約多少？
What is the approximate number of people?

領隊 包括領隊我在內，共 30 人。
A total of 30 people including me as the team leader.

服務員 我知道了，請稍候。我幫您查詢適合的車種。
Got it, please wait a moment. I will check for suitable vehicle options.

領隊 謝謝。我希望盡可能讓旅客坐得舒適。
Thank you. I want to make my guests as comfortable as possible.

▸ 1-28

服務員 久等了。這段期間可為您提供車子使用。
Thank you for your patience. During that period, we can provide a vehicle for you.

領隊 謝謝，是否可提供報價單呢？
Thank you. Can you provide a quotation, please？

服務員 報價內容必須視客人的行程而定，可以先請您寄送客人的行程嗎？
The quotation will depend on the guests' itinerary. Could you please send us the guests' itinerary？

領隊 好的，之後會寄送過去。
Okay. I will send it to you later.

服務員 好的，一旦確認行程後即為您寄出報價單。
Alright, once we confirm the itinerary, we will send you the quotation.

領隊 謝謝您的協助。
Thank you for your assistance.

服務員 不客氣。
It's my pleasure.

情境 23 行程確認 Confirming the Itinerary

領隊 您好，我是臺灣○○旅遊的領隊。我們有預約 10 月 15 日至 10 月 19 日共五天的包車，請問是司機約翰先生嗎？
Hello. I'm the tour leader from ○○ Travel in Taiwan. We have booked a charter vehicle for five days from October 15th to October 19th. Are you Mr. John, our designated driver？

司機 您好，我是約翰，這趟旅程的司機。
Hello, this is John speaking, the driver for this trip.

領隊 我想先與您確認明天起的行程。
I would like to confirm the itinerary starting from tomorrow.

司機 好的，您們明天是早上 10 點抵達○○機場嗎？
Alright. Will you be at ○○ Airport at 10:00 a.m. tomorrow？

領隊 沒錯，抵達後我將立即與您聯繫，之後預計前往國家博物館。
That's correct. Once we arrive, I will contact you immediately, and we plan to head to the National Museum afterwards.

司機 好的。不過，那一帶較難停車，下車與上車地點可能會離國家博物館有一段距離。
Alright. However, it is difficult to park in that area, so the drop-off and pick-up locations may be some distance away from the National Museum.

領隊 那不是問題。
That's not a problem.

司機 再者，大型巴士禁止長時間暫停，請務必準時。
Also, long-term parking is not allowed for coaches, so please make sure that the group is puntcual.

領隊 我知道了，我會告訴客人。
No problem, I will inform the passengers.

司機 國家博物館參觀後，接著先到當地餐廳用完午餐，再回到○○飯店嗎？
Λfter visiting the National Museum, we will proceed to a local restaurant for lunch and then return to ○○ Hotel, right ?

領隊 對的，沒錯。午餐時間預計在餐廳停留一小時左右。
Yes, that's right. We expect to stop at the restaurant for about an hour during lunch time

司機 好的。接著第二天，10 月 16 日，因那間飯店前面較混亂無秩序，可以麻煩您們在隔壁停車場出口處集合嗎？
Okay, one more thing. The next day, October 16th, because the front area of that hotel is a little bit chaotic. Can I ask you to gather at the exit of the neighboring parking lot ?

領隊 好的，接下來要前往著名的市立公園觀光。
Alright, next we will proceed to the famous City Park for sightseeing.

司機 是的，當天...（下略）行程就是這樣沒錯吧？
Yes, on that day...... the itinerary is as you described, right ?

領隊 是的。明天起麻煩您了。我到機場再與您聯繫。
That's right. Thank you for your assistance. I will contact you when arriving at the airport.

司機 好的，明天見。
Alright, see you tomorrow.

▸ 1-30

★ 交通 TRAFFIC

單字	中文	單字	中文
subway station	地鐵站	periodic ticket	定期票
platform	月台	monthly ticket	月票
coin locker	投幣式置物櫃	one-way ticket	單程票
route map	路線圖	round-trip ticket	來回票
timetable	時刻表	refund	退票
peak time	尖峰時段	transfer	轉乘
turnstile	驗票閘口	transportation	交通車輛
ticket vending machine	自動售票機	shuttle	接駁車
fare	(交通工具的)票價, 車(船)費	bus stop	巴士站
sightseeing bus	觀光巴士	chartered car	包車
rent a car	租車	priority seat	博愛座
taxi	計程車	cabinet	座艙
high-speed road	高速公路	turbulence	亂流
tollbooth	收費站	sailing	航行(在海上)
toll	過路費	port / wharf	港口 / 碼頭
traffic accident	交通意外	ferry	渡輪
speeding	超速	carsickness	暈車
drunk driving	酒駕	seasickness	暈船
driver's license	駕照	budget	廉價的
vehicle registration card	行車執照	airport service	機場接送服務
destination	目的地	conductor	車掌, 隨車服務員
first class	頭等車廂		

餐 食
MEAL

情境 24 預約餐廳 Making Restaurant Reservation

導遊 您好，我是○○旅遊的領隊。我想為台灣來的團體旅客預約座位。
Hello, I am the tour leader from ○○ Travel. I would like to make a reservation for a group of tourists from Taiwan.

服務員 好的，請問日期與時間？
Sure, may I know the date and time？

導遊 7 月 1 日星期五晚上 7 點，共有 20 人。
Friday, July 1st, at 7 PM. There are a total of 20 people.

服務員 好的，請稍等。
Alright, please wait a moment.

讓您久等了，這一天晚上的團體包廂要從 8 點後才能使用，8 點可以嗎？
Thank you for waiting. The private room for groups on that evening is only available after 8 PM. Would 8 PM be acceptable？

導遊 沒問題，那就 8 點吧！
No problem, 8 PM is fine!

服務員 好的，團體名稱就用○○旅遊可以嗎？
Great, can we use the group name ○○ Travel？

導遊 可以。另外，可以先提供菜單給我們嗎？
Yes, that's fine. Also, can you provide us with the menu in advance?

▶ 1-32

服務員 好的，用電子郵件寄送可以嗎？
Sure, can we send it via email ?

導遊 好的，請寄至～。
Yes, please send it to [email address].

服務員 好的。我們待會將為您寄送套餐的菜單，再麻煩您確認。若能在來店前一天以前提供點餐內容，會讓我們更快準備您的餐點，麻煩您。
Alright. We will send you the set menu shortly, please confirm it. If you can provide us with the order details before one day prior to your visit, it would help us prepare your meal better. Thank you in advance.

導遊 好的。我確認後將再與您聯繫，謝謝。再見。
Okay. I will contact you again after confirming. Thank you. Goodbye.

服務員 再見。
Goodbye.

情境 25 點餐 Ordering

服務員 歡迎光臨，我帶您到座位上。
Welcome, please follow me to your table.

這是您預定的包廂。
This is the private room you reserved.

旅客 麻煩請提供給我菜單。
Could you please give me the menu ?

服務員 好的，在這邊。
Sure, here you go.

決定好要點什麼了嗎？
May I take your order now?

旅客 今日有什麼推薦的餐點嗎？
What are today's specials?

服務員 今日特餐是清蒸魚。您可以在魚上灑些檸檬和鹽，它附贈一份手做甜點，要不要試試？
Today's special is steamed fish. You can sprinkle the lemon and salt on the fish. It comes with a handmade dessert. Would you like to try it ?

旅客 好的，我們要在主菜清蒸魚和牛排前，加點兩道開胃菜，有雞翅、莫札瑞拉起司條、沙拉和湯，以及兩杯紅酒。
Sure, we'll order two appetizers, chicken wings and Mozzarella sticks, salad and soup before the main dishes, the steamed fish, one steak, with two glasses of red wine.

服務員 好的。請問您的牛排要如何烹調？
Okay. How would you like your steak ? /How would you like that cooked/done?

旅客 一分熟 / 三分熟 / 五分熟 / 七分熟 / 全熟。
Rare / medium rare / medium / well done.

服務員 好的，紅酒要先上嗎？
Alright, would you like the red wine served first ?

旅客 好的，麻煩您了。
Yes, please. Thank you.

服務員 這是意見調查表，再請您撥空幫我們填寫。為了符合顧客的期望並能提高餐飲的品質，您的意見對我們來說十分重要。
This is the questionnaire of the restaurant. Please take some time to finish it. To meet customers' expectations and to improve the quality of the meals, your opinion is very important to us.

情境 26 付費 Payment

旅客 我想要結帳。
Can we have the bill, please?/ Check, please.

服務員 好的，請稍等。
Okay, please wait a moment.

費用總共是 150 美元。
The total amount is US$150 dollars.

旅客 可以用信用卡支付嗎？
Do you take credit cards?/Can I pay with a credit card?

▸ 1-34

服務員 可以的，收取您的信用卡。
Yes, we take credit card.

請確認這邊的金額，再麻煩您在這裡簽名。
Please confirm the amount here, and sign on this side .

旅客 不好意思，這餐點只收費 150 美元，但收據卻顯示 250 美元，我想我是被多收費用了。
Sorry, the meal only costs US$150, but the receipt shows US$250. I think I was overcharged.

服務員 很抱歉 ，我現在馬上幫您處理。
Sorry, I am taking care of this right now.

旅客 好的，麻煩也提供給我收據。
Alright, may I have the receipt, please ?

服務員 好的，先歸還您信用卡。這邊是您的發票，感謝您光臨。
Okay. I'll return your credit card first. Here is your receipt. Thank you for dining with us.

餐食相關需求

- 不好意思，這道菜和我點的不一樣。
  Excuse me, this dish is different from what I ordered.
- 這道菜有奇怪的味道。
  There is a strange taste in this dish.
- 可以幫我將這些盤子先收下去嗎？
  Can you please clear these plates for me ?
- 可以整理一下桌面嗎？
  Could you tidy up the table, please ?
- 可以外帶嗎？
  Can I have this to take away/to go ?
- 餐點可以上快一點嗎？
  Can we have the meals served faster, please ?

★ 餐食 MEAL

單字	中文	單字	中文
supermarket	超市	convenience store	超商
buffet	自助式	wine	葡萄酒
street vendor	路邊攤	beer	啤酒
fast food	速食	curry rice	咖哩飯
fried food	油炸物	pasta	義大利麵
menu	菜單	gratin	焗烤
appetizer	開胃菜	omurice	蛋包飯
pickles	醃漬物	stew	燉菜
panna cotta	奶酪	pound cake	磅蛋糕
sundae	聖代冰淇淋	herb juice	青草茶
white gourd drink	冬瓜茶	caviar	魚子醬
ranch dressing	田園醬	mustard	黃芥末醬
mayonnaise	美乃滋	oyster sauce	蠔油
sesame oil	麻油	eggplant	茄子
white fungus	白木耳	spinach	菠菜
shaddock/pomelo	柚子 / 文旦	pitaya	火龍果
durian	榴槤	wax-apple	蓮霧
tangerine/mandarine	橘子	abalone	鮑魚
seaweed	海草	eggs benedict	班尼迪克蛋
chicken breasts	雞胸肉	chicken thighs	去骨雞腿肉
chop	切絲	dice	切塊
smoked	煙燻	numb	麻感
for here	內用	to go	外帶
snack	點心	alcoholic drinks	酒

▶ 1-36

情境 27 購物 Shopping

旅客 不好意思，這個可以試穿嗎？
Excuse me, can I try this on?

服務員 可以的，試衣間請直走到底，然後右轉。
Sure, the fitting rooms are straight ahead and then turn right at the end.

旅客 這件藍色的襯衫太寬鬆了，你有比較小的尺寸可以試穿嗎？
This blue blouse is too loose. Do you have a smaller one to try?

服務員 有的，而且今天購買可有 8 折的折扣。
Yes, here you are. And if you purchase it today, you can enjoy a 20% discount.

旅客 那請問這件藍色還有新的嗎？
Can I ask if you have a new one in this blue color?

服務員 有的。
Yes, we do.

旅客 這樣啊，那就買這件和那個紅色手提袋吧。
I see, then I'll purchase this and that red tote bag.

服務員 好的，您還需要什麼嗎？
Alright. Do you need anything else？

旅客 不用，就這樣了。
No, that will be all.

服務員 好的，請問有會員嗎？
Okay. Do you have a membership？

旅客 不，我沒有。
No, I don't.

服務員 好的，這些商品共五件，總共是 100 美元。請問要刷卡還付現？
Sure, there are five items, and the total amount of purchases is US$100. Would you like to pay by card or cash？

旅客 刷卡。
By card, please.

服務員 如果你想用信用卡支付，你可以直接在設備上刷卡。除了折扣外，我們還可以保留收據，到機場時領取增值稅退稅。
If you want to pay with a credit card, you can directly swipe the card on the device. Besides the discount, we can also keep the receipts to get a VAT (value-added tax) refund at the airport.

旅客 太好了。
That's great.

服務員 請記得在出發前三小時抵達機場進行退稅申請。
Please remember to arrive at the airport three hours prior to your departure time for tax refund.

旅客 好的，謝謝您的提醒。
Alright, thank you for the reminder.

情境 28 退貨 Return・換貨 Exchange

領隊 不好意思，我是○○旅遊的領隊。我們的客人在這裡購買吸塵器，是否能退貨或換貨呢？
Excuse me, I'm the tour leader from ○○ Travel. Our guest purchased a vacuum cleaner here and would like to know if it is possible to return or exchange it.

▶ 1-38

店員 這個商品有什麼問題嗎？
Is there any issue with the product ?

領隊 他幫朋友買到錯誤的產品型號了。
He bought the wrong type for his friend.

店員 他們有使用過嗎？
Have they used it ?

領隊 沒有，而且還沒有拆封。
No, it hasn't been unpacked yet.

店員 請問他們有保留收據嗎？
Do they have the receipt with them ?

領隊 有，在這裡。
Yes, here it is.

店員 馬上為您處理。很不幸地，本店只能換貨，無法退貨！
I will take care of this right now. Unfortunately, our store only allows exchanges, not returns.

領隊 沒關係。可以將這台吸塵器換成這個產品嗎？
That's fine. Can we exchange this vacuum cleaner for this product ?

店員 好的，不過價格不太一樣，請支付不足的部分。
Sure, but the price is different, so you'll need to pay the insufficient part.

領隊 沒問題，謝謝。
No problem, thank you.

購物相關需求

- 這是日本製的嗎？
  Is this made in Japan ?
- 有特價 / 折扣嗎？
  Is there any special price or discount ?

- 有附保證書嗎？
  Does it come with a warranty certificate？
- 這個價格含稅還未稅？
  Does the price include tax or exclude tax？
- 有中文說明書嗎？
  Is there a Chinese instruction manual？
- 可以將這個寄送到其他國家嗎？
  Can this be shipped to another country？

★ 購物 Shopping

單字	中文	單字	中文
department store	百貨公司	credit card	信用卡
wholesaler	批發商	installment payment	分期付款
auction	拍賣	pay off	一次付清
duty free shop	免稅品店	sign	簽名
business hours	營業時間	receipt	發票
business day	營業日	sales tax	消費稅
public holiday	公休日	tax included	含稅
returned	退貨	untaxed	未稅
exchanged	換貨	excluding tax	不含稅
tax refund procedure	退稅手續	cash	現金
price	價格	change	找零
cost	費用	size	尺寸
discount	打折	color	顏色
checkout counter	收銀台	fit on	試穿
payment	付款	defective	有瑕疵的
coupon	優惠券	warranty	保固

▶ 1-40

情境 29 購買票券 Purchase Tickets

旅客 請給我三張門票。
Please give me three tickets.

服務員 沒問題。
No problem.

旅客 今天還有快速通關券嗎？
Are there any fast-pass tickets available today ?

服務員 今天的快速通關券還剩下 7 項及 4 項，這裡是這兩種的介紹，要購買嗎？
There are only Express Pass with 4 items and Express Pass with 7 items left today. Here's the introduction of both types. Would you like to purchase any ?

旅客 請給我三張 4 項快速通關券。
Please give me three premium Express Pass 4.

服務員 好的，一共是 175 美元。
Alright, that will be US$175 dollars.

旅客 好的，我要用信用卡支付。
Okay, I'll pay by credit card.

服務員 收取您的信用卡。請在這邊簽名。
Sure, I'll take your credit card. Please sign here.

好的，這是您的門票。這是 4 項快速通關券。謝謝您。
Okay, here are your tickets and your four fast pass tickets. Thank you.

購物相關需求

- 有投幣式置物櫃嗎？
  Is there a coin locker ?
- 醫護室 / 洗手間在哪裡？
  Where is the medical room / restroom ?
- 哪一個設施比較空？
  Which facility is less crowded ?
- 出場後還可以再次入場嗎？
  Can I re-enter after exiting ?
- 有外文地圖嗎？
  Do you have a map in English ?
- 我的孩子迷路了，請幫幫我。
  My child is lost, please help me.
- 我想借嬰兒車。
  I'd like to borrow a stroller.
- 有 ATM 嗎？
  Is there an ATM ?
- 秀 / 電影 / 遊行 / 煙火大會 / 比賽是幾點開始？
  What time does the show / movie / parade / fireworks display / competition start ?
- 集合地點在這邊，集合時間為晚上九點整。
  The meeting point is here, and the meeting time is at exactly 9:00 PM.

▸ 1-42

情境 30 預約導覽 Reserve a Guided Tour

領隊 不好意思，我是〇〇旅遊的領隊。我們 10 月 16 日預計前往，是否可預約中文導覽呢？
Excuse me, I'm the tour leader from 〇〇 Travel. We are planning to visit your place on October 16th. Is it possible to make a reservation for a Chinese tour？

服務員 好的，大約有多少人呢？
Sure, how many people are there in the group？

領隊 全團共 30 人。
There are a total of 30 people in the group.

服務員 好的，我們可提供中文導覽，請在抵達前 30 分鐘再次以電話告知。對了，您們可先下載我們的 APP，科技技術允許客人在手機上進行虛擬遊覽，在抵達前可先瀏覽參觀博物館、世界遺產和其他景點。
Okay. We can provide a Chinese language tour, but please inform us again by phone 30 minutes before your arrival. By the way, you can download the app first before arrival, technology allows guests to go on virtual tours on their phones to see museums, world heritage sites, and other attractions before their visit.

領隊 請問有團票優惠嗎？
Is there a discount price for the group?

服務員 博物館給予學生和老年人提供優惠價。進入博物館前，請在寄物處寄存所有貴重物品和行李。
The museum offers concessions/lower price for students and elders. And before entering the museum, please check in all valuables and bags at the cloakroom.

★ 娛樂 ENTERTAINMENT

單字	中文	單字	中文
bakery	西點麵包店	shopping mall	購物中心
coffee shop	咖啡屋	department store	百貨公司
grocery store	雜貨店	train station	火車站

單字	中文
convenience store	便利商店
supermarket	超級市場
health club / gym	健身俱樂部
library	圖書館
museum	博物館、美術館
post office	郵局
hardware store	五金行
amusement park	遊樂園
theme park	主題樂園
art gallery	美術館
museum	博物館
aquarium	水族館
stadium	球場；體育場
competition	比賽
gym	健身房
massage	按摩
foot massage	腳底按摩
spa	溫泉
salon	沙龍
hair salon	美髮沙龍
stone spa	岩盤浴
yoga	瑜珈
camp	露營
hiking	登山
skiing	滑雪
group tour	團體旅遊

單字	中文
bus station	公車站
barber shop	理髮店
video store	錄影帶店
movie theater	電影院
drug store / pharmacy	藥房
clinic	診所
hospital	醫院
child-care center	托兒所 / 幼稚園
hair salon	美容院
tourist attraction	觀光地
sightseeing spot	景點
fishing	釣魚
fireworks show	煙火大會
flower viewing	賞花
moon viewing	賞月
festival	祭典
autumn leaves viewing	賞楓
ruin	遺跡
historical site	史跡
cultural heritage	文化遺產
world heritage site	世界遺產
wheelchair	輪椅
lost child	走失兒童
diaper changing station	尿布更換處（育嬰室）
admission fee	入場費用
admission ticket	入場券

▸ 1-44

單字	中文
independent travel	自由行
tourist	觀光客
travel agency	旅行社
tour guide	導遊
tour leader	領隊
free time	自由時間

單字	中文
ticket office	售票處
ticket machine	售票機
observation deck	展望台
cable car	纜車
aerial tramway	空中纜車
guidebook	旅遊書；旅遊指南

急難救助 EMERGENCY

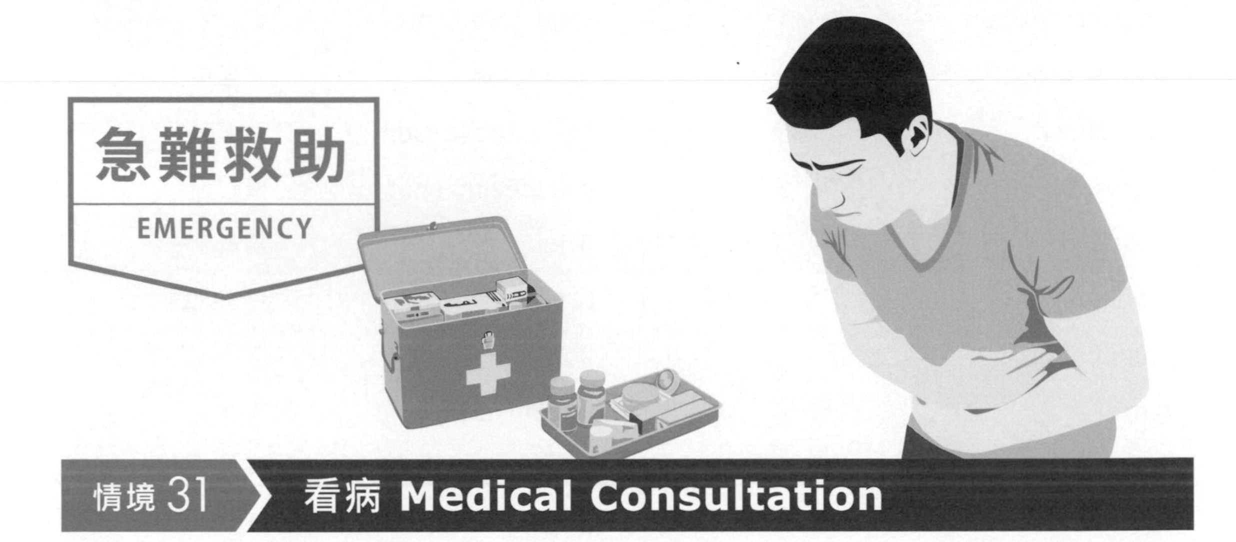

情境 31 看病 Medical Consultation

旅客 自從上星期一加入旅遊團後，我就感到身體不適。
I haven't been feeling well since I joined a tour group last Monday.

醫生 你有什麼症狀？
What are the symptoms？

旅客 我肚子不舒服，還有感冒和發燒。
Well, I have an upset stomach. I also have a cold [1] and fever.

【註 ❶】a cold 感冒、a fever 發燒、a sharp pain 刺痛、diarrhea 拉肚子、food poisoning 食物中毒、high blood pressure 高血壓、low blood pressure 低血壓、a toothache 牙齒痛、a runny nose 流鼻水、a stuffy nose 鼻塞、a high temperature 發高燒

醫生 有感覺疼痛嗎？
Do you feel any pain？

是否還有其他症狀？
Are there any other symptoms ?

旅客 肚臍這一帶會痛，也沒有食慾，有拉一點肚子，感覺噁心想嘔吐。
I feel pain around my belly button, I have no appetite, I've had some diarrhea, and I feel nauseous and want to vomit.

醫生 有吃了什麼不新鮮的食物嗎？
Have you eaten any spoiled food ?

旅客 不，我的朋友都沒有問題。只有我有這些症狀。
No, my friends don't have any issues. Only I have these symptoms.

醫生 這可能是腸胃炎。飲食請盡量清淡，像是少量稀飯或吐司，也請按時服藥。
This could be gastroenteritis. Try to stick to a light diet, such as small amounts of rice porridge or toast. Please also take your medication on time.

旅客 我會注意的，謝謝。
I will take note of that. Thank you.

情境 32 詢問醫院 Ask for a Hospital

領隊 不好意思，我是○○旅遊的領隊。請問這附近有醫院嗎？
Excuse me, I'm the tour leader for the group. Is there a hospital nearby ?

服務員 身體不舒服嗎？有什麼問題呢？
Are you feeling unwell? What seems to be the problem ?

領隊 6018 房的旅客胃很痛，似乎無法忍耐了。
The guest in room 6018 is experiencing severe stomach and seems not to endure it anymore.

服務員 距離這裡 15 分鐘車程處有間腸胃科醫院。
There is a gastroenterology hospital about 15 minutes drive from here.

領隊 可以幫我叫計程車嗎？
Could you please call a taxi for me ?

▸ 1-46

服務員 好的，請稍等。
Okay, please wait a moment.

領隊 非常感謝您的幫忙。
Thank you so much for your help.

服務員 計程車再 5 分鐘會抵達，請先讓客人到大廳等候。
The taxi will arrive in 5 minutes. Please ask the guest to come to the lobby first.

領隊 好的，我現在去叫喚他。
Alright, I will go and notify him now.

情境 33 緊急醫療 Emergency Medical

領隊 不好意思，我是○○旅遊的領隊。6020 號房的客人身體不舒服，可以幫我們叫救護車嗎？
Excuse me, I'm a tour leader from ○○ travel. A guest in room 6020 seems not feeling well. Could you please call an ambulance for us ?

醫護員 請問怎麼了嗎？
What's wrong ?

領隊 他說心臟很痛。
He says he's suffering from heart disease.

醫護員 本來心臟就有什麼疾患嗎？
Does he have any heart disease ?

領隊 他有高血壓，通常飯後就會吃藥，但今天忘記吃藥，藥物也放在家裡。
He has hypertension, and he needs to takes medicine after meals everyday, but he forgot to take it today, and the medicine is at home.

醫護員 好的。現在會送往距離這裡最近的醫院，請領隊一同前往。
I see. The guest will be taken to the nearest hospital. The tour leader please come together.

領隊 好，謝謝您的幫忙。
Thank you, I appreciate your help.

情境 34 掛號 Register

櫃員 下一位。
Next, please.

領隊 這位先生是台灣來的旅客，並沒有購買旅行保險。
This gentleman is a tourist from Taiwan and does not have travel insurance.

櫃員 這樣的話費用會比較貴喔，沒關係嗎？
In that case, the cost will be relatively higher. Is that okay？

領隊 沒關係，因為痛到實在無法忍耐，我想還是先請醫師看一看比較好。
It's okay. The pain is unbearable, and I think it's better to have a doctor take a look first.

櫃員 那請填寫這份表格。另外，請提供患者的護照。
Then please fill out this form. Also, please provide the patient's passport.

領隊 好的。
Sure.

櫃員 這樣就可以了。請在那邊稍等一下。
That's all we need. Please wait over there for a moment.

領隊 好的，謝謝。
Okay, thank you.

情境 35 領藥 Getting Medication

旅客 醫生給了我一張處方箋，讓我到藥房拿藥。
The doctor wrote me a prescription and asked me to get it filled at the pharmacy.

藥劑師 好的。請問是 Emma 小姐嗎？
Alright. Is it Miss Emma？

旅客 是的。請問我一天要吃幾次藥？
Yes. How many times a day should I take this？

▶ 1-48

藥劑師 藥袋裡有使用說明，使用前請仔細閱讀。
The directions are in the medicine bag. Read them carefully before you use it.

旅客 好，謝謝。
Okay, thank you.

情境 36 報案 Report a Crime

旅客 不好意思，我想報案遺失物，我在旅途中遺失了護照。
I would like to report a lost item. I lose my passport during the trip.

警察 我明白了。請先冷靜下來，告訴我發生了什麼事。
I see. Please calm down and tell me what happened.

旅客 好的。我今天下午一點左右從機場出境，晚上回到飯店才發現護照不見了。
Yes. I left the airport around 1 PM today and when I returned to the hotel in the evening, I noticed my passport was missing.

警察 有沒有可能掉在什麼地方？
Is it possible that you dropped it somewhere？

旅客 我記得出境後就收進包包，完全想不起來掉在哪裡。
I remember putting it back in my bag after leaving the airport, but I can't recall where it might have fallen out.

警察 請先用英語填寫這份文件。接著，請與台北經濟文化辦事處聯絡。
Please start by filling out this form in English. Next, please get in touch with the Taipei Economic and Cultural Representative Office.

旅客 好的，勞您費心了。
Thank you. I'm sorry for the trouble.

警察 回國後，必須到大使館重新申辦一本新的護照。
You must go to the embassy to renew your passport after returning to your country.

★ 急難救助 EMERGENCY

單字	中文	單字	中文
hospital	醫院	burn	燒燙傷
clinic	診所	frostbite	凍傷
ambulance	救護車	atopic dermatitis	過敏性皮膚炎
emergency room	急診室	period pain	生理痛
physician	醫師; 內科醫師	pregnancy	懷孕
registration counter	掛號櫃台	miscarriage	流產
health insurance card	健保卡	disease / illness / sickness	疾病
medical certificate	診斷書	virus	病毒
examination	檢查	symptom	症狀
consultation	診察	pain / ache	疼痛
hospitalization	住院	headache	頭痛
surgery	手術	fever	發燒
discharge	出院	sore throat	喉嚨痛
nursing	看護	stomachache	肚子痛
hurt; injured	受傷	toothache	牙齒痛
seriously hurt / serious injury	重傷	chest pain	胸痛
minor injury	輕傷	arm pain	手臂痛
abrasion / scrape	擦傷	leg pain	腳痛
sprain	扭傷	cough	咳嗽
fracture	骨折	runny nose	流鼻水
convulsion / spasm	痙攣	allergy	過敏
pharmacy	藥局	influenza	流行性感冒
drugstore	藥妝店	vomit	嘔吐

▶ 1-50

單字	中文	單字	中文
first aid kit	急救箱	diarrhea	腹瀉
prescription	處方箋	food poisoning	食物中毒
side effect	副作用	indigestion	消化不良
earthquake	地震	gastritis	胃炎
typhoon	颱風	contagion	傳染病
volcanic eruption	火山爆發	capsule	膠囊
thunder	打雷	syrup	藥水
falling stone	落石	cold medicine	感冒藥
mudslide	土石流	analgesic	解熱鎮痛劑
snowslide	雪崩	antibiotics	抗生素
fire alarm	火災警報器	smoke detector	煙霧偵測器

| **Right** 的由來 |

Right 是右邊的、正確的意思。在西方，人們普遍認為右邊代表吉利，左邊則代表凶兆。在觀鳥占卜時，如果鳥從右側飛入代表吉利，稱為「**dexter**」，表示右邊的、幸運的意思；如果鳥從左側飛入則表示凶象，稱為「**sinister**」，表示左邊的、凶兆的意思。

同樣在 **Right** 一詞，既表示右邊，也有正確的意思；而 **left** 則表示左邊，也有弱、愚蠢、卑賤的含義。在聖經中，末日審判時，神讓善人站在右邊，表示上天堂；而惡人站在左邊，則下地獄。另一方面，在多數國家的婚禮，新娘站在新郎的左邊，有女性屬於次要地位的象徵。

Unit .

02.

文法篇

文法的規則，
目的在快速拆解句子，破解題型，
使考生有更充裕的時間作答。
文法其實並不難，
本單元整理常考『九十種文法規則』，
即使看不懂單字，也能輕鬆破題！

Chapter. 01 | 文法 | 動詞

善用動詞規則及時態，正確表達句意

動詞

■ 動詞為句子的靈魂，用來表示主詞動作或狀態的詞，也就是說，沒有動詞就不能構成一個完整的句子。了解動詞的種類與其時間狀態，就能知道句子所代表的語態、語氣及意義。

使役動詞

文法 01 完全及物動詞（需要有受詞）

❶ **S + get + O +** [**to Vr (active)** / **Vpp. (passive)**]

❷ **S +** [**make** / **have**] **+ O +** [**Vr (active)** / **Vpp. (passive)**]

❸ **S + let + O +** [**Vr (active)** / **be Vpp. (passive)**]

❹ **S + be + made + to + V**

❺ **S + help + O +** [**(to) + Vr** / **with + N**]

說明 使另一個動作發生的動詞(let,make,have,bid,help)，即稱為使役動詞 (Causative Verb)。使役動詞亦屬於連綴動詞，其後的受詞補語若是動詞，原形動詞表主動狀態(不可用現在分詞)，過去分詞表被動狀態，help之後亦可使用不定詞。

小試一下

( ) 1. Please get someone _____ the air-conditioner in my room. 94導
(A)fixed (B)fixing (C)to fix (D)fix 答 C
(請找個人修理我房間的冷氣。)

不定詞

文法 02 Verb + to Vr

want 想要	**need** 需要	**would like** 想要	+ to Vr
learn 學習	**fear** 害怕	**mean** 表示...的意思	
pretend 假裝	**attempt** 企圖	**offer** 提供	
refuse 拒絕	**promise** 允諾	**endeavor** 努力	
manage 管理	**get** 帶領	**believe** 相信	
introduce 引進	**cause** 引起	**teach** 教導	
lead 領導	**enable** 使能夠		

說明「句子裡如果有兩個動詞(V1和V2)在一起，一定會打架」，因此句子裡不允許有兩個動詞碰在一起。避免兩個動詞打架的方法有兩種：

❶在 V2 後面加上「ing」→「V1 + V2ing」，Ving為動名詞。

❷用「to」將兩者分開→「V1 to V2」，「to V」為不定詞。

- 「to V」全稱為「動詞不定詞」，不受主語的人稱和數的限制，是一種非限定動詞。不定詞具有動詞、名詞、形容詞和副詞的特徵，雖有「一般態」、「進行態」、「完成態」的變化，卻不受「現在、過去、將來」的時間限制。

補充 做為獨立用法的重要片語：

To begin with	首先	To be brief	簡言之
So to speak	可以這麼說	To make the story short	簡言之
Needless to say	不用說	To be frank with you	坦白地說
To do (sb) justice	公平而論	To be plain with you	坦白地說
Suffice it to say that	不提別的	To say nothing of	毋庸置疑
To make matters worse	更糟的是	Not to mention	毋庸置疑

意志動詞

文法 03 意志動詞

S + [verb] + that + S + (should) + Vr / O + (not) to Vr

advise 勸告	**move** 提議
advocate 提倡	**propose** 提議
agree 同意	**prefer** 寧願
allow 允許	**pray** 懇求
appoint 下令	**provide** 規定
arrange 安排	**permit** 允許
argue 主張	**persist** 堅持
ask 要求	**petition** 請願
command 命令	**persuade** 說服
claim 要求	**warn** 告誡
compel 強迫	**request** 要求
decide 決定	**recommend** 提議
decree 命令	**require** 要求
demand 要求	**resolve** 決心
desire 請求	**tell** 吩咐
determine 決定	**remind** 提醒
direct 命令	**order** 命令
dictate 命令	**object** 反對
expect 希望	**sentence** 判決
forbid 禁止	**specify** 指定
force 強迫	**suggest** 建議
insist 堅持	**stipulate** 規定
intend 打算	**urge** 主張
legislate 立法	**wish** 希望
maintain 主張	**hope** 希望

+ **that + S + (should) + Vr**
+ **O + (not) to Vr**

說明 「命令、建議、要求、堅持、強迫、希望、勸告」意味的字，不論是名詞、動詞或形容詞，其所接句子中的動詞都要用「Vr」或「should+Vr」，其中，should常被省略，所接受詞之後，要接不定詞to做為受詞補語。

小試一下

( ) 1. Now that our passports have been stolen, Officer, what do you recommend ____?
(A)to us doing (B)us do (C)us to do (D)we will do 95導
(既然我們的護照已被偷，警官，你建議我們去做些什麼？)
答 C

情緒動詞

文法 04 情緒動詞

❶ 物 + 情緒動詞 + 人 (事物使人)

- **His words *surprised* me.**

❷ 物 + be+情緒動詞-ing + to + 人 (事物令人)

說明 現在分詞當形容詞使用，用來修飾物。

- **His words *were surprising to* me.**

❸ 人 + be+情緒動詞-ed + Prep. + 物 (人對事物感到)

說明 過去分詞當形容詞使用，用來修飾人。

- **I *was surprised at* his words.**

■ 情緒動詞：用來修飾人或物喜怒愛樂

bore	使無聊	**inspire**	鼓舞	**satisfy**	使滿意
excite	使興奮	**insult**	污辱	**awaken**	喚醒
stun	使震驚	**attract**	吸引	**exhaust**	耗盡
tire	使厭倦	**humiliate**	羞辱	**embarrass**	使尷尬
scare	使害怕	**charm**	迷惑	**disappoint**	使失望
amuse	娛樂	**surprise**	使驚訝	**discourage**	使氣餒
interest	興趣	**depress**	使沮喪	**encourage**	鼓勵
appeal	吸引	**amaze**	使驚訝	**entertain**	娛樂

小試一下

( ) 1. Having secured political and economic stability and overcome severe flooding, Thailand's ability to bounce back is ______ to investors. 102導

(A)annoying (B)enduring (C)appealing (D)scaffolding 答 C

(有著穩當的政治和經濟安定並克服了嚴重的洪水氾濫，泰國有能力在受挫折後恢復原狀是因為吸引投資者。)

動名詞

文法 05 動名詞可做為主詞、受詞及補語

❶ 動名詞做主詞：***Smoking* is bad for health.** 抽菸對身體不好

❷ 動名詞做受詞：**My sister is busy (in) *cleaning* up the room.**
(妹妹正忙著收拾房間)

❸ 動名詞做補語：**Seeing is *believing*.** 眼見為憑

註 Her favorite hobby is dancing. (動名詞做be的補語，不是進行式)
She is dancing with her friends now. (現在分詞和be動詞構成進行式)

說明 動名詞是具「動詞的外表」與「名詞的內涵 」的詞類，也就是將動詞名詞化，也就是說動詞當名詞用，亦具有進行和主動的意思。

文法 06 動名詞和現在分詞做形容詞時，意義上的差異

❶ 動名詞做形容詞，表示其所修飾的名詞，非行為者

- a checking counter (= a counter for checking) 收銀臺
- drinking water (= water for drinking) 飲用水

❷ 現在分詞做形容詞，表示其所修飾的名詞，即行為者

- a smoking man. (= a man who is smoking.) 吸菸的男人
- I prefer to read than play. (= I prefer reading to playing.)
(我較喜歡讀書，勝於玩耍。)

註 like to + V「現在去做」; like V-ing 「某事」。

文法 07 動詞後用動名詞與不定詞而意義不同者

1 forgot

- I forgot to turn the light off. (我忘了關燈。)

  → I forgot turning the light off. (我有關燈卻忘了。)

  註 forget to + V「忘了去做」; forget V-ing「忘了做過的事」。

2 remember

- I will remember to see that movie. (我會記得去看那部電影。)

  → I remember seeing that movie. (我記得看過那部電影。)

  註 remember to + V「記得去做」; remember V-ing「記得做過的事」。

3 stop

- After working all day, he stopped (working) to take a rest.

  → He stopped running when he felt tired.

  註 stop to + V「停下手邊的事去做別的事」; stop V-ing「停下手邊的事」。

4 try

- I never do this before, but I'll try my best to do it. (=make an attempt)

  → I did it before, let me try (doing it). (= make an experience)

  註 try to + V表示「之前沒經驗」; try V-ing表示「之前有經驗」。

5 go

- My father ***goes*** to sleep at 10 every night.

  → My father ***goes*** jogging every morning.

  註 go to + V表示去做「例行公事」; go V-ing表示去「休閒娛樂」。

6 go on

- After math, he went on to study English. (讀數學後他繼續讀英文。)

  → He went on studying English for 2 hours. (他一口氣讀了兩小時英文。)

  註 go on to + V表示接著去做「另一事」; go on V-ing表示繼續「同一事」。

7 **regret**

- I regret to say that. (我真不願去這麼說 [可是不得不說，還沒說]。)
  → I regret saying that. (我真後悔這麼說 [可是已經說]。)
- I regret not to do that. (我真後悔沒去做那件事。)
  → I don't regret doing that. (我不後悔這麼做。)

  註 regret not to + V「後悔沒去做」； do not regret + V-ing「不後悔做了」

文法 08 動詞後可以接不定詞或動名詞

like 喜歡	**begin** 開始	**dislike** 不喜歡
love 喜愛	**stand** 忍受	**endure** 忍受
start 開始	**resist** 忍受	**tolerate** 忍受
bear 忍受	**abhor** 憎恨	**detest** 憎恨
hate 討厭	**dread** 害怕	**intend** 意欲、打算
omit 省略	**cease** 停止	**disdain** 不屑
commence 開始	**continue** 繼續	**prefer** 偏好
neglect 忽略	**regret** 後悔	**be worthwhile** 值得

文法 09 動詞後接不定詞當受詞，具未來定義（尚未開始做）

ask 要求	**decide** 決定	**need** 必須
advise 忠告	**deserve** 值得	**order** 命令
allow 允許	**encourage** 鼓勵	**seem** 似乎
appear 顯得	**expect** 期待	**refuse** 拒絕
agree 同意	**force** 強制	**teach** 教導
beg 乞求	**prepare** 準備	**want** 想要
care 在乎	**promise** 承諾	**tell** 告訴
command 命令	**hope** 希望	**wish** 希望
desire 渴望	**help** 幫助	

文法 10 動詞後接動名詞（已經開始做，但尚未做完之意）

keep 繼續	**enjoy** 享受	**finish** 完成
deny 拒絕	**quit** 終止	**miss** 錯過
escape 逃避	**imagine** 想像	**defer** 延遲
postpone 延後	**practice** 練習	**avoid** 避免
consider 考慮	**appreciate** 欣賞	

- You must avoid making the same mistakes.
- If you want to gain good grades, you have to keep studying hard.

文法 11 Verb + Ving（接 Ving 當受詞的動詞）

enjoy 享受	**practice** 練習	**consider** 考慮	
mind 介意	**avoid** 避免	**suggest** 建議	
spend 花費	**admit** 允許	**appreciate** 感激	
risk 冒險	**miss** 錯過	**stand** 處於...狀態	
recall 回想	**delay** 延遲	**anticipate** 預料	
resist 抵抗	**excuse** 辯解	**imagine** 想像	**+ Ving/N.**
deny 否認	**fancy** 幻想	**propose** 提議	
keep 保持	**postpone** 延遲	**resent** 厭惡	
forgive 原諒	**recollect** 回憶	**give up** 放棄	
involve 涉入	**stop** 停止	**feel like** 想要	
finish 完成	**escape** 躲避		

- Would you mind opening the window? 開個窗透透氣好嗎?

have +
- **difficulty** (對…事情有困難)
- **trouble** (對…事情有難題)
- **problems** (對…事情有問題)
- **fun** (享受)
- **pleasure** (愉悅的做某事)
- **a good/ hard time** (開心的 / 艱困的做某事)

+ (in) + Ving/N.

- I have more and more fun doing my math exercises. 數學題越做越有趣。
- I have trouble doing my math exercises. 數學題越做越頭大。

情境篇 文法篇 片語篇 測驗篇 口試篇

when it comes to (當涉及到) **look forward to (期待)**	] **+ Ving/N.**

說明 介詞後以動名詞做受詞，不可用不定詞

I feel like *crying*. (○)
I feel like *to cry*. (X)

小試一下

( ) 1. The school boys stopped ____ the stray dog when their teacher went up to them.
(A)bully (B)bullied (C)to be bullying (D)bullying 101領
(學校的男孩中止欺凌流浪狗，當他們老師走向他們的時候。) 答 D

文法 12 Verb... from + Ving

keep 保持 **stop** 停止 **deter** 阻止 **prevent** 預防 **hinder** 阻礙 **defend** 辯護 **protect** 保護 **save** 挽救 **rescue** 拯救 **shelter** 庇護 **forbid** 禁止 **protect** 保護 **ban, bar** 阻擋 **restrain** 抑制 **discourage** 阻礙 **dissuade** 勸阻	] **+ sb./sth. + from + N/Ving**

分詞

- 分詞是由動詞分出來。因需求不同時，有不同的稱呼，於是把動詞加「-ing」變成名詞，當遇到英文又詞窮，欠缺的不是名詞，而是形容詞時，分詞就是由動詞變出來的形容詞。
- 現在分詞，會在動詞加上「-ing」；而過去分詞則是在動詞加上「-ed」。

文法 13 分詞

說明 分詞不可單獨做為本動詞，需依賴助動詞(be, have, has, had)以形成進行式，被動式或完成等時態的本動詞，單獨使用時僅用做為形容詞或副詞。

- The wind blowing from the South is so cold. (從南邊吹來的風好冷。)
- The flowers blooming lively looks so beautiful. (這些盛開的花看起來好美。)
- Gymnastics is a kind of exercise requiring great durance.
(體操是一種需要堅強耐力的運動。)

文法 14 現在分詞作受詞補語

說明 一般說來，現在分詞表示動作過程的一部分，即動作在進行。

- She saw him stealing into the bank at night.
(她看見他夜晚溜進銀行。) [現在分詞 stealing 作受詞補語表示動作在進行]

文法 15 主動詞為經常性動作，不定詞或現在分詞同義

- We often see her walk (walking) along the river bank by herself.
(我們常常看見她獨自沿著河岸散步。)

時態

- 基本時式 (Primary Tense)：動詞因動詞或狀態的時間不同而分現在、過去、未來三種時式，稱為基本時式。在主動的直述法中，英文的動詞共有十二種時式。

▶ 2-12

文法16 現在簡單式 Simple Present Tense

S + V

1 表示主語現在的性格、特徵、能力

2 現在的動作或狀態

3 現在習慣的動作或職業

- I often go to gym on Saturday. (我常常星期六上健身房。)

4 不變的真理或格言

- Light goes faster than sound. (光的傳播速度比聲音快。)

5 代替未來

❶ 來去動詞，即表示「出發」、「開始」、「來往」的動詞，可用現在式代替未來式。

- The plane starts at 10 o'clock in the morning. (飛機將在早上十點出發。)

❷ 表「時間或條件」的副詞子句，其未來的動作要用現在式表示(這種情況常與連接詞when當...的時候, as soon as一...就, before在...之前, after在...之後, until直到..., if如果,等引導的時間副詞子句或條件副詞子句連用。)

- I will clean up the room before my mother comes home.
  (我會在我媽媽回家前整理好房間。)

文法17 現在進行式 Present Progressive Tense

be + Ving

1 表示現在正在進行的動作

2 表示在最近的未來、即將發生，通常表「來去」的動詞，常與表未來之時間副詞連用，可代替未來式

- Is Max departing soon? (馬克思很快就要啟程了嗎？)

3 表示現在的安排或計畫未來要做的事

- I am going to see a movie with Max on Sunday.
  (我星期天將與馬克思去看電影。)

4 表示現在的感情與情緒

- Why are you looking so sad? (為什麼你看起來如此沮喪？)

文法 18 現在完成式 Present Perfect Tense

have , has + P.P.

1 表示現在剛剛完成之動作

2 表示過去繼續到現在的動作或狀態

- He has played the skateboard for 10 years. (他玩滑板已有十年之久。)

3 表過去某時發生的動作，其結果影響到現在，或某狀態繼續到現在。

- I am sorry I have lost the key. I can't open the door.

  (對不起我把鑰匙弄丟了。門打不開。)

  [鑰匙是什麼時候弄丟得不知道。重點是結果：沒有鑰匙打不開門。]

4 常伴隨時間副詞出現

❶ **for +** 一段時間

- She has lived here for a year. (我在這裡住了一年。)

❷ **since +** 過去時間

- She has lived here since last year. (她住在這裡，從去年起。)

❸ **have gone to +** 地點：表示到了某地或正在去某地的途中 **(**該人不在現場**)**

- Sam is away on holiday. He has gone to Japan.

  (山姆去渡假，他到日本去了。)

❹ **have been to +**地點**/**位置副詞：表示曾經到過某地 **(**表經驗，該人在現場**)**

- Sam came back from holiday. He has been to Japan.

  (山姆渡假回來了，他去了日本。)

小試一下

(　　) 1. The number of independent travelers ______ steadily since the new policy was announced. 99領

(A)rose (B)has risen (C)arose (D)has arisen

(自由行旅客的人數穩定地上升，自從新政策被公布以來。)　答 B

文法19 過去簡單式 Simple Past Tense

S + Ved (有清楚交待時間)

1 過去的動作或狀態

2 過去的習慣動作

文法20 過去進行式 Pass Progressive Tense

was / were + Ving

1 表在過去某一時候正在進行的動作

2 表過去兩個動作一起在進行時，應為過去進行式與過去簡單式聯用

- My sister was talking on the phone while I was taking a shower.
(我在洗澡的時候，我妹妹在講電話。)

文法21 過去完成式 Pass Perfect Tense

had + Vpp.

1 在過去的某一時間內做過的事

2 在過去某時之前完成的動作或在另一動作發生之前所先完成的動作

- Tom told me that he had passed all the final exams.
(湯姆告訴我他通過了所有的期末考試。)

- I found the train had left when I got to the station.
(當我抵達車站時，我發現火車已經離開了。)

3 表示過去兩個不同時間發生的動作、狀態，先發生的用過去完成式，後發生的用過去簡單式

- When I arrived at the bus station, the bus had already left.
(當我到達公車站時，公車早已離開了。)

4 過去曾經做的事，現在已經不做

- I had taught English since 1985 to 2000. (從1985到2000年間，我在教英文。)

5 用於關係子句，表示早於過去式之前的事

- I found the money which I had lost yesterday. (我找到我昨天丟掉的錢。)

文法 22 未來式 Future Tense

will (shall) + Vr

1 單純表示未來的動作或狀態，或自然的結果，或非出自於自由意志的

2 意志未來

❶ 表說話者的意志 (You shall)

❷ 詢問對方的意志 (Will you?)

❸ 表主詞的意志 (You will)

文法 23 未來進行式 Future Progressive Tense

will (shall) + be + Ving

1 表示未來某點或某段時間將要進行的動作

- I shall be having an interview this time tomorrow.
  (明天的這個時候，我正在面試。)

小試一下

( ) 1. This time next year I _____ in France. 102導
(A)am traveling (B)have been traveling (C)will be traveling (D)have traveled
(明年的這個時候，我將去法國旅行。)
答 C

文法 24 未來完成式 Future Perfect Tense

will (shall) have + Vpp.

1 未來某時間之前，或另一未來動作前，已經完成之動作

- By the time Max retires, his daughter will probably have got married.
  (馬克思退休時，他的女兒可能已結婚了。)

2 敘述到未來某時已存在的經驗

- My sister will have graduated from college this time next year.

(明年的這個時候我妹妹將從大學畢業。)

文法 25 現在完成進行式 Present Perfect Progressive Tense

have/has been + Ving

1 表示從過去某時間開始一直繼續到現在仍在進行的動作(強調持續性質)

- The novelist has been writing the novel since last night.

(自從昨晚，小說家一直在寫小說。)

文法 26 過去完成進行式 Past Perfect Progressive Tense

had been + Ving

1 表示從較早的過去繼續到過去某時，並強調該動作在過去某時還在繼續進行

- Iris had been crying whole night for she was dumped by her boyfriend.

(愛莉絲被男友甩了，她哭了整晚。)

文法 27 未來完成進行式 Future Perfect Progressive Tense

will (shall) + have been + Ving

1 敘述某動作將繼續到未來某時，並暗示該動作在未來某時可能還在繼續進行

- I will have been working for 15 hours when you pay me a visit.

(當你來訪時，我將已工作15個小時了。)

小試一下

( ) 1. Those who _____ a quake _____ life more. 98領

(A)survives…cherishes (B)have survived…will cherish

(C)are surviving…are cherished (D)are survivals of…had cherished

(那些在地震中的倖存者，將會更珍惜他們的生命。) 答 B

語氣 Mood

■ 語法就是表達思想的方法，可分為「直述語氣」、「祈使語氣」、「假設語氣」三種。

文法 28 直述語氣 Indicative Mood

用以敘述事實或詢問事情

小試一下

( ) 1. If the world's tropical rain forests continue to disappear at it present rate, many animal species ___________. 94領

(A)will be extinct (B)have extincted (C)extinct (D)extincted 答 A

(如果世界上的熱帶雨林繼續消失，以其目前的速度，許多動物種類都將滅絕。)

文法 29 祈使語氣 Imperative Mood

❶ 當主詞「**you**」**(**你、你們**)**時，**you**通常會被省略，只留下原形動詞

❷ 用原形動詞

說明 用以表達命令、請求、希望、禁止、禱告、勸告...

- Mind your language. (注意你的言語。)
- Please be polite to others. (請對他人有禮貌。)
- Don't say dirty words. (請勿說髒話。)
- Wish a wonderful trip. (祝福你有個美好的旅程。) 102導
- Let me show you some good manners. (讓我告訴你合適的規矩。)

小試一下

( ) 1. _____ go on a trip with him, Susan. 93導

(A)Not (B)Doesn't (C)Don't (D)Won't 答 C

(不要跟他去旅行，蘇珊。)

假設語氣 Subjunctive Mood

- 用以表達不可能實現的願望、假設、目的、想像等，一為條件子句，一為主要子句。
- 假設語氣與時間的關係可分為「文法30 與現在事實相反」、「文法31 與過去事實相反」和「文法32.33 與未來事實相反的假設」三種：

文法 30 與現在事實相反的假設（指現在的假設）

條件子句	主要子句
If + S + 過去式 V / were,	**S + should (might, would, could) + Vr**

- If I were a billionaire, I would buy all the things that I never have.
  (如果我是個億萬富翁，我會買下所有我從未擁有的東西。)
  [事實是：I am not a billionaire.]
- If I bought that car, I would be very happy.
  (我若買了那輛車，我一定會很開心。) [事實是：I do not buy it.]

小試一下

( ) 1. She acts as if she _____ the principal of the school. 93導
(A)is (B)had been (C)should be (D)were 答 D
(她裝出猶如她就是學校的校長。)

文法 31 與過去事實相反的假設（指過去的假設）

條件子句	主要子句
If + S + had + Vpp,	**S + should (might, would, could) + have + Vpp**

- If I had won the lottery, I would have been a billionaire.
  (如果我[當時]中了彩券，我[現在已經]是億萬富翁。) [事實是：I didn't win the lottery.]
- If I had bought that stock, I would have been rich.
  (我若曾買那支股票，早就已經發財了。) [事實是：I didn't buy the stock.]

小試一下

( ) 1. If I had called to reserve a table at Royal House one week earlier, we ____ a gourmet reunion dinner last night. 101領

(A)can have (B)will have had (C)would have had (D)would have eating 答 C

(如果我提早一週打去Royal House訂位，我們昨晚就會有美味的團圓飯。)

( ) 2. The interpreter talked as if he _____ how to fly like a bird. 100領

(A)knew (B)would know (C)had known (D)has known 答 C

(口譯員講的好像他知道如何像鳥兒一樣會飛。)

文法 32 與未來事實相反的假設(表示絕不可能)

條件子句		主要子句
If + S +	過去式 **were to + Vr** (表示未來絕對不可能)	+ **S + should (might, would, could) + Vr**

- If you were to be a better man, I would marry you.
  (如果你是更好的男人，我會嫁給你。) [事實是：你不是好男人，我也不會嫁給你。]
- If I were to go to America, I would take the same flight with you.
  (若我是要去美國，那我就會和你搭同班飛機了。)
  [事實是：我不是要去美國，也不會和你搭同班飛機。]

文法 33 與未來事實相反的假設(可能性極小)

條件子句		主要子句
If + S +	**should + Vr** 「萬一」，表可能性極小	+ 祈使句 **shall (will, can, may) + Vr** **should (would, could, might) + Vr**

- If it should rain tomorrow, don't expect me. (如果明天下雨，不用等我。)

情境篇
文法篇
片語篇
測驗篇
口試篇

分詞片語

- 有限定用法，只能放在其所修飾的名詞之後以修飾該名詞，不能用逗點分開句號。

文法 34 關係代名詞後接 be 動詞，刪除關係代名詞和 be 動詞，即成為分詞片語

N + 關係代名詞 + Be動詞 = N + Ving

- The girl who is dancing on the stage is my sister.
  = The girl dancing on the stage is my sister.
- Take a look at the painting which is hung on the wall.
  = Take a look at the painting hung on the wall.

文法 35 關係代名詞後無 be 動詞，刪除關係代名詞和 be 動詞，即成為分詞片語

N + 關係代名詞 + V = N + Ving

- People who live here are very friendly to tourists.
  = People living here are very friendly to tourists.
- The dress which was bought at night market could not be refunded.
  = The dress (being) bought at night market could not be refunded.

分詞構句 Participial Construction

- 分詞構句是一種複合句(compound sentence)，也就是把兩句單句合成一句compound sentence，讓句子更簡潔。
- 可代替合句中的另一對等子句，其作用是說話者對主要子句的敘述，加以補充說明。

文法 36 對等子句改為分詞構句

S1 + V1... and S1 + V2... → S1 + V1..., V2ing... 前後句主詞相同

1 對等子句主詞相同時，保留一主詞即可，即and (+主詞)+V=~ing

- Max sat at the bus stop and wait for the arrival of his girlfriend.
  =Max sat at the bus stop, waiting for the arrival of his girlfriend.

S1 + V1... and S2 + V2... → S2 + V1..., S2 + V2ing... 前後句主詞不同

1 前後不相同的情況(帶有意義上主詞的分詞片語，稱為獨立分詞構句。此片語不可能來自補述用法的形容詞子句，與主要子句的主詞無關，故稱之獨立分詞構句。)

2 對等子句主詞不同時，改為獨立分詞構句，兩個主詞都保留。

- Max is watching TV, and his girlfriend is reading a book beside him.
  = Max is watching TV, his girlfriend reading a book beside him.

小試一下

(　　) 1. __________, the little girl did not open the door. 95領
(A)Not being recognized who was the man (B)Not recognized who the man was
(C)Not recognizing who was the man (D)Not recognizing who the man was 答 D
(【由於】無法認出誰是那名男子，小女孩沒有開門。)

(　　) 2. Cursive II is a recent work of Taiwan's master choreographer Lin Hwai-min. He created Cursive, with its title _____ from Chinese calligraphy. 100導
(A)authorized (B)derived (C)evacuated (D)generalized 答 B
(Cursive II 是臺灣名編舞家林懷民近期的作品，他創造了Cursive，其名稱源自於中國書法。)

(　　) 3. Passengers ____ to other airlines should report to the information desk on the second floor. 101領
(A)have transferred (B)transfer (C)are transferred (D)transferring 答 D
(乘客轉換到其他航空公司，應向二樓的詢問處報到。)

■ 與分詞有關的常見格言：

▸ A drowning man will grasp at straws.
(一個快淹死的人，連根稻草都不放過【急不暇擇】。)

▸ A rolling stone gathers no moss. (滾石不生苔；轉業不積財。)

- Barking dogs seldom bite. (會叫的狗不咬人。)
- Let sleeping dogs lie. (不要惹事生非。)
- A burnt child dreads the fire. (一朝被蛇咬，十年怕草繩。)

同義：Once bitten, twice shy.

文法 37 分詞構句的表示法

S+Vt+O

1 如何寫分詞構句：

❶ 將引導副詞子句的連接詞去掉

❷ 判斷兩句話主詞是否一樣。主詞相同，去掉副詞子句的主詞；主詞不同，則兩句話的主詞皆保留。

❸ 任何動詞(包括be動詞)均為現在分詞(如進行式，則需把be動詞去掉)。

❹ 分詞為being和having been時，可把它省略掉。

❺ 如遇到否定詞，則放在分詞前(否定詞+分詞)。

❻ 其餘照抄。

2 有時為了明確表示原來引導副詞子句的連接詞的意義，將原本在分詞構句中已經刪除的從屬連接詞予以保留，此類連接詞為從屬連接詞，包括：

❶ 表示「時間」：when, while, before, after...等

❷ 表示「原因」：because, since, as...等

❸ 表示「條件」：if, unless, once...等

❹ 表示「讓步」：although, though

- Though Max knew his little sister was sleeping, he spoke rather loudly.

  =Though knowing his little sister was sleeping, Max spoke rather loudly.

文法 38 副詞子句改為分詞構句

連接詞 **+ S + V1..., S + V2... → (**連接詞 **+) Ving/ Vpp, S + V2...**

說明 副詞子句改為分詞構句時，若主要子句的動詞為現在式，副詞子句的動詞為過去式，為了要表示副詞子句的動詞動作時間早於主要子句的動詞，應改為完成式分詞，表示比主要子句動詞的動作先發生。

- As Max was idle in his youth, he has to work hard in his old age.
  = (Having been) idle in his youth, Max has to work hard in his old age.

小試一下

(　) 1. ______ a good cellist, she was hired by the orchestra.　93領
(A)Having been　(B)As　(C)Being　(D)Such　答 C
(作為一個優秀的大提琴家，她被聘請於樂團。)

(　) 2. ____ more manpower and fund, we'll complete the task within two months.
(A)Give　(B)Given　(C)Giving　(D)To give　95領　答 B
(【由於】給予更多的人力和資金，我們將完成任務，在兩個月內。)

(　) 3. ____ unemployed for almost one year, Henry has little chance of getting a job.
(A)Having been　(B)Be　(C)Maybe　(D)Since having　101領　答 A
(【由於】已經失業將近一年了，亨利找到工作的機會不大。)

補充 無人稱獨立分詞構句

- Judging from (由...判斷)
- Seeing that (既然...)
- frankly speaking = honestly speaking (坦白說)
- generally speaking (一般說來)
- broadly speaking = roughly speaking (大致說來)
- strictly speaking (嚴格說來)
- considering + N (就...而論)
- regarding / concerning / respecting + N (關於...)
- provided / providing / supposing that + S + V (假如...)
- given + N / given that + S + V (若考慮到；若假設)
- speaking of (說到...)

Chapter. 02 | 文法 | 名詞

了解名詞的用法是構成句子的基石

名詞

- 名詞指的就是「有名字的」，凡是「人、事物、地」的名字都是名詞。其中名詞可分為「可數名詞(CN, Countable Nouns)」和「不可數名詞(UN, Uncountable Nouns)」。

可數名詞

文法 39 可數名詞

1 單數(Singular Number)前面一定要加「a/an/one」表示「一個」。

- a girl (一個女孩), an apple (一顆蘋果)

2 可數名詞若在兩個或兩個以上稱「複數或多數(Plural Number)」，要在字尾加上「s」或「es」；有些名詞複數形為「不規則變化」。

- a man → men (男人們), a child → children (小孩們)

3 可數名詞的種類：

❶ 普通名詞(Common Noun)

- student (學生), rabbit (兔子)

❷ 集合名詞(Collective Noun)：同種類的人或動物等的集合體的名稱叫做集合名詞。

- family (家庭), police (警察), people (人們), crowd (群眾), army (軍隊), class (班級), nation (國家), party (黨), team (隊), mankind (人類)

不可數名詞

文法 40 不可數名詞

1 不可數名詞因不能數，故無單複數之別。若真要算，必須用「計量詞」來計算。

- a cup of tea (一杯茶), a loaf of bread (一條麵包)

2 雖然本身無法加s，但計量詞是複數時要加上「s」或「es」。

- two cups of tea (兩杯茶), five loaves of bread (五條麵包)

3 表示量的形容詞也可以放在前面。

- little time (很少時間), much money (很多錢)

4 不可數名詞的種類：

❶ 專有名詞(Proper Noun)：專有名詞需以大寫字母起首、通常不加冠詞「a, an, the」等，通常無複數。

人名	Avril Lavgane (艾薇兒), Miss Chen (陳小姐)
地名	Taipei (臺北), Hong Kong (香港), California (加州)
國名	Taiwan (臺灣), America (美國)
國民、國語名稱	Chinese (中國人), American (美國人)
月名、週日名、節日名	March (三月), Friday (星期五), Halloween (萬聖節)

❷ 物質名詞(Material Noun)：沒有一定型態的物質的名稱叫做物質名詞。

食物、飲料	food (食物), rice (米), wheat (小麥), flour (麵粉), bread (麵包), meat (肉), fish (魚), sugar (糖), salt (鹽), butter (奶油), milk (牛奶), tea (茶), coffee (咖啡), wine (酒), beer (啤酒), water (水), fruit (水果)
材料	wood (木), stone (石), grass (草), coal (煤), brick (磚), gold (金), silver (銀), copper (銅), iron (鐵), metal (金屬), cotton (棉花), cloth (布), paper (紙), glass (玻璃), chalk (粉筆), money (錢)
液體、氣體	air (空氣), gas (氣體), oil (油), ink (墨水), rain (雨), snow (雪)

❸ 抽象名詞(Abstract Noun)：性質、狀態、動作、概念等的名稱叫做抽象名詞。

diligence (勤勉), health (健康), honesty (誠實), kindness (仁慈), peace (和平), knowledge (知識), wisdom (智慧), grammar (文法), history (歷史), movement (動作), freedom (自由), height (高度)

*抽象名詞如用指特定的事物，則須加the

5 總稱用法：Happiness cannot be bought with money. (幸福是用金錢買不到的)

6 特定用法：People envy the happiness of my relationship. (人們羨慕我感情幸福)

Chapter. 03 文法 代名詞

代名詞豐富句子的表達、增加層次

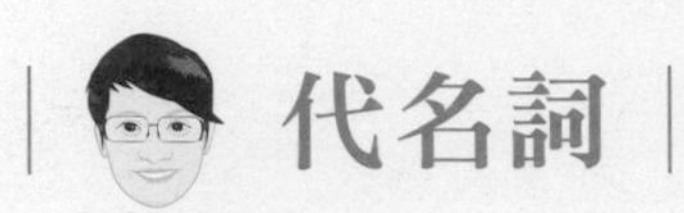

代名詞

- 人稱代名詞指人或事物的代名詞。有人稱、數、格的變化。第三人稱單數的人稱代名詞還有性別的變化。

人稱代名詞 Personal Pronoun

文法 41 人稱代名詞

類型			人稱代名詞		所有格代名詞		反身代名詞
			主格	受格	形容詞	代名詞	
第一人稱	單數		I	me	my	mine	myself
	複數		we	us	our	ours	ourselves
第二人稱	單數		you		your	yours	yourself
	複數						yourselves
第三人稱	單數	陽性	he	him	his	his	himself
		陰性	she	her	her	hers	herself
		中性	it	it	its	its	itself
	複數		they	them	their	theirs	themselves

小試一下

( ) 1. Members of the design team were not surprised that Ms. Wang created the company logo ____. 101領

(A)itself (B)herself (C)themselves (D)himself 答 B

(設計團隊成員並不感到意外，對於王女士自己創建公司標誌。)

( ) 2. Those wishing to be considered for paid leave should put ____ requests in as soon as possible. 94領

(A)they (B)them (C)theirs (D)their 答 D

(那些有意被考慮列為帶薪休假的人，應盡快提交他們的要求。)

指示代名詞 Demonstrative pronoun

■ 表示指定的人或事物時使用的代名詞稱為指示代名詞。有this, these, that, those, such, same, so。

文法 42 指示代名詞

this, these, that, those

說明

❶ this, these指較近的人或物。that, those指較遠的人或物。

❷ that, those為避免重複可代替前面已說過的名詞。this, these不可做這種用法。

- The ears of rabbit are longer than those (the ears) of a bear.
  (兔子的耳朵比熊的[耳朵]長。)

❸ those... these... (複數) / that... this... (單數)
= the former... the latter... (前者...後者...)

文法 43 such

such

- Such was the case. (情形是這樣。)
- I don't like such a man. (我不喜歡那樣的人。)

說明 such可以用作感嘆的意味，與what一樣，接名詞。

- He is such a loser! (他真是個輸家！)

such ~as (=like) 像~那樣的

- I have never seen such a man as he (is).
  (我從未見過像他那樣的人。)

such as (=like, for example)

- Western food, such as French or Italian food, is very common here.
  (西方食物，例如法式或義式料理，在這裡非常普遍。)

小試一下

( ) 1. A: I ‘d like to visit Taipei. Could you tell me some interesting spots? 95導

B: There are many interesting places, ______ CKS Memorial Hall, Taipei 101, etc.

(A)as (B)as such (C)like as (D)such as 答 D

(A：我想參訪臺北。你能告訴我一些有趣的景點嗎？

B：有許多有趣的地方，如中正紀念堂，臺北101等。)

不定代名詞

- 表示數量或對象不確定的人或事物時，所使用的代名詞，稱為不定代名詞。

文法 44 不定代名詞

some 一些	**any** 任何	**both** 兩者都
either 兩者中之任一	**neither** 兩者中無一	**all** 全部
one 任何人、某人、某事	**each** 各個	**most** 大部分的
few 極少數	**little** 極少量	**none** 無一人
much 多量	**other** 其他	**every** 每一
more 更多的	**enough** 充分	**several** 一些
many 很多	**each** 各個	

小試一下

( ) 1. Despite facing an imminent labor shortage as its population ages, Japan has done _____ to open itself up to immigration. 100導

(A)small (B)little (C)none (D)less 答 B

(由於人口老齡化，儘管面臨著勞動力短缺，日本仍開放一些移民。)

( ) 2. In southern Taiwan, people's ties to rural folk culture are strongest. Local gods are more fervently worshipped. Tainan, for instance, has a temple heritage second to _____. 100導

(A)one (B)none (C)any (D)some 答 B

(在臺灣南部地區，人們與鄉村民間文化有很大的密切關係。尤其地方神祇崇拜更熱切。例如，位於臺南的一個寺廟遺產並不亞於其他古蹟。)

文法 45 some 或 any 和 -thing, -body, -one, -where 等結合

everything 每一物	**nobody** 無一人	**nothing** 無一物
someone 某人	**somebody** 某人	**something** 某物
anyone 任何人	**anybody** 任何人	**anything** 任何物
everyone 每人	**everybody** 每人	

說明 在肯定句、否定句、疑問句，條件句中的用法，大致和**some**與**any**的用法相同。

~body, ~one , ~thing + 單數動詞(is...)

- Something goes wrong. (有一點毛病。)

~body, ~one , ~thing + 形容詞

- I have nothing else to give you. (我沒有別的東西可以給你。)

小試一下

( ) 1. The exam results were poor. ________ passed. 100導

(A)Almost all (B)A few people (C)Hardly anyone (D)Just about everyone 答 C

(考試的成果不佳。幾乎沒有人通過。)

文法 46 不定代名詞的慣用語

- anything but 並不；絕不
  - Iris is anything but beautiful. (愛莉絲並不美。)
- nothing but 只；不過
  - Iris is nothing but skin and bones. (愛莉絲非常瘦，只有皮包骨。)
- do nothing but + Vr 除了...之外什麼都不做；只是
  - Iris does nothing but fool around all day.
    (愛莉絲除了整日遊手好閒，什麼都不做。)
- have nothing to do but (or except) + Vr 除...之外別無辦法
  - I have nothing to do but wait here. (我除了在這裡等之外，別無辦法。)

- have something to do with 與...有關
  - The affair has something to do with Iris. (這件婚外情跟愛莉絲有關係。)
- all in = very tired = exhausted 很疲倦
  - My mother is all in. (我母親很疲倦。)
- all but = almost 幾乎
  - The classroom is all but empty. (教室裡幾乎全空了。)
- all in all (A)完全地 (B)一般說來
  - (A) Trust me not at all, or all in all. (要嘛不相信我，否則就完全相信我。)
  - (B) All in all, they are not likely to be in a relationship.
    (一般說來，他們不可能交往。)
- all at once = every one at one time 同時；一下子
  - He did the homework all at once for he wanted to hang out with friends on weekends. (他一下子就把功課做完了，因為他週末想跟朋友們出去玩。)
- all right 妥善；無恙
  - Everything is going to be alright. (一切將會無恙。)
- all over = finish = throughout 結束；遍佈
  - I dream of traveling all over the world. (我夢想著環遊世界。)
- all the same = still; however 仍然；不過
  - He is no longer handsome, but I love him all the same.
    (他不那麼帥了，可是我還是很愛他。)
- all the same to 對...都一樣
  - It is all the same to him. (對他而言，這都是一樣的。)
- all alone = completely alone 獨自地
  - He solved the problem all alone. (他獨自地解決問題。)
- all together 全部；一起
  - We are all in this together. (我們全部在一起。)
- all gone = nothing/nobody left 無物/人留下
  - By the time I was there, people were all gone. (我到達時，大家都走了。)

- all along = all the time; from the beginning 從一開始
  - I knew it all along. (我從一開始就知道了。)
- above all 最重要的是
  - The girl is cute, innocent and, above all, polite. No wonder everybody likes her. (女孩可愛、天真，最重要的是她有禮貌。難怪每個人都喜歡她。)
- after all = after all is said and done 畢竟
  - After all, he is just a kid. (畢竟，他只是個小孩。)
- at all 用在疑問、條件、消極及否定句上，作“in any way” (全然)解
  - He is not at all responsible. (他一點都不負責任。)
- in all = all together 總共
  - There are ten of them in all. (他們總共有十個人。)
- once (and) for all 只此一次；斷然地
  - Don't mention this person, once and for all. (永遠別再提到這個人。)

文法 47 Other 與 Another（非特定對象）

❶ **one... another... still another** (三個以上)	一個...，另一個...，另一個
❷ **one... others / other Ns**	一個...，另一些...
❸ **some..., others (; still others)** **= some... some... (; some...)**	有些...，有些...

小試一下

( ) 1. Smokers who insist on lighting up in public places are damaging not only their own health but also that of ____. 101領

(A)another (B)each other (C)one another (D)others 答 D

(吸菸者堅持在公共場所點菸，損害的不僅是自己的健康，也【損害】其他人。)

( ) 2. If you lose your passport, you should try to _____ immediately. 100導

(A)apply for another one (B)apply to the other one

(C)apply for the other (D)apply to another one 答 A

(如果你遺失了你的護照，你應該立即嘗試申請另一本。)

情境篇 文法篇 片語篇 測驗篇 口試篇

文法48 Other 與 Another（特定的對象）

❶ **one...; the other...**	(兩個之中) 一個；另一個
❷ **one..., another..., the other...**	(三個之中) 一個，一個，另一個
❸ **one...; the others.../ the other Ns**	(三個以上) 一個；其餘的
❹ **some...; the others.../ the other Ns...**	(四個以上) 一些；另一些

- the other day = a few days ago 前幾天
  - I went to Taipei the other day. (我前幾天去臺北。)
- every other day (or month, year...) 每隔一天/月/年...
  - I am requested to check the e-mail every other day. (我被要求每兩天收一次電子郵件。)
- on the other hand 在另一方面；反之
  - I like to hang out with friends; on the other hand, my sister likes to stay at home. (我喜歡跟朋友出去；反之，我妹妹喜歡待在家裡。)
- some day or other = sooner or later 總有一天；遲早
  - Whoever does something bad would be punished by God some day or other. (任何人做壞事，總有一天會被上帝處罰。)
- one after the other 兩者相繼地
  - His friends left him one after the other because he took drugs. (他的朋友相繼地離開他，由於他使用毒品。)
- another day 改天
  - Tomorrow is another day. (明天是嶄新的一天。)
- one way and another 用種種方法
- one way or another 無論如何
- one after another 三者以上相繼地
  - His plans failed one after another. (他的計畫相繼地失敗。)

疑問代名詞 Interrogative Pronoun

- 表示疑問時使用的代名詞稱為疑問代名詞，有who, which, what通常置於疑問句句首。

文法 49 疑問代名詞

主格	所有格	受格
Who	Whose	Whom
What	-	What
Which	-	Which

說明 Who? (指人)；What? Which? (指事、物)；Whose? (誰的)

口語中常用who來代替whom。

- What is it? (那是什麼?)
- Who are they? (他們是誰?)
- Which one is better? (哪個比較好?)

關係代名詞

關係代名詞	**who, whom, which, whose, that, what**
複合關係代名詞	**whoever, whomever, wherever, whatever, whichever, however**
準關係代名詞	**as, but, than**

說明 關係代名詞兼有代名詞與連接詞的作用，用來代替前面提過的名詞，並連接兩個句子。關係代名詞有who, which, that, what, whoever, whichever, whatever, as, but, than等。

文法 50 關係代名詞

關係代名詞的所有格	**sth. (,) + whose + N...** **= sth. (,) + the N of which...** **= sth. (,) + of which the N...**

- The room, whose walls are painted pink, is mine.

  = The room, the walls of which are painted pink, is mine.

  = The room, of which the walls are painted pink, is mine.

  (牆壁被漆成粉紅色，是我的房間。)

文法 51 限定用法與補述用法

限定用法 (Restrictive use)	非限定用法 (Continuative use)
用形容詞子句把其先行詞限定於某一個特殊狀態	用以補充說明先行詞的意思
關係代名詞之前沒有逗號	關係代名詞之前有逗號
作受格的關係代名詞可省略	關係代名詞不可省略
可用that	不能用that

1 限定用法：表示它至少還有一個女兒住在別處。

- He has two daughters who live in the US. (他有兩個住在美國的女兒。)

2 非限定用法：表示他只有兩個女兒。

- He has two daughters, who live in the US. (他有兩個女兒，他們住在美國。)

文法 52 非限定形容詞子句

N + all/most/some/... of + whom/which + V/Vpp 關係子句

- She has two daughters, ***both of whom study*** abroad.

N + and + all/most/some/... of + it/them + V/Vpp 對等子句

- She has two daughters, ***and both of them study*** abroad.

N + all/most/some/... of + it/them + Ving/Vpp 分詞構句

- She has two daughters, ***both of them studying*** abroad.
  她有兩個女兒，兩個都在國外念書。

小試一下

( ) 1. Finding an accountant ____ specialty and interests match your needs is critically important. 101領
(A)who (B)which (C)whose (D)whom　答 C
(尋找一個會計師，他的專業和興趣能滿足您的需求是極為重要的。)

( ) 2. The hotel ____ for the conference featured a nine-hole golf course. 101領

(A)that he selected (B)that he selected it (C)that selected (D)he selected it 答 A

(他選擇此次會議的飯店，是以一個九個洞的高爾夫球場為特色。)

( ) 3. As a collector, Mr. Strachwitz has built _____ is believed to be the largest private collection of Mexican-American and Mexican music. 96導

(A)that (B)what (C)who (D)which 答 B

(身為一位收藏家，Strachwitz先生建立一座被認為是墨西哥裔美國人和墨西哥音樂最大的私人收藏。)

情境篇
文法篇
片語篇
測驗篇
口試篇

文法 53 複合關係代名詞

引導名詞子句	引導副詞子句
whoever = any one who	whoever = no matter who
whichever = any that	whichever = no matter which
whatever = anything that	whatever = no matter what
whomever = any one whom	whomever = no matter whom
whosever = any one whose	

說明 複合關係代名詞，可引導副詞子句與名詞子句。

- 引導名詞子句時，子句為不完整子句，表達「~任何人；任何~的人/~任何事物；任何~的事物/事物~的任一個」之意，其意等於先行詞+關係代名詞
- 引導副詞子句時，子句為完整子句，表達「無論何人/何事/何時/何處/如何」之意，其意等於no matter +疑問詞

小試一下

( ) 1. ____ is first to arrive in the office is responsible for checking the voice mail. 101領

(A)The person (B)Who (C)Whoever (D)Whom 答 C

(無論是誰第一個到達辦公室都要負責檢查語音郵件。)

( ) 2. I have absolutely no intention _____ to hide the truth from you. 97導

(A)whereas (B)whether (C)however (D)whatsoever 答 D

(我絕對無意對你隱藏任何真相。)

Chapter. 04 | 文法 | 副詞
副詞可使句型多樣化、句意更完整

 副詞

- 副詞主要用來修飾動詞、形容詞及其他副詞。
- 修飾動詞時，單字副詞一般放在句尾，如放在句中則在be動詞或助動詞之後或一般動詞之前；放在句首則用來修飾整句，若be動詞或助動詞一併前調主詞前，則成倒裝句；副詞片語和副詞子句放在句尾則必定用來修飾動詞，放在句首則用逗號與主句隔開；修飾形容詞及其他副詞時必定放在被修飾者之前。

表時間的副詞

文法 54 Time

now (現在), **lately** (最近), **soon** (不久之後), **at once** (立刻), **long ago** (很久以前), **today** (今天), **yesterday** (昨天), **tomorrow** (明天), **next year** (明年), **recently** (最近), **presently** (目前), **nowadays** (現今), **already** (已經), **before** (之前), **early** (早), **late** (晚), **directly** (直接地), **immediately** (立即地), **afterward** (後來), **beforehand** (預先), **then** (當時), **very +** 時間 **, next +** 時間 **, last +** 時間 **, this +** 時間 **, that +** 時間

1 every前不可加介系詞

- I take a shower ***every morning***. (O)
  I take a shower ***in the morning every day***. (O)
  I take a shower ***in every morning***. (X)

2 Time (時候)：可用作when (什麼時候)的答語

- I will show up ***on Sunday***. (O)
  I will show up ***this Sunday***. (O)
  I will show up ***on this Sunday***. (O)
  I will show up ***on next Sunday***. (X)

3 next前不可加介系詞

小試一下

( ) 1. Some tourists like to make plans and reservations for local tours after they have arrived. They prefer not to have every day of their vacation planned _____. 98導

(A)behind (B)afterward (C)late (D)ahead 答 D

(有些遊客在他們抵達之後，喜歡[做]計劃和預訂當地的旅行團。他們不喜歡事先計劃好每天的假期。)

文法 55 Duration 持續期間

long (很久), **forever** (永遠), **all day** (整天), **for ten years** (十年之久)...

說明 Duration (期間)：用來作how long (多久)的答語

文法 56 Repetition 重複期間

once (一次), **rarely** (很少), **seldom** (很少), **at times** (有時候), **sometimes** (有時候), **scarcely** (不常), **occasionally** (偶爾), **once in a while** (偶爾), **often** (常常), **always** (總是), **usually** (通常), **frequently** (經常), **daily** (每天), **continually** (持續地), **regularly** (定期地), **hardly ever** (幾乎不會), **never** (絕不)......

說明 Repetition (反覆)：用來作how often (幾次)的答語，也可稱為頻率副詞

- seldom、never具否定意義
  - ▸ seldom = hardly ever = rarely = scarcely
- ever多用於完成式的疑問句
- always、usually、often、sometimes具肯定意義；always、usually、often若用於否定，只做為部分否定，其義等於sometimes。
  - ▸ always = all the way = all the time
  - ▸ usually = regularly = frequently
  - ▸ often = less frequently
  - ▸ sometimes = at times = from time to time = on and off = off and on

小試一下

( ) 1. Take your time. I don't need an answer _____. 101導

(A)consistently (B)regularly (C)immediately (D)frequently 答 C

(慢慢來。我不需要馬上有答案。)

文法 57 Order 順序

first (最先), **next** (其次), **last** (最後)...

說明 頻率副詞著重於動作出現的機率，次數副詞則著重於動作出現的實際次數，通常放句尾；次數副詞：once、twice、thrice、firstly、secondly、thirdly、again。

表示程度的副詞

文法 58 表程度的副詞

very (很), **rather** (相當), **quite** (十分地), **much** (非常), **greatly** (非常), **nearly** (幾乎), **almost** (幾乎), **completely** (完全地), **entirely** (全部地), **perfectly** (完美地), **absolutely** (絕對地), **thoroughly** (徹底地), **extremely** (極端地), **exactly** (確切地), **partly** (部分地), **slightly** (稍微地), **so** (那麼), **too** (太), **just** (正是), **scarcely** (幾乎不), **awfully, terribly, frightfully** (相當；很), **utterly** (全然地), **enormously** (非常地)...

小試一下

( ) 1. That dessert looks ______ delicious. 95導

(A)absolutely (B)fully (C)nicely (D)sincerely 答 A

(那甜點看起來新鮮又美味。)

表示地方的副詞

文法 59 表地方的副詞

here (這裡), **there** (那裡), **far** (遠), **near** (近), **out** (在外面), **away** (離開), **off** (離開),

outside (在外面), **inside** (在裡面), **to and fro** (來來回回), **across** (越過), **back** (向後), **backwards** (向後), **forwards** (向前), **over** (在...之上), **under** (在...之下), **above** (在上面), **hither** (在這裡), **thither** (在那裡), **thence** (從那裡), **home** (在家), **upstairs** (在樓上), **downstairs** (在樓下), **somewhere** (某處), **nowhere** (無處)...

說明 地方副詞和時間副詞中通常會含有介詞，但是有些地方、時間本身同時既是名詞也是副詞，則其前不可加介詞。

- The child goes home immediately after school every day. (○)
- The child goes to home immediately after school every day. (X)

  ※ 回到自己家，不使用「to」。

- The child goes to my home immediately after school every day. (○)
- The child goes my home immediately after school every day. (X)

  ※ 到我家，須加上「to」。

疑問副詞 Interrogative Adverbs

說明 用以詢問所提之情況、時間、地方等副詞的問句。

- 疑問副詞有when, where, how, why：
  - when 表時間的疑問副詞
  - where 表地方的疑問副詞
  - why 表原因的疑問副詞
  - how

文法 60 表示方法或狀態的疑問副詞

How about	用以徵求同意
How often	用以問次數頻率

- How can you speak English so well? 如何你說英文(說的)這麼好？

文法 61 表示程度或數量的疑問副詞

How well	用以問程度	**How old**	用以問年齡
How long	用以問耗時和長度	**How fast**	用以問速度
How wide	用以問寬度	**How many**	用以問數量
How tall	用以問身高	**How much**	用以問價錢
How high	用以問高度		

- How much money does it cost? (它的成本是多少錢？)

文法 62 疑問副詞 (How 的疑問副詞)

How + 助動詞 **+ S +** 連綴動詞 **?**

- A: How does it taste?
  B: It tastes sweet.

文法 63 疑問副詞 (What 的疑問副詞)

What + 助動詞 **+ S +** 連綴動詞 **+ like ?**

- A: What does the tea taste like?
  B: It takes like mint.

關係副詞 Relative Adverbs

文法 64 關係副詞

(the place) where + S + V	~ 的地方
(the time) when + S + V	~ 的時間
(the reason) why + S + V	~ 的理由
How + S + V	~ 的方式

小試一下

( ) 1. A: Why do you travel to Taitung so often? 95導

B: Taitung is the city ______ my parents live.

(A)that (B)where (C)which (D)in where

答 B

(A：為什麼你到臺東旅遊如此頻繁？

B：臺東是我父母所居住的城市。)

複合關係副詞

文法 65 複合關係副詞

whenever = no matter when	無論何時
wherever = no matter where	無論何處
however = no matter how	無論如何

小試一下

( ) 1. _____ there is a holiday, we always go hiking. 100領

(A)During (B)Whatever (C)Whenever (D)While

答 C

(當有假期時，我們總是去爬山。)

副詞子句相關子句

文法 66 副詞子句

so... that + S + V & so... as to V	如此...以至於...
such + N + that + S + V	如此...以至於

小試一下

( ) 1. It's _________that we'd better go hiking in Yang-ming Mountain. 95領

(A)a such lovely day (B)a so lovely day (C)such lovely a day (D)so lovely a day

(這是多麼美好的一天，我們最好去陽明山遠足。)

答 D

Chapter. 05 | 文法 | 形容詞

形容詞使名詞表達的更細膩及生動

形容詞

- 形容詞為修飾者(modifier)之一，於句中專門用來形容、修飾名詞謂之限定用法，作為補述用法謂之非限定用法，而形容詞本身亦可接受副詞的修飾。
- 形容詞種類可分為六種：專有(Proper)、性狀(Descriptive)、表量(Quantitative)、數詞(Numeral)、指示(Demonstrative)及個別(Distributive)，而冠詞(Article) 亦歸類於形容詞。
- 修飾名詞時，單字形容詞放在名詞之前(前位修飾)，而形容詞片語和形容詞子句，則放在名詞之後(後位修飾)；修飾代名詞時，一律放在代名詞之後(後位修飾)。
- 限定用法：專門用來形容、修飾名詞(Attributive use)，謂之定語。

形容詞比較級

文法 67 原級

...as adj./adv. as...	像...一樣
not as/so adj./adv. as...	不像...一樣

小試一下

( ) 1. Do not be afraid to eat with your hands here. When in Rome, do ______ the Romans do. 100領

(A)for (B)as (C)of (D)since 答 B

(在這裡不要害怕用手吃飯，要入境隨俗。)

( ) 2. A: How do you like the tour? 95導

B: I hate it ______ you do.

(A)as much as (B)so much as (C)so much so (D)so much like 答 A

(A：你覺得這個旅行如何？ B：我討厭它[旅行]就跟你一樣。)

文法 68 比較級 (Comparative degree)

A + is	**~ er** / **more ~**	**+ than B (is)**	A較B為~

說明 兩主詞的比較均用主格，than前面需接比較級。

小試一下

( ) 1. The Franklin stove, which became common in the 1790s, burned wood _______ an open fireplace. 94領

(A)efficiently much more than (B)much more efficiently than

(C)much more than efficiently (D)more efficiently much than

答 B

(富蘭克林爐逐漸普遍在1790年代，比起開放式的壁爐，燒木材更加有效率。)

( )2. Our music teacher said that ______ of chamber music was the string quartet. 94領

(A)most the form famous (B)the form most famous

(C)the most famous form (D)the famous most form

答 C

(我們的音樂老師說，最有名的室內音樂形式是弦樂四重奏。)

文法 69 兩者中較 ~ 者

The +	**~ er** / **more ~**	**+ of the two**	二者中較~者

文法 70 其他詞表示比較級

be +	**superior/inferior**	**+ to + N/Ving**	比...好/差
	prior/posterior		比...之前/之後
	senior/junior		比...年長/年輕

小試一下

( ) 1. If you have to extend your stay at the hotel room, you should inform the front desk at least one day ____ your original departure time. 101領

(A)ahead to (B)forward to (C)prior to (D)in front of 答 C

(如您需要延長飯店房間的停留時間，在原定的離開時間，應提前一天告知櫃檯。)

文法 71 愈...就愈...

The + 比較級 (+N) (+S1 + V1), the + 比較級 (+N) (+S2 + V2)

小試一下

( ) 1. ____ the offer is, the more pressure we will have to bear. 101領

(A)The greatest (B)The greater (C)More of (D)Most of 答 B

(開價越大，我們將要承受越多的壓力。)

( ) 2. The higher the altitude, the lower ____ temperature. 96導

(A)the (B)has (C)it is (D)is 答 A

(海拔越高，溫度越低。)

文法 72 喜歡...勝於

prefer...to
= prefer to V1 rather than V2

小試一下

( ) 1. A: Which do you like better? Singing or dancing? 95導

B: Well, I prefer singing ______ dancing.

(A)for (B)over (C)than (D)to 答 D

(A：哪一個你比較喜歡？唱歌還是跳舞？
B：嗯，我喜歡唱歌勝過跳舞。)

文法 73 最高級（無範圍）

The +	~est most~	最~的

小試一下

( ) 1. Giant pandas are among the _____ animals in the world. There are only some 1,860 in the world, and two are residing in Taipei Zoo now. 98導

(A)busiest (B)rarest (C)smartest (D)barest

答 B

(大熊貓在世界上是最稀有的動物之一。目前世界上約有1,860隻，並且目前有兩隻居住在臺北市立動物園。)

文法 74 最高級（有範圍）

The +	~est most~	+ of +	the three all	三者中最~者 全體中最~者

補充 最高級形容詞的慣用語

- at first (起初)
- at last (最後)
- at (the) latest (最遲)
- at (the) most (最多)
- at least (至少)
- at best (充其量不過)
- at one's best (全盛時期)
- do one's best (盡力)
- for the most part (多半；大部分)
- make the most (or best) of (善加利用)
- not in the least = not at all (一點也不)
- at (the) worst (最壞也不過)

Chapter. 06 | 文法 | 連接詞

連接詞是句子間的橋樑，讓句子更生動

連接詞

- 連接詞(Conjunctions)，可分成對等連接詞及從屬連接詞兩種。
- 連接詞於句中為連接字與字，片語與片語，甚至句與句，使句子的意義得以更加豐富，對等連接詞連接的是為上下文接續的作用，從屬連接詞連接的依其功能可為名詞子句，形容詞子句，及副詞子句。

對等連接詞 Coordinators

文法 75 對等連接詞

對等連接詞：**and, but, or, nor, so, for,...**

併合對等連接詞：

not only...but also	(不是...而是...)
as well as	(和...一樣)
either...or	(不是...就是...)
neither...nor	(兩者都不是...)
both...and	(既...又)
whether...or...	(是否)

說明 A as well as B (動詞和A一致)
= not only B but (also) A
= not only B but A as well

小試一下

( ) 1. In the interests of safety, passengers should carry ____ dangerous items nor matches while on board. 101領
(A)either (B)or (C)neither (D)not

答 C

(為了安全起見，當在飛機上時，旅客不應隨身攜帶危險的物品或火柴。)

( ) 2. Neither you, nor I, nor he _____ in Mr. Brown's class. 100領

(A)am (B)is (C)are (D)be 答 B

(既不是你，也不是我或他在布朗先生的班級。)

從屬連接詞 Subordinators

- 從屬連接詞所引導的子句，稱為從屬子句，必須依附主要子句，不能獨立存在。
- 一個連接詞只能連接兩個子句，不能有兩個連接詞。
- 從屬連接詞和對等連接詞不可並用：
  - (×) although…but… 雖然…但是…

    (×) because/as/since…so… 因為…所以…

    (×) unless…or… 除非…否則…

    (×) if…and… 那麼…則…

小試一下

( ) 1. The Internet is creating social isolation ____ people are spending more time on computer. 101領

(A)unless (B)so that (C)though (D)as 答 D

(網路正造成社會隔離，因為人們花費更多的時間在電腦上。)

( ) 2. While courts in the U.S. generally favor the mother in the event of a divorce, Taiwan family and divorce laws will grant custody to the father, _____ some other agreement is reached. 100導

(A)unless (B)regardless (C)until (D)considering 答 A

(雖然在美國，對於離婚事件法院普遍青睞於母親，在臺灣的家庭和離婚的法律將授予監護權優先給父親，除非達成其他的協議。)

( ) 3. _____ there is more than one Paris in the world, there's really only one Paris in the world. It is the capital of France. 100領

(A)Although (B)Already (C)However (D)And 答 A

(雖然世界有超過不只一個巴黎，但只有一個真正的巴黎在世界上。它是法國首都。)

Chapter. 07 文法 介系詞

貫徹動詞意志，串起受詞文意的幫手

介系(繫)詞

- 介系詞是不及物動詞和受詞之間產生連貫意義的介面，連繫整句的語義，以貫徹動詞的動作，而構成動詞片語；就其字義亦譯為前置詞，即位在某位置、時間之前的字，中文語意「在...」之意。
- 英文中有半數以上的動詞，需要介系詞的協助方能行使動詞的功能，構成動詞片語的介詞之後必接受詞，而受詞必為名詞；每逢介詞之後有動詞，一定用動名詞(V-ing)，介詞之後不可接不定詞(to+V)。
- 介詞和名詞所構成的介詞片語，可作副詞或形容詞使用。簡單來說，介系詞若非和不及物動詞構成動詞片語，便是以介詞片語作形容詞或副詞使用。

介系詞的種類

文法 76 at

1 地方，強調一精確的地點，常用來表示小地方**(在...地點)**

- I live at a villa. (我住在一棟別墅。)

2 時間 **(在...時間)**

- I usually get up at 7 o'clock. (我通常都七點起床。)

3 從事於某種活動 **(正在做...)**

- I am at work. (我正在工作。)

4 目的或方向 **(對準...；向...)**

- Don't yell at me. (別對著我吼叫。)

5 速度 **(以...的速度)**

- My dad drove at the rate of 80 miles an hour. (我爸爸開車，以時速八十。)

6 價格 **(以...的價格)**

- I bought the dress at a good price. (我買這件洋裝，以一個好價錢。)

7 年齡 **(在...的年齡)**

- The girl earned her own living at the age of ten.
  (小女孩在十歲的時候自食其力養活自己。)

小試一下

( ) 1. I am so happy that Nick is coming to visit us. Please tell him to make himself _____ home. (A)inside (B)in (C)on (D)at 100領 答 D
(我很開心尼克要來拜訪我們。請告訴他把這裡當自己家。)

( ) 2. We offer high-quality car-rental service _____ reasonable prices. 97導
(A)in (B)at (C)on (D)by 答 B
(我們提供高品質的汽車租賃服務，以合理的價格。)

文法 77 by

1 靜態的位置 **(在...的旁邊)**

- The boy sat by the girl. (男孩坐在女孩旁邊。)

2 動態的位置 **(經過)**

- As time goes by, they became stranger. (隨著時間流逝，他們成了陌生人。)

3 方法、方式 **(藉...；以...)**

- The package was sent by express. (包裹以快遞運送。)

4 數量單位 **(以...計)**

- The part-timer is paid by the hour. (兼差工作者被以時薪支付【薪水】。)

5 相差的程度 **(至...的程度)**

- My sister is younger than I by two years. (我妹妹比我小兩歲。)

6 期限 **(最遲在...之前；到...的時候已經)**

- I will be home by 9pm. (我最晚會在晚上九點以前回家。)

小試一下

(　　) 1. Now you can purchase a seat and pick up your boarding pass at the airport on the day of departure ____ simply showing appropriate identification. 101領
(A)together (B)for (C)by (D)with 答 C
(現在您可以在出發當天在機場購買座位並拿登機牌，只需出示適當的身份證件。)

文法 78 for

1 目的地或方向 **(**向...；往...**)**

- I am going to leave for Taipei later. (我晚點將前往臺北。)

2 期限 **(**經過...的時間**)**

- The prisoner has been jailed for 5 years. (犯人已經被囚禁五年了。)

3 原因或理由 **(**因為；由於**)**

- He was sentenced to death for smuggling. (他被判死刑，由於走私。)

4 代表、代替

- She is the supervisor for the five-star hotel. (她是五星級飯店的監督人。)

5 目的

- The lady worked for her living. (這位女士為了她的生計而工作。)

6 交換

- I paid 100 hundred dollars for breakfast. (我付一百元買早餐。)

7 作「當作」解

- He takes his girlfriend for future wife. (他把他的女朋友當作未來的妻子。)

8 for + (代)名詞，造成不定詞意思上的主詞

- It is time for him to go. (他是時間該走了。)

文法 79 from

1 地方的起點

- Let's start from here. (我們由此出發。)

2 時間的起點

- He likes the plan from the very beginning. (他喜歡這個計畫，從一開始。)

3 區別

- I can hardly tell jackfruit from durian.
  (我幾乎無法分辨波羅蜜與榴槤的差別。)

4 原料

- Wine is made from grapes. (紅酒是葡萄釀成的。)

5 原因 (因為)

- The cause of the accident results from the driver's carelessness.
  (意外的發生，是因為司機的不小心。)

文法 80 in

1 地方

- My mom is in the kitchen. (我媽媽在廚房。)

2 時間，或「再過...時間」

- I will be there in 5 minutes. (我再過五分鐘將會到那裡。)

3 狀態

- The room was in a mess. (房間一團亂。)

4 穿著

- James looks cool in a black suit. (詹姆士穿著一套黑色西裝，看起來很帥。)

5 方法

- He paid the bill in cash. (他用現金付帳單。)

文法 81 on

1 地方 (在...上)

- She put the vase on the table. (她把花瓶放在桌上。)

2 日期、星期或特定的時間

- My birthday is on July, 18th. (我的生日在7月18日。)

3 作「關於；論及」解

- The teacher asked us to make some comments on his lecture.
  (老師叫我們做一些評論，關於他的授課。)

4 狀態

- The house is on fire. (房子著火了。)

5 方向，朝向 (對...)

- The window looks on the street. (窗戶面對馬路。)

6 表示與線的接觸 (在...旁；沿...邊)

- He stood on my left. (他站在我的左邊。)

7 在某事發生的時候，或緊接著某事之後 (一...)

- She fainted on hearing the bad news. (她一聽到壞消息就昏倒了。)

8 支持 (信賴；以...為生；支撐)

- Man goes on two legs, brutes on four. (人類以兩腳走，獸以四肢。)

文法 82 of

1 所有

- The roofs of the house have been destroyed by typhoon.
  (房子的屋頂被颱風毀壞了。)

2 部分關係

- Max is one of my best friends. (馬克斯是我最好的朋友之一。)

3 材料製成成品後的性質不變

- The house is made of brick. (房子是由磚塊建成的。)

4 出身

- He was a graduate of Harvard University. (他是哈佛大學的畢業生。)

5 情緒上或生病、死亡的原因

- My grandfather died of liver cancer. (我的祖父因肝癌逝世。)

6 剝奪、奪去

- Slaves are robbed of liberty. (奴隸被奪取了自由。)

7 組成

- The organization consists of people from all walks of life. (這個組織由各行各業的人組成。)

8 關係、涉及

- What are you thinking of? (你想起什麼？)

9 of + 抽象名詞，當形容詞片語用

- Angel is a woman of ability. (安琪是有能力的女人。)

文法 83 to

1 目的地；方向

- We are heading to the airport. (我們正前往機場。)

2 時間的終點 (至...；到...)

- The student studied from morning to night. (這學生讀書，從早到晚。)

3 結果

- The refugees starved to death. (難民們飢餓死了。)

4 行為的對象

- Be nice to others. (對他人友善點。)

文法 84 with

1 「和…一起」

- The elder shared his life experience with us.
  (這位年長者與我們分享他的人生經歷。)

2 同時，或隨著

- The little girl dances with the music happily. (小女孩隨著音樂開心地跳舞。)

3 帶在身上

- I have no money with me. (我身上沒有錢。)

4 原因、理由 (因為；由於)

- Children laughed out loud with joy. (孩子們因為高興而大聲地笑。)

5 工具、媒介 (用…；以…)

- She had her meal with fork. (她以叉子用餐。)

6 具有、附有

- The girl with pink skirt is my sister. (那女孩穿著粉紅裙子是我妹妹。)

7 狀態，後面常與抽象名詞連用，可等於副詞

- The hunk picked up the heavy box with ease.
  (健美男子不費力地舉起重箱子。)

文法 85 take, cost, spend

❶ **It takes (+sb.) +時間 + to V** **= N/Ving + take (+sb.) +時間**

❷ **It costs (+sb.) +金錢 + to V** **= N/ving + cost (+sb.) +金錢**

❸ **sb. + spend + 時間/金錢 + Ving/on + N** 某人花時間/金錢在…

文法 86 until

It is not until... that + S + V

= S + be/助動詞 + not (+V)... + until... 一直到...時候才做...

= Not until... + be/助動詞 + S (+V)...

文法 87 倒裝句

never, seldom, rarely, little, hardly, scarely, no way,

under no circumstances, by no means, on no account, in no situation,

not until... ; no sooner... than... ; hardly/scarcely... when/before,

not only... , but also (**not only**銜接的子句要倒裝，逗點後面的主要子句則不需要)

說明 否定副詞 (片語)/否定副詞子句放句首

- Little did I know where he had been. (我一點也不知道，他去了哪裡。)
- Not until my mother called me did I go home. (直到媽媽打給我，我才回家。)

說明 only放句首，只有主要子句需倒裝。後面通常接：

❶ 時間副詞

❷ 介係詞片語

- Only by studying hard can you pass the final exams.
  (只有藉由用功讀書，你才能通過期末考試。)

❸ 副詞子句

- Only where there is life can there be hope. (留得青山在，不怕沒材燒。)

文法 88 ...不...，...也不...(否定句)

Nor	+	**be + S...**
and + nor/neither		助動詞 **+ S + V**

- I didn't oppose the project, nor did I support it.

  (我不反對這項計畫，我也不支持它。)

- Iris didn't tell the truth, nor did her boyfriend.

  = Iris didn't tell the truth, and neither did her boyfriend.

  = Iris didn't tell the truth; neither / nor did her boyfriend.

  = Iris didn't tell the truth. Neither / Nor did her boyfriend.

  (愛莉絲沒有說實話，她的男朋友也沒有。)

文法 89 間接問句

S + ask , wonder + if / whether/ wh- / how + S + V

- The boy asked his mother if he could turn on the TV.

  (小男孩問他的媽媽，是否他可以打開電視。)

- I wonder why it doesn't work.

  (我納悶為什麼它行不通。)

說明 如果為**wh-**問句，則保留疑問詞，在間接問句中，句子不倒裝。

文法 90 直接問句

引導的名詞子句，通常用「**Do you know**」或「**Can you tell me**」開頭，

然後接**5W1H(when, where, what, why, who, how)**或**whether/if**

- Who is she? (直接問句)

  = I have no idea who she is.

- Which way should I go? (直接問句)

  = Can you tell me which way I should go?

小試一下

( ) 1. Do you know ________ to walk through that forest alone at night? 94領

(A)how it is terrible (B)how terrible is it (C)it is how terrible (D)how terrible it is

(你知道這有多可怕嗎？當你晚上獨自一個人穿過那片森林。) 答 D

Unit .

03.

片語篇

單字及片語，
一直是學習英語必備的工具。
句子，是由許多個字詞所組成，
為避免被單一字詞誤導整句的意思，
藉由片語的輔助，就如同中文的成語，
判斷句子正確的句意、結構及句型。

Chapter. 01 | 片語 | 歷年重要片語彙整

學習片語，更快判斷句意及句型結構

片語精選

	片語	中文
A -	a black day	沮喪的一天, 大禍臨頭的那天, 黯淡的日子
	a period of 112領 108領	一段時間
	a variety of 108導 107導	各種各樣的
	abide by	遵守, 服從, 堅持
	above all	最重要的; 尤其
	account for 109領	占; 說明(原因)
	accuse sb. of 107領	控告某人犯了..., 責備
	accustomed to	習慣於
	and so on 112領 108導	等等; 諸如此類
	ahead of 107領	提前
	aim at 110領	瞄準; 以...為目的, 立志
	aim to 112領	旨在
	all the way 107導	整個途中, 全部時間
	all over 112領	到處, 各處；正像所說的人一樣; 全部結束
	apply for 109導 107領	申請, 應徵
	around the corner 109領	在附近；即將來臨
	arrive at 108導	到達(小地方)
	arrive in 107導	到達, 來到(大地方)
	as a result 110領 110導 109領 108領	結果, 因此
	aside from 112導	除了

	片語	中文
	ask for 107領	要求見某人, 要求與某人談話, 要某事物
	at all cost	無論如何
	at all times 108領	總是, 隨時, 永遠
	at first sight 109導	初見; 乍看之下
	at high risk of 112領 108領	高風險
	at large	逍遙法外; 詳細
	at the cost of 107領 107導	以...為代價
	at the expense of	由...支付費用
	attend to 110領	注意; 致力於; 照顧
B -	back up	支持
	bail out	保釋, 幫助...擺脫困境; 跳傘; 汲水
	bargain for 109導 108導	預料到, 期待
	base on 112領	根據
	be a staple of 112領	為某物的一個主要成分
	be able to 112領 107領	能夠, 有...能力, 勝任
	be about to 109導	即將
	be addicted to 109導	沈迷於...
	be allergic to 112領 110領 110導 109領	對...過敏
	be aware of	意識到
	be charged with 112領 110領	被收取
	be committed to 112導	致力於
	be dedicated to 109導 108導	奉獻於, 獻身於, 題獻給
	be due to 110導 108領 107導 107領	因為; 由於
	be eligible to 112領 107領	具備條件的；有資格的
	be expected to 112導 108領	預計

▶ 3-4

片語	中文
be good at	擅長於, 精通
be irritated by 109導	被...激怒
be known as 109導 108導 107導	作為...而聞名遐邇; 被稱為
be made up of 110導 108導	由...組成
be obliged to 112導	非常感謝
be referred to 112領 107導	提及
be renowned for 112導 107導	以...聞名
be satisfied with 112導 109領	對...感到滿意
be sensitive to 108導	對...敏感; 易受傷害
be suitable for 110導	適合
be surrounded by 112領 108導	被...環繞
bear down on	逼近; 對(某人)施加壓力, 襲擊; 強調
belong to 112領	屬於
bend over 107導	俯身於...
break down 109領 107導	失敗; 故障; 分解
break into	闖入; 打斷; 突然...起來
break through 108導	突破(障礙); 克服
break up	崩潰; 分離, 分手; 解散
bring up	培養; 嘔吐; 提出
brush up	溫習(語言); 改良, 熟練
buckle up 108領	繫好安全帶
build up	建立; 積累, 增加
build-in	嵌入的; 固定的; 內建的
burn down	完全燒毀, 火力減弱
butter up	討好; 奉承

	片語	中文
	by all means 107領	無論如何
	by all odds	毫無疑問
	by and by	不久, 馬上
	by and large	基本上, 大概
	by chance	偶然地; 意外地
	by leaps and bounds	突飛猛進, 大幅度地, 急速地
	by no means	絕不是, 決不, 絲毫不
C -	call for 110領	呼喚, 需要, 號召
	calm down 112領 110領	冷靜
	carry on 109領 109導	繼續; 進行; 經營
	carry out	完成; 實行
	carry over	保存, 持續; 推遲
	cash in on	利用; 賺錢
	catch on	流行; 抓住; 掛在...上; 理解
	catch up with	趕上
	cater to 112領	迎合
	change for	交換
	check up	核對, 檢查
	come across	巧遇; 照辦
	come through	成功; 出現; 傳來; 經歷
	come to light	暴露, 真相大白
	come up 107導	開始; 發生; 上樓; 被提出討論, 發芽; 出現
	come up with	趕上; (針對問題)想出; 提出
	consist of	由...構成
	contribute to 108領	貢獻; 撰稿; 投稿; 捐助; 促進

▶ 3-6

	片語	中文
	cope with	對付; 處理; 克服; 與...抗衡
	count on	依靠, 依賴, 信賴; 指望
	cut down	削減; 奪去某人的健康
D -	date back	回溯至
	deal out	分配, 給予...
	deal with 109領 107導 107領	應付; 處理
	depend on 112領 110領	取決於
	derive from	起源於; 從...獲得..., 來自...
	devoted to	專心致力於(工作); 深愛(人)
	disguise as 109導	偽裝成,化裝成...
	dress up 112領	打扮
	drive back	趕回去, 擊退
E -	entitle to 109領	有資格
F -	fall apart 107導	破裂; 破碎; 散開
	fall short of	射不中; 達不到; 不符合
	fall through	失敗, 無法實現, 成為泡影
	far from 107領	遠離
	fed up 107導	感到厭煩的
	figure out	演算出; 計算出; 揣測, 斷定
	file for	提起訴訟; 申請, 報名參加
	fill in 112導 110領	填寫
	fill out 108導 107導	發胖; 填寫(表格、申請書等)
	fill up	裝滿, 填補, 淤積
	filled with 112導 110領 108領 107導	充滿
	find fault with	挑剔; 抱怨

	片語	中文
	find out	發現, 查明; 想出
	fly-by-night	不可靠的, 騙人的
	for example 112領 108導 107導	舉例來說
	for fear of 107領	惟恐; 以免(發生危險)
	for good	永久地; 永遠
	for the sake of	為了...的利益; 由於, 為了
G -	get along with	與...和睦相處; 進展
	get around 108領 107領	避開; 說服; 爭取
	get off 110領 108領	動身; 下車
	get on 110領 109領 108導	進展; 上車
	get over	克服
	get rid of	擺脫, 消滅
	give away	贈送; 分發; 洩露
	give in 107導	讓步, 屈服
	give up 107導	放棄, 認輸
	go a long way 107領	經用, 用很長時間, 經花; 叫人受不了
	go against the grain	違背意願
	go along	進行; 繼續; 同意
	go astray	誤入歧途
	go bananas	失常; 不正常
	go Dutch 109導	分開付帳
	go on 110領 109領	繼續下去
	go over	檢查; 複習
	go through 108導	(指法律、法案等)被正式通過或接受, 貫穿
	go together	相配

▶ 3-8

	片語	中文
	go up	上升；被建造起來
	go with 112領 109領	搭配
	grow up	(指人或動物)長大；成年；成熟，發展
H -	**hand in** 109導 107導	提出；繳交
	hang around	閒混，遊蕩
	hang out 112領	閒晃
	hang up	掛斷電話；拖延
	head back	回去一開始出門的地點
	head down	由北方往南方前進
	head for	向某方向，某地點而去，對準某地而去
	head off	攔截；阻止；阻擋
	head out	離開前往某處
	head over	前往特定的目的地或明確的地點
	head up	由南方往北方前進
	high on	熱衷於
	hold on	不掛斷電話，繼續；抓牢，堅持
I -	**in accordance with**	與...一致；依照
	in addition to 112導 110領 108導	此外
	in advance 109領	在前面；預先
	in case 109領	以防萬一
	in case of 110導 107導	假使，如果發生
	in charge of	負責
	in compliance with 108領	依照；順從；與...一致
	in contrast	相反地
	in favor of	支持；有利於；支付給

	片語	中文
	in front of 112領 107領	在...之前
	in general 112領 107領	一般來說
	in light of	按照; 根據
	in no time	很快; 立即
	in order to 109領 108領 107領	為了...
	in regard to 107導	關於
	in respect to	關於, 至於; 就...而言; 在...方面
	in secret	偷偷的, 秘密的, 私下的
	in shape	處於良好健康狀態
	in spite of	儘管, 不管
	in terms of	在...方面, 根據, 按照; 從...角度
	in tune with 107導	音高或調子正確; 協調; 融洽
	insist on	堅決地宣告; 督促, 強烈地要求
	instead of 109領 108領	代替; 寧願
	interfere with 108導	打擾; 妨礙
	iron out	消除
J -	jump on	撲向, 襲擊, 攻擊; 斥責
K -	keep abreast of	與...並駕齊驅
	keep afloat	維持; 對付, 應付自如
	keep in touch	保持聯繫
	keep the change 109導	(零錢)不用找了
	keep track of	了解...的動態(或線索); 記錄
	keep up 109領 109導	(使)不停止; 保持; 熬夜
	knock off	撞倒; 打掉, 敲掉
L -	lapse into	陷入

▶ 3-10

	片語	中文
	lay aside	把...放在一邊; 積蓄
	lay down	放下; 規定; 建造; 主張
	lay waste to	損壞
	let alone	更不用說
	let off 108導	下車; 放開, 開; 釋放
	let on 112導 108導	假裝; 洩露
	live up to 110導	實踐; 遵守, 堅持; 無愧於
	live with	與...同居; 接受, 承認; 忍受
	look for 109導 109領 107領	尋求; 期待
	look forward to	盼望
	look into 109導	在...裡查資料; 深入地檢查, 研究; 調查
	look out	朝外看; 提防; 照料; 搜尋
	look through 109領	穿過...看去; 瀏覽
	look up	查詢; 拜訪, 好轉
M -	**make for**	為使; 走向, 駛向; 有助於; 導致
	make up 109領 108導	補足; 捏造; 和解; 組成; 發明; 杜撰; 化妝
	make use of 108導	使用; 利用
	make way for	為...騰出地方; 讓位於, 被...所替代
	move on	前進; 出發; 離開
N -	**nail down**	確定; 敲定; 要明確表態, 使履行諾言
	no later than	不晚於
	no less than	不少於
	no more than	不多於; 僅僅
	no longer 112領	不再
	no sooner than	一...就...

	片語	中文
	not to mention	更不必說
	now that 107領	既然; 因為; 而今
O -	off the hook 107領	脫身, 擺脫窘境
	on account of 109領 108導	由於; 因為, 為了...
	on and off 108導	斷斷續續
	on behalf of	代表, 為了...
	on display 108領 107導	展出, 陳列著
	on leave	在休假中
	on the contrary	反而
	on the house 109導	【俚語】免費(由酒吧及餐廳等請客)
	on the other hand 112領 107領	另一方面
	one of these days	總有一天
	one-of-a-kind 112領	獨一無二
	opt for	選擇, 選修, 選中, 作出...抉擇
	out of order	發生故障
P -	pay a visit to	參觀; 訪問
	pay attention to	注意; 關心
	pay off	償清債務; 帶來好結果, 成功, 行得通
	pick up 108領	用汽車搭載某人或接某人, 撿起, 振作, 加快
	pile up	增多; 積累
	plenty of 110導	很多; 大量
	plug in	插上...的插頭以接通電源
	pop in 109領	偶然來訪
	popular with	受歡迎
	prick on	驅使, 激勵, 鼓勵

▸ 3-12

	片語	中文
	prior to 112領 108領	優先
	pull off 107導	(使勁)摘掉, 脫掉; 成功完成
	pull over 107導	靠邊停車; 把...拉過來, 靠岸
	put in	加進; 提交; 放入; 插入; 進入
	put off 110導	推遲; 拖延; 阻止, 勸阻; 脫掉; 去掉
	put on 110導 107導	上演; 穿上
	put out	放出; 伸出; 挖出; 生產, 出版; 發布; 撲滅
	put up	建造; 推舉, 提名
Q -	**qualified for**	有...的資格
	queue up 107導	排隊等候
R -	**raise concerns** 112領	喚起注意
	range from...to... 109領	在從...到...的範圍內變化
	refer to 109領 108領 107導	提到; 談論; 意指; 參考
	regard as	把...看作
	rely on	依靠, 信賴
	responsible for 109領	對...負責; 是...的原由
	result in 108導	導致; 結果是
	return to 112導 109導	返回
	rule out 109領	把...排除在外, 排除...的可能性
	run over 109領	壓過, 輾過; 快速閱讀; 溫習或演習
S -	**safe and sound**	安然無恙
	seem to 112領 110領 109領 107領	似乎
	sell out 108領	賣光
	set off 108導	出發; 使爆發; 隔開; 襯托
	set on 108導	攻擊; 唆使; 決定

	片語	中文
	set out	動身, 開始; 提出, 移植
	settle down	安下心來做某事, 開始做...
	shop around 107導	逐店選購; 貨比三家; 搜尋
	sit back	坐下來休息; 不採取行動
	sort out 109領	解決(問題等); 挑出; 分開
	spare time 107導	業餘時間
	speak up	不顧忌地道出; 大聲說
	stand someone up	放某人鴿子
	stay away from 112導	離開; 不接近...
	stay up	不去睡覺, 熬夜
	step down	辭職; 減少
	step out	加快腳步, 加速
	stop off	中途稍作停留(做某事)
	suffer from 109領 108導	受...之苦; 患有某種疾病
	sum up 107導	形成看法; 總結; 計算; 歸納證詞或雙方論點
	summon up	鼓起; 引起
T -	**take a detour** 112領 108導	繞路
	take a stroll	散步, 漫步, 閑逛
	take actions 112領	採取行動
	take advantage of 108導	利用, 占...的便宜
	take after 109領	像; 與...相似
	take away 110領	拿走, 帶走; 除去; 沒收
	take care of 109領	照顧; 處理
	take in	接受; 理解
	take notice of 108導	注意; 理會

▶ 3-14

	片語	中文
	take off 112領	脫下; 起飛; 休假
	take over	接管, 繼任
	take turns	輪流
	take up	拿起, 抬起, 舉起; 開始從事
	tied up	(人)脫不了身; 忙得不可開交
	tighten up on sth.	變得更小心(或警惕、嚴格)
	turn down 109領	拒絕; 調低, 向下翻轉
	turn in	出現, 被發現; (指機會)出現, 到來
	turn out	交上; 歸還
	turn to 109導	結果是; 證明是; 出席; 關掉
	turn up 109導	求助於; 轉向; 參考
U -	ups and downs	盛衰
W -	ward off 109導	避開; 擋住; 防止
	ways and means	辦法
	wear off 109領	磨損; 漸漸減少, 逐漸消失; 消逝
	wear on	消逝; 使惱火
	wide array 107領	各式各樣
	wind up	上弦; 結束; 環繞; 吊起來
	worst-case scenario	最壞的情況

| Go Bananas 的由來 |

俚語「**Go bananas**」相當於 **Go crazy**，有瘋狂、發瘋的意思。形容人們的反應就像猴子看到香蕉那樣的瘋狂。通常在兩種情況下，會使用 **Go bananas** ：

❶「並不是什麼壞事」亢奮之表現，例如：**When the pop diva appeared, the fans went bananas.**（當這位流行歌后一出場，粉絲們就瘋掉了。）

❷「並不是什麼好事」激動之表現，例如：**The parents went bananas when they knew that their teenage daughter was <u>in the family way</u>.**（得知正當年少的女兒<u>懷孕</u>，雙親瘋掉了）。

Unit .

04.

測驗篇

考試要高分，
不只是累積『單字量』及熟悉『文法規則』，
不斷加強練習考試題型，
才能善將單字及文法規則運用在考題上。
先熟讀各年度一百個重要單字，再進入測驗，
是不是更容易答題了呢！

Chapter. 01 | 測驗 | 109年度導遊試題

掌握關鍵單字，更快作答70%考題！

重要單字彙整

掃描 QR code 或登入網址
www.magee.tw/istudy
用聽的也能背單字！

本單元針對**109～112**年度導遊、領隊試題，依各年度題型之重要程度，歸納出**100**個必讀單字及單字出現次數統計(分析100年以前的試題與現今考法差異較大，考生可將重心放在近年題型為主)。建議先熟記單字，再進行試題測驗，更能提升作答實力！

由於領隊、導遊在單字部分並無明顯範圍區別，建議報考導遊類組的考生，領隊篇單字也須熟記。同時，因應命題趨勢，特別收錄「同義詞」及「反義詞」彙整，幫助聯想記憶，進而累積單字量。

實力應證法 先將**109～111**年共六章的單字熟讀，再進行**112**年度試題測驗，試試看能認得多少個單字呢！

單字學習法 背單字的方法有很多，本書另提供老師線上語音導讀，帶著大家一起背單字

	單字	出現	音標	中文	詞性
1	**landmark**	8	[ˋlænd͵mɑrk]	(顯而易見的)地標, 陸標 同義詞 turning-point, milestone	名詞
2	**accommodation**	30	[ə͵kɑməˋdeʃən]	住宿; 適應; 調節; 膳宿	名詞
3	**range**	12	[rendʒ]	(數量、種類等變化的) 範圍, 幅度, 區域 同義詞 limit, extent, distance, length	名詞
4	**sandal**	5	[ˋsændL]	涼鞋; 拖鞋	名詞
5	**irritate**	6	[ˋɪrə͵tet]	使惱怒; 使煩躁; 使不舒服; 使難受 同義詞 annoy, incite, agitate, provoke	動詞
6	**confuse**	7	[kənˋfjuz]	使困惑; 把...混同, 混淆	動詞
7	**addict**	10	[əˋdɪkt]	使沉溺; 使醉心; 使成癮 同義詞 complicate, mistake, bewilder 反義詞 compose 使安定	動詞
8	**aware**	14	[əˋwɛr]	知道的, 察覺的, 意識到的 同義詞 knowing, conscious, realizing 反義詞 ignorant 無知的; unaware 未察覺的	形容詞

	單字	出現	音標	中文	詞性
9	**beware**	7	[bɪˋwɛr]	當心; 小心; 注意; 提防 同義詞 be careful, guard against	動詞
10	**attack**	9	[əˋtæk]	進攻, 襲擊; 抨擊; 責難 同義詞 bombard, charge, ambush, assault 反義詞 defend 防禦, protect 保護	動詞
11	**rumor**	9	[ˋrumɚ]	謠言, 謠傳; 傳聞, 傳說 同義詞 gossip, broadcast, circulate	名詞
12	**plastic**	13	[ˋplæstɪk]	塑膠的; 塑性的; 造型的; 塑造的	形容詞
13	**firecracker**	9	[ˋfaɪrˏkrækɚ]	爆竹, 鞭炮	名詞
14	**replica**	11	[ˋrɛplɪkə]	複製品; 複寫; 酷似 同義詞 copy, reproduction, duplicate	名詞
15	**exhibit**	28	[ɪgˋzɪbɪt]	展示, 陳列; 表示; 顯出 同義詞 demonstrate, display, present	名詞
16	**maintain**	8	[menˋten]	維持; 保持; 使繼續; 維修; 保養 同義詞 uphold, possess, sustain, preserve	動詞
17	**payment**	7	[ˋpemənt]	支付, 付款	名詞
18	**campfire**	5	[ˋkæmpˏfaɪr]	營火, 篝火	名詞
19	**budget**	22	[ˋbʌdʒɪt]	預算; 預算費; 生活費, 經費	名詞
20	**schedule**	18	[ˋskɛdʒʊl]	時間表; 課程表	名詞
21	**peak**	10	[pik]	最高的, 高峰的	形容詞
22	**nightmare**	7	[ˋnaɪtˏmɛr]	惡夢; 夢魘般的經歷 同義詞 bad dream, horrid dream	名詞
23	**pack**	7	[pæk]	包裝貨物; 整理行裝	動詞
24	**bonus**	9	[ˋbonəs]	獎金; 額外津貼; 特別補助	名詞
25	**tax**	12	[tæks]	稅金	名詞
26	**fare**	3	[fɛr]	(交通工具的)票價, 車(船)費	名詞
27	**tip**	26	[tɪp]	小費; 告誡; 提示 同義詞 gratuity, bonus, premium	名詞

▸ 4-4

	單字	出現	音標	中文	詞性
28	**exclude**	7	[ɪk`sklud]	把...排除在外; 不包括 反義詞 include 包括	動詞
29	**megapixel**	3	[ˈmegəpɪksl]	百萬畫素	名詞
30	**complete**	20	[kəm`plit]	完整的; 全部的; 完成的; 結束的 同義詞 finish, conclude, terminate	形容詞
31	**commentary**	5	[`kamən͵tɛrɪ]	評論, (對某一著作)系統的註釋 同義詞 explanation, exegesis, elucidation	名詞
32	**commencement**	7	[kə`mɛnsmənt]	開始, 發端; 學位授予典禮	名詞
33	**curb**	5	[kɝb]	路邊, (人行道旁的)鑲邊石, 邊欄	名詞
34	**tunnel**	9	[`tʌnəl]	隧道, 地道; (礦場的)坑道, 石巷	名詞
35	**corporation**	7	[͵korpə`reʃən]	公司 同義詞 industry, company, business	名詞
36	**rough**	6	[rʌf]	粗糙的; 表面不平的; 毛茸茸的; 蓬亂的 同義詞 uneven, bumpy, rocky, rugged 反義詞 smooth 柔軟的, even 平坦的	形容詞
37	**hoarse**	5	[hors]	(嗓音)嘶啞的; 粗啞的 同義詞 rough, gruff, harsh, husky	形容詞
38	**administration**	9	[əd͵mɪnə`streʃən]	管理, 經營; 政權	名詞
39	**goodness**	2	[`gʊdnɪs]	善良; 仁慈; 美德; 精華 反義詞 badness 壞, 不好	名詞
40	**blame**	7	[blem]	責備, 指責 同義詞 charge, accuse, impeach, indict 反義詞 praise 讚揚	動詞
41	**nostalgia**	6	[nas`tældʒɪə]	鄉愁; 懷舊之情	名詞
42	**geologic**	5	[dʒɪə`ladʒɪk]	地質學上的, 地質的	形容詞
43	**marvelously**	5	[`ma:vləsli]	令人驚訝地; 奇妙地	副詞
44	**volcano**	6	[val`keno]	火山; 隨時可能爆發的狀態	名詞
45	**procession**	4	[prə`sɛʃən]	沿著街道行進; 遊行	動詞

	單字	出現	音標	中文	詞性
46	**embody**	3	[ɪm`bɑdɪ]	體現, 使具體化, 包含, 收錄 同義詞 include, comprise, contain	動詞
47	**prolong**	4	[prə`lɔŋ]	延長, 拉長; 拖延; 拖長(音節等)的發音 同義詞 extend, stretch, lengthen	動詞
48	**refresh**	4	[rɪ`frɛʃ]	使清新, 使清涼; 消除...疲勞 同義詞 renew, revive, reanimate 反義詞 exhaust 精疲力盡, weary 疲倦的	動詞
49	**merely**	3	[`mɪrlɪ]	只是, 僅僅, 不過 同義詞 simply, only, purely, barely	副詞
50	**respect**	10	[rɪ`spɛkt]	敬重, 尊敬, 重視 同義詞 adore, appreciate, admire, esteem 反義詞 dishonor 不尊敬, insult 侮辱	動詞
51	**cherish**	5	[`tʃɛrɪʃ]	珍惜; 撫育; 愛護 同義詞 adore, worship, treasure, protect 反義詞 neglect, ignore 無視	動詞
52	**inscribe**	4	[ɪn`skraɪb]	題寫; 印; 牢記, 銘記 同義詞 write, engrave, mark, imprint	動詞
53	**propel**	3	[prə`pɛl]	推進, 推; 推動; 驅策, 激勵 同義詞 drive, move, motivate, stimulate	動詞
54	**furniture**	6	[`fɝnɪtʃɚ]	傢俱; (工廠等的)設備	名詞
55	**craftsmanship**	4	[`kræftsmən͵ʃɪp]	工藝	名詞
56	**transcribe**	3	[træns`kraɪb]	抄寫, 謄寫; 把(資料)改錄成另一種形式	動詞
57	**assembly**	1	[ə`sɛmblɪ]	集會; 集合; (因特定目的)聚集在一起的人	名詞
58	**launch**	9	[lɔntʃ]	開始; 發射 同義詞 start, introduce, spring	動詞
59	**illuminate**	6	[ɪ`lumə͵net]	照亮; 照射; 用燈裝飾(房屋等) 同義詞 light, brighten, spotlight	動詞
60	**confront**	5	[kən`frʌnt]	迎面遇到; 面臨; 遭遇 同義詞 oppose, face, encounter	動詞
61	**revive**	4	[rɪ`vaɪv]	甦醒; 復甦; 恢復精力; 恢復生機	動詞

▶ 4-6

	單字	出現	音標	中文	詞性
62	**central**	15	[`sɛntrəl]	中心的, 主要的, 核心的; 重要的 同義詞 main, chief, leading, principal	形容詞
63	**destination**	39	[ˌdɛstə`neʃən]	目的地, 終點; 目標, 目的	名詞
64	**lounge**	7	[laʊndʒ]	休息室	名詞
65	**vendor**	4	[`vɛndɚ]	小販; 供應商; 自動售貨機	名詞
66	**valet**	4	[`vælɪt]	(飯店或餐廳的)代客泊車者	名詞
67	**cashier**	4	[kæ`ʃɪr]	出納員	名詞
68	**porter**	5	[`portɚ]	行李員; (車站, 機場等的)搬運工人	名詞
69	**delight**	10	[dɪ`laɪt]	感到高興; 欣喜, 愉快 同義詞 gratify, gladden, please	動詞
70	**donate**	11	[`donet]	捐獻, 捐贈 同義詞 contribute, present, bestow, award	動詞
71	**valuable**	8	[ˈvæl.jə.bəl]	值錢的, 貴重的; 有用的, 有價值的 同義詞 costly, expensive, priceless	形容詞
72	**sponsor**	9	[`spɑnsɚ]	發起; 主辦; 倡議; 贊助	動詞
73	**inspect**	7	[ɪn`spɛkt]	檢查; 審查; 檢閱; 視察	動詞
74	**accompany**	5	[ə`kʌmpənɪ]	陪同, 伴隨; 隨著...發生, 伴有 同義詞 associate, affiliate, syndicate	動詞
75	**entrance**	8	[`ɛntrəns]	門口; 進入, 登場, 就任	名詞
76	**concession**	5	[kən`sɛʃən]	優惠價格; 讓步; 特許權, 專利權 同義詞 privilege, exception	名詞
77	**contend**	5	[kən`tɛnd]	爭奪, 競爭; 全力對付; 搏鬥; 奮鬥 同義詞 fight, struggle, argue, quarrel	動詞
78	**regret**	7	[rɪ`grɛt]	懊悔; 因...而遺憾; 感到後悔; 感到抱歉	動詞
79	**functional**	7	[ˈfʌŋk.ʃən.əl]	實用的; 功能性的; 在起作用的	形容詞
80	**sophisticated**	6	[sə`fɪstɪˌketɪd]	富有經驗的; 老於世故的; 精通的	形容詞
81	**definition**	6	[ˌdɛfə`nɪʃən]	定義; 釋義; 限定; 定界; 規定 同義詞 delimitation, circumscription	名詞

	單字	出現	音標	中文	詞性
82	**delivery**	9	[dɪ`lɪvərɪ]	投遞, 傳送, 交付, 交貨	動詞
83	**airflow**	3	[`ɛəfləu]	(飛機等產生的)氣流; 空氣的流動	名詞
84	**turbulence**	10	[`tɝbjələns]	亂流; 湍流; (氣體等的)紊流	名詞
85	**carriage**	3	[`kærɪdʒ]	運輸; 運費; 四輪馬車	名詞
86	**identification**	6	[aɪˌdɛntəfə`keʃən]	認出; 識別; 鑑定; 身分證明; 身分證	名詞
87	**translation**	4	[træns`leʃən]	翻譯; 調任; 轉移 同義詞 transliteration, transcription	名詞
88	**nationality**	3	[ˌnæʃə`nælətɪ]	國籍; 民族	名詞
89	**hesitant**	5	[`hɛzətənt]	遲疑的; 躊躇的; 猶豫不定的	形容詞
90	**reluctant**	4	[rɪ`lʌktənt]	不情願的; 勉強的 同義詞 unwilling, grudging, disinclined 反義詞 willing 情願的, 願意的	形容詞
91	**suspicious**	5	[sə`spɪʃəs]	猜疑的, 疑心的; 多疑的 同義詞 suspecting, doubtful, questionable	形容詞
92	**rescue**	6	[`rɛskju]	援救; 營救; 挽救 同義詞 release, retrieve, salvage, extricate	動詞
93	**irrational**	1	[i`ræʃənəl]	無理性的; 不合理的; 不明事理的 反義詞 rational 合理的	形容詞
94	**relationship**	7	[rɪ`leʃən`ʃɪp]	關係, 關聯; 人際關係	名詞
95	**fountain**	3	[`faʊntɪn]	噴泉; 水源; 人造噴泉; 噴水池 同義詞 spring, spout, spray	名詞
96	**invisible**	3	[in`vizəbl]	無形的; 看不見的; 不顯眼的 同義詞 imperceptible, concealed, veiled	形容詞
97	**unreliable**	1	[`ʌnri`laiəbl]	不可靠的; 不可信任的; 靠不住的 反義詞 reliable 可信賴的	形容詞
98	**headline**	3	[`hɛdˌlaɪn]	頭版頭條新聞 同義詞 caption, heading, superscription	名詞
99	**reflect**	10	[rɪ`flɛkt]	反映, 反射; 照出, 映出	動詞
100	**indication**	1	[ˌɪndə`keʃən]	指示; 指點; 表示; 徵兆; 跡象	名詞

109年導遊筆試測驗

● 本書採用英語邏輯思維[中譯]
幫助更快看懂句子，拆解字義

題型分析	單字 40	片語 11	對話 14	情境命題	景物 6	餐飲 3	住宿 5	交通 9	機場 7
	文法 5	閱測 10			生活 26	民俗 2	產業 6	職能 0	購物 6

單選題 [共80題，每題1.25分]

( ) 1. Reservation: Hello, Hotel Four Corners. How may I help you?
John: Hello, I would like to _______ a room for three days.
(A)place (B)order (C)book (D)conserve 住宿 單字

[中譯] 櫃檯：四角飯店您好，有什麼能為您服務的嗎？ John：你好，我想預訂一間房入住三天。
(A)放置 (B)命令 (C)預訂 (D)保存 答 C

( ) 2. Local tour guide: Good morning everyone. Today, I will take you touring the city to some famous _______, such as Taipei 101, National Palace Museum, Chiang Kai Sheck Memorial Park, and many more.
(A)areas (B)shops (C)restaurants (D)**landmarks**[1] 景物 單字

[中譯] 當地導遊：早安各位。今天，我會帶你們去遊覽這個城市的一些著名地標，例如臺北101、故宮博物院、中正紀念堂和其他景點。
(A)地區 (B)商店 (C)餐廳 (D)地標 答 D

( ) 3. Visitor: How often does the bus run from here to the airport?
Receptionist: _______
(A)The plane leaves in an hour. (B)Every 20 minutes.
(C)It will take off very soon. (D)The bus goes straight to the airport. 交通 對話

[中譯] 遊客：從這裡到機場的巴士多久發車一次？ 接待員：每20分鐘一班。
(A)飛機會在一小時內離開 (B)每20分鐘一班 (C)它將很快起飛 (D)巴士直達機場 答 B

( ) 4. Visitor: I'd like some information about **accommodations**[2], please.
Information center: _______
(A)The hotel price in this area **ranges**[3] from 2,000 to 3,000 NT dollars.
(B)There are a lot of foreign visitors from Japan and Korea.
(C)You might want to stay for a few more days.
(D)The room service is 24 hours a day. 住宿 對話

[中譯] 遊客：我想要一些關於住宿的資訊。
服務中心：這個區域的飯店價格落在新台幣2000元到3000元之間。
(A)這個區域的飯店價格落在新台幣2000元到3000元之間。
(B)有很多外國遊客來自日本和韓國。
(C)您可能想再多住幾天。
(D)客房服務全天24小時。 答 A

( ) 5. Guest: I'd like to reserve a table for a party of five tonight at 7 o'clock, please.
Receptionist: _______
(A)Yes, it is 120 dollars.
(B)Oh, that will be too much.
(C)Sorry, I'm afraid we are all booked up for tonight.
(D)No, can you come back tomorrow? 生活 對話

[中譯] 客人：我想預訂一張5人桌在今晚7點。 接待員：抱歉，今晚座位恐怕都已被預訂了。
(A)好的，120美金 (B)哦，那太多了
(C)抱歉，今晚座位恐怕都已被預訂了 (D)不行，您明天可以回來嗎？ 答 C

( ) 6. Person A: Is the next seat taken? Person B: _______
(A)Don't worry. (B)You don't want to know.
(C)I prefer to sit by myself. (D)That's a problem. 生活 對話

[中譯] 人物A：旁邊的座位有人了嗎？ 人物B：我喜歡自己一個人坐。
(A)不要擔心 (B)你不會想知道 (C)我喜歡自己一個人坐 (D)那是個問題 答 C

( ) 7. Today's lunch special is beef lasagna. It _______ a medium coke.
(A)looks into (B)takes over (C)comes with (D)gives in 餐飲 片語

[中譯] 今天的特色午餐是牛肉千層麵，它附贈一杯中杯可樂。
(A)調查 (B)接管、繼任 (C)附贈 (D)讓步、投降 答 C

( ) 8. In some restaurants, there may be a _______. You cannot just turn up with your shorts and **sandals**[4].
(A)reservation (B)dress code (C)reception (D)popular starter 生活 片語

[中譯] 在一些餐廳，可能會有穿著要求，你不能只穿著短褲和涼鞋出席。
(A)預訂 (B)著裝守則 (C)接待 (D)招牌前菜 答 B

( ) 9. Willie _______ coffee. He must drink at least five cups of coffee every day.
(A)is dedicated to (B)is **irritated**[5] by (C)is **confused**[6] with (D)is **addicted**[7] to
生活 片語

[中譯] Willie對咖啡上癮，他每天需要喝至少五杯咖啡。
(A)致力於 (B)惱怒 (C)混淆 (D)對...上癮 答 D

( ) 10. Chinese New Year is _______. I have a lot of shopping to do in just a few days.
(A)around the corner (B)months away (C)drawing new (D)cutting the corner
生活 片語

[中譯] 農曆新年即將來臨，我最近幾天要買許多東西。
(A)即將來臨 (B)在幾個月後 (C)畫新的 (D)走捷徑 答 A

( ) 11. I will keep you _______ the weather condition tomorrow.
(A)**aware**[8] (B)**beware**[9] of (C)updated with (D)dated of 生活 文法

[中譯] 我會持續和你更新明天的天氣狀態。
(A)察覺的 (B)注意、小心 (C)更新 (D)日期 解 P2-9. 文法11 答 C

解 (A)aware為形容詞，keep後接Ving，應改為keep you being aware of ...。

( ) 12. _______ that a monster called ‘Nian’ **attacked**[10] people and animals in the village.
(A)It said (B)Hearing (C)**Rumor**[11] has it (D)Saying 生活 片語

[中譯] 據說，有一個叫做“年”的怪物襲擊了村裡的人和動物。
(A)它說 (B)聽到 (C)傳言 (D)諺語、格言 答 C

( ) 13. People decorate their homes with **plastic**[12] **firecrackers**[13] to _______ bad luck.
(A)wait for (B)disguise as (C)look for (D)ward off 生活 片語

[中譯] 人們運用塑料鞭炮裝飾他們的家，以擋住壞運。
(A)等待 (B)偽裝成 (C)尋找、期待 (D)擋住、避開 答 D

( ) 14. At the end of the tour, you’ll see a _______ with **replicas**[14] of almost every item in the **exhibit**[15].
(A)restroom (B)souvenir shop (C)ticket counter (D)information center
產業 單字

[中譯] 旅程結束時，你會看到一家紀念品商店，裡面陳列著幾乎所有展品的複製品。
(A)洗手間 (B)紀念品商店 (C)售票處 (D)服務中心 答 B

( ) 15. Inside the museum, flash photography is strictly _______.
(A)allowed (B)**maintained**[16] (C)prohibited (D)encouraged 景物 單字

[中譯] 在博物館裡，閃光燈拍照是被嚴格禁止的。
(A)允許的 (B)維護的 (C)禁止的 (D)被鼓勵的 答 C

( ) 16. If you wish to return the product within 7 days, most stores will give you a _______ with no questions asked.
(A)check (B)refund (C)**payment**[17] (D)answer 購物 單字

[中譯] 如果您希望在7天內退貨，多數商家都會無條件退款給您。
(A)支票；檢查 (B)退款 (C)付款 (D)回答 答 B

( ) 17. _______ a **campfire**[18] is the most classic outdoor activity for camping.
(A)Setting up (B)Setting aside (C)Going off (D)Putting out 生活 片語

[中譯] 搭起營火是露營很典型的戶外活動。
(A)搭起、建造 (B)置...於一旁 (C)爆炸、離開 (D)撲滅、逐出 答 A

( ) 18. We are _______, so we want to plan a vacation that doesn't cost too much.
(A)on a tight **budget**[19] (B)in a tight budget
(C)in a big hurry (D)in a tight **schedule**[20] 生活 片語

[中譯] 我們預算有限，所以想要規劃一個不需要花太多錢的假期。
(A)(B)預算有限 (C)急忙 (D)行程緊湊 答 A

( ) 19. You can get a lower rate when taking a vacation during the _______.
(A)holiday season (B)low season (C)**peak**[21] season (D)high season 產業 片語

[中譯] 在淡季度假時，你可以取得較低的價格。
(A)聖誕假期 (B)淡季 (C)旺季 (D)旺季 答 B

( ) 20. _______ for a vacation is a **nightmare**[22]. I wish someone could do it for me. It took me so long to get everything needed in place.
(A)Looking (B)**Packing**[23] (C)Waiting (D)Walking 生活 單字

[中譯] 為了度假打包行李是一場噩夢， 我希望有人能幫我搞定，我得花很長時間才能將一切所需準備就緒。
(A)尋找 (B)打包、收拾(行李) (C)等待 (D)走路 答 B

( ) 21. When you tell the driver to "keep the change," you are giving the change as a _______.
(A)**bonus**[24] (B)**tax**[25] (C)**fare**[26] (D)**tip**[27] 生活 單字

[中譯] 當你告訴司機"不用找零了"，代表你給零錢作為小費。
(A)獎金 (B)稅金 (C)票價 (D)小費 答 D

( ) 22. Guest: Why is my order taking so long? Server: I'm sorry, sir. _______
(A)I'll check on it right now. It shouldn't be too long.
(B)I have nothing to do with this delay.
(C)What can I do for you?
(D)Can I get you anything? 生活 對話

[中譯] 客人：為什麼我的訂單花上這麼長時間？
服務員：我很抱歉，先生，我馬上確認，不應該這麼久的。
(A)我馬上確認，不應該這麼久的 (B)這個延誤與我無關
(C)我可以為您做什麼？ (D)我可以幫您什麼？ 答 A

( ) 23. Guest: Is the tip included in the bill? Server: _______
(A)The tip is extra, sir. (B)Tipping is appreciated.
(C)The bill is **excluded**[28]. (D)A tip is possible. 生活 對話

[中譯] 客人：請問小費包含在帳單裡嗎？ 服務員：小費是外加的，先生。
(A)小費是外加的，先生 (B)非常感謝您的小費 (C)拒收的 (D)有可能有小費 答 A

( ) 24. One simplest way to mean splitting the bill can be "_______."
(A)On the house (B)Go Dutch (C)Pay cash (D)Cash or charge 生活 片語

[中譯] 最簡單的方式去表達分攤帳單可以說 "各付各的"。
(A)免費提供的 (B)各付各的 (C)支付現金 (D)現金或刷卡 答 B

( ) 25. A: Excuse me. I ordered a Big Mac, not a chicken sandwich.
B: _______ I'll get your order fixed right now.
(A)What did you say? (B)Did you say that?
(C)Sorry about that. (D)That's not my fault. 餐飲 對話

[中譯] A：不好意思，我點的是大麥克，不是雞肉三明治。
B：我很抱歉，我將立刻更正您的訂單。
(A)您說什麼？ (B)你有說嗎？ (C)我很抱歉 (D)這不是我的錯 答 C

( ) 26. A: Would you like anything to drink? B: _______
(A)To go, please. (B)Sure, it is free.
(C)Sorry about that. (D)Yes, a coke, please. 餐飲 對話

[中譯] A：您想要喝些什麼嗎？ B：好，請給我一杯可樂。
(A)麻煩外帶 (B)當然，是免費的 (C)我很抱歉 (D)好的，請給我一杯可樂 答 D

( ) 27. A: How big is the memory card? B: _______
(A)It is 128 kg. (B)It is 36 **megapixels**[29].
(C)Twice the size. (D)As large as it can be. 生活 單字

[中譯] A：這個記憶卡有多大？ B：它是36百萬像素。
(A)它是128公斤 (B)它是36百萬像素 (C)兩倍的大小 (D)要多大有多大 答 ABCD

( ) 28. Usually the hotel offers guests with two bottles of drinking water free of charge. They are _______.
(A)complimentary (B)**complete**[30] (C)**commentary**[31] (D)**commencement**[32]
住宿 單字

[中譯] 通常飯店提供客人兩瓶免費的瓶裝水。它們是附贈的。
(A)附贈的 (B)完成的 (C)評論(n.) (D)開端 答 A

( ) 29. A: I'm kind of in a hurry. Could you please drive a little faster?
B: Sorry, I'm already going very fast, close to the _______.
(A)**curb**[33] side (B)**tunnel**[34] end (C)police car (D)speed limit 交通 單字

[中譯] A：我有點趕時間，可以請你開再快一點嗎？
B：抱歉，我已經開得非常快了，接近限速。
(A)路邊 (B)隧道盡頭 (C)警車 (D)限速 答 D

( ) 30. When shopping for clothing, you can try the items on in _______ before buying them.
(A)fitting rooms (B)restrooms (C)sitting rooms (D)waiting rooms 購物 單字

[中譯] 購買服裝時，在購買前您可以在試衣間試穿衣服。
(A)試衣間 (B)洗手間 (C)起居室 (D)等候室 答 A

( ) 31. The pants I bought yesterday are too long. I would like to have them _______.
(A)changed (B)shortened (C)ironed (D)cut 生活 單字

[中譯] 我昨天買的這條褲子太長了，我想要去改短它們。
(A)更改 (B)改短 (C)熨燙 (D)切割 答 B

( ) 32. The Taipei Rapid Transit **Corporation**[35] planned to change the harsh mechanical beeping of the card readers at the entry gates to the Taipei Metro system to a _______ piano tone, thereby making a small change in the soundscape design of the city.
(A)**rough**[36] (B)high (C)soft (D)**hoarse**[37] 交通 單字

[中譯] 台北捷運公司計劃將台北捷運入口處讀卡機發出的刺耳的機械嗶音改為柔和的鋼琴音調，進而對城市的音景設計進行一些改變。
(A)粗糙的 (B)高的 (C)柔和的 (D)沙啞的 答 C

( ) 33. Taiwan Railways **Administration**[38] offers bento, the Japanese name for a boxed meal, transporting memories, _______ for home, and tales of **goodness**[39].
(A)crowd (B)rush (C)**blame**[40] (D)**nostalgia**[41] 產業 單字

[中譯] 台灣鐵路管理局提供的鐵路「便當」(盒裝餐點的日文)傳承著回憶，對家的懷舊之情，和美好的故事。
(A)人群 (B)匆忙 (C)責備 (D)懷舊之情 答 D

( ) 34. Taiwan's North Coast provides a special cycling experience because it features a winding coastline, **geologic**[42] _______, and **marvelously**[43] shaped rocks.
(A)landscapes (B)**volcanos**[44] (C)patties (D)villages 景物 單字

[中譯] 台灣北海岸提供特殊的騎行體驗，因為它的特色蜿蜒海岸線，地質景觀和奇石巨岩。
(A)景觀 (B)火山 (C)小餡餅 (D)村莊 答 A

( ) 35. The **procession**[45] for the goddess Mazu is a century-old tradition that _______ the collective memories of Taiwanese people.
(A)extends (B)**embodies**[46] (C)**prolongs**[47] (D)**refreshes**[48] 民俗 單字

[中譯] 媽祖繞境遊行是一個百年歷史的傳統，體現了台灣人民的群體記憶。
(A)擴張 (B)體現 (C)延長 (D)恢復精神 答 B

情境篇 文法篇 片語篇 測驗篇 口試篇

( ) 36. Chishang's Autumn Rice Harvest Arts Festival is not **merely**[49] an arts event, but also a meaningful one _______ its locality.
(A)celebrated (B)celebrating (C)celebrates (D)celebrate 產業 單字

[中譯] 池上秋收稻穗藝術節不僅是一項藝術活動，更是對深化在地性之意義深長。
(A)著名的 (B)深耕 (C)(D)慶祝 答 B

( ) 37. Glove puppetry is Taiwan's cultural treasure that we should **respect**[50] and _______.
(A)resemble (B)**cherish**[51] (C)**inscribe**[52] (D)**propel**[53] 民俗 單字

[中譯] 布袋戲是台灣文化的珍寶，我們應該要尊敬並且珍惜它。
(A)像、類似 (B)珍惜 (C)題寫 (D)驅策、推進 答 B

( ) 38. Bamboo **furniture**[54] is popular in Latin America as a result of bamboo-weaving **craftsmanship**[55] _______ from Taiwan.
(A)**transcribed**[56] (B)transferred (C)assigned (D)**assembled**[57] 產業 單字

[中譯] 由於台灣竹編織工藝的傳入，竹製家具在拉丁美洲深受歡迎。
(A)抄寫 (B)傳入 (C)指定 (D)集合、召集 答 B

( ) 39. The Trending Taiwan channel on YouTube _______ in 2015 presents short films that share the impressive scenes of Taiwan and its people with people around the globe.
(A)**launched**[58] (B)appeared (C)**illuminated**[59] (D)counted 產業 單字

[中譯] 2015年在YouTube開張的Trending Taiwan頻道是透過短片與世界各地的人們分享令人印象深刻的台灣風情與民情。
(A)開始從事 (B)出現 (C)被照亮的 (D)計算 答 A

( ) 40. To share the sights of his native Taiwan, Chen Guan-zhou used over 40,000 Lego pieces to make Long-shan Temple, which made him _______ to fame in the field.
(A)rocket (B)rockets (C)rocketed (D)rocketing 生活 文法

[中譯] 為了分享祖國台灣的景象，陳冠州用超過40,000個樂高積木製作了龍山寺，這使他從此聲名大噪。
(A)(B)(C)(D)聲名大噪 解 P2-2. 文法01 答 A

解 使役動詞的文法為 make + O + Vr；其他常見使役動詞有let, make, have, help等。

( ) 41. The National Taiwan Museum as the gateway to 228 Memorial Park tells Taiwan's stories, _______ her history, and serves as a museum truly for and about the people.
(A)**confronts**[60] (B)encounters (C)records (D)**revives**[61] 景物 單字

[中譯] 國立台灣博物館是通往228紀念公園的入口，講述著台灣的故事，記錄著台灣的歷史，是為人們所設的人類相關博物館。

(A)面臨 (B)遭遇 (C)記錄 (D)復活 答 C

( ) 42. The airport is a huge _______, a **central**[62] area where many flights come and connect to other flights.

(A)**destination**[63] (B)concourse (C)hub (D)**lounge**[64] 機場 單字

[中譯] 機場是一個巨大的樞紐，是許多航班往返於並與其他航班相連的集中區域。

(A)目的地 (B)大堂 (C)樞紐 (D)(機場的)候機室 答 C

( ) 43. Customs officer: What is the purpose of your visit?

Tourist: _______

Customs officer: No problem.

(A)My uncle lives here. (B)I've booked a hotel for my trip.

(C)My friend will pick me up. (D)I was just here to transit. 機場 對話

[中譯] 海關員：您此次旅行的目的是什麼？

遊客：我只是在這裡過境。

海關員：沒問題。

(A)我的叔叔住在這裡 (B)我已經為我的旅途預定了一個旅館

(C)我的朋友會來接我 (D)我只是在這裡過境。 答 D

( ) 44. If you drove to a hotel, there might be a _______, who will take your car and park it for you.

(A)**vendor**[65] (B)**valet**[66] (C)**cashier**[67] (D)retailer 住宿 單字

[中譯] 如果您開車去飯店，可能會有代客泊車員，他會接手並將您的車停好。

(A)小販 (B)代客泊車員 (C)出納員 (D)零售商 答 B

( ) 45. A hotel usually has a _______, who will help you organize a local tour, make a restaurant reservation, buy tickets to the theatre or sports games—anything you want to do outside the hotel.

(A)concierge (B)**porter**[68] (C)bellhop (D)maid 住宿 單字

[中譯] 飯店通常會有櫃台人員，他們會協助您安排在地觀光，預訂餐廳，購買劇院門票或體育比賽—任何您想在飯店以外進行的活動。

(A)櫃台人員 (B)行李員 (C)(旅館)服務生 (D)少女 答 A

( ) 46. In addition to your passport, you need a _______ that lets you pass through security and into the airport.

(A)reservation card (B)carry-on backpack (C)boarding pass (D)baggage tag

機場 單字

[中譯] 除了護照外，你還需要登機證來通過安檢和進入機場。
(A)預訂卡 (B)手提背包 (C)登機證 (D)行李掛牌 答 C

( ) 47. A: Excuse me. Could you please tell me the way to the Empire State Building?
B: ________
(A)It's in the heart of the city. (B)Bus number 24 goes there.
(C)A railway station is nearby. (D)Take exit 4 and you'll see it across the street.
交通 對話

[中譯] A：不好意思，可以請你告訴我去帝國大廈的路嗎？B：走4號出口，然後你會看到它在對街。
(A)它是城市的中心 (B)公車24號到那裡
(C)在火車站附近 (D)走4號出口，然後你會看到它在對街 答 D

( ) 48. A: ________
B: Go down this street, turn left, and you should see it on your right.
(A)Excuse me. How do I get to the modern gallery center by bus?
(B)I'm going to the city library. Can you show me which train to take?
(C)Hi, do you know where the nearest subway station is?
(D)What's the best way to the airport? 交通 對話

[中譯] A：您好，請問您知道最近的地鐵站在哪裡嗎？
B：沿著這條街走，向左轉，應該會看到它在您的右邊。
(A)不好意思， 我該如何搭乘公車去現代美術館中心呢？
(B)我要去市立圖書館，你能告訴我坐哪班火車去嗎？
(C)您好，請問您知道最近的地鐵站在哪裡嗎？
(D)前往機場的最佳方式是什麼？ 答 C

( ) 49. A: Excuse me. Where can I find some jackets?
B: ________
A: Medium should be fine.
(A)Do you want to request a refund?
(B)What size do you wear?
(C)Would you like to apply for a store credit card?
(D)Do you like to try them on? 購物 對話

[中譯] A：不好意思，請問我在哪裡可以找到一些外套？ B：您穿什麼尺寸呢？
A：中等尺寸應該就可以了。
(A)您想要要求退款嗎？ (B)您穿什麼尺寸呢？
(C)您想要申請商店信用卡嗎？ (D)您想試穿一下嗎？ 答 B

( ) 50. A: Do I need tickets for Taiwan Culinary Exhibition? B: _______
(A)We would be **delighted**[69] to see you there.
(B)You can **donate**[70] five dollars to the museum.
(C)It's free and open to the public.
(D)They also have a regular exhibition. 生活 對話

[中譯] A：我需要票券去台灣烹飪展覽會嗎？
B：它是免費的並對公眾開放。
(A)我們很高興在那裡見到你 (B)您可以捐贈五美元給博物館
(C)它是免費的並對公眾開放 (D)他們也有定期展覽 答 C

( ) 51. Before entering the museum, please _______ all **valuables**[71] and bags at the cloakroom.
(A)check in (B)request (C)set up (D)provide 生活 單字

[中譯] 進入博物館之前，請在寄物處寄存所有貴重物品和行李。
(A)寄存 (B)要求 (C)建造 (D)提供 答 A

( ) 52. Let me remind you that all children must be _______ by an adult in the art center.
(A)**sponsored**[72] (B)**inspected**[73] (C)connected (D)**accompanied**[74] 生活 單字

[中譯] 容我提醒您，在藝術中心內所有孩童都必須有成年人陪同。
(A)贊助 (B)檢查 (C)連接 (D)陪同 答 D

( ) 53. Visiting the museum of modern art, a lady turned to an attendant _______ nearby and asked about the painting.
(A)stood (B)stand (C)standing (D)stands 生活 文法

[中譯] 一位女士在參觀現代藝術博物館時，向站在附近的服務人員詢問了這幅畫。
(A)(B)(C)(D)站著 解 P2-20. 文法35 答

解 本題文型為 N + 關係代名詞 + V = N + Ving，依題可拆解成兩個子句 "A lady turned to an attendant and asked about the painting." 以及 "An attendant stood nearby."。因為 an attendant 是指人，關係代名詞要用 who，句子應改為 A lady turned to an attendant who stood nearby and asked about the painting. = A lady turned to an attendant standing nearby and asked about the painting.

( ) 54. A: Where does the tour start off？ B: _______
(A)It begins at 1:30. (B)We'll join the group at 2 o'clock.
(C)At the main **entrance**[75]. (D)Please keep up with the schedule. 交通 對話

[中譯] A：旅程從哪裡出發呢？ B：從正門口。
(A)從1:30開始 (B)我們將在2點加入這個小組 (C)從正門口 (D)請遵守行程表 答 C

( ) 55. The museum offers **concessions**[76] for students and elders.
(A)agreement (B)lower price (C)higher price (D)disagreement 景物 單字

[中譯] 博物館給予學生和老年人提供優惠價格。
(A)同意 (B)較低的價格 (C)較高的價格 (D)不同意 答 B

( ) 56. I heard books are on sale in the store this month. Maybe we can get a good _______ there.
(A)specialty (B)account (C)bargain (D)clearance 購物 單字

[中譯] 我聽說這個月書籍在商店有折扣，也許我們可以在那裡買到一些特價品。
(A)專業 (B)帳戶 (C)特價品 (D)清算 答 C

( ) 57. You can get a 15% discount if you buy it today. I can _______ it's the lowest you will get.
(A)prove (B)guarantee (C)**contend**[77] (D)**regret**[78] 購物 單字

[中譯] 如果今天購買的話，您可以享有15%的折扣，我可以保證這會是您得到的最低價格。
(A)證明 (B)保證 (C)爭奪 (D)懊悔 答 B

( ) 58. This new type of smart phone is very easy to operate. It is _______.
(A)**functional**[79] (B)user-friendly (C)complicated (D)**sophisticated**[80]
生活 單字

[中譯] 這種新型的智慧手機非常容易操作， 它很人性化的。
(A)實用的 (B)人性化的 (C)複雜的 (D)富有經驗的 答 B

( ) 59. May I have immigration card and custom _______ card?
(A)**definition**[81] (B)declaration (C)**delivery**[82] (D)departure 機場 單字

[中譯] 可以給我入境卡和海關申報單嗎？
(A)定義 (B)(納稅品等的)申報 (C)投遞 (D)出發 答 B

( ) 60. Please fasten your seatbelt and remain _______.
(A)sit (B)seated (C)sitting (D)seat 交通 文法

[中譯] 請繫緊您的安全帶並保持就座。
(A)(C)坐 (B)就坐的 (D)座位 答 B

解 (B) seat 是及物動詞，表示「就座」，常見用法為 be seated；而 sit 是「坐下」的動作。

( ) 61. We are now crossing a zone of _______. Please return to your seats and keep your seat belts fastened.
(A)atmosphere (B)**airflow**[83] (C)**turbulence**[84] (D)circulation 交通 單字

[中譯] 我們現在正通過亂流區。請回到你的座位上，並繫好安全帶。
(A)大氣層 (B)氣流 (C)亂流 (D)環流 答 C

( ) 62. A: My suitcase didn't appear on the _______.
B: Do you have your claim ticket? I need to get your tag number.
(A)circle (B)carousel (C)delivery (D)**carriage**[85] 機場 單字

[中譯] A：我的行李箱沒有出現在轉盤上。 B：您有行李憑條嗎？ 我需要取得您的掛牌號碼。
(A)圓圈 (B)行李傳送帶(轉盤) (C)投遞 (D)馬車 答 B

( ) 63. I am not feeling _______. Is there a hospital nearby?
(A)tired (B)well (C)ill (D)busy 生活 單字

[中譯] 我覺得不舒服，這附近有醫院嗎？
(A)疲憊 (B)舒服 (C)生病 (D)忙碌 答 B

( ) 64. No worries. The doctor gave him a/an ______ for his cold.
(A)operation (B)transition (C)prescription (D)**identification**[86] 生活 單字

[中譯] 別擔心，醫生針對他的感冒給他開了一份處方。
(A)操作 (B)轉換 (C)處方 (D)識別 答 C

( ) 65. A: Do you need anything else? B: No, that will be _______. Thanks.
(A)nice (B)all (C)mine (D)sure 購物 單字

[中譯] A：您還需要什麼嗎？ B：不用，就這樣了，謝謝。
(A)好 (B)全部 (C)我的 (D)當然 答 B

( ) 66. This is a routine stop check. Your driver's license and vehicle _______ card, please.
(A)registration (B)**translation**[87] (C)**nationality**[88] (D)society 交通 單字

[中譯] 這是例行的停車檢查。 請提供您的駕駛執照和行車執照。
(A)執照 (B)翻譯 (C)國籍 (D)社會 答 A

( ) 67. A: I lost my passport! B: Did you notice anyone _______?
(A)**hesitant**[89] (B)**reluctant**[90] (C)skeptical (D)**suspicious**[91] 生活 單字

[中譯] A：我弄丟我的護照了！ B：你有注意到任何可疑的人嗎？
(A)遲疑的 (B)不情願的 (C)疑神疑鬼的 (D)可疑的 答 D

( ) 68. If you find your baggage _______ after the arrival of your flight, report to the Airport Service Office immediately.
(A)damaged (B)damages (C)damage (D)damaging 機場 文法

[中譯] 如果航班抵達後您發現您的行李遭到損害，請立即向機場服務台申報。
(A)(B)(C)(D)損害、毀壞 解 P2-20. 文法35 答 A

補 If you find your baggage (which is) damaged...，其中句型省略 which is。

( ) 69. Customs officer: How long will you be staying? Tourist: _______.
(A)A week (B)New York (C)Once a week (D)Tomorrow 機場 片語

[中譯] 海關員：您將停留多長時間？ 遊客：一個禮拜。
(A)一個禮拜 (B)紐約 (C)一週一次 (D)明天 答 A

( ) 70. Caoling was attacked by the 1999's Jiji Earthquake, but its new "flying mountain" and barrier lake attracted the attention of the general public, sparking a new wave of _______.
(A)disorder (B)**rescue**[92] (C)tourism (D)perspective 景物 單字

[中譯] 草嶺在1999年的集集地震遭受毀壞，但新景點〞飛山〞和堰塞湖吸引大眾的注意，燃起新一波的觀光熱潮。
(A)混亂 (B)援救 (C)觀光 (D)透視的 答 C

閱讀測驗一

For some museums in the world, love is in the air all year round.

The Palazzo Filomela in Venice is better known as the Museum of Love. This museum was once the private home of a famous 16th-century singer. On the walls, you can see paintings of legendary lovers, such as the god Cupid and his lover, Psyche.

For many, love and chocolate go hand in hand, so a visit to the Chocolate Museum in Cologne, Germany, makes sense. There, visitors can learn about the history of chocolate and watch chocolate bars being made. The museum also gives out wafers that were dipped in chocolate from a three-meter-high chocolate fountain.

What is more, the Diamond Museum Amsterdam in Holland is the place to go when your're ready to take your love to the next level. At this museum, you can learn about diamonds, including how to tell a real one from a fake one. You may also get some ideas about which diamond to buy when you're getting engaged.

Shakespeare once wrote, "Love looks not with the eyes, but with the mind." Thanks to these special museums, we can all open our minds to, and fill our hearts with, love.

對於世界上的一些博物館來說，愛是一年到頭佈滿在空氣中的。

威尼斯的菲洛梅拉宮更是被稱為愛的博物館。這個博物館曾是16世紀著名歌手的私人住宅。在牆上，您可以看到傳奇戀人的畫作，例如愛神丘比特和他的戀人賽姬。

對於許多人來說，愛與巧克力是息息相關的，因此參觀德國科隆的巧克力博物館就顯得非常有意義。在那裡，遊客可以了解巧克力的歷史並觀看巧克力塊的製作過程。博物館還贈送從三米高巧克力噴泉中浸滿巧克力的威化餅。

更甚者，當您準備好將您的愛意提升到下一層次時，荷蘭阿姆斯特丹的鑽石博物館是您應到訪的地方。在這裡，您可以了解鑽石，包括如何分辨真假鑽石。您甚至可以了解該買何種鑽石，當您到時候訂婚時。

莎士比亞曾寫道：〞愛不是在於眼所見，而是在於心所感。〞感謝這些特別的博物館，我們可以敞開心房，讓我們的內心充滿，愛。

( ) 71. Where is the museum which was once the home of a famous 16th century singer?
(A)Amsterdam (B)Cologne (C)Venice (D)Shakespeare

[中譯] 曾經是16世紀著名歌手的家的博物館在哪裡？
(A)阿姆斯特丹 (B)科隆 (C)威尼斯 (D)莎士比亞 答 C

( ) 72. What do you think Shakespeare means in " Love looks not with the eyes, but with the mind?"
(A)Love is blind and **irrational**[93].
(B)Love is not what you see neither what you think.
(C)Love is not seeing the appearance but the inside of a person.
(D)Love at first sight is not reliable.

[中譯] 如何解讀莎士比亞說的 "愛不是在於眼所見，而是在於心所感" 這句話？
(A)愛是盲目和不合理的
(B)愛不是你看到的，也不是你所想的
(C)愛不是透過外表看到的，而是在一個人的內心
(D)一見鐘情並不可靠 答 C

( ) 73. According to the article, which museum would you go if you were about to ask someone to marry you?
(A)Palazzo Filomela (B)Chocolate Museum
(C)Museum of **Relationship**[94] (D)Diamond Museum Amsterdam

[中譯] 根據這篇文章，如果您想請求某人與您結婚，應該去哪個博物館？
(A)菲洛梅拉宮 (B)巧克力博物館 (C)關係博物館 (D)阿姆斯特丹鑽石博物館 答 D

( ) 74. Why is the author writing about a chocolate museum in this article?
(A)Because people love to learn the history of chocolate.
(B)Because handmade chocolate is the best way to express love.
(C)Because there is a huge chocolate **fountain**[95].
(D)Because many people believe that love and chocolate are closely connected.

[中譯] 為什麼作者寫有關巧克力博物館的內容在這篇文章中？
(A)因為人們喜歡學習巧克力的歷史 (B)因為手工巧克力是最佳方式來表達愛意
(C)因為有一個巨大的巧克力噴泉 (D)因為許多人認為愛情和巧克力是緊密相連的 答 D

( ) 75. In the article, what do you think "Love is in the air" mean?
(A)Love is everywhere. (B)Love is like the air.
(C)Love is **invisible**[96]. (D)Love is so **unreliable**[97].

[中譯] 在這篇文章中，如何解讀 " 愛佈滿在空氣中 " 的意思？
(A)愛無處不在 (B)愛就像空氣 (C)愛是無形的 (D)愛是如此不可靠的 答 A

閱讀測驗二

As a flood of news **headlines**[98] highlighting overtourism, it's easy to think that the planet is simply full. But away from the well-worn tourist trails, you'll discover another travel story entirely different.

In much of the world, there are places that are eager to welcome tourists. Based on the most recent data by the United Nations World Tourism Organization (UNWTO), in 2017, nearly 87 million international tourists arrived in France; yet mere 2,000 international tourists visited the South Pacific country of Tuvalu, where it's easy to find a beach -- or even an entire island -- to yourself. The same data **reflect**[99] many of the world's least-visited countries and territories, where you'll find gorgeous natural beauty, culture and history without pushing through **bunches of selfie sticks.**

Imagine lounging on Sierra Leone beaches, exploring Liechtenstein's mountaintop castles or shipwreck diving in the South Pacific! How rewarding it can be to leave the popular sites behind. If you can't picture a week in Kiribati or imagine the flavor of Timor Leste's traditional cuisine, it's OK. By **spinning the globe and booking a flight to a country you know little about**, you'll infuse the journey with a sense of wonder. That, after all, is what travel is for.

在如洪水般的新聞標題突顯過度旅遊之下，很容易地聯想到地球已經飽和。但是，當遠離那些舊有的旅遊路線，您會發現另一個完全與眾不同的旅行故事。

在這個世界上很多地方，都非常期待接待遊客。2017年，根據聯合國世界旅遊組織(UNWTO)的最新數據，將近8,700萬外國旅客造訪法國；然而，卻僅有2,000名外國旅客造訪南太平洋國家吐瓦魯(Tuvalu)，在這裡你可以輕易找到海灘 -- 或者甚至整個島嶼 -- 給你自己。相同的數據反映出在世界上這些造訪次數最少的國家和地區，在這裡您可以發現美麗的自然風光，文化和歷史而不需要擁擠地穿過**一堆自拍棒**。

想像一下閒逛在獅子山共和國的海灘上，探索列支敦士登的山頂城堡或在南太平洋的沉船中潛水！將熱門地點拋在腦後是件非常值得的事情。如果您無法在吉里巴斯(Kiribati)待上一個禮拜，或者無法想像東帝汶(Timor Leste)傳統的菜餚風味，沒關係。透過**轉動地球儀，然後預訂航班飛往一個你知道甚少的國家**，會給您的旅程注入驚奇感。畢竟，這就是旅行。

( ) 76. The number shown in the data of UNWTO concerning international tourists to France is an indication of _______.
(A)Wonderful trip (B)Romantic tour
(C)Overtourism (D)Gorgeous experience

[中譯] 聯合國世界旅遊組織(UNWTO)的數據顯示有關法國外國旅客過度旅遊的跡象。
(A)美妙之旅 (B)浪漫之旅 (C)過度旅遊 (D)華麗體驗

答 C

( ) 77. What is common between Sierra Lione and Tuvalu, as described in this passage?
(A)Sandy beaches (B)Traditional cuisine
(C)Shipwreck diving (D)Mountain trails

[中譯] 根據本文描述，在獅子山共和國和吐瓦魯之間有什麼共同點？
(A)沙灘 (B)傳統菜餚 (C)海灘潛水 (D)山徑 答 A

( ) 78. "Bunches of selfie sticks" is an **indication**[100] of _______.
(A)high technology (B)tourist crowd (C)tourist attraction (D)tour information

[中譯] "一堆自拍棒"用來表示成群遊客。
(A)高科技 (B)成群遊客 (C)觀光景點 (D)旅遊資訊 答 B

( ) 79. In the article, the author seems to encourage the reader to _______.
(A)visit well-worn trails (B)travel to least-visited countries
(C)go to the beaches (D)go mountain hiking

[中譯] 在這篇文章裡，作者似乎鼓勵讀者去造訪數最少的國家旅遊。
(A)造訪舊有的路線 (B)造訪數最少的國家旅遊 (C)去海灘 (D)去爬山 答 B

( ) 80. "Spinning the globe and booking a flight to a country you know little about" is a promotion of _______.
(A)business travel (B)cruise travel (C)holiday travel (D)adventure travel

[中譯] "轉動地球儀並預訂航班飛往一個你知道甚少的國家"是對探險旅遊的一種推廣。
(A)商務旅遊 (B)郵輪旅遊 (C)假日旅遊 (D)探險旅遊 答 D

情境篇 文法篇 片語篇 測驗篇 口試篇

| Coffee 的由來 |

傳說在阿拉伯有一個牧羊人，看見他的羊群在啃食一種乾果後，行為出現反常。因此牧羊人決定品嘗看看，卻產生了異常興奮，便將這件事告訴其他的牧羊人。不久之後，阿拉伯人學會將這種灌木的新鮮果實，瀝乾並以煎煮的方式調成飲料，稱之為「**Qahwa**」，立即在穆斯林引起騷動。

按伊斯蘭教的教義規定，伊斯蘭教徒是不准飲酒的。一些教徒認為**Qahwa**帶有刺激作用，屬於酒類，必須禁飲。有一些教徒為使在作禮拜時不致睏倦，會偷偷飲用這種飲料。然而，同樣是信仰伊斯蘭教的土耳其人，卻欣然接受，並將此飲料稱之為「**Kahve**」。之後傳到了法國，將其稱為「**Cafe**」。後又傳到英國，而有「**Coffee**」一詞產生。

Chapter. 02 | 測驗 | 110年度導遊試題

掌握關鍵單字，更快作答70%考題！

重要單字彙整

	單字	出現	音標	中文	詞性
1	**organized**	8	[ˋɔrgən͵aɪzd]	有條理的；有系統的 同義詞 systematic	形容詞
2	**punctual**	2	[ˋpʌŋktʃuəl]	精確的；正確的；準時的 反義詞 unpunctual 不守時的	形容詞
3	**disease**	14	[dɪˋziz]	疾病；病害 同義詞 sickness, malady 反義詞 health 健康；健康狀況	名詞
4	**border**	3	[ˋbɔrdɚ]	邊界，國界 同義詞 frontier	名詞
5	**bond**	2	[bɑnd]	債券；公債；契約；束縛；聯結	名詞
6	**destination**	50	[͵dɛstəˋneʃən]	目的地，終點；目標，目的	名詞
7	**promise**	4	[ˋprɑmɪs]	承諾，諾言；希望	名詞
8	**pointer**	1	[ˋpɔɪntɚ]	指針；指示物 同義詞 infringe	名詞
9	**violate**	3	[ˋvaɪə͵let]	違反；侵犯	動詞
10	**fine**	9	[faɪn]	罰款，罰金	名詞
11	**permit**	5	[pɚˋmɪt]	許可，允許 同義詞 allow, consent, let, admit	動詞
12	**prove**	2	[pruv]	證明；表現，顯示 同義詞 verify, confirm, justify, certify	動詞
13	**ban**	8	[bæn]	禁止；禁忌	名詞
14	**inspire**	3	[ɪnˋspaɪr]	啟發；鼓舞 同義詞 stimulate, hearten, encourage	動詞

	單字	出現	音標	中文	詞性
15	**pandemic**	12	[pæn`dɛmɪk]	(疾病)全國流行的; 普遍的 同義詞 notify, tell, apprise, report	形容詞
16	**inform**	3	[ɪn`fɔrm]	通知, 報告; 告發 同義詞 prevent,avoid	動詞
17	**avert**	2	[ə`vɝt]	避免, 防止; 避開 同義詞 consent, license, permit, approval	動詞
18	**restriction**	5	[rɪ`strɪkʃən]	限制; 約束; 限定	名詞
19	**increase**	33	[ɪn`kris]	增加; 增強 同義詞 augment, multiply, add, annex	動詞
20	**indicate**	6	[`ɪndə͵ket]	指出; 顯示表明; 象徵 同義詞 show, exhibit, display, hint	動詞
21	**compromise**	6	[`kɑmprə͵maɪz]	妥協, 和解 同義詞 yield	名詞
22	**consume**	10	[kən`sjum]	消耗, 花費; 耗盡	動詞
23	**cruise**	10	[kruz]	乘船遊覽 同義詞 sail	名詞
24	**intricate**	2	[`ɪntrəkɪt]	錯綜複雜的; 難理解的 同義詞 complicated, complex, confused 反義詞 simple 簡單的, 簡易的	形容詞
25	**savor**	4	[`sevɚ]	品味; 品嚐; 欣賞 同義詞 relish, enjoy	動詞
26	**scenario**	1	[sɪ`nɛrɪ͵o]	設想的情況; 局面; 情節; 劇本	名詞
27	**miserable**	1	[`mɪzərəb!]	痛苦的; 悲慘的 同義詞 poor, wretched, sorry	形容詞
28	**predict**	6	[prɪ`dɪkt]	預言; 預料; 預報 同義詞 foretell, prophesy, forecast	動詞
29	**territory**	6	[`tɛrə͵torɪ]	領域; 領地; 領土 同義詞 domain	名詞
30	**afford**	2	[ə`ford]	負擔得起; 有足夠的……; 給予	動詞

▸ 4-26

	單字	出現	音標	中文	詞性
31	**dip**	5	[dɪp]	下降; 浸; 泡 同義詞 immerse, dunk	動詞
32	**slip**	4	[slɪp]	滑動; 滑落; 洩漏 同義詞 slide, glide	動詞
33	**instructor**	1	[ɪn`strʌktɚ]	教練; 教師; 指導者	名詞
34	**rescue**	7	[`rɛskju]	援救; 營救; 挽救 同義詞 salvage, extricate, save	動詞
35	**besiege**	1	[bɪ`sidʒ]	圍攻; 包圍; 圍困 同義詞 siege	動詞
36	**benefit**	10	[`bɛnəfɪt]	利益, 優勢; 津貼 同義詞 advantage, good, avail	名詞
37	**raise**	11	[rez]	提高; 增加; 升起 同義詞 lift, increase, elevate, hoist	動詞
38	**situation**	8	[ˌsɪtʃʊ`eʃən]	處境; 情況; 局面 同義詞 circumstances, condition	名詞
39	**premium**	2	[`primɪəm]	【商】優惠; 獎金; 津貼 反義詞 discount 打折扣	名詞
40	**elusive**	1	[ɪ`lusɪv]	難以理解的; 逃避的 同義詞 intangible, impalpable	形容詞
41	**negligible**	1	[`nɛglɪdʒəb!]	無關緊要的; 微不足道的	形容詞
42	**primary**	5	[`praɪˌmɛrɪ]	主要的; 初級的; 基本的 同義詞 first, fundamental, foremost	形容詞
43	**define**	5	[dɪ`faɪn]	定義, 解釋; 規定 同義詞 explain	動詞
44	**decline**	12	[dɪ`klaɪn]	減少; 下降; 婉拒 同義詞 refuse, reject	動詞
45	**decay**	1	[dɪ`ke]	腐敗; 腐爛; 衰退	名詞
46	**declaration**	4	[ˌdɛklə`reʃən]	申報; 宣布; 聲明 同義詞 announcement	名詞

	單字	出現	音標	中文	詞性
47	**alcoholic**	3	[ˌælkəˋhɔlɪk]	含酒精的 同義詞 nonalcoholic 不含酒精的	形容詞
48	**accelerate**	5	[ækˋsɛləˌret]	加快；增長；增加 同義詞 hasten, quicken	動詞
49	**avoid**	22	[əˋvɔɪd]	避免；避開 同義詞 shun, evade, eschew	動詞
50	**temptation**	2	[tɛmpˋteʃən]	誘惑，引誘	名詞
51	**purchase**	23	[ˋpɝtʃəs]	購買；贏得，獲得 同義詞 buy, shop	動詞
52	**impulse**	2	[ˋɪmpʌls]	衝動；刺激 同義詞 push, pressure	名詞
53	**impact**	24	[ɪmˋpækt]	衝擊，碰撞；壓緊	動詞
54	**impression**	1	[ɪmˋprɛʃən]	印象；影響；效果	名詞
55	**immune**	2	[ɪˋmjun]	免疫者；免除者	名詞
56	**financial**	5	[faɪˋnænʃəl]	財政的；金融的 同義詞 pecuniary, monetary	形容詞
57	**encourage**	6	[ɪnˋkɝɪdʒ]	鼓勵；促進；激發 同義詞 urge, inspire	動詞
58	**participate**	3	[pɑrˋtɪsəˌpet]	參加；分享 同義詞 partake	動詞
59	**customs**	1	[ˋkʌstəmz]	海關；關稅；報關手續 同義詞 light, brighten, spotlight	名詞
60	**emigration**	1	[ˌɛməˋgreʃən]	移民；移居 同義詞 oppose, face, encounter	名詞
61	**festival**	28	[ˋfɛstəvḷ]	節日；音樂節，戲劇節；慶祝活動 同義詞 holiday	名詞
62	**spiritual**	3	[ˋspɪrɪtʃuəl]	精神(上)的；神聖的	形容詞
63	**therapeutic**	2	[ˌθɛrəˋpjutɪk]	有療效的；有益於健康的	形容詞
64	**cuisine**	29	[kwɪˋzin]	菜餚；烹飪	名詞

▶ 4-28

	單字	出現	音標	中文	詞性
65	**authentic**	9	[ɔ`θɛntɪk]	可靠的; 真正的, 非假冒的 同義詞 true, real, reliable	形容詞
66	**spurious**	1	[`spjʊrɪəs]	偽造的; 欺騙性的; 虛假的	形容詞
67	**emergency**	7	[ɪ`mɝdʒənsɪ]	緊急情況; 突然事件 同義詞 exigency	名詞
68	**supply**	7	[sə`plaɪ]	供應量; 庫存; 生活用品; 補給品	名詞
69	**debt**	2	[dɛt]	借款; 負債; 恩情	名詞
70	**remove**	10	[rɪ`muv]	移動; 消除; 調動	動詞
71	**install**	7	[ɪn`stɔl]	安裝, 設置; 任命	動詞
72	**incense**	1	[`ɪnsɛns]	香; 焚香時的煙; 香味	名詞
73	**inscription**	3	[ɪn`skrɪpʃən]	題詞; 銘刻; 刻印文字	名詞
74	**complimentary**	11	[ˏkɑmplə`mɛntərɪ]	贈送的; 贊賞的; 表示敬意的	形容詞
75	**treasure**	6	[`trɛʒɚ]	珍寶; 財富貴重物品 同義詞 fortune, wealth	名詞
76	**application**	12	[ˏæplə`keʃən]	申請書; 請求; 運用 同義詞 petition	名詞
77	**source**	13	[sors]	來源; 根源 同義詞 origin, beginning	名詞
78	**hybrid**	1	[`haɪbrɪd]	混合源物; 雜種; 混血兒	名詞
79	**refund**	15	[rɪ`fʌnd]	退款; 退還; 償還 同義詞 repay, reimburse	名詞
80	**annul**	1	[ə`nʌl]	廢除, 取消; 宣告...無效 同義詞 disannul, abolish, revoke, nullify	動詞
81	**claim**	14	[klem]	要求; 聲稱; 主張	動詞
82	**negate**	3	[nɪ`get]	取消; 否認定; 使無效	動詞
83	**nullify**	1	[`nʌləˏfaɪ]	使無效; 廢棄; 取消	動詞
84	**souvenir**	14	[`suvəˏnɪr]	伴手禮; 紀念品 同義詞 keepsake, memento, relic, token	名詞

	單字	出現	音標	中文	詞性
85	**variety**	14	[və`raɪətɪ]	多樣化, 變化 同義詞 diversity	名詞
86	**product**	23	[`prɑdəkt]	產品; 產量; 出產; 成果 同義詞 production, produce	名詞
87	**expatriate**	2	[ɛks`petrɪˌet]	移居國外者; 被流放（國外）者	名詞
88	**indigenous**	9	[ɪn`dɪdʒɪnəs]	本地的; 土產的 同義詞 native, original 反義詞 exotic 異國情調的; 外來的	形容詞
89	**collection**	12	[kə`lɛkʃən]	收集; 收藏品; 募捐 同義詞 accumulation, heap, amassment	名詞
90	**paradigm**	2	[`pærəˌdaɪm]	範例; 模範 同義詞 unwilling, grudging, disinclined	名詞
91	**pilgrimage**	2	[`pɪlgrəmɪdʒ]	朝聖; 旅行; 漫遊	名詞
92	**construction**	10	[kən`strʌkʃən]	建造; 建築物; 解釋 同義詞 architecture, building	名詞
93	**foundation**	3	[faʊn`deʃən]	基礎; 建立, 創辦 同義詞 establishment	名詞
94	**diverse**	8	[daɪ`vɝs]	多種多樣的; 多變化的; 不同的 同義詞 different, unlike, distinct 反義詞 same 同樣的; 同一的	形容詞
95	**highlight**	9	[`haɪˌlaɪt]	最突出(或最精彩)的部分; 最明亮部分	名詞
96	**influence**	8	[`ɪnflʊəns]	影響; 影響力; 勢力	名詞
97	**development**	32	[dɪ`vɛləpmənt]	發展; 生長; 進化 同義詞 growth, evolution, enlargement	名詞
98	**isolation**	2	[ˌaɪs!`eʃən]	隔離; 孤立; 脫離	名詞
99	**understanding**	9	[ˌʌndɚ`stændɪŋ]	理解; 領會; 共議; 同情心 同義詞 understanding	名詞
100	**prevent**	9	[prɪ`vɛnt]	預防; 阻止; 妨礙 同義詞 prohibit, preclude, stop, block	動詞

110年導遊筆試測驗

● 本書採用英語邏輯思維[中譯]
幫助更快看懂句子，拆解字義

題型分析			情境命題				
單字 55	片語 3	對話 3	景物 11	餐飲 8	住宿 2	交通 6	機場 2
文法 9	閱測 10		生活 21	民俗 4	產業 9	職能 2	購物 5

單選題［共80題，每題1.25分］

( ) 1. The greatest tour guides are ________ and **organized**[1], helping their guests get to where they need to be on time.
(A)tardy (B)**punctual**[2] (C)arrogant (D)deceptive 職能 單字

[中譯] 最棒的導遊是準確及有條理地協助客人們準時抵達他們需要到的地方。
(A)遲鈍的 (B)準確的 (C)傲慢的 (D)虛偽的 答 B

( ) 2. Many countries closed their ________ to flights from the UK due to a new variant of the **disease**[3] COVID-19 that had been spreading in London and the southeast of England.
(A)booths (B)bombs (C)**borders**[4] (D)**bonds**[5] 生活 單字

[中譯] 由於COVID-19的新型變種病毒正在倫敦和英格蘭東南部傳播開來，許多國家對來自英國的航班關閉了邊界。
(A)攤位 (B)炸彈 (C)邊界 (D)債券 答 C

( ) 3. Telluride, a Victorian-era mining town in Colorado, is a winter ________ offering plenty to do and isn't as crowded as some of Colorado's other **destinations**[6].
(A)**promise**[7] (B)phase (C)**pointer**[8] (D)paradise 景物 單字

[中譯] Telluride是一座位於科羅拉多州維多利亞時代的礦業小鎮，是一個提供多元活動的冬季天堂，且不像同州其他類似景點般地擁擠。
(A)承諾 (B)階段 (C)指標 (D)天堂 答 D

( ) 4. Taiwan has become the first country in Asia to totally ________ the eating of dog and cat meat, and **violating**[9] the rule is punishable by up to $8,000 in **fines**[10].
(A)**permit**[11] (B)**prove**[12] (C)**ban**[13] (D)**inspire**[14] 生活 單字

[中譯] 台灣已成為亞洲第一個完全禁止食用狗肉和貓肉的國家，違反該規定將被處以最高8,000美元的罰款。
(A)許可 (B)證明 (C)禁止 (D)啟發 答 C

( ) 5. During the COVID-19 **pandemic**[15], travelers should remember to share their previous travel history with their health care providers and make every effort to ________ them by phone before visiting a medical facility. 生活 單字
(A)refer (B)**inform**[16] (C)**avert**[17] (D)pose

[中譯] 在COVID-19流行期間，旅行者應記得與醫療人員分享近期旅遊史，並在造訪醫療機構前盡可能地透過電話告知。

(A)指點 (B)通知 (C)防止 (D)提出　答 B

( ) 6. Despite global ________ on travel due to the coronavirus pandemic, travel between the United States and Mexico has continued relatively unchecked through 2020.

(A)supports (B)permission (C)fashion (D)**restrictions**[18] 生活 單字

[中譯] 儘管全球旅遊在冠狀病毒流行期間大受限制，但2020年美國與墨西哥間的旅行相對不受限。

(A)支持 (B)許可 (C)流行 (D)限制　答 D

( ) 7. Air travel in the US took its biggest ________ since World War II at the beginning of the pandemic in 2020. The number of passengers dropped from 2.3 million on Mar. 1 to a low of 87,500 on Apr. 14.

(A)**increase**[19] (B)dive (C)slope (D)shape 產業 單字

[中譯] 自2020年疫情爆發以來，美國的航空旅行經歷了自第二次世界大戰以來最大的急速下滑。旅客人數從3月1日的230萬人次下降到4月14日的低點87,500人次。

(A)增加 (B)急速下滑；俯衝 (C)傾斜 (D)形態　答 B

( ) 8. A report **indicates**[20] that Taiwanese people ________ almost 7.9 kilograms of apples per person every year, comparable to the quantity of bananas a Taiwanese has a year.

(A)cost (B)**compromise**[21] (C)confuse (D)**consume**[22] 購物 單字

[中譯] 一項報告指出，台灣人每年每人消費近7.9公斤的蘋果，相當於每人香蕉的平均消費數量。

(A)花費 (B)妥協 (C)混淆 (D)消耗　答 D

( ) 9. Summer time is ________ the best time to visit Penghu Islands. There are eateries open the whole day, and mini **cruise**[23] ships would take you to fascinating places.

(A)doubtfully (B)definitely (C)suspiciously (D)slightly 景物 單字

[中譯] 夏季毫無疑問地是遊覽澎湖群島的最佳時間。餐館全天開放，小型遊艇帶您前往各個迷人的地方。

(A)懷疑地 (B)毫無疑問地 (C)可疑地 (D)輕微地　答 B

( ) 10. Before the pandemic, micro trips were becoming ________ common because fares were cheap and the sharing economy, like Airbnb, was booming.

(A)dully (B)eternally (C)increasingly (D)unfortunately 產業 單字

[中譯] 在疫情之前，微旅行變得越來越普遍，因為票價便宜且共享經濟如Airbnb正急速發展。

(A)呆滯地 (B)永恆地 (C)越來越多地 (D)不幸地　答 C

( ) 11. Coronavirus has been described as an ________ bullet, silently piercing human's vital organs.
(A)insensible (B)**intricate**[24] (C)invisible (D)invaluable 生活 單字

[中譯] 冠狀病毒被描述為一種看不見的子彈，無聲地穿透人體內的重要器官。
(A)不可思議的 (B)錯綜複雜的 (C)看不見的 (D)不可估量的 答 C

( ) 12. We don't really know what's going to happen, but we need to plan for the worst-case ________.
(A)**savor**[25] (B)saint (C)**scenario**[26] (D)slang 生活 片語

[中譯] 我們真的不知道會發生什麼，但我們需要做最壞的打算。
(A)情趣 (B)聖徒 (C)局面 (D)情況 答 C

補 worst-case scenario 最壞的情況

( ) 13. Unexpectedly, a ________ number of people turned out at the debut of the movie and made the director laugh with tears.
(A)**miserable**[27] (B)surprising (C)decimal (D)minimal 生活 單字

[中譯] 令人驚訝的人數出現在這部電影的首映，這使得導演笑到流淚。
(A)悲慘的 (B)令人驚訝的 (C)十進位的 (D)最小的 答 B

( ) 14. It is hard to **predict**[28] the success of space travel since it is an ________ **territory**[29].
(A)unexplored (B)unlucky (C)unsuitable (D)un**afford**able[30] 產業 單字

[中譯] 太空旅行的成功很難預測，因為它是一個未經探索的領域。
(A)未探測的 (B)不幸的 (C)不合適的 (D)負擔不起的 答 A

( ) 15. The temperature has ________ so low that the mountain is blanketed with snow.
(A)**dipped**[31] (B)hiked (C)**slipped**[32] (D)increased 景物 單字

[中譯] 氣溫下降得如此之低，以至於山上覆蓋著雪。
(A)下降 (B)增加 (C)滑動 (D)增強 答 A

( ) 16. It takes the joint efforts of both the government and the general public to ________ the spread of the virus.
(A)drop (B)push (C)spark (D)halt 生活 單字

[中譯] 遏止該病毒的傳播需要政府和公眾共同合作。
(A)降低 (B)推動 (C)引起；誘發 (D)遏止 答 D

( ) 17. The yoga **instructor**[33] believes that yoga should be ________ to all people regardless of body-type, level of athleticism, and age.
(A)accessible (B)excusable (C)inconsiderable (D)incontrollable 生活 單字

[中譯] 瑜珈教練認為，瑜珈應該是適合所有人的，無論體型，運動能力和年齡。
(A)可得到的 (B)可諒解的 (C)無足輕重的 (D)不能控制的 答 A

( ) 18. The Atacama Desert in Peru and Chile ________ Mars in many ways. Soil samples taken from Mars have been found to be surprisingly similar to those taken from this desert.
(A)resigns (B)resents (C)resembles (D)**rescues**[34] 景物 單字

[中譯] 秘魯和智利的阿他加馬沙漠在許多方面都類似於火星。從火星上採集的土壤樣本被發現與從此沙漠中採集的樣本驚人地相似。
(A)放棄 (B)憤慨 (C)與...相似 (D)援救 答 C

( ) 19. Although there is an intentional absence of maintenance, the garden remains a pleasing sight to ________.
(A)**besiege**[35] (B)behave (C)**benefit**[36] (D)behold 景物 單字

[中譯] 儘管有意不進行維護，花園仍是令人賞心悅目。
(A)圍住 (B)表現 (C)得益 (D)注視 答 D

補 incredible sight of behold 嘆為觀止

( ) 20. The winner of five Olympic medals participating in the vicious riot was a ________ to his sport and his country.
(A)disgrace (B)glory (C)**raise**[37] (D)abyss 生活 單字

[中譯] 奧運五項獎牌得主參加這場嚴重暴動是對他的專業和國家的恥辱。
(A)恥辱 (B)榮耀 (C)增加；加薪 (D)深淵 答 A

( ) 21. In Taiwan, you don't have to worry about traveling far to find beautiful places that ________ perfect for a winter vacation.
(A)are (B)is (C)was (D)had been 景物 文法

[中譯] 在台灣，您不必擔心要走遠才能找到適合寒假去的美麗景點。
(A)(B)(C)(D)是 答 A

解 that 後接動詞，依that前面的主詞來判斷，其中beautiful places為複數，故動詞用are。

( ) 22. Vacations are a much-needed break from life at work and home, but they can cause ________ because many vacation packages include all-you-can-eat and all-you-can-drink options.
(A)weight gain (B)hunger awareness (C)back pain (D)test anxiety 生活 單字

[中譯] 假期是在工作與家庭生活外非常需要的休憩，但它可能造成體重增加，因為許多套裝行程包含了 "吃到飽" 及 "喝到飽" 的選項。
(A)體重增加 (B)飢餓關注 (C)背痛 (D)考試焦慮 答 A

情境篇 文法篇 片語篇 測驗篇 口試篇

( ) 23. Do we want to become a country where the top tier remains wealthy ________, and the rest are working in jobs that help make the lives of the rich more comfortable?
(A)beyond imagination (B)under construction
(C)under consideration (D)beyond the call of duty 生活 單字

[中譯] 我們是否想變成那種頂層階級保有超乎想像的富裕，而其餘的人都在從事有助富人生活更加舒適工作的國家？
(A)超乎想像 (B)施工中 (C)考慮中 (D)超出職責範圍 答 A

( ) 24. A beautiful wild hot spring in Taiwan's east, Lisong is ________ away in Taitung's mountains.
(A)hid (B)hide (C)hiding (D)hidden 景物 文法

[中譯] 栗松是台灣東部美麗的野溪溫泉，隱藏在台東的群山之中。
(A)(B)(C)(D)隱藏 解 P2-11. 文法13 (過去分詞) 答 D

解 本題文型為過去分詞 be + P.P.。

( ) 25. ________ the pandemic **situation**[38], getting out of the city and social distancing up in the hills has never been a better idea in Taiwan.
(A)Giving (B)Given (C)To give (D)Give 生活 文法

[中譯] 在疫情流行之下的台灣，離開城市和遠離眾人到山間從來都不是一個好主意。
(A)(B)(C)(D)假如 答 B

( ) 26. Maokong in Taipei produces more than 60 tons of tea per year, most of ________ is used up in the tea houses spread across Maokong's hillsides.
(A)that (B)this (C)which (D)where 產業 文法

[中譯] 台北貓空每年生產60噸以上的茶，其大部分用於分布在貓空山坡上的茶館。
(A)那個 (B)這個 (C)哪個 (D)在哪裡 解 P2-34. 文法52 答 C

( ) 27. The ________ chocolate is a must-buy souvenir for tourists.
(A)humble (B)undistinguished (C)**premium**[39] (D)unsavory 購物 單字

[中譯] 頂級巧克力是遊客必買的紀念品。
(A)粗糙的；謙虛的 (B)無分別的 (C)優質的 (D)難吃的 答 C

( ) 28. Tour guides' ________ responsibility is to make sure the tour is safe for the group of tourists.
(A)**elusive**[40] (B)minor (C)**negligible**[41] (D)**primary**[42] 職能 單字

[中譯] 導遊主要的職責是確保團體旅客的行程安全。
(A)難以捉摸的 (B)次要的 (C)無關緊要的 (D)主要的 答 D

( ) 29. In recent years, food tourism has been _____ by a single phrase: "Eat like a local."
(A)deterred (B)**defined**[43] (C)**declined**[44] (D)**decayed**[45] 產業 單字

[中譯] 近年來，美食旅遊可用一句話來定義："食如在地"。
(A)制止 (B)定義 (C)減少 (D)腐敗 答 B

( ) 30. Flight attendant: Do you want a can, Sir?
Passenger: ________
(A)Where is seat 30E? (B)One extra blanket, please.
(C)A diet coke, please. (D)I need a Customs **Declaration**[46] Form. 餐飲 對話

[中譯] 空服員：先生，您要飲料嗎？ 乘客：請給一罐健怡可樂。
(A)30E座位在哪裡？(B)請多給一條毯子 (C)請給一罐健怡可樂 (D)我需要一張海關申報表
答 C

( ) 31. Where do we store carry-on baggage ________ the plane?
(A)at (B)on (C)in (D)above 交通 文法

[中譯] 我們要將隨身行李放在飛機上的什麼地方？
(A)在 (B)在 (C)在 (D)以上 解 P2-52. 文法81 答 B

( ) 32. As a rule of thumb, you need to be at the airport at least 3 hours before ________ when flying international.
(A)Gate 20 (B)Terminal A (C)the official time of departure (D)boarding pass

[中譯] 根據經驗法則，搭乘國際線航班時，您需要在正式起飛時間前至少3個小時抵達機場。
(A)20號登機門 (B)A航站 (C)正式起飛時間 (D)登機證 交通 片語 答 C

補 a rule of thumb 經驗法則

( ) 33. Would you like something to drink? We have ________ drinks and **alcoholic**[47] drinks.
(A)firm (B)medium (C)soft (D)mixed 餐飲 單字

[中譯] 您想喝點什麼嗎？我們有不含酒精飲料和含酒精飲料。
(A)堅硬的 (B)中等的 (C)非酒精的 (D)混合的 答 C

( ) 34. ________ can his car **accelerate**[48]?
(A)How far (B)How long (C)How tall (D)How fast 交通 文法

[中譯] 他的汽車可以開多快？
(A)多遠 (B)多長時間 (C)多高 (D)多快 解 P2-40. 文法61 答 D

( ) 35. I will fly to Rome from London on ________.
(A)2 weeks (B)the 24th of January (C)12:35 a.m. (D)July 交通 文法

[中譯] 我將於1月24日從倫敦飛往羅馬。
(A)2週 (B)1月24日 (C)上午12:35 (D)7月 解 P2-52. 文法81 答 B

( ) 36. Could you tell me where ________ ?
(A)is the check-in counter for Lufthansa (B)the check-in counter for Lufthansa is
(C)has the check-in counter for Lufthansa (D)the check-in counter for Lufthansa has 機場 對話

[中譯] 您能告訴我漢莎航空的報到櫃檯在哪裡嗎？
(A)(B)(C)(D)漢莎航空的報到櫃檯 答 B

( ) 37. Can I ________ to business class?
(A)upstream (B)uprising (C)upload (D)upgrade 交通 單字

[中譯] 我可以升等到商務艙嗎？
(A)上游 (B)起義 (C)上傳 (D)升級 答 D

( ) 38. Passenger: What is the baggage allowance? Officer: ________
(A)It is 20 kg for the economy class. (B)It is NTD 1,000.
(C)Prices may vary on routes. (D)You can pay with credit card. 機場 對話

[中譯] 乘客：請問行李的限額是多少？ 官員：經濟艙是20公斤。
(A)經濟艙是20公斤 (B)新台幣1,000元 (C)價格可能因航線而異 (D)您可以用信用卡付款 答 A

( ) 39. When I was in London, I ________ usually walk along the Piccadilly Circus after dinner.
(A)has (B)have (C)will (D)would 生活 文法

[中譯] 當我在倫敦時，我通常會在晚餐後沿著皮卡迪利廣場散步。
(A)有 (B)有 (C)將會 (D)會 解 P2-14. 文法19 答 D

( ) 40. I am allergic to pork. Is there ________ in this Pepper Bun?
(A)any (B)each (C)every (D)some 餐飲 文法

[中譯] 我對豬肉過敏。這個胡椒包中有任何含在裡面嗎？
(A)任何 (B)各個 (C)每一個 (D)一些 解 P2-52. 文法81 答 A

( ) 41. While many people are ________ by the smell of stinky tofu, those who take the plunge are usually won over by its unique taste.
(A)pull on (B)put on (C)put off (D)suit up 餐飲 片語

[中譯] 雖然許多人都對臭豆腐的氣味所困擾，但那些決心嘗試的人通常會被它獨特的味道所吸引。
(A)穿上 (B)穿上 (C)推遲 (D)裝扮 答 C

解 take the plunge （經考慮後）決心冒險，打定主意

( ) 42. Planning how to spend next month's income will help you to save money and **avoid**[49] the **temptation**[50] to make an ________ **purchase**[51].
(A)**impulse**[52] (B)**impact**[53] (C)**impression**[54] (D)**immune**[55] 生活 單字

[中譯] 計劃如何支出下個月的收入將有助於你省錢，避免誘惑而造成衝動性消費。
(A)衝動 (B)衝擊 (C)印象 (D)免疫 答 A

( ) 43. In response to the current virus pandemic, the Tourism Bureau is providing **financial**[56] aid to city and county governments to **encourage**[57] hotels to **participate**[58] in the "Epidemic Prevention ________ Hotels" program.
(A)**Customs**[59] (B)**Emigration**[60] (C)Kosher (D)Quarantine 產業 單字

[中譯] 為因應當前的病毒大流行，觀光局正向市、縣政府提供財政援助，以鼓勵旅館加入"防疫隔離旅館"計劃。
(A)海關 (B)移出的移民 (C)符合猶太教飲食戒律的 (D)檢疫；隔離 答 D

( ) 44. The "Yehliu Geopark" is one of the most famous ________ of Taiwan.
(A)feline parks (B)**festivals**[61] (C)landmarks (D)parking lots 景物 單字

[中譯] "野柳地質公園"是台灣最著名的地標之一。
(A)貓科動物公園 (B)節日 (C)地標 (D)停車場 答 C

( ) 45. These Herbal Mineral Springs provide herbal ________ springs and beautifying mineral baths.
(A)corporeal (B)**spiritual**[62] (C)surgical (D)**therapeutic**[63] 生活 單字

[中譯] 這些草本礦物泉提供草藥療效和美容礦物浴。
(A)實質的 (B)心靈的 (C)外科的 (D)治療的 答 D

( ) 46. The restaurant is well known for its ________ Taiwanese **cuisines**[64] to receive three Michelin stars for two consecutive years.
(A)**authentic**[65] (B)copy (C)hoax (D)**spurious**[66] 餐飲 單字

[中譯] 這家餐廳以其正宗的台灣菜餚而聞名，連續兩年獲得米其林三星。
(A)正統的 (B)複製 (C)騙局 (D)不實的 答 A

( ) 47. Rain ________ are known for producing rain-like sprays.
(A)bathtubs (B)bidets (C)dryers (D)shower heads 生活 單字

[中譯] 雨淋式蓮蓬頭以製造類似雨水的噴霧而著稱。
(A)浴缸 (B)下身清洗盆/坐浴盆 (C)吹風機 (D)蓮蓬頭 答 D

( ) 48. In case of ________, open the transparent plastic cover and press the red button to stop the escalator.
(A)calmness (B)closure (C)**emergency**[67] (D)tranquility 生活 單字

[中譯] 緊急情況下，打開透明的塑膠蓋，然後按下紅色按鈕以停止電扶梯。
(A)平靜 (B)封閉 (C)緊急 (D)平和寧靜的 答 C

( ) 49. Every station has a ticket gate for the ________, wheelchair users, or passengers with strollers or bulky packages.
(A)able-bodied (B)disabled (C)robust (D)sturdy 產業 單字

[中譯] 每個車站都有一個驗票口供身障人士、輪椅使用者或攜帶嬰兒推車或大件包裹的乘客使用。
(A)體格健全的 (B)身障的 (C)強健的 (D)健壯的 答 B

( ) 50. According to a newspaper report, blood ________ are running low across Taiwan, with blood banks reporting an average of less than five days of stock.
(A)needs (B)**supplies**[68] (C)shortages (D)**debts**[69] 生活 單字

[中譯] 根據報章報導，全台灣的血液供應量缺乏，血庫報告顯示平均庫存不足五天。
(A)需求 (B)供應量 (C)短缺 (D)債務 答 B

( ) 51. Guide signs are ________ to direct disabled passengers to the trains.
(A)**removed**[70] (B)separated (C)**installed**[71] (D)taken off 交通 單字

[中譯] 引導號誌已安裝，以指引身障乘客搭乘火車。
(A)移除 (B)分開 (C)安裝 (D)取下 答 C

( ) 52. The temple is unique in that the burning of ________ is banned in the interest of the environment.
(A)diesel oil (B)essential oil (C)**incense**[72] (D)polymers 產業 單字

[中譯] 這座寺廟的獨特之處在於為了保護環境而禁止焚香。
(A)柴油 (B)精油 (C)香 (D)聚合物 答 C

補 in the interest of 為某事物的緣故；為了...的利益

( ) 53. One of the most popular pieces of jade ________ in the museum is the Jadeite Cabbage.
(A)calligraphy (B)carvings (C)etchings (D)paintings 景物 單字

[中譯] 博物館中最受歡迎的玉雕作品之一是翠玉白菜。
(A)書法 (B)雕刻 (C)蝕刻 (D)繪畫 答 B

( ) 54. The interior surface of the Mao Gong Ding is covered in a/an ________ of 500 characters.
(A)**inscription**[73] (B)lyric (C)melody (D)subtitle 景物 單字

[中譯] 毛公鼎的腹內刻有500字的銘文。
(A)銘文 (B)歌詞 (C)旋律 (D)字幕 答 A

( ) 55. Use of the fitness center is restricted to ________ guests and members only.
(A)in-situ (B)in-vitro (C)in-vivo (D)in-house 住宿 單字

[中譯] 健身中心僅限入住的房客和會員使用。
(A)在原處 (B)在體外 (C)在體內 (D)內部的 答 D

( ) 56. A ________ room is a guest room for which no charge is made.
(A)**complimentary**[74] (B)laundry (C)maid (D)meeting 住宿 單字

[中譯] 免費房是不收取任何費用的客房。
(A)贈送的 (B)洗衣房 (C)女傭 (D)會議 答 A

( ) 57. By combining traditional culture with ________ technology, Taiwan Lantern Festival presents itself as a shining fest compatible with its international counterparts.
(A)atrocious (B)substandard (C)top-notch (D)unsatisfactory 民俗 單字

[中譯] 台灣燈會結合傳統文化及頂尖科技，呈現出與其他國際上同類型並列媲美的璀璨盛典。
(A)差勁的 (B)不合格的 (C)一流的 (D)令人不滿的 答 C

( ) 58. The National Palace Museum houses the world's largest ________ of priceless Chinese art **treasures**[75].
(A)collection (B)crowd (C)flock (D)herd 景物 單字

[中譯] 國立故宮博物院收藏著世界上最多無價珍寶的中國藝術珍藏。
(A)收藏品 (B)人群 (C)羊群；人群 (D)獸群 答 A

( ) 59. The Visitor Visa **Application**[76] Form can be ________ from the website of the Bureau of Consular Affairs, Ministry of Foreign Affairs.
(A)back loaded (B)downloaded (C)overloaded (D)reloaded 生活 單字

[中譯] 訪客簽證申請表可以從外交部領事事務局網站下載。
(A)推遲 (B)下載 (C)超載 (D)重新裝載 答 B

( ) 60. The cultures of Taiwan are a ________ of various **sources**[77].
(A)flock (B)**hybrid**[78] (C)pocket (D)board 民俗 單字

[中譯] 台灣文化是多樣化的來源所組合的混合體。
(A)人群 (B)混合物 (C)口袋 (D)木板 答 B

( ) 61. To ________ the tax **refund**[79], foreign travelers can apply at the port of their departure from Taiwan.
(A)**annul**[80] (B)**claim**[81] (C)**negate**[82] (D)**nullify**[83] 購物 單字

[中譯] 要索取退稅，外國旅客可以在離開台灣港口時提出申請。
(A)廢除 (B)要求 (C)取消 (D)使無效 答 B

( ) 62. Pineapple cakes have become one of the top-selling ________ in Taiwan.
(A)cargos (B)facilities (C)fruits (D)**souvenirs**[84] 購物 單字

[中譯] 鳳梨酥已成為台灣最暢銷的伴手禮之一。
(A)貨物 (B)設施 (C)水果 (D)紀念品 答 D

( ) 63. Taiwanese peanut ________ are traditional Taiwanese candy with peanuts.
(A)breads (B)cakes (C)pies (D)nougats 產業 單字

[中譯] 台灣花生牛軋糖是台灣傳統的花生糖。
(A)麵包 (B)蛋糕 (C)餡餅 (D)牛軋糖
答 D

( ) 64. Mochi or muah chee is a sweet and chewy dessert made of ________ rice.
(A)black (B)brown (C)glutinous (D)wild 餐飲 單字

[中譯] (麻糬)Mochi或Muah Chee，是由糯米製成的一種甜而有嚼勁的甜點。
(A)黑色 (B)棕色 (C)黏 (D)野生
答 C

( ) 65. Taiwanese Pork ________ are made of pork mixed with almond in the form of a crisp as thin as a piece of paper.
(A)Chops (B)Knuckles (C)Nougats (D)Sheets 餐飲 單字

[中譯] 台灣豬肉紙是由豬肉和杏仁混合而成，酥脆又像紙一樣薄。
(A)排骨 (B)指關節 (C)牛軋糖 (D)薄片
答 D

( ) 66. ________ is a tea-based drink with chewy tapioca balls.
(A)Bubble tea (B)Herbal tea (C)Oolong tea (D)Pu-erh tea 餐飲 單字

[中譯] 珍珠奶茶是一種有耐嚼粉圓的茶飲料。
(A)珍珠奶茶 (B)青草茶 (C)烏龍茶 (D)普洱茶
答 A

( ) 67. Taiwan's ________ tribes produce a wide **variety**[85] of **products**[86] in their local villages and sell as souvenirs.
(A)alien (B)**expatriate**[87] (C)outer (D)**indigenous**[88] 購物 單字

[中譯] 台灣原住民部族在當地部落生產種類繁多的產品，並做為紀念品銷售。
(A)外籍的 (B)僑民 (C)在外的 (D)土生土長的
答 D

( ) 68. Organized crime has ________ rampant due to the inaction of the government.
(A)fallen (B)driven (C)raised (D)run 生活 單字

[中譯] 由於政府的無所作為，組織犯罪活動已然猖獗。
(A)下降 (B)驅動 (C)上升 (D)運行
答 D

( ) 69. The Mazu ________ from Dajia's Zhenlan Temple takes place during the third month of the Chinese lunar calendar.
(A)**collection**[89] (B)fraternization (C)**paradigm**[90] (D)**pilgrimage**[91] 民俗 單字

[中譯] 大甲鎮瀾宮媽祖繞境在農曆三月舉行。
(A)募捐；收藏 (B)親善 (C)模範 (D)朝聖
答 D

( ) 70. The ________ of the Plague God Boat is a folk ritual practiced by fishermen in southwestern Taiwan.
(A)burning (B)**construction**[92] (C)soaking (D)sinking 民俗 單字

[中譯] 燒王船是台灣西南部漁民的一種民間儀式。
(A)燃燒 (B)建造 (C)浸泡 (D)下沉 答 A

閱讀測驗一

Traveling in Taiwan is a luxury that anyone can enjoy without spending a fortune. A small country, Taiwan is like a world in miniature that has much to offer. In fact, it is possible to find something that suits your liking the whole year round. Being an island, Taiwan has a wealth of seaside possibilities for both beachgoers and sea lovers. With its special terrain, Taiwan is home to many breathtaking mountains, hills, and valleys. In addition, the unique Taiwanese culture is a magnet that attracts new and repeated tourists to the beautiful island.

Taiwan has several metropolises where people of different ethnicities have formed the **foundation**[93] of the rich Taiwanese culture. As you make your way through **different**[94] **destinations**[95], you are bound to encounter a cultural mosaic of diverse highlights, traditions, and events. As the social landscape of Taiwan grows increasingly heterogeneous, Taiwan will open up more opportunities for visitors with different cultural appreciation.

One best way to appreciate a culture is through food. With its multicultural characteristics and abundant food sources, Taiwan boasts kaleidoscopic cuisines to live up to its name of a food paradise. From local delicacies to exotic culinary delights, Taiwan offers a whole array of food choices that cater to all tastes. As a dream destination, Taiwan is capable of appealing to sight, taste, and other senses of its visitors. Welcome to Taiwan to discover the gem of your own!

在台灣旅行是一種無需花大筆錢就能享受的奢侈品。台灣是一個小國，就像一個微型的世界，可以提供很多服務。實際上，一年四季都能找到適合自己喜好的東西。作為一個島嶼，台灣為海灘遊客和海洋愛好者提供海濱豐富的可能性。由於台灣地形特殊，擁有許多令人嘆為觀止的山脈、丘陵和山谷。此外，獨特的台灣文化吸引著新遊客和既有遊客到這個美麗的島嶼。

台灣有幾個大都市，不同種族的人構成了豐富的台灣文化的基礎。當您穿越不同的目的地時，您必然會遇到由各種亮點、傳統和事件構成的文化馬賽克。隨著台灣社會景象的日益多元化，台灣將為欣賞不同文化的遊客開啟更多機會。

欣賞文化的一種最佳途徑是透過食物。台灣以其多元文化特色和豐富的食物來源，擁有千變萬化的美食，不辜負其美食天堂的美譽。從當地美食到異國風味的美食，台灣提供了一系列各式各樣的食物選擇，可以滿足所有味蕾。台灣是理想的旅遊地，能夠吸引遊客的視覺、味覺和其他感官。歡迎來到台灣，發現自己的瑰寶！

( ) 71. According to the passage, what can be the key that makes Taiwan a favorable tourist attraction?
(A)diversity (B)hospitality (C)generosity (D)universality

[中譯] 根據本篇文章，什麼是使台灣成為受歡迎的旅遊勝地的關鍵？
(A)多樣性 (B)熱情好客 (C)慷慨 (D)大學 答 A

( ) 72. Which of the following explains "Taiwan is home to many breathtaking mountains, hills, and valleys"?
(A)Many people in Taiwan build homes in the breathtaking mountains, hills, and valleys.
(B)Taiwan calls breathtaking mountains, hills, and valleys home.
(C)Taiwan has many breathtaking mountains, hills, and valleys.
(D)Taiwanese see breathtaking mountains, hills, and valleys as homes.

[中譯] 下列哪一項解釋了"台灣擁有許多令人嘆為觀止的山脈、丘陵和山谷"？
(A)許多人在台灣建造房子在壯麗的山脈、丘陵和山谷中。
(B)台灣稱作令人嘆為觀止的山脈、丘陵和山谷。
(C)台灣有許多令人嘆為觀止的山脈、丘陵和山谷。
(D)台灣人將壯麗的山脈、丘陵和山谷視為家園。 答 C

( ) 73. Which of the following may replace "you are bound to" in the second paragraph of the above passage?
(A)you are headed to (B)you are certain to
(C)you are oriented to (D)you are wounded up to

[中譯] 下列哪一項可以代替上述段落第二段中的"你必然會"？
(A)你將前往 (B)你一定會 (C)你被導向 (D)你生氣、焦慮 答 B

( ) 74. Which of the following is NOT related to "cultural mosaic" or "cultural appreciation"?
(A)Cultures made up of people of the same kind.
(B)Eagerness to explore diverse cultural elements.
(C)Inclusion of culturally diverse groups.
(D)Coexistence of contrasting cultures.

[中譯] 下列哪一項與"文化多元景象"或"文化欣賞"無關？
(A)由同一種族的人組成的文化。 (B)渴望探索各種文化元素。
(C)包含文化上不同的群體。 (D)差異文化並存。 答 A

( ) 75. Which of the following does NOT support or imply the idea of "multicultural characteristics" of Taiwan?
(A)Kaleidoscopic cuisines.
(B)From local delicacies to exotic culinary delights.
(C)A whole array of food choices.
(D)A world in miniature with special terrain.

[中譯] 下列哪一項是指台灣"多元文化特徵"的概念 ？
(A)千變萬化的美食。 (B)從當地美味到異國風情美食。
(C)各式各樣的食物選擇。 (D)具有特殊地形的微型世界。 答 D

閱讀測驗二

At a personal level, the COVID-19 pandemic has **influenced**[96] individuals of all ages. The first and foremost is change in social life. Social life of youngsters and youths has been greatly compromised when school learning moved online. Rather than meeting up with others in class and studying jointly as a cohort, most students have been taking classes remotely in a home environment. It is quite concerning to think about how virtual learning might impact students' socialization and **development**[97].

Amid the practice of social distancing, curfews, and lockdowns, it is very difficult for ordinary people to stay mentally sane and physically fit. In some cities, seated dining is an exception rather than the norm, home parties are discouraged or banned altogether, and group gatherings are prohibited. Mandatory mask-wearing may impede the drive to communicate, and the constant fear of contagion may lead to social **isolation**[98]. Nonetheless, most people have tapped into their ingenuity and creativity to maintain a decent social life during the trying times.

In fact, new **understanding**[99] has been reached as a result of the impact of the pandemic. While there has been a huge drop in work and household travel overseas, people have come to realize the fun and beauty of domestic outings. While people have shuttled back and forth attending meetings, they are now participating in numerous meetings via online platforms with more efficiency and effectiveness. Indeed, in this ongoing war against the pandemic, we have seen the resilience and power of mankind.

在個人層面上，COVID-19疫情影響了所有年齡層的人。首先，也是最重要的是社會生活改變。當學校學習轉移到網路上時，青少年的社交生活受到相當損害。大多數學生不是與其他人在課堂上見面並一群人共同學習，而是在家庭環境中遠距上課，而虛擬學習可能對學生的社會化和發展影響是相當令人擔憂的。

在執行社交距離，宵禁和封城的措施時，普通人很難保持精神健全和身體健康。在某些城市，就座用餐是一種特例而非正常，家庭聚會不受鼓勵甚至禁止，群聚則是完全禁止。強制戴口罩可能會阻礙交流的動力，對傳染病的持續恐懼可能會導致社會孤立。儘管如此，大多數人還是利用自己的匠心巧思與創造力維持合宜的社交生活在這段艱難時期。

實際上，由於疫情的影響，人們已有了新的認知。儘管在海外工作和家庭旅行大幅減少的同時，人們意識到國內旅遊的樂趣和美麗；人們來回奔波於會議之間，現在透過線上平台以更高的效率和效力參加了許多會議。在這場持續對抗疫情的戰爭中，我們看到了人類的韌性和力量。

( ) 76. According to the passage, what makes it hard for people to stay mentally sound?
(A)Difficulty in managing time with online learning.
(B)The requirement to participate in meetings via online platforms.
(C)Reduced opportunities for normal socialization.
(D)Constant fear of being uncreative.

[中譯] 根據這篇文章，是什麼使人們難以保持身心健康呢？
(A)難以透過線上學習來管理時間。 (B)被要求透過線上平台參加會議。
(C)減少了正常社交的機會。 (D)一直擔心自己會失去創造力。 答 C

( ) 77. What does the word "impede" mean?
(A)**Prevent**[100]. (B)Encourage. (C)Trigger. (D)Initiate.

[中譯] "阻礙"一詞是什麼意思？
(A)妨礙 (B)鼓勵 (C)觸發 (D)創始 答 A

( ) 78. What message does the author intend to convey in the last paragraph?
(A)Domestic sightseeing is better than traveling overseas.
(B)There is a silver lining to the devastating corona pandemic.
(C)Meeting in person is a waste of time.
(D)The pandemic has seriously compromised the power of humans.

[中譯] 作者在最後一段中，想要傳達什麼訊息？
(A)國內旅遊勝過出國旅遊。 (B)徹底摧毀疫情有一線希望。
(C)親自見面是浪費時間。 (D)疫情嚴重削弱了人類的力量。 答 B

( ) 79. What may not be the reason of seated dining a normal practice in some cities?
(A)Social distancing. (B)Curfews. (C)Domestic outings. (D)Lockdowns.

[中譯] 何者並非是在某些城市就座用餐不是正規做法的原因？
(A)社交距離 (B)宵禁 (C)國內旅遊 (D)封鎖 答 C

( ) 80. Which of the following explains why "trying times" is used to describe the fight against coronavirus?
(A)It is a time that stifles human ingenuity.
(B)It is a time that people are advised to maintain an active social life.
(C)It is a time to experiment online learning at school settings.
(D)It is a time of struggle, hardship, and challenge.

[中譯] 下列哪一項可解釋為什麼用"艱難時期"來描述與冠狀病毒的鬥爭？
(A)這是扼殺人類創造力的時期。 (B)建議人們保持積極的社交生活。
(C)現在是在學校環境中試驗線上學習的時期。(D)這是一個充滿掙扎、艱辛和挑戰的時代。
答 D

| **Breakfast** 的由來 |

Fast是「齋戒、封齋」的意思。伊斯蘭教在一年中，有一個月為「齋戒月」，把齋的人在白天不進飲食，只在一早一晚，即兩頭不見太陽的時候進餐。

當齋戒月結束時，稱為「開齋」，是伊斯蘭教徒十分隆重的節日。**Breakfast**原意為**Break the fast**，即「打破齋戒或開齋」，而早餐即是打破齋戒的第一餐，**Breakfast** 一詞，由此而來。

Chapter. 03 | 測驗 | 111年度導遊試題

掌握關鍵單字，更快作答70%考題！

重要單字彙整

	單字	出現	音標	中文	詞性
1	**vegetarian**	6	[ˌvɛdʒəˋtɛrɪən]	素食主義者	名詞
2	**carnivore**	1	[ˋkɑrnəˌvɔr]	肉食主義者；肉食性動物	名詞
3	**confer**	1	[kənˋfɝ]	商談，協商 同義詞 consult, discuss	動詞
4	**enable**	1	[ɪnˋeb!]	使能夠；使可能	動詞
5	**entitle**	2	[ɪnˋtaɪt!]	享有權利；命名	動詞
6	**empower**	1	[ɪmˋpaʊɚ]	授權；允許；使能夠 同義詞 authorize, allow, commission	動詞
7	**manipulate**	1	[məˋnɪpjəˌlet]	操作，運用 同義詞 influence, control, direct	動詞
8	**perpetuate**	2	[pɚˋpɛtʃʊˌet]	永存；延續；不朽	動詞
9	**quarry**	1	[ˋkwɔrɪ]	挖掘；採石	動詞
10	**vary**	4	[ˋvɛrɪ]	不同；變化；改變 同義詞 change, differ, alter	動詞
11	**consequent**	4	[ˋkɑnsəˌkwɛnt]	由此引起的；隨之而來的 同義詞 resulting, following, ensuing 反義詞 inconsequent 不合理的；矛盾的	形容詞
12	**frequent**	4	[ˋfrikwənt]	頻繁的，時常發生的 同義詞 common, repeated, usual 反義詞 infrequent 不頻發的；罕見的	形容詞
13	**sequent**	2	[ˋsikwənt]	連續的；依次的	形容詞
14	**subsequent**	2	[ˋsʌbsɪˌkwɛnt]	隨後的；接著發生的 同義詞 following, later, succeeding 反義詞 antecedent 前情	形容詞

	單字	出現	音標	中文	詞性
15	**disable**	4	[dɪs`eb!]	失靈; 失去能力; 傷殘 同義詞 cripple, weaken, debilitate	動詞
16	**import**	2	[`ɪmport]	輸入, 進口; 重要性	名詞
17	**export**	4	[`ɛksport]	輸出, 出口	名詞
18	**alleviate**	3	[ə`livɪˌet]	減輕; 使緩和 同義詞 ease, reduce, relieve	動詞
19	**impose**	2	[ɪm`poz]	課徵; 徵收; 強加	動詞
20	**mitigate**	1	[`mɪtəˌget]	減輕; 緩和下來 同義詞 aggravate, deteriorate, worsen	動詞
21	**relieve**	6	[rɪ`liv]	減輕, 緩解; 解除 同義詞 ease, soothe, alleviate 反義詞 intensify 加強, oppress 壓迫	動詞
22	**denunciation**	2	[dɪˌnʌnsɪ`eʃən]	檢舉; 告發	名詞
23	**implication**	1	[ˌɪmplɪ`keʃən]	涉及; 牽連; 暗示	名詞
24	**refutation**	1	[ˌrɛfjʊ`teʃən]	反駁; 辯駁	名詞
25	**proclaim**	1	[prə`klem]	表明; 宣告; 讚揚 同義詞 declare, announce, herald	動詞
26	**agritourism**	1	['ægrɪtʊrɪzəm]	農業旅遊; 農業觀光	片語
27	**culinary**	32	[`kjulɪˌnɛrɪ]	食物的; 烹飪的, 烹調的	形容詞
28	**geotourism**	11	[dʒiːəʊ'tuərɪzəm]	生態旅遊; 地質旅遊	名詞
29	**nautical**	2	[`nɔtək!]	航海的; 海上的	形容詞
30	**brand**	27	[brænd]	品牌; 商標; 標記 同義詞 mark, label, tag	名詞
31	**mark**	4	[mɑrk]	記號; 痕跡; 標記 同義詞 sign, evidence, indication	名詞
32	**stigma**	1	[`stɪgmə]	污名; 惡名; 恥辱	名詞
33	**captain**	6	[`kæptɪn]	飛機機長; 長官; 首領 同義詞 chief, leader, head	名詞

▶ 4-48

	單字	出現	音標	中文	詞性
34	**committee**	2	[kə`mɪtɪ]	委員會; 監護人 同義詞 group, delegation, board	名詞
35	**eject**	1	[ɪ`dʒɛkt]	驅逐; 排除; 噴射 同義詞 remove, eliminate, expel	動詞
36	**harbor**	7	['hɑ:bə]	懷有; 藏匿; 窩藏	動詞
37	**deceive**	3	[dɪ`siv]	欺騙; 哄騙 同義詞 beguile, trick, lie 反義詞 undeceive 使醒悟	動詞
38	**conclusion**	6	[kən`kluʒən]	結論; 結尾; 結束	名詞
39	**concrete**	2	[`kɑnkrit]	具體的; 實質性的 同義詞 specific, precise, explicit 反義詞 abstract 抽象的	形容詞
40	**rudimentary**	1	[ˌrudə`mɛntəri]	基本的, 初步的	形容詞
41	**enforce**	5	[ɪn`fors]	實施; 執行	動詞
42	**essential**	8	[ɪ`sɛnʃəl]	不可缺的, 必要的; 重要的	形容詞
43	**convert**	5	[kən`vɝt]	轉化; 兌換; 換算 同義詞 change, transform	動詞
44	**revert**	1	[rɪ`vɝt]	恢復; 回復 同義詞 regress, reverse, return	動詞
45	**prey**	1	[pre]	獵物; 犧牲品 同義詞 quarry, game, kill	名詞
46	**decoy**	1	[dɪ`kɔɪ]	誘餌; 引用 同義詞 bait, lure	名詞
47	**trap**	4	[træp]	陷阱; 圈套 同義詞 catch, snare, hook	名詞
48	**discipline**	5	[`dɪsəplɪn]	訓練; 懲罰 同義詞 train, drill, exercise	動詞
49	**religious**	3	[rɪ`lɪdʒəs]	宗教的; 虔誠的; 認真的	形容詞
50	**endangered**	5	[ɪn`dendʒɚd]	瀕臨絕種的; 快要絕種的	形容詞
51	**conservation**	6	[ˌkansɚ`veʃən]	保存; 保護, 管理	名詞

	單字	出現	音標	中文	詞性
52	**alien**	3	[`elɪən]	外國人; 外星人	名詞
53	**extrinsic**	1	[ɛk`strɪnsɪk]	外來的; 外在的; 非固有的 反義詞 intrinsic 本身的	形容詞
54	**snitch**	1	[snɪtʃ]	告密者; 告發者	名詞
55	**benchmark**	1	[`bɛntʃˌmark]	基準點; 參照點	名詞
56	**postmark**	2	[`postˌmark]	郵戳	名詞
57	**trademark**	1	[`tredˌmark]	商標; 特點 同義詞 brand, stamp, label	名詞
58	**attribute**	5	[`ætrəˌbjut]	屬性; 特性, 特質 同義詞 characteristic, feature, nature	名詞
59	**credit**	15	[`krɛdɪt]	信用; 貸款 同義詞 belief, trust, faith 反義詞 discredit 敗壞名聲	名詞
60	**tribute**	3	[`tribju:t]	債務; 恩情 同義詞 contribution, subscription	名詞
61	**defect**	3	[dɪ`fɛkt]	缺點, 缺陷 同義詞 fault, flaw, weakness 反義詞 merit 價值	名詞
62	**forte**	2	[fort]	強項; 特長; 專長	名詞
63	**anonymity**	1	[ˌænə`nɪmətɪ]	匿名; 作者不詳	名詞
64	**proximity**	2	[prɑk`sɪmətɪ]	鄰近, 接近; 親近	名詞
65	**consulate**	2	[`kɑns!ɪt]	領事館	名詞
66	**headquarter**	2	[`hɛd`kwɔrtɚ]	設立總部	動詞
67	**elementary**	2	[ˌɛlə`mɛntərɪ]	基本的; 初級的 同義詞 fundamental, basic, primary	形容詞
68	**fulfill**	3	[fʊl`fɪl]	實現; 達到; 滿足 同義詞 perform, complete, satisfy	動詞
69	**vanish**	3	[`vænɪʃ]	消失; 失蹤 同義詞 disappear, fade, perish 反義詞 appear 出現	動詞

▶ 4-50

	單字	出現	音標	中文	詞性
70	**aboriginal**	27	[ˌæbəˋrɪdʒən!]	土生土長的; 原始的	形容詞
71	**amateur**	1	[ˋæməˌtʃʊr]	業餘的; 外行的	形容詞
72	**luggage**	11	[ˋlʌgɪdʒ]	行李 同義詞 baggage, valises, bags	名詞
73	**crave**	1	[krev]	渴望; 熱望	動詞
74	**carve**	10	[kɑrv]	雕刻; 切割 同義詞 cut, slice, incise	動詞
75	**depart**	22	[dɪˋpɑrt]	離開; 出發; 去世 同義詞 die, decease, perish 反義詞 arrive 抵達	動詞
76	**insert**	1	[ɪnˋsɝt]	插入, 添寫 同義詞 introduce, inject, enter	動詞
77	**strike**	12	[straɪk]	打擊; 攻擊; 罷工 同義詞 hit, knock, jab	動詞
78	**settle**	24	[ˋsɛt!]	結算, 支付; 安頓 同義詞 determine, decide, resolve 反義詞 unsettle 使心神不寧	動詞
79	**skeptical**	3	[ˋskɛptɪk!]	懷疑的, 多疑的	形容詞
80	**interactive**	2	[ˌɪntɚˋæktɪv]	互動的; 相互交流的	形容詞
81	**calculation**	3	[ˌkælkjəˋleʃən]	計算; 估計; 盤算	名詞
82	**etiquette**	3	[ˋɛtɪkɛt]	禮儀; 規矩 同義詞 manners, formalities	名詞
83	**posture**	1	[ˋpɑstʃɚ]	姿勢, 姿態 同義詞 position, carriage, bearing	名詞
84	**employment**	4	[ɪmˋplɔɪmənt]	僱用; 受僱; 職業 同義詞 hiring, engaging	名詞
85	**reasonable**	2	[ˋriznəb!]	合理的; 適當的 同義詞 sensible, appropriate, fair 反義詞 unreasonable 不講理的	形容詞

	單字	出現	音標	中文	詞性
86	**asset**	3	[`æsɛt]	財產, 資產 同義詞 accounts, resources, property	名詞
87	**option**	14	[`ɑpʃən]	選擇; 選項 同義詞 choice, alternative, substitute	名詞
88	**undo**	1	[ʌn`du]	解開, 打開; 取消 同義詞 unfasten, untie, disassemble	動詞
89	**spare**	2	[spɛr]	節省; 抽出; 剩下 同義詞 relinquish, omit	動詞
90	**pilfer**	1	[`pɪlfɚ]	偷竊 同義詞 steal, thieve, rob	動詞
91	**license**	10	[`laɪsns]	執照; 許可證 同義詞 permit, pass, certificate	名詞
92	**complain**	15	[kəm`plen]	抱怨, 發牢騷	動詞
93	**receipt**	11	[rɪ`sit]	發票; 收據; 收入 同義詞 voucher, quittance	名詞
94	**significant**	7	[sɪg`nɪfəkənt]	重要的; 有意義的 同義詞 momentous, eventful, fateful 反義詞 insignificant 地位低微的	形容詞
95	**tendency**	1	[`tɛndənsɪ]	潮流; 傾向; 天分 同義詞 inclination, leaning, bent	名詞
96	**negative**	8	[`nɛgətɪv]	負面的; 消極的; 否定的 同義詞 nullifying, voiding, canceling	形容詞
97	**positive**	7	[`pɑzətɪv]	正面的; 積極的; 明確的 同義詞 definite, certain, absolute	形容詞
98	**infrastructure**	8	[`ɪnfrə͵strʌktʃɚ]	基礎建設; 公共建設	名詞
99	**profit**	5	[`prɑfɪt]	利潤; 利益; 收益 同義詞 gain, benefit, advantage 反義詞 loss 喪失	名詞
100	**interaction**	2	[͵ɪntə`rækʃən]	互動; 互相影響	名詞

111年導遊筆試測驗

●本書採用英語邏輯思維[中譯]
幫助更快看懂句子, 拆解字義

題型分析			情境命題				
單字 45	片語 8	對話 4	景物 6	餐飲 6	住宿 2	交通 7	機場 5
文法 13	閱測 10		生活 21	民俗 1	產業 9	職能 7	購物 6

單選題 [共80題, 每題1.25分]

( ) 1. It was so obvious that he was just trying to butter ____ his boss in order to get a raise.
(A)at (B)on (C)over (D)up 職能 片語

[中譯] 很明顯，他只是為了加薪想討好老闆。
(A)在 (B)上 (C)多 (D)向上
補 to butter up 巴結某人 / 釋出善意給某人，希望得到有利的回應 答 D

( ) 2. I went to the amusement park last week and had a ______.
(A)blast (B)bless (C)boost (D)boast 景物 片語

[中譯] 我上週去了遊樂園，而且玩得很盡興。
(A)爆炸 (B)祝福 (C)提升 (D)吹噓
補 to have a blast 很開心、很愉快、很盡興 答 A

( ) 3. Buying a second-hand car may save you some money, but make sure you don't buy a (an) ______.
(A)apple (B)banana (C)lemon (D)melon 購物 片語

[中譯] 購買二手車可能會為你省下一些錢，但須確保不會買一輛狀況很多的車。
(A)蘋果 (B)香蕉 (C)檸檬 (D)甜瓜
補 to buy a lemon 買一輛狀況很多的車 答 C

( ) 4. Jimmy learns everything so fast! He is indeed a smart ______.
(A)cake (B)cookie (C)cracker (D)muffin 職能 片語

[中譯] Jimmy學得真快！他確實是一個聰明的人。
(A)蛋糕 (B)曲奇餅 (C)餅乾 (D)鬆餅
補 smart cookie 聰明人；tough cookie 硬漢、不動感情的人 答 B

( ) 5. What do we call someone who refrains from consuming meat, eggs, dairy products, and any other animal-derived substances?
(A)**vegetarian**[1] (B)vegan (C)**carnivore**[2] (D)flexitarian 餐飲 單字

[中譯] 我們如何稱呼那些不吃肉、蛋、奶製品和任何其他動物源性物質的人？
(A)素食主義者 (B)嚴格素食主義者 (C)肉食性動物 (D)彈性素食者 答 B

( ) 6. If your flight has been canceled by the airline, you are ______ to a refund that only applies to services you have not received.
(A)**conferred**[3] (B)**enabled**[4] (C)**entitled**[5] (D)**empowered**[6] 交通 單字

[中譯] 如果您的航班被航空公司取消，您有權獲得退款，但僅適用於您尚未接受的服務。
(A)賦予 (B)配有(某種設備或技術)的 (C)有權做...的 (D)經授權的 答 C

( ) 7. The amount of alcohol passengers are allowed to carry onto a plane ______ from country to country.
(A)**manipulates**[7] (B)**perpetuates**[8] (C)**quarries**[9] (D)**varies**[10] 交通 單字

[中譯] 允許乘客攜帶上飛機的酒精含量因國家/地區而異。
(A)操縱 (B)延續 (C)採石 (D)不同 答 D

( ) 8. Please pay close attention to the safety instructions even if you are a ______ flyer.
(A)**consequent**[11] (B)**frequent**[12] (C)**sequent**[13] (D)**subsequent**[14] 交通 單字

[中譯] 即使您是飛行常客，也請密切注意安全說明。
(A)由此引起的 (B)頻繁的 (C)順序的 (D)隨後的 答 B

( ) 9. Federal law prohibits _____ any smoke detector installed in any airplane lavatory.
(A)**disable**[15] (B)to disable (C)disabling (D)disabled 交通 文法

[中譯] 聯邦法律禁止任何安裝在飛機廁所中的煙霧探測器失靈。
(A)(B)(C)(D)使失靈 解 P2-9. 文法11 答 C

( ) 10. Customs Duty is a tax ______ on **imports**[16] and **exports**[17] of goods in accordance with the Customs Import Tariff.
(A)**alleviated**[18] (B)**imposed**[19] (C)**mitigated**[20] (D)**relieved**[21] 產業 單字

[中譯] 關稅是根據海關進口關稅對進出口貨物徵收的稅。
(A)緩解 (B)徵收 (C)減輕 (D)緩和 答 B

( ) 11. A: May I have your passport and customs ______ form, please?
B: Sure, here you are.
(A)declaration (B)**denunciation**[22] (C)**implication**[23] (D)**refutation**[24] 機場 單字

[中譯] A：請給我您的護照和報關單，好嗎？ B：當然，給您。
(A)聲明 (B)檢舉 (C)涉及 (D)反駁 答 A

( ) 12. You can get to Baggage ____ by going down the escalator and following the signs.
(A)Acclaim (B)Claim (C)Exclaim (D)**Proclaim**[25] 機場 單字

[中譯] 您可以沿著自動手扶梯向下走，按照指示牌前往行李認領。
(A)好評 (B)認領 (C)喊叫 (D)宣布 答 B

( ) 13. The last thing you want on a vacation is to find out _____ fees that you must pay.
(A)hiding (B)hid (C)hidden (D)hides 生活 文法

[中譯] 休假時，你最不想做的就是找出你必須支付的隱藏費用。 解 P2-11. 文法13 答 C
補 hidden fees 被隱藏的費用

( ) 14. ______ is the exploration of food as the purpose and destination.
(A)**Agritourism**[26] (B)**Culinary**[27] tourism
(C)**Geotourism**[28] (D)**Nautical**[29] tourism

[中譯] 美食觀光是以美食為目標及目的地的探索。 產業 單字
(A)農業觀光 (B)美食觀光 (C)地質觀光 (D)航海觀光 答 B

( ) 15. Tourism is vital to the economy of a country; as a result, the National Tourism Authorities always try to promote its national ______ image.
(A)**brand**[30] (B)flag (C)**mark**[31] (D)**stigma**[32] 產業 單字

[中譯] 旅遊業對一個國家的經濟至關重要；因此，國家旅遊局總是試圖宣傳其國家品牌形象。
(A)品牌 (B)旗幟 (C)標記 (D)汙名 答 A

( ) 16. Customers are very much in the ______ seat today given all the options for choosing what's in their favor on the internet.
(A)**captain**'s[33] (B)driver's (C)passenger's (D)rider's 購物 片語

[中譯] 客戶今天可以完全掌控，在網路上選出他們喜歡的所有選項。
(A)(飛機的)機長；隊長 (B)駕駛 (C)乘客 (D)騎士
補 be in the driving seat 負責，處於控制（或管理）地位 答 B

( ) 17. Many **committee**[34] members actually ___ suspicions about his intention to resign.
(A)embrace (B)**eject**[35] (C)**harbor**[36] (D)**deceive**[37] 生活 單字

[中譯] 許多委員會的成員實際上對他請辭的意圖心存懷疑。
(A)擁抱 (B)驅逐 (C)心懷；藏匿；庇護 (D)欺騙 答 C

( ) 18. It is hard to come to any **conclusion**[38] given the ______ knowledge we have at this stage.
(A)**concrete**[39] (B)delicate (C)**rudimentary**[40] (D)thorough 生活 單字

[中譯] 鑒於我們現階段掌握的初步知識，很難得出任何結論。
(A)具體的 (B)脆弱的 (C)初步的 (D)仔細的 答 C

( ) 19. Identifying the problem is the first step to help us make an ______ decision.
(A)abreast (B)informed (C)**enforced**[41] (D)erudite 生活 單字

[中譯] 識別問題是幫助我們做出明智決定的第一步。
(A)並肩而行 (B)有根據的 (C)實行 (D)有學問的 答 B

( ) 20. Shopping has ______ into an **essential**[42] factor for many tourists when choosing a travel destination.
(A)**converted**[43] (B)extroverted (C)inverted (D)**reverted**[44] 產業 單字

[中譯] 購物已成為許多遊客在選擇旅遊目的地時必要的因素。
(A)轉換 (B)外向 (C)顛倒 (D)回覆 答 A

( ) 21. Many tourists can easily fall ____ to the pickpockets in some crowded tourist spots.
(A)bait (B)**prey**[45] (C)**decoy**[46] (D)**trap**[47] 景物 單字

[中譯] 許多遊客在一些擁擠的旅遊景點容易成為扒手的獵物。
(A)誘餌 (B)獵物 (C)誘騙 (D)陷阱 答 B

( ) 22. When you **discipline**[48] your staff, try not to make them feel they are being told ____.
(A)in (B)on (C)off (D)out 職能 片語

[中譯] 當你教導你的員工時，盡量不要讓他們覺得自己被指責了。
(A)在 (B)上 (C)關 (D)出
補 tell sb off 責備，斥責（某人） 答 C

( ) 23. ______ tourism is an umbrella term which refers to a specific tourism product tailored to the needs of a particular audience.
(A)Mass (B)**Religious**[49] (C)Niche (D)Top-notch 產業 單字

[中譯] 小眾旅遊是一個總括性術語，指的是根據特定受眾的需求量身訂製的特定旅遊產品。
(A)大量的 (B)宗教的 (C)利基的 (D)第一流的 答 C

( ) 24. Many people suffer from ______ and therefore never switch off their cellphones.
(A)acrophobia (B)claustrophobia (C)nomophobia (D)xenophobia 生活 單字

[中譯] 許多人患有無手機焦慮症，因此從不關掉手機。
(A)懼高症 (B)幽閉恐懼症 (C)無手機焦慮症 (D)排外主義 答 C

( ) 25. He was so mad at the salesclerk's attitude but tried very hard not to make a(an) ______ in public.
(A)act (B)blow (C)mark (D)scene 購物 片語

[中譯] 他對銷售員的態度非常生氣，但試著很努力地不在公共場合鬧事。
(A)行為 (B)吹動 (C)標記 (D)場面
補 make a scene 大吵大鬧 答 D

( ) 26. The Formosan black bear is a species ______ to Taiwan and currently listed as "**endangered**[50]" under Taiwan's Wildlife **Conservation**[51] Act.
(A)**alien**[52] (B)**extrinsic**[53] (C)indigenous (D)invasive 景物 單字

[中譯] 臺灣黑熊是臺灣本土物種，根據臺灣目前的野生動物保護法被列為「瀕危」物種。
(A)外國人；僑民 (B)外來的 (C)本土的 (D)侵入的 答 C

( ) 27. The annual Dajia Matsu Pilgrimage procession went off without a ____ this year!
(A)ditch (B)hitch (C)**snitch**[54] (D)stitch 民俗 片語

[中譯] 一年一度的大甲媽祖繞境之旅行今年順利進行！
(A)拋棄 (B)繫住 (C)揭發 (D)縫線
補 go (off) without a hitch 順利進行 答 B

( ) 28. In order to enhance our service, we need to be ______ against the leading hotels with a reputation for high quality.
(A)**benchmarked**[55] (B)embarked
(C)**postmarked**[56] (D)**trademarked**[57] 產業 單字

[中譯] 為了提升我們的服務，我們需要以高品質盛譽領先的飯店為目標基準。
(A)基準 (B)登船 (C)郵戳 (D)商標 答 A

( ) 29. Those who gave valedictory speeches paid their ______ to one of the most iconic figures in the history of contemporary music.
(A)**attribute**[58] (B)**credit**[59] (C)debt (D)**tribute**[60] 職能 單字

[中譯] 那些發表告別演說的人向當代音樂史上最具代表性的人物之一致敬。
(A)特性 (B)讚揚 (C)借款 (D)致敬 答 D

( ) 30. Given her angelic voice, there is no doubt that singing is her ______.
(A)**defect**[61] (B)**forte**[62] (C)track (D)weakness 職能 單字

[中譯] 鑑於她天使般的聲音，唱歌是她的強項毫無疑問。
(A)缺點 (B)強項 (C)軌道 (D)弱點 答 B

( ) 31. Okinawa is quite a popular vacation destination because of its ______ to Taiwan.
(A)**anonymity**[63] (B)longevity (C)**proximity**[64] (D)sublimity 景物 單字

[中譯] 由於鄰近臺灣，沖繩是一個非常受歡迎的度假勝地。
(A)匿名 (B)壽命 (C)鄰近 (D)崇高 答 C

( ) 32. You should contact the nearest embassy or ______ for assistance if your passport is lost or stolen while traveling abroad.
(A)conventions (B)**consulate**[65] (C)**headquarters**[66] (D)heritage 生活 單字

[中譯] 如果您的護照在國外旅行時遺失或被竊，您應該聯繫最近的大使館或領事館尋求協助。
(A)會議 (B)領事館 (C)總部 (D)遺產 答 B

( ) 33. Our last holiday was a five-day trip to Bali. We enjoyed ______ weather during our vacation on the tropical island.
(A)literary (B)heavenly (C)jumpy (D)**elementary**[67] 景物 單字

[中譯] 我們上一個假期是巴里島五天的旅行。在熱帶島嶼度假期間我們享受天堂般的天氣。
(A)文學的 (B)天堂般的 (C)提心吊膽的 (D)基本的 答 B

( ) 34. In Taiwan, people ______ tap water first before drinking it; however, in Japan, people don't have to.
(A)bump (B)solve (C)boil (D)drop 生活 單字

[中譯] 在臺灣，人們先將自來水煮沸後再飲用；然而，在日本，人們不必這樣做。
(A)碰撞 (B)思考 (C)煮沸 (D)丟下 答 C

( ) 35. People from Australia, where the air is usually dry, have a tough time getting used to the______ weather in Taiwan.
(A)humid (B)arid (C)bare (D)crispy 景物 單字

[中譯] 澳洲的空氣通常很乾燥，來自那裡的人，很難適應台灣潮濕的天氣。
(A)潮濕的 (B)乾燥的 (C)赤裸的 (D)酥脆的 答 A

( ) 36. National parks can ______ the important function of preservation of the natural environment.
(A)huddle (B)**fulfill**[68] (C)distract (D)**vanish**[69] 產業 單字

[中譯] 國家公園能發揮保護自然環境的重要功能。
(A)擠成一團 (B)實踐 (C)干擾 (D)絕跡 答 B

( ) 37. No one knows how to operate this airport e-Gate Enrollment system because the instruction is rather______.
(A)complicated (B)**aboriginal**[70] (C)**amateur**[71] (D)hilarious 機場 單字

[中譯] 沒有人知道如何操作這個機場的入出國自動查驗通關註冊系統，因為操作指示相當複雜。
(A)複雜的 (B)土生土長的 (C)業餘愛好的 (D)非常滑稽的
補 e-Gate Enrollment System 入出國自動查驗通關註冊系統 答 A

( ) 38. Our plane will take off in twenty minutes, so we'd better ____ to the departure gate.
(A)hurry (B)notice (C)pause (D)check 機場 單字

[中譯] 我們的飛機將在二十分鐘後起飛，所以我們最好快點到登機口。
(A)加快 (B)注意到 (C)暫停 (D)檢查 答 A

( ) 39. Before going abroad, make sure that your passport must be ______ for another six months before you depart for international travel.
(A)related (B)plain (C)insulting (D)valid 生活 單字

[中譯] 在出國之前，請確保您的護照在您出發至國際旅行前須至少6個月有效。
(A)相關的 (B)簡單的 (C)無禮的 (D)有效的 答 D

( ) 40. Please empty ______ your pocket. Put your bag, phone and other electronic devices, belt or metal objects on the tray. 機場 文法
(A)up (B)in (C)out (D)for

[中譯] 請清空你的口袋。將您的包包、手機和其他電子設備、皮帶或金屬物品放在托盤上。
(A)向上 (B)在 (C)出去 (D)為了 解 P2-48. 文法76 答 C

( ) 41. Don't bring too much ______ if you want to travel light.
(A)percent (B)**luggage**[72] (C)cloak (D)server 生活 單字

[中譯] 如果您想輕裝旅行，請不要帶太多行李。
(A)百分比 (B)行李 (C)斗篷 (D)伺服器 答 B

( ) 42. I feel terribly ______. Please give me an aspirin for airsickness.
(A)refreshing (B)scrambled (C)reasonable (D)uncomfortable 生活 單字

[中譯] 我感到非常不舒服。請給我一顆阿斯匹靈減緩暈機。
(A)提神的 (B)移動的 (C)合理的 (D)不舒服的 答 D

( ) 43. Do you feel like ______ a cup of hot tea?
(A)had (B)having (C)to have (D)have 餐飲 文法

[中譯] 您想喝杯熱茶嗎？ 解 P2-9. 文法11 答 B

( ) 44. Would you like another ______ of bread?
(A)**craving**[73] (B)setting (C)serving (D)**carving**[74] 餐飲 單字

[中譯] 你想再來一份麵包嗎？
(A)渴望 (B)一套 (C)一份 (D)雕刻品 答 C

( ) 45. Did Alex's flight to Taipei ______ on time?
(A)**depart**[75] (B)**insert**[76] (C)oppose (D)**strike**[77] 交通 單字

[中譯] Alex飛往台北的航班準時起飛嗎？
(A)起飛 (B)插入 (C)反對 (D)攻擊 答 A

( ) 46. You have a superior room ______ for three nights.
(A)reserve (B)reserves (C)reserving (D)reserved 住宿 文法

[中譯] 您預訂了三晚的高級客房。
(A)(B)(C)(D)預訂 解 P2-20. 文法35 答 D
補 You have a superior room (which is) reserved...，其中句型省略 which is。

( ) 47. I'd like to leave early tomorrow morning. Can I ______ my bill now?
(A)**settle**[78] (B)remove (C)reserve (D)seat 住宿 單字

[中譯] 我明天一早想先離開。可以現在結算我的帳單嗎？
(A)結算 (B)移除 (C)保留 (D)給...安排座位 答 A

( ) 48. Were those eggs fried or ______?
(A)poached (B)packed (C)teased (D)tingled 餐飲 單字

[中譯] 那些雞蛋是油煎的還是水波的？
(A)去殼水煮的 (B)擁擠的 (C)取笑 (D)刺痛 答 A

( ) 49. The museum of nature science's ______ exhibits provides children with a hands-on experience and immediate feedback.
(A)flat (B)vocal (C)**skeptical**[79] (D)**interactive**[80] 產業 單字

[中譯] 自然科學博物館的互動展品為孩子們提供手動體驗和即時反饋。
(A)水平的 (B)嗓音的 (C)懷疑的 (D)互動的 答 D

(　　) 50. Alex has such a strong ______ for art that he spends most of his spare time in museums and galleries.
(A)**calculation**[81] (B)anxiety (C)temper (D)passion 生活 單字

[中譯] Alex對藝術有著如此強烈的熱情，以至於他將大部分空閒時間都花在博物館和畫廊裡。
(A)算計 (B)擔心 (C)脾氣 (D)熱情 答 D

(　　) 51. Mary's pictures look all the same because she always adopts the same ______ for the camera.
(A)awe (B)**etiquette**[82] (C)**posture**[83] (D)**employment**[84] 生活 單字

[中譯] Mary的照片看起來都一樣，因為她總是對著鏡頭擺相同的姿勢。
(A)驚奇 (B)禮儀 (C)姿勢 (D)受僱 答 C

(　　) 52. Would you be willing to help Karen ______ information about our new product in this catalog?
(A)found (B)finding (C)have found (D)find 職能 文法

[中譯] 你願意協助Karen在這個目錄中找到我們新產品的資訊嗎？
(A)(B)(C)(D)找到 解 P2-2. 文法01 答 D
補 使役動詞的文法為 make + O + Vr；其他常見使役動詞有let, make, have, help等。

(　　) 53. I didn't think the price was too high at all; in fact, it seemed quite ______.
(A)fascinated (B)**reasonable**[85] (C)demanding (D)eloquent 購物 單字

[中譯] 我根本不認為價格過高；事實上，這似乎很合理。
(A)入迷的 (B)合理的 (C)苛求的 (D)有說服力的 答 B

(　　) 54. Jane ______ an international collect call to her friend yesterday.
(A)made (B)hung (C)printed (D)sent 生活 片語

[中譯] Jane昨天打了一通國際對方付費電話給她的朋友。
(A)做了 (B)掛著 (C)印刷 (D)發送 答 A

(　　) 55. You can make big ______ with your credit card. That way, you don't have to carry large amounts of cash.
(A)**assets**[86] (B)purchases (C)moments (D)**options**[87] 購物 單字

[中譯] 您可以使用信用卡進行大額購買。這樣，您就不必攜帶大量現金。
(A)資產 (B)購買 (C)瞬間 (D)選擇 答 B

(　　) 56. If you are trapped in an elevator, ______ as much energy as you can and call 9-1-1 with your cell phone if you have service.
(A)**undo**[88] (B)abandon (C)**spare**[89] (D)**pilfer**[90] 生活 單字

[中譯] 如果您被困在電梯中，請盡量節省體力，如果您的手機有行動服務，請撥打9-1-1。
(A)解開 (B)放棄 (C)節省 (D)偷竊 答 C

( ) 57. Please remove your driver's ______ from your wallet and hand me your ID.
(A)**license**[91] (B)quill (C)method (D)garage 生活 單字

[中譯] 請從你的皮夾取出你的駕駛執照，然後將它交給我。
(A)許可 (B)羽毛筆 (C)方法 (D)車庫 答 A

( ) 58. A: Is it OK if we sit by the window? B: ______
(A)Sure, I'll help you move over there. (B)I'll give you a cup of water.
(C)Yes, that's right. (D)I am sorry. But we have a two-hour limit. 生活 對話

[中譯] A：如果我們坐在窗戶旁邊可以嗎？ B：當然可以，我會幫您搬過去。
(A)當然可以，我會幫您搬過去。 (B)我會給您一杯水。
(C)是，這是正確的。 (D)我很抱歉。但是我們有兩個小時的限制。 答 A

( ) 59. A: I'm thirsty. Can I have a glass of water? B: ______
(A)Yes, we'll be closed at 10:00 p.m. (B)Yes, I'll give it to you right away.
(C)No, I'm afraid we are full at the moment. (D)No, it's too cold here. 餐飲 對話

[中譯] A：我渴了。可以給我一杯水嗎？ B：好的，我馬上給您。
(A)是，我們將在晚上10:00關門休息。 (B)好的，我馬上給您。
(C)不，恐怕我們現在已經客滿了。 (D)不，這裡太冷了。 答 B

( ) 60. Could you help me ______ an arrangement?
(A)do (B)ticket (C)encase (D)make 生活 文法

[中譯] 你能幫我做安排嗎？
(A)做 (B)售票 (C)把...包住 (D)做 解 P2-2. 文法1 答 D
補 make an arrangement 做安排

( ) 61. Don't drink the cola in the refrigerator in the hotel, ______ you will be charged for the drink.
(A)when (B)or (C)but (D)yet 餐飲 文法

[中譯] 不要喝放在飯店冰箱裡的可樂，否則你將會被收費。
(A)當...時 (B)否則 (C)但 (D)尚未 解 P2-46. 文法75 答 B

( ) 62. ______a map with you in case you get lost.
(A)Enter (B)Take (C)Stay (D)Raise 生活 片語

[中譯] 隨身攜帶地圖以防迷路。
(A)進入 (B)帶 (C)停留 (D)舉起 答 B

( ) 63. It is raining cats and dogs outside, because there is a typhoon ______ Taiwan now.
(A)hanging (B)putting (C)hitting (D)giving 生活 單字

[中譯] 外面正在傾盆大雨，因為有颱風襲擊台灣。
(A)懸掛 (B)造成 (C)襲擊 (D)給予 答 C

( ) 64. When Lisa ______ about the slow service, the manager apologized.
(A)**complained**[92] (B)amused (C)bored (D)laughed 生活 單字

[中譯] 當Lisa抱怨服務太慢的時候，經理道歉了。
(A)抱怨 (B)被逗樂 (C)感到無聊的 (D)大笑 答 A

( ) 65. Tony is a ______ tour guide. He brings a destination to life with his passion, storytelling and wit.
(A)first-hand (B)cut-rate (C)convertible (D)first-rate 職能 片語

[中譯] Tony是一流的導遊。他用自身的熱情、講故事敘事能力和機智，將景點活靈活現。
(A)第一手的 (B)打折的 (C)可改變的 (D)一流的 答 D

( ) 66. A: Can I pick up the car at the airport? B: ______
(A)Yes. Make sure you go as fast as you can.
(B)No, but we can arrange for transportation to our lot.
(C)Actually, I'm still not done.
(D)The price depends on the kind of car you rent. 交通 對話

[中譯] A：我可以在機場取車嗎？ B：不，但我們可以安排交通工具到我們的停車場。
(A)是的。確保你盡可能地快走。
(B)不，但我們可以安排交通工具到我們的停車場。
(C)其實，我還沒說完。
(D)價格取決於您租用的汽車類型。 答 B

( ) 67. I couldn't return this item because I had lost the ______.
(A)toll (B)period (C)**receipt**[93] (D)gate 購物 單字

[中譯] 我無法退回這件商品，因為我遺失了收據。
(A)通行費 (B)一段時間 (C)收據 (D)大門 答 C

( ) 68. ______ one do you like, orange, apple or banana?
(A)Where (B)How (C)What (D)Which 生活 文法

[中譯] 你喜歡哪一種，橘子、蘋果還是香蕉？
(A)哪裡 (B)如何 (C)什麼 (D)哪一 解 P2-38. 文法59 答 D

( ) 69. A: ______ is the taxi stand nearby?
B: It's just one mile away. You can walk there if you want.
(A)How old (B)How far (C)How tall (D)How much 交通 對話

[中譯] A：附近的計程車招呼站有多遠？
B：就在一英里之外。如果你願意，你可以步行到那裡。
(A)年紀多大 (B)多遠 (C)多高 (D)多少 解 P2-39. 文法60 答 B

情境篇 文法篇 片語篇 測驗篇 口試篇

( ) 70. Taiwan is famous ______ its rich fruit supply.
(A)for (B)on (C)at (D)in 產業 文法

[中譯] 臺灣以其豐富的水果供應而聞名。
(A)為了 (B)在...上面 (C)在...上 (D)在...裡面
補 be famous for 以...聞名

答 A

閱讀測驗一

In recent decades, we have seen the cumulative effects and **significant**[94] impacts generated by tourism in economic, environmental, and social-cultural aspects. Unfortunately, there is a **tendency**[95] to believe that the economic impacts are often put forward in a positive light, the environmental impacts seen as **negative**[96], and the social-cultural impacts sometimes misunderstood or ignored. In fact, there can be both **positive**[97] and negative impacts.

To begin with, it is evident that tourism industry has the power to improve and **vitalize** local economies. Such effects include improved tax revenue and personal income, increased standards of living, improvement in local **infrastructures**[98], and more employment opportunities. However, let's not be naïve about the downside of it, including the seasonal and low-paying jobs and the fact that most **profits**[99] go to the multinational and internationally-owned corporations. Secondly, tourism does help with the protection and conservation of natural environment. Nevertheless, there are also issues such as increase in water and energy consumption, excessive pollution, and disruption of wildlife behavior. Finally, tourism allows for cross-cultural **interaction**[100] which leads to further understanding and appreciation as well as tolerance of cultural differences. For example, the inclusion of LGBT travel, investment in arts and culture, celebration of Indigenous peoples, and community pride. Nonetheless, it also brings the change or loss of indigenous identity and values, culture clashes, and ethical issues (such as an increase in sex tourism or the exploitation of child workers).

In a nutshell, tourism is always a double-edged sword. While reaping the benefits, we should raise our awareness and take actions to cope with the several negative impacts of tourism.

近幾十年來，我們看到了旅遊業在經濟、環境和社會文化方面產生的累積效應和重大影響。不幸的是，人們往往認為經濟影響是積極的，環境影響被視為消極的，而社會文化影響有時被誤解或忽視。事實上，正面影響和負面影響都可能存在。

首先，旅遊業顯然具有改善和**振興**當地經濟的能力。這些影響包括稅收和個人收入的提高、生活水平的提高、當地**基礎設施**的改善以及提供更多就業機會。然而，我們不應天真地看待它的負面影響，包括季節性的工作和低工資，以及大部分的利潤流向跨國性和國際性獨資公司。其次，旅遊業確實有助於保護和保育自然環境。然而，也存在像是水和能源消耗的增加、過度污染和破壞野生動物行為等問題。最終，旅遊業促進了跨文化互動，進一步增進對不同文化的理解、欣賞及尊重。例如，將 LGBT 觀光納入其中、對藝術和文化的投資、原住民的慶典活動及社會遊行。儘管如此，它也可能帶來原住民身份和價值觀的改變或喪失、文化衝突和道德問題（例如色情旅遊的增加或對童工的剝削）。

總而言之，旅遊業始終是一把雙刃劍。在獲得收益的同時，我們應提高意識，以及採取行動去應對旅遊帶來的若干負面影響。

( ) 71. What is NOT true about the impacts of tourism in the first paragraph?
(A)Tourism does not always boost economic growth.
(B)All environmental impacts are detrimental.
(C)There is misunderstanding about the social-cultural impacts.
(D)Tourism actually brings both positive and negative impacts.

[中譯] 第一段中關於旅遊業的影響何者為非？
(A)旅遊業並不總能促進經濟增長。
(B)所有的環境影響都是有害的。
(C)對社會文化影響存在誤解。
(D)旅遊業實際上帶來了正面和負面的影響。 答 B

( ) 72. Which of the following words does NOT mean "**vitalize**"?
(A)aggravate (B)energize (C)invigorate (D)stimulate

[中譯] 下列哪一個詞不是"**振興**"的意思？
(A)更嚴重 (B)激勵 (C)活躍 (D)刺激 答 A

( ) 73. Which of the following statements is NOT true about the **infrastructures** in line three of paragraph two?
(A)It refers to the basic physical and organizational structures and facilities.
(B)It can include buildings, roads, power supplies, transportation systems, and so on.
(C)Communication networks are not included in infrastructures.
(D)Infrastructures can be beneficial to both locals and tourists.

[中譯] 關於第二段第三行文中的**基礎設施**，下列敘述何者不正確？
(A)指基本的實體和組織結構和設施。
(B)它可以包括建築物、道路、電源、交通系統等。
(C)通訊網絡不包括在基礎設施中。
(D)基礎設施對當地人和遊客都有好處。 答 C

( ) 74. What might NOT be considered as a positive social-cultural impact of tourism?
(A)The inclusion of LGBT tourism.
(B)More cultural festival activities of indigenous peoples.
(C)A growing sense of pride in one's own heritage.
(D)Increased job opportunities for locals, both adults and children alike.

[中譯] 何者可能不被視為旅遊業的積極社會文化影響？
(A)將 LGBT 觀光納入其中。
(B)增加原住民文化節慶活動。
(C)對自己的傳統越來越感到自豪。
(D)增加當地人的就業機會，包括成人和兒童。 答 D

(　　) 75. Which of the following statements is FALSE according to the author?
(A)Tourism, which only comes with positive impacts, is not a double-edged sword.
(B)Culture clashes refer to the integration among different cultures.
(C)Wildlife behaviors can be disrupted as a result of negative impacts of tourism.
(D)Actions should be taken to avoid the deprivation of under-aged workers.

[中譯] 根據作者的說法，下列敘述何者錯誤？
(A)旅遊業只有積極影響，不是一把雙刃劍。
(B)文化衝突是指不同文化之間的融合。
(C)旅遊業的負面影響可能會破壞野生動物的行為。
(D)應採取措施以避免未成年工人的權利被剝奪。

 A

閱讀測驗二

"There isn't a train I wouldn't take, no matter where it's going." The poet who wrote these words knew the joy and excitement of train rides. Train travels grant passengers access to sights that are often missed when traveling by plane or car.

On the Blue Train, tourists can experience the wild beauty of the South African landscape in comfort. During the 27-hour trip, passengers view vineyards, sunflower farms and the ostrich-filled Karoo Desert. Off-train excursions include a stop in Kimberley, a historical diamond-rush town.

The journey over the roof of Norway on the Bergen Line connects Bergen and Oslo. This 300-mile line is northern Europe's highest railroad. The seven-hour trip gives tourists breathtaking views of snow- capped mountains, glaciers and fjords. Passengers can get off at ski resorts or charming mountain villages along the route.

Take the Kuranda Scenic Railway if you want to see tropical forests. In Australia's Barron Gorge National Park, you'll travel through unspoiled rainforest and past spectacular waterfalls on an amazing journey. When you get at Kuranda, the journey doesn't end there. The Koala Gardens, the Australian Butterfly Sanctuary, and BirdWorld Kuranda are among the many attractions in this picturesque village.

One of the world's highest railway trips takes you to Machu Picchu, the ruins of an ancient city located in the Andes Mountains of South America. Your journey will begin at the city of Cuzco. You'll take local PeruRail trains to the "Lost City of the Incas" from there. Your ride will be bumpy, but it will offer unforgettable views of thick jungle and spectacular peaks.

「無論去哪裡，我都會坐火車。」寫下這些話的詩人深知乘坐火車的喜悅和興奮。火車旅行讓乘客可以參觀乘坐飛機或汽車旅行時，經常錯過的景點。

在藍色列車上，遊客可以舒適地體驗南非風景的狂野美景。在27小時的旅程中，乘客可以觀賞葡萄園、向日葵農場和充滿鴕鳥的卡魯沙漠。途中下車遊覽，包括停留在金伯利，一座曾有採鑽熱的歷史名鎮。

卑爾根路線上的挪威屋頂之旅連接卑爾根和奧斯陸。這條300英里長的鐵路是北歐地區地勢最高的鐵路。七小時的旅程讓遊客可以欣賞到雪山、冰川和峽灣的壯麗景色。乘客可以在沿途的滑雪勝地或迷人的山村下車。

如果您想觀賞熱帶森林，請乘坐庫蘭達觀光列車。在澳洲的巴倫峽谷國家公園，您將穿越未受破壞的熱帶雨林和壯觀的瀑布，展開一段奇妙的旅程。當您抵達庫蘭達時，這趟旅程並沒有就此結束。考拉花園、澳洲蝴蝶保護區和庫蘭達鳥類世界是這個風景如畫的村莊的眾多景點之一。

其中一個世界上最高的鐵路之旅將帶您前往馬丘比丘，位於南美洲安第斯山脈的一座古城遺址。您的旅程將從名為庫斯科的城市開始。您將從那裡乘坐當地的秘魯鐵路列車前往「失落的印加城市」。您的旅程將會很顛簸，但它會提供令人難忘的茂密叢林和壯觀山峰的景色。

( ) 76. According to the article, from the Blue Train, what kind of fruit can you see?
(A)Grapes (B)Bananas (C)Litchi (D)Mangos

[中譯] 根據文章，從藍色列車上，你能看到什麼樣的水果？
(A)葡萄 (B)香蕉 (C)荔枝 (D)芒果

答 A

( ) 77. According to the article, in which community can you see lots of wildlife?
(A)Kimberley (B)Oslo (C)Kuranda (D)Cuzco

[中譯] 根據文章，您可以在哪一個社區看到大量野生動物？
(A)金伯利 (B)奧斯陸 (C)庫蘭達 (D)庫斯科

答 C

( ) 78. Which trip will probably be less comfortable than the other three?
(A)The trip on the Blue Train. (B)The trip on the Bergen Line.
(C)The trip on the Kuranda Scenic Railway. (D)The trip on PeruRail.

[中譯] 哪一種旅行可能不如其他三種舒適？
(A)藍色列車之旅。 (B)卑爾根路線之旅。 (C)庫蘭達觀光列車之旅。 (D)秘魯鐵路之旅。

答 D

( ) 79. Which railway can probably offer opportunities to enjoy winter views and sports?
(A)The Blue Train (B)The Bergen Line
(C)The Kuranda Scenic Railway (D)The local PeruRail trains

[中譯] 哪一條鐵路可能提供欣賞冬季景色和運動的機會？
(A)藍色火車 (B)卑爾根路線 (C)庫蘭達觀光鐵路 (D)當地的秘魯鐵路列車

答 B

( ) 80. In which magazine would you most likely find this article?
(A)People (B)Adventures Abroad (C)Sport (D)World Movie Magazine

[中譯] 你最有可能在哪一類雜誌上找到這篇文章？
(A)人物 (B)國外冒險 (C)體育 (D)世界電影雜誌

答 B

Chapter. 04 | 測驗 | 112年度導遊試題

掌握關鍵單字，更快作答70%考題！

重要單字彙整

	單字	出現	音標	中文	詞性
1	**flavor**	9	[`flevɚ]	味道；風味，韻味 同義詞 taste, savor, tang	名詞
2	**dressing**	1	[`drɛsɪŋ]	調味品；穿衣，化妝 同義詞 sauce, seasoning	名詞
3	**orient**	3	[`orɪənt]	使朝向；熟悉環境	動詞
4	**strive**	4	[straɪv]	努力，奮鬥；鬥爭 同義詞 struggle, contend, battle	動詞
5	**undergo**	5	[͵ʌndɚ`go]	接受治療；經歷；忍受 同義詞 experience, suffer, endure	動詞
6	**certificate**	5	[sɚ`tɪfəkɪt]	證明書；結業證書；執照 同義詞 document, certification	名詞
7	**require**	16	[rɪ`kwaɪr]	需要；要求，命令 同義詞 demand, command 反義詞 refuse 拒絕	動詞
8	**assemble**	2	[ə`sɛmb!]	集合，聚集；收集 同義詞 congregate, group, crowd 反義詞 disperse, dismiss 解散	動詞
9	**dissemble**	1	[dɪ`sɛmb!]	掩飾；假裝	動詞
10	**resemble**	5	[rɪ`zɛmb!]	相似，類似 同義詞 approximate 反義詞 differ 不同	動詞
11	**accumulate**	3	[ə`kjumjə͵let]	累積，積聚 同義詞 gather, amass, compile 反義詞 dissipate, waste 使消散	動詞
12	**prevailing**	1	[prɪ`velɪŋ]	流行的；普遍的；土要的	形容詞

	單字	出現	音標	中文	詞性
13	**conduct**	5	[kən`dʌkt]	引導, 帶領; 實施 同義詞 manage, direct, guide, lead	動詞
14	**gateway**	2	[`get͵we]	通道; 入口處; 途徑 同義詞 door, portal, enteral	名詞
15	**getaway**	1	[`gɛtə͵we]	逃走	名詞
16	**impair**	1	[ɪm`pɛr]	損害; 削弱; 減少 同義詞 damage, harm, weaken	動詞
17	**intensify**	1	[ɪn`tɛnsə͵faɪ]	增強, 強化; 變激烈	動詞
18	**amenity**	5	[ə`minətɪ]	便利設施; 舒適; 愉快	名詞
19	**immunity**	1	[ɪ`mjunətɪ]	免疫力; 免除, 豁免	名詞
20	**lodging**	4	[`lɑdʒɪŋ]	寄宿; 住所	名詞
21	**particular**	6	[pɚ`tɪkjəlɚ]	特定的; 特殊的; 特有的 同義詞 special, unusual, different 反義詞 general 一般的, ordinary 平常的	形容詞
22	**assimilate**	3	[ə`sɪm!͵et]	同化; 消化; 吸收 同義詞 absorb, digest	動詞
23	**configure**	1	[kən`fɪgɚ]	配置; 安裝; 裝配	動詞
24	**customize**	2	[`kʌstəm͵aɪz]	訂做; 改造	動詞
25	**renown**	6	[rɪ`naʊn]	名聲；聲望	名詞
26	**boutique**	5	[bu`tik]	精品店; 流行女裝商店	名詞
27	**bazaar**	2	[bə`zɑr]	市集; 義賣; 商店街 同義詞 market, mart, rialto	名詞
28	**fabric**	2	[`fæbrɪk]	織物, 織品; 布料 同義詞 textile, cloth, material	名詞
29	**pottery**	1	[`pɑterɪ]	陶器; 製陶手藝	名詞
30	**crop**	4	[krɑp]	作物; 收成; 大量 同義詞 produce, yield, harvest	名詞
31	**staple**	4	[`step!]	日常必需品; 主要商品; 纖維	名詞
32	**stature**	4	[`stætʃɚ]	身高, 身材; 高度 同義詞 height, loftiness	名詞

▶ 4-68

	單字	出現	音標	中文	詞性
33	**statue**	16	[\`stætʃʊ]	雕像; 塑像 同義詞 figure, sculpture, monument	名詞
34	**status**	6	[\`stetəs]	地位, 身分; 情形 同義詞 position, rank, condition	名詞
35	**statute**	1	[\`stætʃʊt]	法令, 法規; 條例 同義詞 law, regulation, legislation	名詞
36	**gratitude**	3	[\`grætə͵tjud]	感激之情, 感謝 同義詞 gratefulness, appreciation	名詞
37	**gratuity**	2	[grə\`tjuətɪ]	小費; 慰勞金, 遣散費	名詞
38	**donor**	1	[\`donɚ]	贈送人; 捐贈者	名詞
39	**ecological**	5	[͵ɛkə\`lɑdʒɪkəl]	生態的; 生態學的	形容詞
40	**ancestry**	1	[\`ænsɛstrɪ]	祖先; 血統; 名門出身	名詞
41	**dedication**	3	[͵dɛdə\`keʃən]	奉獻; 專心致力	名詞
42	**remission**	1	[rɪ\`mɪʃən]	寬恕; 豁免; 減輕	名詞
43	**commitment**	3	[kə\`mɪtmənt]	承諾; 託付, 交託	名詞
44	**commission**	6	[kə\`mɪʃən]	佣金; 委託 同義詞 compensation, consignment	名詞
45	**command**	1	[kə\`mænd]	命令; 指揮, 統率 同義詞 direct, instruct, demand	動詞
46	**comfort**	4	[\`kʌmfɚt]	安逸, 舒適; 使人舒服的設備 同義詞 ease, relieve 反義詞 discomfort 不安, affliction 悲傷	名詞
47	**commemorate**	1	[kə\`mɛmə͵ret]	慶祝; 紀念 同義詞 honor, celebrate, observe	動詞
48	**appraise**	1	[ə\`prez]	估計, 估量; 估價	動詞
49	**accessory**	4	[æk\`sɛsərɪ]	附件, 配件; 附加物件 同義詞 extra, addition, supplement	名詞
50	**chemical**	4	[\`kɛmɪk!]	化學製品; 化學藥品	名詞
51	**topping**	3	[\`tɑpɪŋ]	配料	名詞

	單字	出現	音標	中文	詞性
52	**abandon**	12	[ə`bændən]	丟棄; 拋棄; 放棄 同義詞 quit, desert, relinquish 反義詞 maintain, retain 保持	動詞
53	**persevere**	2	[ˌpɝsə`vɪr]	堅持不懈; 不屈不撓 同義詞 persist, endure, keep on	動詞
54	**appreciate**	7	[ə`priʃɪˌet]	感謝, 感激; 欣賞 同義詞 acknowledge, admire, praise 反義詞 depreciate, despise 鄙視	動詞
55	**dealer**	1	[`dilɚ]	業者, 商人; 發牌者	名詞
56	**description**	3	[dɪ`skrɪpʃən]	描寫; 敘述; 說明書	名詞
57	**transport**	14	[`trænsˌport]	運輸; 交通工具; 運輸船 同義詞 transit, shipment, freightage	名詞
58	**complementary**	1	[ˌkɑmplə`mɛntərɪ]	補充的; 互補的; 相配的 同義詞 complemental, correlative	形容詞
59	**compensatory**	1	[kəm`pɛnsəˌtorɪ]	賠償的; 補償的	形容詞
60	**deposit**	6	[dɪ`pɑzɪt]	押金; 訂金; 存款 同義詞 pledge, stake	名詞
61	**consent**	4	[kən`sɛnt]	同意, 贊成, 答應 同義詞 permit, assent, accept 反義詞 dissent 異議, refuse 拒絕	動詞
62	**intention**	2	[ɪn`tɛnʃən]	意圖, 意向, 目的 同義詞 purpose, aim, objective	名詞
63	**occasion**	4	[ə`keʒən]	場合, 時刻; 盛典; 時機, 機會 同義詞 condition, situation	名詞
64	**affection**	1	[ə`fɛkʃən]	影響; 屬性	名詞
65	**spectacular**	6	[spɛk`tækjəlɚ]	壯觀的; 引人注目的 同義詞 dramatic, sensational	形容詞
66	**spectacle**	3	[`spɛktək!]	精彩的表演; 壯觀的場面	名詞
67	**expire**	3	[ɪk`spaɪr]	滿期, 屆期; 終止	動詞
68	**conspire**	1	[kən`spaɪr]	同謀, 密謀; 共同促成 同義詞 plot, scheme	動詞

▶ 4-70

	單字	出現	音標	中文	詞性
69	**loan**	2	[lon]	借出; 貸款 同義詞 lend, advance, give	名詞
70	**apparatus**	3	[ˌæpəˋretəs]	設備, 裝置; 儀器 同義詞 equipment, furniture	名詞
71	**approach**	15	[əˋprotʃ]	接近, 靠近; 通道, 入口	名詞
72	**appendix**	2	[əˋpɛndɪks]	附錄, 附件; 附加物 同義詞 index, supplement, addendum	名詞
73	**cater**	13	[ˋketɚ]	提供飲食; 承辦宴席; 迎合 同義詞 provide, serve, indulge	動詞
74	**guarantee**	12	[ˌgærənˋti]	保證; 擔保; 保障 同義詞 promise, secure, assure	動詞
75	**deport**	2	[dɪˋport]	驅逐; 放逐	動詞
76	**refrain**	3	[rɪˋfren]	忍住; 抑制, 節制 同義詞 avoid, abstain	動詞
77	**forecast**	4	[ˋforˌkæst]	預測, 預報; 預言 同義詞 predict, foretell, prophesy	動詞
78	**withdraw**	3	[wɪðˋdrɔ]	撤回; 取消; 移開 同義詞 retreat, recede, retire	動詞
79	**reconfirm**	1	[ˌrikənˋfɝm]	再證實; 再確認; 再確定	動詞
80	**accommodate**	5	[əˋkɑməˌdet]	能容納; 使適應; 通融 同義詞 oblige, adapt, conform	動詞
81	**apologize**	3	[əˋpɑləˌdʒaɪz]	道歉; 認錯; 辯解	動詞
82	**signal**	2	[ˋsɪgn!]	信號; 暗號; 交通指示燈 同義詞 guidepost, indication, symbol	名詞
83	**sight**	10	[saɪt]	視覺, 視力	名詞
84	**element**	3	[ˋɛləmənt]	元素; 要素, 成分 同義詞 component, constituent	名詞
85	**category**	1	[ˋkætəˌgorɪ]	種類; 部屬; 類型 同義詞 classification, variety, species	名詞

	單字	出現	音標	中文	詞性
86	**spread**	14	[sprɛd]	使伸展, 使延伸; 展開 同義詞 unfold, extend, sprawl	動詞
87	**fragile**	10	[`frædʒəl]	易碎的; 易損壞的; 精細的 同義詞 delicate, frail, slight 反義詞 sturdy, tough, strong 牢固的	形容詞
88	**edible**	6	[`ɛdəb!]	可食的, 食用的 同義詞 eatable, comestible, esculent	形容詞
89	**portable**	2	[`portəb!]	便於攜帶的, 手提式的；輕便的 同義詞 transferable, conveyable 反義詞 stationary, ponderous 笨重的	形容詞
90	**appropriate**	5	[ə`proprɪˌet]	適當的, 恰當的, 相稱的 同義詞 suitable, becoming, proper	形容詞
91	**maximum**	2	[`mæksəməm]	最大的; 最多的; 最高的 同義詞 largest, highest, greatest 反義詞 minimum 最小的	形容詞
92	**excess**	5	[ɪk`sɛs]	過量的; 額外的; 附加的 同義詞 additional, extra, surplus	形容詞
93	**surcharge**	1	[`sɝˌtʃɑrdʒ]	超載; 額外費	名詞
94	**purpose**	12	[`pɝpəs]	目的, 意圖; 用途 同義詞 aim, intention, object	名詞
95	**aircraft**	5	[`ɛrˌkræft]	航空器; 飛機, 飛艇 同義詞 aeroplane, plane, jet	名詞
96	**detector**	3	[dɪ`tɛktɚ]	探測器; 發現者	名詞
97	**chain**	28	[tʃen]	連鎖; 鏈條; 項圈	名詞
98	**electric**	1	[ɪ`lɛktrɪk]	用電的; 導電的; 電動的 同義詞 cordless	形容詞
99	**contributor**	3	[kən`trɪbjʊtɚ]	捐贈者; 捐款人; 貢獻者 同義詞 donor, presenter, subscriber	名詞
100	**establish**	8	[ə`stæblɪʃ]	建立; 創辦; 確立 同義詞 settle, build, organize 反義詞 destroy, demolish, ruin 破壞	動詞

112年導遊筆試測驗

● 本書採用英語邏輯思維[中譯]
幫助更快看懂句子, 拆解字義

題型分析	單字 47	片語 3	對話 15	情境命題	景物 4	餐飲 14	住宿 6	交通 7	機場 9
	文法 5	閱測 10			生活 23	民俗 2	產業 1	職能 3	購物 1

單選題 [共80題, 每題1.25分]

( ) 1 I'll like the mixed green salad. What kind of ______ do you have?
(A)seasonings (B)**flavors**[1] (C)**dressings**[2] (D)tastes 餐飲 單字

[中譯] 我想要一份綜合生菜沙拉。你們有哪些種類的調味佐料？
(A)調味料 (B)口味 (C)調味佐料 (D)味道 答 C

( ) 2 Tourists may ______ themselves in the city if there is a giant map at the exit of each MRT station in Taipei.
(A)attend (B)**orient**[3] (C)pursue (D)**strive**[4] 生活 單字

[中譯] 如果台北每個捷運站出口都有一張巨大的地圖，遊客就可以在城市中找到方向。
(A)參加 (B)辨識 (C)追求 (D)努力 答 B

( ) 3 ______ all COVID-19 restrictions lifted, overseas visitors to Taiwan won't be required to **undergo**[5] any kind of quarantine.
(A)As (B)While (C)Because (D)With 機場 文法

[中譯] 隨著COVID-19相關限制的解除，來台的海外旅客將不需要進行任何形式的隔離檢疫。
(A)由於 (B)當 (C)因為 (D)隨著 解 P2-54. 文法84 答 D

( ) 4 Foreigners without an ROC (Taiwan) Resident **Certificate**[6] are **required**[7] to ______ an Arrival Card.
(A)check in (B)fill in (C)settle down (D)look after 機場 片語

[中譯] 未持有中華民國 (台灣) 居留證的外國人需要填寫入境卡。
(A)報到 (B)填寫 (C)安頓 (D)照顧 答 B

( ) 5 Guabao, a steamed sandwich, ______ a hamburger that has a soft white bun filled with braised pork, pickled vegetables, peanut powder, and cilantro.
(A)**assembles**[8] (B)**dissembles**[9] (C)**resembles**[10] (D)**accumulates**[11] 餐飲 單字

[中譯] 刈包是一種類似漢堡的蒸式三明治，柔軟的白麵包內填滿滷肉、醃漬蔬菜、花生粉和香菜。
(A)組裝 (B)掩飾 (C)類似 (D)累積 答 C

( ) 6 Tomorrow morning, Clement will fly from Taoyuan International Airport and stop in Istanbul ______ to his country, Nigeria.
(A)en masse (B)bon voyage (C)bon mot (D)en route 機場 單字

[中譯] 明早，Clement將從桃園國際機場出發，途中經停伊斯坦堡，再前往他的國家奈及利亞。
(A)【法】全體集合 (B)【法】一路順風 (C)【法】妙語如珠 (D)【法】途中 答 D

( ) 7. She is now looking for ____ airline tickets in order to return to her homeland soon.
(A)ludicrous (B)exorbitant (C)**prevailing**[12] (D)affordable 生活 單字

[中譯] 她現在正在尋找價格合理的機票，以便盡快回到她的家鄉。
(A)荒唐可笑的 (B)過度的 (C)盛行的 (D)負擔得起的 答 D

( ) 8. When traveling abroad, you should carefully choose the money changers to ______ currencies.
(A)converge (B)convert (C)**conduct**[13] (D)replace 生活 單字

[中譯] 當出國旅行時，你應仔細選擇外幣兌換商，以進行貨幣兌換。
(A)聚合 (B)轉換 (C)進行 (D)替換 答 B

( ) 9. A day to Yilan is the ideal holiday ______ for you to stay away from the frenetic pace of life in Taipei.
(A)portal (B)**gateway**[14] (C)**getaway**[15] (D)shortcut 生活 單字

[中譯] 宜蘭一日遊是你遠離台北繁忙生活的理想度假勝地。
(A)入口 (B)通道 (C)度假勝地 (D)捷徑 答 C

( ) 10. ______ you have any questions regarding the loss of your wallet and passport abroad, feel free to contact us anytime during office hours.
(A)Should (B)Had (C)Were (D)Would 生活 文法

[中譯] 如果您對於在國外遺失錢包和護照有任何問題，請隨時在辦公時間內與我們聯繫。
(A)如果 (B)曾經 (C)在 (D)將要 解 P2-19. 文法33 (倒裝) 答 A

( ) 11. You must remain seated while the fasten-seat-belt signals are ______ during turbulence.
(A)illustrated (B)**impaired**[16] (C)**intensified**[17] (D)illuminated 交通 單字

[中譯] 遇到亂流時，當安全帶燈號亮起，你必須保持坐在座位上。
(A)描述 (B)損壞 (C)加劇 (D)點亮 答 D

( ) 12. Most premium airlines provide passengers with superior levels of comfort, seats, ______ ,and luggage management.
(A)**amenities**[18] (B)**immunity**[19] (C)**lodging**[20] (D)intensity 交通 單字

[中譯] 大多數高級航空公司提供旅客卓越的舒適度、座椅、設施和行李管理。
(A)設施 (B)免疫力 (C)住宿 (D)強度 答 A

( ) 13. Do I need to dial the international ______ while making a call abroad?
(A)zip code (B)barcode (C)QR code (D)area code 生活 單字

[中譯] 在海外撥打國際電話時，我需要撥國際區號嗎？
(A)郵遞區號 (B)條碼 (C)QR碼 (D)地區號碼 答 D

( ) 14. Most foreigners find Taipei summertime intolerable because the majority of summer days are ______.
(A)placid (B)muggy (C)bleak (D)murky 生活 單字

[中譯] 大多數外國人認為台北的夏天令人難以忍受，因為很悶熱。
(A)平靜的 (B)悶熱的 (C)蒼涼的 (D)混濁的 答 B

( ) 15. After days of nonstop rain, it finally ______ today.
(A)lay up (B)lay on (C)let up (D)let on 生活 片語

[中譯] 經過連日不間斷的下雨，今天終於停了下來。
(A)靠岸 (B)接續 (C)停止 (D)透露 答 C

( ) 16. Simply give our customer service a call, and we will gladly ______ your trips to match any **particular**[21] requirements or interests you may have.
(A)accustom (B)**assimilate**[22] (C)**configure**[23] (D)**customize**[24] 職能 單字

[中譯] 只需打電話給我們的客戶服務，我們很樂意根據您的任何特殊需求或興趣來定制您的旅行。
(A)使適應 (B)同化 (C)配置 (D)定制 答 D

( ) 17. Yingge District in New Taipei City has been **renowned**[25] for its ______ for a long time, but recently, tourists have realized that this area offers so much more.
(A)**boutique**[26] (B)**bazaar**[27] (C)**fabric**[28] (D)**pottery**[29] 民俗 單字

[中譯] 新北市鶯歌區一直以陶瓷聞名，但近來，遊客意識到這個地區提供了更多樣化的選擇。
(A)精品店 (B)市集 (C)織物 (D)陶瓷 答 D

( ) 18. You can't call a trip to Tainan complete without tasting the city's two breakfast ______ : milkfish congee and beef soup.
(A)**crops**[30] (B)ingredients (C)**staples**[31] (D)clips 餐飲 單字

[中譯] 如果你沒有嚐過台南的兩種招牌早餐：虱目魚粥和牛肉湯，就不能算是完整的台南之旅。
(A)農作物 (B)原料 (C)必備品 (D)片段 答 C

( ) 19. ______ beef may seem like a great choice for holidays and other special occasions, some research suggests it may not be the healthiest option.
(A)Since (B)While (C)When (D)What 餐飲 文法

[中譯] 雖然牛肉在節日和特殊場合似乎是不錯的選擇，但一些研究建議這可能不是最健康的選擇。
(A)因為 (B)雖然 (C)當 (D)什麼 解 P2-22. 文法37 答 B

( ) 20. The Duomo di Milano in Italy has over 3,400 sculptures, making it the place with the most ______ in the world.
(A)**statures**[32] (B)**statues**[33] (C)**status**[34] (D)**statutes**[35] 景物 單字

[中譯] 位於義大利的米蘭大教堂擁有超過3,400座雕像，使其成為世界上雕像最多的地方。
(A)身材 (B)雕像 (C)地位 (D)法令 答 B

( ) 21. In many countries, it is customary to leave a ______ while dining out.
(A)tip-off (B)**gratitude**[36] (C)**gratuity**[37] (D)rip-off 餐飲 單字

[中譯] 在許多國家，用餐時留下小費是一種慣例。
(A)告密 (B)感激 (C)小費 (D)敲詐 答 C

( ) 22. It is not uncommon to find street ______ selling tasty and inexpensive food on the streets in Taiwan.
(A)**donors**[38] (B)creditors (C)vendors (D)pitchers 餐飲 單字

[中譯] 在台灣，很常見到街頭巷尾販賣美味又便宜的小吃攤販。
(A)捐贈者 (B)債權人 (C)攤販 (D)投手 答 C

( ) 23. ______ tourism is a sort of tourism in which tourists visit locations where they may learn family history and develop family connections.
(A)**Ecological**[39] (B)**Ancestry**[40] (C)Collective (D)Spiritual 生活 單字

[中譯] 祖先旅遊是一種旅遊方式，遊客造訪可能了解家族歷史並建立家族聯繫的地方。
(A)生態的 (B)祖先的 (C)集體的 (D)精神的 答 B

( ) 24. Most tour guides earn ______on sales in addition to their base salary.
(A)**dedication**[41] (B)**remission**[42] (C)**commitment**[43] (D)**commission**[44] 職能 單字

[中譯] 大多數導遊除了基本薪資外，還會根據業績銷售獲得提成。
(A)奉獻 (B)減免 (C)承諾 (D)佣金 答 D

( ) 25. To compensate for the loss of foreign tourists caused by COVID-19 restrictions, Taiwanese travel businesses have shifted ______ towards domestic trips.
(A)gears (B)**commands**[45] (C)handles (D)wheels 產業 單字

[中譯] 為彌補COVID-19限制措施所造成的外國遊客減少，台灣旅行業已轉向國內旅遊。
(A)齒輪 (B)命令 (C)處理 (D)車輪 答 A

( ) 26. The Dragon Boat Festival ______ Qu-Yuan, an old poet who drowned himself when a ruler ignored his advice.
(A)chastises (B)**comforts**[46] (C)**commemorates**[47] (D)**appraises**[48] 生活 單字

[中譯] 端午節是為紀念古代詩人屈原，在當時的統治者無視他的忠告，他選擇投江自盡。
(A)譴責 (B)安慰 (C)紀念 (D)評價 答 C

( ) 27. People in Taiwan like eating shaved ice with fruit or other delicious ______.
(A)**accessories**[49] (B)**chemicals**[50] (C)**toppings**[51] (D)crops 餐飲 單字

[中譯] 台灣人喜歡在刨冰上加水果或其他美味的配料。
(A)配件 (B)化學物質 (C)配料 (D)農作物 答 C

( ) 28. Taiwan's ______shows have reached a new level of creativity and artistic excellence through the hard work of the Huang family in Yuenlin.
(A)figurine (B)dragon dancing (C)beehive (D)puppet 民俗 單字

[中譯] 台灣的布袋戲透過雲林黃家的努力，達到了新的創意和藝術卓越水準。
(A)人形 (B)舞龍 (C)蜂窩 (D)布袋戲 答 D

( ) 29. Much of Taiwan's natural beauty and wealth are ____ on the east coast of the island.
(A)consumed (B)**abandoned**[52] (C)**persevered**[53] (D)conserved 景物 單字

[中譯] 台灣許多的自然美景和豐富資源都被保留在島嶼的東海岸。
(A)消耗 (B)拋棄 (C)保持 (D)保存 答 D

( ) 30. A: Does your restaurant supply a continental breakfast? B: ______
(A)We serve it from 6:00 a.m. to 10:00 a.m.
(B)Yes, it is.
(C)Yes, we do, and it's served in a buffet style.
(D)It costs $9.99 for adults and is free for children under 12. 餐飲 對話

[中譯] A：你們的餐廳提供歐陸式早餐嗎？ B：是的，我們有提供，並以自助餐形式供應。
(A)我們早上6:00到10:00供應 (B)是的
(C)是的，我們有提供，並以自助餐供應 (D)成人每位$9.99美元，12歲以下兒童免費 答 C

( ) 31. A: How does Mexican cuisine taste? B: ______
(A)Taco and burrito. (B)It has a spicy and heavy flavor.
(C)I like it medium. (D)It has a lot of different fillings. 餐飲 對話

[中譯] A：墨西哥菜的味道如何？ B：它有辣味和重口味。
(A)墨西哥玉米餅和捲餅 (B)它有辣味和重口味
(C)我喜歡中等口味 (D)它有很多不同的餡料 答 B

( ) 32. A: Can I use my EasyCard to rent YouBikes? B: ______
(A)Yes, it can be purchased at any convenience store.
(B)It costs 5 dollars for the first 30 minutes.
(C)Yes, you can use it on subways, buses and YouBikes.
(D)Yes, it's easy and convenient to ride a YouBike. 交通 對話

[中譯] A：我可以用悠遊卡租借YouBike嗎？ B：是的，你可以在捷運、公車和YouBike上使用。
(A)是的，它可以在任何便利商店購買 (B)前30分鐘費用是5元
(C)是的，你可以在捷運、公車和YouBike上使用 (D)是的，騎YouBike非常容易和方便 答 C

( ) 33. A: I'm Emily Smith in 316. I'm checking out. B: ______
(A)Very good. The invoice is included.
(B)I'll be right over, Ms. Smith.
(C)Can I pay with a traveler's check?
(D)Just one moment. I'll check on you later. 住宿 對話

[中譯] A：我是316號房的艾米莉．史密斯。我要退房。 B：我馬上過來，史密斯女士。
(A)很好，發票已包含在內 (B)我馬上過來，史密斯女士
(C)我可以用旅行支票付款嗎？ (D)稍等片刻，我稍後會關注您 答 B

( ) 34. A: I love this breeze. B: ______
(A)Is there a tornado coming?
(B)I didn't know that.
(C)I agree that a stuffy day would be best for an outing.
(D)And it is cool. It is neither too hot nor too cold. 生活 對話

[中譯] A：我喜歡這陣微風。 B：而且很涼爽，既不太熱也不太冷。
(A)是否有龍捲風來襲？ (B)我不知道那件事
(C)我同意，悶熱的天氣最適合外出 (D)而且很涼爽，既不太熱也不太冷 答 D

( ) 35. A: You've traveled to Europe before. B: ______
(A)Maybe. Where would you like to visit?
(B)Yes, that's true. Do you want to go on a trip?
(C)How much time do you want to spend?
(D)I **appreciate**[54] your curiosity. 生活 對話

[中譯] A：你之前去過歐洲旅行。 B：是的，沒錯。你想去旅行嗎？
(A)也許吧。你想去哪裡旅行？ (B)是的，沒錯。你想去旅行嗎？
(C)你想花多少時間？ (D)我很感激你的好奇心 答 B

( ) 36. A: Have you had any issues renewing your visa? B: ______
(A)Good idea, I'm ready. (B)No, nothing worked out for me.
(C)Yes, I'd like to find a **dealer**[55]. (D)Not yet. 生活 對話

[中譯] A：你續簽簽證有遇到什麼問題嗎？ B：還沒有。
(A)很好，我已經準備好了 (B)不，對我來說沒有用
(C)是的，我想找一家經銷商 (D)還沒有 答 D

( ) 37. The doctor wrote me a/an ______. I need to get it filled at the pharmacy.
(A)operation (B)reception (C)prescription (D)**description**[56] 生活 單字

[中譯] 醫生給我開了一張處方箋，我需要去藥局拿藥。
(A)手術 (B)接待處 (C)處方箋 (D)描述 答 C

( ) 38. Usually a ______ passenger will change from one plane to another and stop over at a midpoint for at most 24 hours before continuing the next journey.
(A)transformed (B)transfer (C)**transport**[57] (D)transplant 交通 單字

[中譯] 通常轉機旅客會從一架飛機轉乘到另一架飛機，在中途停留最多24小時，繼續下一段旅程。
(A)轉換的 (B)轉機 (C)運輸 (D)移植 答 B

( ) 39. All our VIP customers will receive a ______ bottle of wine without charge.
(A)complimentary (B)**complementary**[58]
(C)contemplative (D)**compensatory**[59] 生活 單字

[中譯] 我們所有的VIP客戶將免費獲得一瓶贈送的葡萄酒。
(A)贈送的 (B)補充的 (C)沉思的 (D)補償的 答 A

( ) 40. If passengers have anything that needs to be declared, they should go through ____.
(A)Quarantine (B)Airport Terminals
(C)Transit Lounges (D)Customs 機場 單字

[中譯] 如果旅客有任何需要申報的物品，他們應該通過海關。
(A)檢疫 (B)機場航廈 (C)中轉候機室 (D)海關 答 D

( ) 41. Sir, we need your ______ for a confirmed and guaranteed reservation.
(A)balance (B)arrival (C)**deposit**[60] (D)**consent**[61] 生活 單字

[中譯] 先生，我們需要您的押金來確認和保證預訂。
(A)平衡 (B)到達 (C)押金 (D)同意 答 C

( ) 42. Every time when I fly to London, I get serious ______. It makes me uneasy.
(A)jet lag (B)**intention**[62] (C)**occasion**[63] (D)**affection**[64] 生活 單字

[中譯] 每當我飛往倫敦時，我都會有嚴重的時差反應，讓我感到不安。
(A)時差反應 (B)意圖 (C)場合 (D)影響 答 A

( ) 43. Niagara Falls is an impressive natural wonder, and I enjoy its ______ view.
(A)spectator (B)**spectacular**[65] (C)**spectacle**[66] (D)spectrum 景物 單字

[中譯] 尼加拉瀑布是一個令人印象深刻的自然奇觀，我喜歡它壯麗的景色。
(A)觀眾 (B)壯觀的 (C)景象 (D)光譜 答 B

( ) 44. Only when David was stopped by a policeman for drunk driving did he realize that his passport had ______ and he was forced to return home.
(A)inspired (B)**expired**[67] (C)**conspired**[68] (D)perspired 生活 單字

[中譯] 直到大衛因酒後駕駛被警察攔下時，他才意識到他的護照已經過期，並被迫返回家中。
(A)富有靈感的 (B)到期 (C)密謀 (D)出汗 答 B

( ) 45. We have been committed to delivering the best service and are always working to conduct business ______ as smoothly as possible.
(A)implants (B)employments (C)discharges (D)transactions 職能 單字

[中譯] 我們一直致力於提供最優質的服務，並且一直努力使業務交易盡可能順利進行。
(A)植入 (B)就業 (C)排放 (D)交易 答 D

( ) 46. If you are not completely satisfied with our product, you can return it for a full ___.
(A)**loan**[69] (B)premium (C)interest (D)refund 購物 單字

[中譯] 如果您對我們的產品不滿意，您可以退貨並全額退款。
(A)貸款 (B)獎金 (C)愛好 (D)退款 答 D

( ) 47. In the travel ______, you'll find information about tours, itineraries, maps, discounts and coupons, or package holidays.
(A)brochures (B)brides (C)brooks (D)brooches 生活 單字

[中譯] 在旅遊手冊中，您可以找到關於旅遊團、行程安排、地圖、折扣券或套裝旅遊的資訊。
(A)手冊 (B)新娘 (C)小溪 (D)胸針 答 A

( ) 48. Mineral fields used to be a marvelous scenic spot but it has lost its ______ in recent years.
(A)**apparatus**[70] (B)**approach**[71] (C)appeal (D)**appendix**[72] 景物 單字

[中譯] 礦場曾是一個令人驚歎的風景區，但近年來失去了吸引力。
(A)設備 (B)接近 (C)吸引力 (D)附錄 答 C

( ) 49. The salespersons ______ that their organic foods do not have preservatives.
(A)**catered**[73] (B)**guaranteed**[74] (C)**deported**[75] (D)**refrained**[76] 餐飲 單字

[中譯] 銷售人員保證他們的有機食品不含防腐劑。
(A)承辦宴席 (B)保證 (C)驅逐 (D)抑制 答 B

( ) 50. You need to ______ your flight 72 hours prior to departure directly with the airline or simply check- in online at the applicable airline's website.
(A)**forecast**[77] (B)**withdraw**[78] (C)compensate (D)**reconfirm**[79] 機場 單字

[中譯] 您須在出發前72小時直接與航空公司重新確認航班，或在可相應的航空公司網站線上登記。
(A)預測 (B)撤回 (C)補償 (D)重新確認 答 D

( ) 51. Designed by British architects, the hotel can ______ more than 700 people.
(A)**accommodate**[80] (B)alienate (C)acquaint (D)**apologize**[81] 住宿 單字

[中譯] 這間由英國建築師設計的飯店可容納超過700人。
(A)能容納 (B)使疏遠 (C)使認識 (D)道歉 答 A

( ) 52. A: Good afternoon. May I help you?
B: We have been waiting in the ______for one and a half hours, but some of our group members still can't find their luggage.
(A)departure lounge (B)boarding gate
(C)baggage claim area (D)the immigration counter 機場 對話

[中譯] A：下午好。有什麼需要幫忙的嗎？
B：我們已經在行李領取區等了一個半小時，但我們的一些團員仍找不到他們的行李。
(A)出境大廳 (B)登機口
(C)行李領取區 (D)入境檢查處 答 C

( ) 53. Tourist: I'd like to make a long distance call to New York.
Hotel Clerk: Yes. ______
Tourist: Yes, I would.
(A)Would you mind holding for a moment?
(B)Can you put me through to Peter Scott?
(C)I'm afraid you've got the wrong number.
(D)Would you like to make a direct-dial call? 住宿 對話

[中譯] 遊客：我想撥打一通到紐約的長途電話。
飯店職員：好的。您想要直撥嗎？
遊客：是的，我想要。
(A)請稍等一下好嗎？ (B)能幫我接 Peter Scott 嗎？
(C)恐怕您打錯電話號碼了 (D)您想直撥嗎？ 答 D

( ) 54. Tourist: Could you tell me the international country code for France, please?
Hotel Clerk: ______
(A)33 is the country calling code assigned to France.
(B)There is no one by Tom Dunkley registered at this hotel.
(C)I will transfer your call to Albert's room.
(D)Would you like to leave a message? 住宿 對話

[中譯] 遊客：請問法國的國際電話區號是多少？
飯店職員：33是法國的指定國際電話區號
(A)33是法國的指定國際電話區號 (B)這家飯店沒有叫Tom Dunkley的人登記過
(C)我會轉接您的電話到Albert的房間 (D)您要留言嗎？ 答 A

( ) 55. Information Desk Clerk: Are you lost? How may I help you? Tourist: ______
(A)I'd like to order take-out here.
(B)A one-way ticket to Chicago, please.
(C)Please show me how to get to Taiwan Taoyuan International Airport.
(D)I'm very much obliged to you. 機場 對話

[中譯] 服務台職員：你迷路了嗎？我能幫你什麼？ 遊客：請告訴我如何前往桃園國際機場。
(A)我想要在這裡外帶 (B)請給我一張去芝加哥的單程票
(C)請告訴我如何前往桃園國際機場 (D)非常感謝您 答 C

( ) 56. Passenger : ______
John: Two dollars one way, three dollars round trip.
(A)How often do the buses run?
(B)What's the bus fare to The Metropolitan Museum of Art?
(C)How much do I owe you?
(D)What's the charge of the express package? 交通 對話

[中譯] 乘客：到大都會藝術博物館的公車票價是多少？
John：單程票2美元，來回票3美元。
(A)公車多久會開一班？ (B)到大都會藝術博物館的公車票價是多少？
(C)我該付多少錢？ (D)快遞包裹的費用是多少？ 答 B

( ) 57. Flight attendant: Ladies and gentlemen, soon we will be landing at O'Hare International Airport. Please fasten your seat belts and observe the ______ sign.
(A)No Spitting (B)No Parking (C)No Admittance (D)No Smoking 交通 片語

[中譯] 空服員：女士們和先生們，我們即將降落奧黑爾國際機場。請繫好安全帶，並注意「禁止吸煙」的標誌。
(A)禁止吐痰 (B)禁止停車 (C)禁止入內 (D)禁止吸菸 答 D

( ) 58. Patient: ______
Pharmacist: The directions are in the medicine bag. Read them carefully before you use it.
(A)How much is the medicine?
(B)How long have you been to the clinic?
(C)How often do I have to go to the clinic?
(D)How many times a day should I take this? 生活 對話

[中譯] 病人：我一天需要服用幾次藥？
藥劑師：藥袋裡有使用說明，使用前請仔細閱讀。
(A)藥費多少？ (B)你在診所待了多久？
(C)我需要多久去一次診所？ (D)一天需要服用幾次？ 答 D

( ) 59. Doctor: What are the ______?
Tiffany: Well, I have an upset stomach. I also have a cold and fever.
(A)signs (B)symptoms (C)**signals**[82] (D)**sights**[83] 生活 單字

[中譯] 醫生：你有什麼症狀？
Tiffany：我肚子不舒服，還有感冒和發燒。
(A)生命跡象 (B)症狀 (C)訊號 (D)景象 答 B

( ) 60. Doctor: Hello, Janet. What seems to be the problem?
Janet: I ______ well since I joined a tour group last Monday.
(A)didn't feel (B)hadn't been feeling
(C)haven't been feeling (D)haven't been felt 生活 文法

[中譯] 醫生：你好，Janet，你有什麼狀況呢？
Janet：自從上星期一加入旅遊團後，我就感到身體不適。
(A)沒有感覺到 (B)從前沒有感覺到 (C)近期感到 (D)沒有被感覺到 答 C

情境篇 文法篇 片語篇 測驗篇 口試篇

( ) 61. A ______ is someone who is employed in a hotel to help guests arrange things, such as local tours, theatre tickets and restaurant reservations.
(A)concierge (B)security guard (C)maintenance worker (D)maid 住宿 單字

[中譯] 禮賓員是指受僱在飯店協助客人安排事宜，例如當地遊覽、劇院門票和餐廳訂位。
(A)禮賓員 (B)保全 (C)維修工人 (D)女傭 答 A

( ) 62. Before going abroad, you need to understand the current exchange rates and have some New Taiwan dollars ______ into U.S. dollars.
(A)convert (B)converting (C)to convert (D)converted 生活 文法

[中譯] 在出國前，你需要了解目前的匯率，並將一些新台幣兌換成美元。
(A)兌換 (B)正在兌換 (C)要兌換 (D)已兌換 解 P2-20. 文法34 答 D
補 ...New Taiwan dollars (which are) converted into ...，其中句型省略 which are。

( ) 63. If you are not hungry, we can order one meal and share it. The _____ are very big.
(A)**elements**[84] (B)portions (C)flavors (D)**categories**[85] 餐飲 單字

[中譯] 如果你不餓的話，我們可以點一份餐點，然後一起分享。份量非常大。
(A)成份 (B)份量 (C)口味 (D)類型 答 B

( ) 64. Today's special is steamed fish. You can ______ the lemon and salt on the fish.
(A)spit (B)splash (C)**spread**[86] (D)sprinkle 餐飲 單字

[中譯] 今天的特餐是清蒸魚。您可以在魚上灑些檸檬汁和鹽。
(A)吐 (B)濺 (C)擴散 (D)灑 答 D

( ) 65. The plastic vegetable leaves on the plate are for decoration only. They are not ____.
(A)**fragile**[87] (B)**edible**[88] (C)**portable**[89] (D)**appropriate**[90] 餐飲 單字

[中譯] 盤子上的塑膠蔬菜葉僅用於裝飾，不可食用。
(A)易碎的 (B)可食用的 (C)可攜帶的 (D)適當的 答 B

( ) 66. Waiter: ______ Guest: Medium-well, please.
(A) May I show you the dessert menu?
(B) Would you like more?
(C) What would you like to order, sir?
(D) How would you like your steak cooked? 餐飲 對話

[中譯] 服務員：您的牛排要如何烹調？ 客人：五分熟，謝謝。
(A)我可以為您展示甜點菜單嗎？ (B)您還要再點些嗎？
(C)先生，您要點什麼菜？ (D)您的牛排要如何烹調？ 答 D

( ) 67. Attendant: Oh, I'm afraid your bag has exceeded the **maximum**[91] baggage ______, so you'll have to pay the **excess**[92] fare.
Mr. Brown: Oh, right.
(A)allowance (B)receipt (C)**surcharge**[93] (D)currency 機場 單字

[中譯] 櫃台人員：噢，恐怕您的行李已經超過最大行李限額，所以您需要支付超額費用。
Brown先生：哦，好的。
(A)行李限額 (B)收據 (C)額外費用 (D)貨幣 答 A

( ) 68. Customs: ______ Vincent: I'm visiting some friends and relatives.
(A)How long do you plan to stay?
(B)Where will you be staying?
(C)Have you got anything to declare?
(D)What's the **purpose**[94] of your visit? 機場 對話

[中譯] 海關：您的來訪目的是什麼？ Vincent：我是來拜訪一些朋友和親戚的。
(A)您計劃停留多長時間？ (B)您會住在哪裡？
(C)您有任何要申報的物品嗎？ (D)您的來訪目的是什麼？ 答 D

( ) 69. Ladies and gentlemen, please be careful while opening the overhead ____ as any items stowed inside might fall out, and take all your personal belongings with you.
(A)**aircraft**[95] (B)compartment (C)instrument (D)**detector**[96] 交通 單字

[中譯] 女士們和先生們，請在打開頂部行李艙時小心，因為內部存放的物品可能會掉落出來，請隨身攜帶您的所有個人物品。
(A)飛機 (B)隔間 (C)器械 (D)探測器 答 B

( ) 70. Hotel clerk: How may I help you?
Guest: Yes. Could you tell me about your hotel ______?
Hotel clerk: We have a bar, a gym, a swimming pool, tennis courts and a buffet restaurant.
Guest: Great. Thanks for the information.
(A)vacancies (B)appointments (C)facilities (D)**chains**[97] 住宿 單字

[中譯] 飯店職員：我能為您效勞嗎？
客人：是的。您能告訴我有關貴飯店的設施嗎？
飯店職員：我們有一個酒吧、健身房、游泳池、網球場和一個自助餐廳。
客人：太好了。謝謝您的資訊。
(A)空位 (B)預約 (C)設施 (D)連鎖店 答 C

閱讀測驗一

In the past few years, most major airlines have announced their plans to use commercial **electric**[98] airplanes. Travelers can soon travel to different places via an electric aircraft. Take United Airlines for example. They will offer fossil fuel-free domestic flights by 2026. In addition, Sweden and Denmark also declared their plans to use fossil fuel-free electric-powered airplanes by 2030. Electric air travel (i.e. traveling with an electric-powered aircraft) is going mainstream. There are various methods to supply electricity; however, the most common way is to use batteries.

The climate crisis has been worsening these past few years. One of the major **contributors**[99] to this environmental problem is air transportation. The aviation sector has released huge amounts of carbon dioxide (CO2) into the atmosphere every year. Unfortunately, airplanes are predicted to triple their CO2 emissions by 2050 if left unchecked now.

Most major airlines have thus signed up to meet the targeted net-zero carbon emissions by 2050. Governments from many different countries are **establishing**[100] policies to help protect the environment. Austria and France have enacted bans on short-haul domestic flights. In the United States of America, the government is also pushing to reduce CO2 emissions through clean-energy transportation.

As presented, the use of small electric airplanes is the first step towards greener air travel. The development of larger electric planes may take several years. Still, you can expect to hear that electric air travel will be going mainstream in the coming years.

在過去幾年裡，大多數主要的航空公司已經宣布他們使用商用電動飛機的計畫。旅客們不久將可以搭乘電動飛機前往不同的地方。以聯合航空公司為例，他們將於2026年提供無化石燃料的國內航班。此外，瑞典和丹麥也宣布了他們在2030年前將採用無化石燃料的電動飛機的計畫。電動航空旅行(即使用電動飛機旅行)正在成為主流。有各種供電方式，然而，最常見的方式是使用電池。

氣候危機近幾年間持續惡化。造成此原因之一是航空運輸。航空業每年釋放大量二氧化碳(CO2)到大氣中。不幸的是，如果現在不加以控制，預測到2050年飛機的二氧化碳排放量將會增加三倍。

大多數主要的航空公司已簽署協議，在2050年前實現零碳排放的目標。許多國家的政府正在制定政策以幫助保護環境。奧地利和法國已經禁止短途國內航班。在美國，政府也在推動通過清潔能源交通減少二氧化碳排放。

正如所述，使用小型電動飛機是實現更環保的航空旅行的第一步。開發大型電動飛機可能需要幾年的時間。然而，您可以期待在未來幾年中電動航空旅行將成為主流。

( ) 71. What is the main idea of the passage?
(A)As science develops, views of travel do not change.
(B)Traveling with an electric-powered aircraft is going mainstream.
(C)It does not suggest a different solution to a problem.
(D)The climate crisis has been worsening these past few years.

[中譯] 這篇文章的主旨是什麼？
(A)隨著科學的發展，旅遊觀點沒有改變。 (B)電動飛機的旅行正成為主流。
(C)它沒有提出不同的問題解決方案。 (D)氣候危機在過去幾年中持續惡化。 答 B

( ) 72. According to the passage, what is the most common way to supply electricity?
(A)To use batteries. (B)To use ocean thermal energy.
(C)To use solar energy. (D)To use wind energy.

[中譯] 根據這篇文章，最常用的供電方式是什麼？
(A)使用電池 (B)利用海洋熱能 (C)利用太陽能 (D)利用風力 答 A

( ) 73. Which of the following is true about commercial electric airplanes?
(A)United Airlines have announced that they will offer fossil fuel-free domestic flights by 2030.
(B)Sweden and Denmark also declared their plans to use fossil fuel-free airplanes by 2026.
(C)Air transportation is one of the major contributors to the worsening environmental problem.
(D)The aviation sector has released huge amounts of oxygen into the atmosphere every year.

[中譯] 關於商業電動飛機，下列敘述何者正確？
(A)聯合航空公司宣布到2030年將提供無化石燃料的國內航班。
(B)瑞典和丹麥也宣布了到2026年使用無化石燃料飛機的計劃。
(C)航空運輸是惡化環境問題的主要因素之一。
(D)航空業每年釋放大量氧氣進入大氣層。

答 C

( ) 74. Which of the following is true about helping protect the environment?
(A)Austria and France have announced their plans to use electric air travel by 2030.
(B)Sweden and Denmark have enacted bans on short-haul domestic flights.
(C)Airplanes are predicted to double their CO2 emissions by 2050 if left unchecked now.
(D)In the United States of America, the government is also pushing to reduce CO2 emissions through clean-energy transportation.

[中譯] 關於保護環境，下列敘述何者正確？
(A)奧地利和法國宣布到2030年使用電動飛行旅遊的計劃。
(B)瑞典和丹麥已經禁止短程國內航班。
(C)如果現在不採取措施，預計到2050年飛機的二氧化碳排放量將翻倍。
(D)在美國，政府也在推動通過清潔能源交通減少二氧化碳排放量。

答 D

( ) 75. What is the advantage of electric air travel?
(A)It is cheaper.
(B)Electric air travel is the first step towards greener air travel.
(C)Electric air travel does not help reduce CO2 emissions.
(D)It is faster.

[中譯] 電動飛行旅遊的優點是什麼？
(A)它更便宜。
(B)電動飛行旅遊是邁向更環保航空旅遊第一步。
(C)電動飛行旅遊無法幫助減少二氧化碳排放。
(D)它更快速。

答 B

閱讀測驗二

I was filled with excitement and awe as our vehicle jolted down the muddy paths of the wildlife reserve. Incredible creatures roamed the savannah, and the sceneries itself were some of the most stunning I've ever seen.

Safari traveling is a thrilling and one-of-a-kind opportunity to take in the splendor and variety of the natural world. In order to see and photograph wild creatures in their natural environment, safari vacationers often visit an African wildlife reserve or national park.

In my experience, seeing iconic and endangered animals like lions, elephants, and gorillas in their natural habitats is expected to be a staple of a safari vacation. My favorite part of the trip was getting to see a group of wild canine animals in their natural habitat. I'd never had such a good look at these endangered creatures before.

Aside from getting an up-close glimpse at the animals, tourists can receive insight into their habits and routines from knowledgeable guides on several safari programs that include guided drives within the park. Safaris sometimes involve more than just visits to zoos and sanctuaries to see animals; they often provide opportunities for hiking, birdwatching, and cultural immersion.

Memories created on the safari journey will last a lifetime since it was truly once in a lifetime opportunity. I think a trip to Africa for a safari would be amazing if you have the chance to go. You won't soon forget this incredible journey.

我們的車子在野生動物保護區的泥濘小徑上顛簸而行，讓我充滿興奮和敬畏。令人難以置信的生物在大草原上自由漫步，這個風景是我見過最迷人的景色之一。

進行野生動物觀察旅行是一個激動人心且獨特的機會，可以欣賞大自然的壯麗和多樣性。為了在它們的自然環境中觀察和拍攝野生生物，野生動物觀察者通常會參觀非洲的野生動物保護區或國家公園。

根據我的經驗，觀察標誌性和瀕危動物，如獅子、大象和大猩猩在它們的自然棲息地中，是野生動物觀察旅行的一個亮點。我在旅行中最喜歡的部分是在它們的自然棲息地中觀察到一群野生犬科動物。這是我第一次如此近距離地觀察到這些瀕臨絕種的生物，讓我非常興奮。

除了近距離觀察動物外，遊客還可以透過博學/知識豐富的導遊在一些野生動物觀察計畫中了解動物的習性和生活習慣。野生動物觀察旅行通常包括在園區內的導覽車輛遊覽，這些導覽可以提供深入的洞察力。野生動物觀察旅行不僅僅是參觀動物園和保護區，它們還經常提供徒步旅行、觀鳥以及文化融入的機會。

在野生動物觀察旅行中創造的回憶將會持續一生，因為這真的是一生中難得的機會。如果您有機會去非洲進行野生動物觀察旅行，我認為這將是一個驚喜的經歷。您不會很快就忘記這段令人難以置信的旅程。

( ) 76. Which is NOT a reason why the author suggests going on a safari vacation?
(A)To achieve a serene vacation.
(B)To discover the diversity of the natural world.
(C)To see animals in their natural environment.
(D)To observe some endangered creatures.

[中譯] 下列哪一項不是作者建議進行野生動物觀察旅行的原因？
(A)獲得寧靜的假期。 (B)探索自然界的多樣性。
(C)在動物的自然環境中觀察。 (D)觀察一些瀕臨絕種的生物。 答 A

( ) 77. What does the word "jolted" mean?
(A)Shattered. (B)Shot. (C)Shook. (D)Shrank.

[中譯] " jolted " 一詞是什麼意思？
(A)破碎的 (B)射擊 (C)搖動的 (D)縮小的 答 C

( ) 78. What was the highlight of the author's safari's trip?
(A)He was surrounded by the most breathtaking landscapes he had ever seen.
(B)He had the chance to see a pack of wild dogs up close.
(C)He could experience the beauty and diversity of the natural world.
(D)He could get close to some of the most famous and endangered animals in the world, like lions and gorillas.

[中譯] 作者在野生動物觀察旅行中的亮點是什麼？
(A)他被他所見過的最壯麗的風景包圍。
(B)他有機會近距離觀察一群野生犬科動物。
(C)他可以體驗自然界的美麗和多樣性。
(D)他可以接近一些世界上最著名和瀕臨絕種的動物，如獅子和大猩猩。 答 B

( ) 79. According to this passage, what can tourists learn from these knowledgeable safari guides?
(A)They can learn about the animals' behavior and habits.
(B)They can learn about endangered animal species.
(C)They can learn about several African wildlife sanctuaries.
(D)They can get knowledge about the splendor of nature.

[中譯] 根據這篇文章，遊客可以從這些知識豐富的野生動物觀察導遊身上學到什麼？
(A)他們可以學習關於動物的行為和習性。
(B)他們可以學習有關瀕危動物物種的知識。
(C)他們可以學習關於幾個非洲野生動物保護區的資訊。
(D)他們可以獲得關於自然的壯麗景色的知識。 答 A

( ) 80. According to this passage, which of the following is NOT included in safari vacations besides animal sightings?
(A)Hiking. (B)Observing birds.
(C)Animal breeding. (D)Cultural encounters. 答 C

[中譯] 根據這篇文章，除了觀察動物外，下列哪一項不包含在野生動物觀察旅行中？
(A)徒步旅行 (B)觀察鳥類 (C)動物繁殖 (D)文化交流

Chapter. 05 | 測驗 | 109年度領隊試題

掌握關鍵單字，更快作答70%考題！

重要單字彙整

掃描 QR code 或登入網址
www.magee.tw/istudy
用聽的也能背單字！

本單元針對**109～112**年度導遊、領隊試題，依各年度題型之重要程度，歸納出**100**個必讀單字及單字出現次數統計(分析100年以前的試題與現今考法差異較大，考生可將重心放在近年題型為主)。建議先熟記單字，再進行試題測驗，更能提升作答實力！

由於領隊、導遊在單字部分並無明顯範圍區別，建議報考領隊類組的考生，導遊篇單字也須熟記。同時，因應命題趨勢，特別收錄「同義詞」及「反義詞」彙整，幫助聯想記憶，進而累積單字量。

實力應證法 先將**109～111**年共六章的單字熟讀，再進行**112**年度試題測驗，試試看能認得多少個單字呢！

單字學習法 背單字的方法有很多，本書另提供老師線上語音導讀，帶著大家一起背單字

	單字	出現	音標	中文	詞性
1	**facility**	15	[fə`sɪlətɪ]	設備, 設施; 能力; 技能 同義詞 edifice, building, structure	名詞
2	**reference**	3	[`rɛfərəns]	參考, 參照; 提及; 涉及 同義詞 mention, notice	名詞
3	**reproach**	3	[rɪ`protʃ]	責備; 批評; 使蒙恥 同義詞 blame, accuse, denounce	動詞
4	**compensate**	6	[`kɑmpən͵set]	補償, 賠償; 酬報	動詞
5	**subtract**	3	[səb`trækt]	減, 減去; 去掉 同義詞 deduct, remove, discount	動詞
6	**simmer**	1	[ˈsɪm.ər]	燉煮; (危機等)即將爆發	動詞
7	**blend**	3	[blɛnd]	混和, 混雜; 交融 同義詞 mix, combine, fuse, mingle	動詞
8	**equip**	4	[ɪ`kwɪp]	裝備, 配備	動詞
9	**govern**	3	[`gʌvən]	治理; 決定, 指導, 影響 同義詞 control, regulate, curb, command	動詞

	單字	出現	音標	中文	詞性
10	**overcome**	2	[ˌovə`kʌm]	克服; 壓倒; 戰勝 同義詞 conquer, defeat, upset, overpower 反義詞 submit 屈服; surrender 投降	動詞
11	**eternal**	1	[i`tə:nəl]	永久的, 永恆的; 無窮的; 永存的, 不朽的 同義詞 perpetual, everlasting 反義詞 submit 屈服; surrender 投降	形容詞
12	**extensive**	3	[ɪk`stɛnsɪv]	廣泛的; 大規模的; 大量的; 龐大的 同義詞 spacious, extended, expanded	形容詞
13	**poisonous**	2	[`pɔɪznəs]	有毒的; 有害的; 惡毒的, 有惡意的 同義詞 toxic, destructive, noxious	形容詞
14	**deck**	4	[dɛk]	甲板; (船的)艙面	名詞
15	**belly**	1	[`bɛlɪ]	腹, 腹部, 腹腔; 肚子	名詞
16	**religion**	4	[rɪ`lɪdʒən]	宗教信仰; 宗教團體	名詞
17	**marital**	4	[ˈmær.ɪ.təl]	婚姻的	形容詞
18	**pharmacy**	1	[`fɑrməsɪ]	藥店, 藥局, 藥房	名詞
19	**prescribe**	5	[prɪ`skraɪb]	開藥方; 給醫囑; 規定, 指定	動詞
20	**detach**	1	[dɪ`tætʃ]	分離, 分開, 拆卸; 派遣, 分遣 同義詞 separate, unfasten, disconnect	動詞
21	**potential**	3	[pə`tɛnʃəl]	潛在的, 可能的 同義詞 possible, promising, hidden	形容詞
22	**restrict**	2	[rɪ`strɪkt]	限制; 限定; 約束 同義詞 confine, limit, bound	動詞
23	**carnival**	1	[ˈkɑ:r.nə.vəl]	嘉年華會, 狂歡節	名詞
24	**various**	5	[`vɛrɪəs]	不同的; 各種各樣的; 許多的 同義詞 several, many, diverse	形容詞
25	**errand**	1	[`ɛrənd]	任務, 使命	名詞
26	**magnet**	1	[`mægnɪt]	磁鐵, 磁石; 有吸引力的人(或物)	名詞
27	**queue**	5	[kju]	排隊	動詞
28	**denomination**	4	[dɪˌnɑmə`neʃən]	(貨幣等的)面額; (度量衡等的)單位	名詞

▶ 4-90

	單字	出現	音標	中文	詞性
29	**knit**	6	[nɪt]	編織; 針織	動詞
30	**compartment**	7	[kəm`pɑrtmənt]	隔間; 置物艙 同義詞 partition, section, division	名詞
31	**amusement**	9	[ə`mjuzmənt]	樂趣; 興味; 娛樂, 消遣; 娛樂活動 同義詞 entertainment, pleasure	名詞
32	**mention**	13	[`mɛnʃən]	提到, 提及, 說起	動詞
33	**recall**	5	[rɪ`kɔl]	回想, 回收 同義詞 remember, recollect, reminisce	動詞
34	**tickle**	2	[ˈtɪk.əl]	逗...笑; 使快樂; 使發癢	動詞
35	**characteristic**	7	[ˌkærəktə`rɪstɪk]	特性, 特徵, 特色 同義詞 nature, feature, attribute	名詞
36	**argument**	7	[`ɑrgjəmənt]	爭論, 爭吵; 辯論	動詞
37	**destruction**	7	[dɪ`strʌkʃən]	破壞; 毀滅; 消滅 同義詞 demolition, wrecking	名詞
38	**tolerant**	3	[`tɑlərənt]	容忍的, 忍受的, 寬恕的	形容詞
39	**enthusiastic**	5	[ɪnˌθjuzɪ`æstɪk]	熱情的; 熱烈的; 熱心的	形容詞
40	**genuine**	5	[`dʒɛnjʊɪn]	名副其實的; 真誠的 同義詞 pure, legitimate, sincere 反義詞 false 不真實的	形容詞
41	**regulate**	8	[`rɛgjəˌlet]	管理; 控制; 為...制訂規章 同義詞 manage, govern, handle	動詞
42	**visible**	9	[ˈvɪz.ə.bəl]	可看見的; 顯而易見的 同義詞 apparent, manifest, noticeable	形容詞
43	**fundamentally**	3	[ˌfʌndə`mentli]	基本地; 重要地	副詞
44	**permanently**	3	[`pɝmənəntlɪ]	永久地; 長期不變地	副詞
45	**oppose**	5	[ə`poz]	反抗; 反對; 妨礙 同義詞 counteract, refute, fight 反義詞 consen 同意, assent 贊成	動詞
46	**squeeze**	5	[skwiz]	榨, 擠壓 同義詞 press, crush, pinch, cram	動詞

	單字	出現	音標	中文	詞性
47	**scramble**	3	[ˈskræm.bəl]	爬行; 混合; 水煮	動詞
48	**poach**	4	[potʃ]	偷獵; 偷捕; 侵佔, 侵犯; 竊取	動詞
49	**allergic**	4	[əˋlɝdʒɪk]	對...過敏; 對...極討厭的	形容詞
50	**receipt**	19	[rɪˋsit]	收據; 收條 同義詞 voucher, acquittance, quittance	名詞
51	**overcharge**	5	[ˋovɚˋtʃardʒ]	對...索價過高; 使過度充電	動詞
52	**grant**	5	[grænt]	同意, 准予 同義詞 allow, permit, consent, admit	動詞
53	**conductor**	5	[kənˋdʌktɚ]	樂團指揮; 列車長 同義詞 director, executive, manager	名詞
54	**swamp**	3	[swamp]	沼澤; 沼澤地	名詞
55	**swallow**	3	[ˋswalo]	吞下, 嚥下; 淹沒, 吞沒; 吞併	動詞
56	**swarm**	3	[swɔrm]	(昆蟲等的)群聚; 蜂群; 成群結隊	名詞
57	**swell**	3	[swɛl]	腫脹, 腫起	動詞
58	**maintenance**	5	[ˋmentənəns]	維修, 保持; 維持, 保養 同義詞 preservation, upkeep	名詞
59	**composition**	6	[ˌkampəˋzɪʃən]	和解協議	名詞
60	**constitutional**	3	[ˌkanstəˋtjuʃən!]	本質的; 基本的; 憲法的; 符合憲法的 同義詞 inherent, intrinsic, inborn	形容詞
61	**utensil**	7	[juːˈten.sɪl]	餐具 同義詞 implement, instrument	名詞
62	**boulevard**	5	[ˋbuləˌvard]	林蔭大道	名詞
63	**entitle**	7	[ɪnˈtaɪ.t̬əl]	有權, 給...權力(或資格) 反義詞 deprive 使喪失	動詞
64	**harbor**	6	[ˋharbɚ]	庇護; 藏匿; 收養(動物等)	動詞
65	**grab**	3	[græb]	攫取, 抓取; 奪取, 霸佔	動詞
66	**margin**	3	[ˋmardʒɪn]	邊沿, 邊緣; 頁邊空白; 欄外 同義詞 border, edge, rim	名詞

▶ 4-92

	單字	出現	音標	中文	詞性
67	**disclose**	3	[dɪs`kloz]	揭露; 透露; 公開 同義詞 reveal, expose 反義詞 conceal 隱藏	動詞
68	**ethical**	3	[ˈeθ.ɪ.kəl]	道德的; 倫理的 同義詞 moral, virtuous, pure, decorous 反義詞 unethical 不道德的	形容詞
69	**browse**	5	[braʊz]	隨意觀看; 瀏覽	動詞
70	**bracelet**	2	[`breslɪt]	手鐲; 手鏈	名詞
71	**obsolete**	5	[`ɑbsəˌlit]	過時的, 老式的; 廢棄的, 淘汰的 同義詞 extinct, dated, outmoded	形容詞
72	**channel**	9	[`tʃænl]	途徑; 手段; 水道, 航道	名詞
73	**conditional**	3	[kən`dɪʃənəl]	附有條件的, 以...為條件的 反義詞 unconditional 無條件的	形容詞
74	**diagnosis**	3	[ˌdaɪəg`nosɪs]	診斷; 診斷結果; 診斷書	名詞
75	**binoculars**	3	[bɪ`nɑkjələ-]	雙筒望遠鏡	名詞
76	**entrepreneur**	4	[ˌɑntrəprə`nɝ]	企業家; 承包人	名詞
77	**rebel**	3	[`rebl]	造反者; 反抗者; 反叛者	名詞
78	**flammable**	4	[ˈflæm.ə.bəl]	易燃的; 可燃的; 速燃的	形容詞
79	**route**	35	[rut]	路線; 路程; 航線 同義詞 course, circuit, path	名詞
80	**cottage**	2	[`kɑtɪdʒ]	農舍, 小屋	名詞
81	**campsite**	8	[`kæmpˌsaɪt]	露營地	名詞
82	**descent**	4	[dɪ`sɛnt]	下降; 下傾; 衰落; 墮落 同義詞 drop, fall, sinking, down-rush 反義詞 ascent 上升	名詞
83	**quarantine**	3	[`kwɔrənˌtin]	隔離; 檢疫	名詞
84	**merchandise**	9	[`mɝtʃənˌdaɪz]	商品, 貨物 同義詞 goods, wares, commodities	名詞

	單字	出現	音標	中文	詞性
85	**entertainment**	13	[ˌɛntɚ`tenmənt]	娛樂, 消遣; 招待, 款待 同義詞 amusement, divertissement	名詞
86	**turbulence**	11	[`tɝbjələns]	亂流; 湍流; (氣體等的)紊流	名詞
87	**occurrence**	3	[ə`kɝəns]	發生; 事件; 事變 同義詞 event, incident, occasion	名詞
88	**installment**	3	[ɪn`stɔlmənt]	就任, 就職; 分期付款	名詞
89	**adopt**	7	[ə`dɑpt]	採用; 採納; 吸收; 過繼, 收養 同義詞 assume, accept as one's own	動詞
90	**scorch**	5	[skɔrtʃ]	飛奔	動詞
91	**deceive**	3	[dɪ`siv]	欺騙, 蒙蔽; 哄騙(某人)做 同義詞 trick, hoax, dupe, betray 反義詞 undeceive 使不受迷惑	動詞
92	**replacement**	5	[rɪ`plesmənt]	更換; 接替; 代替, 取代	名詞
93	**retirement**	3	[rɪ`taɪrmənt]	退休; 退職; 退役 同義詞 retreat, countermarch 反義詞 access 接近, 進入	名詞
94	**recruitment**	5	[rɪ`krutmənt]	徵募; 補充	名詞
95	**escalator**	7	[`ɛskəˌletɚ]	電扶梯	名詞
96	**transparent**	3	[træns`pɛrənt]	透明的; 清澈的; 顯而易見的; 一目了然的 反義詞 opaque 不透明的	形容詞
97	**stow**	5	[sto]	堆裝; 裝載; 貯藏, 收藏 同義詞 pack, load, store	動詞
98	**alter**	8	[`ɔltɚ]	改變; 修改 同義詞 diversify, change, vary, modify 反義詞 preserve 保存; 維持	動詞
99	**drift**	1	[drɪft]	漂浮, 漂泊, 遊蕩 同義詞 wander, roam, stray, meander	動詞
100	**disposal**	3	[dɪˈspəʊ.zəl]	處理, 處置; 配置; 布置; 排列 同義詞 removal, arrangement	名詞

109年領隊筆試測驗

● 本書採用英語邏輯思維[中譯]
幫助更快看懂句子，拆解字義

題型分析	單字 41	片語 10	對話 15	情境命題	景物 0	餐飲 8	住宿 7	交通 19	機場 6
	文法 4	閱測 10			生活 17	民俗 0	產業 4	職能 2	購物 7

單選題 [共80題，每題1.25分]

( ) 1. Sharon told me that cheese wasn't one of the _______ in this dessert.
(A)**facilities**[1] (B)ingredients (C)masterpieces (D)**references**[2] 餐飲 單字

[中譯] Sharon告訴我奶酪並不是這個甜點的成分之一。
(A)設備 (B)成分 (C)傑作 (D)參考 答 B

( ) 2. Lucy had a _______ on her arm while she was walking on a trail.
(A)lane (B)march (C)pitch (D)scratch 生活 單字

[中譯] Lucy走在小徑上時，在手臂上留下了一道刮痕。
(A)小路 (B)進行 (C)投、擲 (D)刮痕 答 D

( ) 3. Do you have anything to _______ the pain of a sore throat?
(A)relieve (B)reform (C)remind (D)**reproach**[3] 生活 單字

[中譯] 你有什麼東西可以緩解喉嚨痛嗎？
(A)緩解 (B)改革 (C)提醒 (D)責備 答 A

( ) 4. Clerk: Could you describe to me what your bag looks like? Traveler: _______
(A)I cannot find my luggage at the carousel.
(B)Two of my carrying bags have been missing.
(C)It's a black duffle bag with a yellow strap.
(D)My bag looks very different from others. 生活 對話

[中譯] 櫃員：可以請您描述一下您的袋子樣式嗎？ 旅客：它是一個有黃色條紋的黑色旅行袋。
(A)我在行李轉盤上找不到我的行李 (B)我的兩個手提包不見了
(C)它是一個有黃色條紋的黑色旅行袋 (D)我的包看起來和別人的非常不同 答 C

( ) 5. Passenger: I cannot find my ticket. I think I have misplaced it.
Ticket collector: _______
(A)The train will reach the destination in ten minutes.
(B)We will have to send you to the fire station.
(C)We will **compensate**[4] for your loss.
(D)You need to purchase a new one. 交通 對話

[中譯] 乘客：我找不到我的車票，我不知道把它放在哪兒了。驗票員：您需要購買一張新的車票。
(A)火車將在十分鐘內抵達終點站 (B)我們必須送您到消防局
(C)我們將會賠償您的損失 (D)您需要購買一張新的 答 D

( ) 6. People live in different time _______. When it's 3 p.m. in Milan, it's 11 p.m. in Seoul. (A)acnes (B)cones (C)wages (D)zones 生活 單字

[中譯] 人們生活在不同的時區。當米蘭是下午三點時，首爾是晚上十一點。
(A)粉刺 (B)圓錐體 (C)薪水 (D)區，地區 答 D

( ) 7. If you _______ 10 from 60 dollars, you only need to pay 50.
(A)**subtract**[5] (B)convince (C)**simmer**[6] (D)attribute 生活 單字

[中譯] 如果你把60元減掉10元，你只需要再支付50元。
(A)減去 (B)說服 (C)煨燉 (D)屬性 答 A

( ) 8. The hotel is _______ with a business center and a gym.
(A)**blended**[7] (B)**equipped**[8] (C)**governed**[9] (D)**overcome**[10] 住宿 單字

[中譯] 這間飯店的設施有商務中心及健身房。
(A)混合 (B)配備 (C)治理 (D)克服 答 B

( ) 9. Clerk: When is your connecting flight? Traveler: _______
(A)I feel nervous about taking the train. (B)I'm flying to Hong Kong.
(C)I'm transiting to Auckland. (D)It comes in three hours. 機場 對話

[中譯] 店員：您的轉機航班是什麼時候？ 旅客：將於三小時內。
(A)對於搭乘火車讓我感到緊張 (B)我要去香港
(C)我要轉機去奧克蘭 (D)將於三小時內 答 D

( ) 10. Although most snakes in the park are not _______, you need to watch carefully where you put your hands and feet.
(A)**eternal**[11] (B)**extensive**[12] (C)**poisonous**[13] (D)prosperous 生活 單字

[中譯] 儘管公園裡大部分的蛇類是沒有毒性的，你需注意手腳擺放的地方。
(A)永恆的 (B)廣泛的 (C)有毒性的 (D)繁榮的 答 C

( ) 11. Some passengers felt seasick, so they went up on the _______ for some fresh air.
(A)**deck**[14] (B)crew (C)alarm (D)**belly**[15] 交通 單字

[中譯] 一些乘客感到暈船，所以他們上到甲板呼吸一些新鮮空氣。
(A)甲板 (B)組員 (C)警報 (D)腹部 答 A

( ) 12. Hotel Guest: Could you tell me how to get to the concert hall? Clerk: _______
(A)Yes, just go outside the hotel and turn left.
(B)No, the traffic is pretty heavy at the moment.
(C)Yes, but I prefer watching a basketball game.
(D)No, I don't think you will like the show. 交通 對話

[中譯] 飯店客人：可以請你告訴我如何前往音樂廳嗎？ 服務員：可以，走出飯店後左轉即可。
(A)可以，只需走出飯店後左轉即可 (B)不可以，交通現在非常地擁擠
(C)可以，但我更傾向於看籃球比賽 (D)不可以，我不認為你會喜歡這個秀 答 A

( ) 13. It is suggested that asking people about their **religion**[16], age, and _______ status be avoided.
(A)lodge (B)luxury (C)**marital**[17] (D)mineral 生活 單字

[中譯] 建議避免去詢問他人的宗教信仰、年齡及婚姻狀況。
(A)投宿 (B)奢華 (C)婚姻的 (D)礦物 答 C

( ) 14. Many medicines must be _______ by a doctor. You cannot buy them at the **pharmacy**[18].
(A)predicted (B)**prescribed**[19] (C)**detached**[20] (D)dismissed 生活 單字

[中譯] 許多藥品必須經由醫師處方。你無法直接在藥局購買。
(A)預計 (B)處方 (C)分離 (D)解散 答 B

( ) 15. Janet uses her _______ flyer miles to get a free flight from Tokyo to Taipei.
(A)constant (B)frequent (C)intensive (D)**potential**[21] 交通 單字

[中譯] Janet 使用她的飛行常客哩數獲得一段東京到台北的免費航程。
(A)固定的 (B)經常的 (C)加強的 (D)潛在的 答 B

( ) 16. Please check with your airline and look at the _______ Articles Guidelines before packing your suitcases.
(A)Reconstructed (B)Reassigned (C)**Restricted**[22] (D)Recreated 機場 單字

[中譯] 在打包你的行李前，請與你的航空公司確認並參照物品限制指南。
(A)重建 (B)再分配 (C)受限制的 (D)再創造 答 C

( ) 17. When going through the security check, you need to put all carry-on luggage on the _______.
(A)contributor (B)conveyor (C)extractor (D)exhibitor 機場 單字

[中譯] 當通過安全檢查時，你需要將所有手提行李置於輸送帶上。
(A)貢獻者 (B)輸送帶 (C)提取器 (D)展示者 答 B

( ) 18. The city is suffering from a(n) _______ lack of rainfall at the moment.
(A)antique (B)**carnival**[23] (C)severe (D)**various**[24] 生活 單字

[中譯] 此時這個城市正遭受嚴重的降雨缺乏。
(A)古代的 (B)嘉年華會 (C)嚴重的 (D)各式各樣的 答 C

( ) 19. The receptionist in the Tourist Information Center asks a guest to _______ the brochure first and then he will answer his inquiry later.
(A)look through (B)rule out (C)take after (D)wear off 產業 片語

[中譯] 旅遊服務中心的接待員先讓旅客瀏覽手冊接著再回答他們的問題。
(A)瀏覽 (B)排除 (C)與....相像 (D)磨損 答 A

( ) 20. The view outside the train was suddenly gone because it went through a(n) _______ and it was dark outside.
(A)**errand**[25] (B)**magnet**[26] (C)**queue**[27] (D)tunnel 交通 單字

[中譯] 火車外面的景色突然消失一片漆黑，因為它正穿越一座隧道。
(A)任務 (B)磁鐵 (C)行列、長隊 (D)隧道 答 D

( ) 21. Customer: What is the exchange rate for Indian rupee? Clerk: _______
(A)One Indian rupee is worth about 1.5 Japanese yen today.
(B)There is no exchange rate for Indian rupees.
(C)Your changes are in a very bad condition.
(D)I'd like bills in small **denominations**[28]. 生活 對話

[中譯] 顧客：印度盧比的兌換匯率為何？ 櫃員：今日匯率為1印度盧比兌換1.5日元。
(A)今日匯率為1印度盧比兌換1.5日元 (B)這裡沒有印度盧比的兌換匯率
(C)你的改變處於非常糟糕的狀態 (D)我想要小張面額的鈔票 答 A

( ) 22. Ian needed to look at the map on his mobile phone several times because he didn't know the _______ to the museum.
(A)**knit**[29] (B)route (C)tablet (D)witness 生活 單字

[中譯] Ian需要數次查看他手機上的地圖，因為他不知道去博物館的路線。
(A)編織 (B)路線 (C)平板 (D)目擊者 答 B

( ) 23. The overhead _______ here seem to be full; we need to see if there is any space in another one.
(A)**compartments**[30] (B)embarkations (C)intersections (D)**amusements**[31]
交通 單字

[中譯] 這個座位上方的置物櫃似乎已經滿了，我們需要看看另一個是否還有空間。
(A)置物櫃 (B)乘坐 (C)交叉 (D)樂趣 答 A

( ) 24. Natalie: I like the atmosphere in your restaurant. It's so bright and cheerful! And everyone leaves with a smile on their face.
Ms. Hall: _______
(A)We offer an expensive buffet in our restaurant.
(B)I'm pleased that you rank our restaurant highly.
(C)There is also a small bar next to our restaurant.
(D)This is a high-class French restaurant. 餐飲 對話

[中譯] Natalie：我喜歡你們餐廳的氛圍。如此明亮和愉悅！每個人離開時都面帶著笑容。
Ms.Hall：我非常開心您給予本餐廳的高度評價。
(A)我們的餐廳提供昂貴的自助餐 (B)我非常開心您給予本餐廳的高度評價
(C)這裡還有一個小酒吧在我們的餐廳旁邊 (D)這是一家高級的法式餐廳 答 B

( ) 25. I would like to _______ the bill. Can I use a credit card to pay for it?
(A)**mention**[32] (B)**recall**[33] (C)settle (D)**tickle**[34] 購物 單字

[中譯] 我想結帳，我可以使用信用卡支付嗎？
(A)提及 (B)回想 (C)結帳 (D)逗.....笑 答 C

( ) 26. Welcome _______ board. This is Captain Cook speaking. Our cabinet crew here will serve you to your satisfaction during your long flight from Taipei to New York. (A)on (B)at (C)for (D)with 交通 文法

[中譯] 歡迎登機。這是機長Cook的廣播。從台北到紐約在您的長程旅途中，我們的座艙組員將提供令您滿意的服務。
(A)在....上 (B)在....地點 (C)為了 (D)與.....一起 解 P2-52. 文法81 答 A

( ) 27. Each country has varying processes and requirements for customs and rules about _______ of items.
(A)declaration (B)**characteristics**[35] (C)convenience (D)**argument**[36] 機場 單字

[中譯] 關於物品申報的規定，每個國家都有不同的通關流程和需求。
(A)申報 (B)特性 (C)便利性 (D)爭論 答 A

( ) 28. The clerk couldn't deal with the guest's complaint, so he asked the manager for help to _______ the problem.
(A)run over (B)sort out (C)turn down (D)warm up 職能 單字

[中譯] 這位店員無法處理客人的抱怨，所以他請求經理的協助以解決問題。
(A)翻轉 (B)解決 (C)拒絕 (D)熱身 答 B

( ) 29. Some tour companies advertise jungle treks, scuba diving, and other _______ as "nature tourism".
(A)expeditions (B)**destructions**[37] (C)registrations (D)nationalities 產業 單字

[中譯] 一些旅遊公司宣傳叢林跋涉、水肺潛水及相關探險導向的"自然觀光"。
(A)探險 (B)破壞 (C)註冊 (D)國籍 答 A

( ) 30. The bedrooms of this luxury hotel are more ____ with quality furnishings and décor.
(A)attentive (B)**tolerant**[38] (C)spacious (D)**enthusiastic**[39] 住宿 單字

[中譯] 這間豪華酒店的臥房更加地寬敞並配有優質的傢俱及裝飾。
(A)注意的 (B)容忍的 (C)寬敞的 (D)熱情的 答 C

( ) 31. Helen treated everyone from the office to that restaurant because she had a _______ for 30% off.
(A)coupon (B)factor (C)option (D)usage 餐飲 單字

[中譯] Helen招待所有辦公室的人到那家餐廳，因為她有七折的優惠券。
(A)優惠券 (B)因素 (C)選項 (D)使用 答 A

( ) 32. The reason why the tour guide was hired was that she could speak _______ languages, including English, Korean, German, and Russian.
(A)**genuine**[40] (B)multiple (C)**regulated**[41] (D)**visible**[42] 職能 單字

[中譯] 這個導遊之所以會被僱用是因為她能說多國的語言，包括英語、漢語、德語及俄語。
(A)真正的 (B)多樣的 (C)規範的 (D)可看見的 答 B

( ) 33. Some people prefer taking a train than a bus because they think they travel more _______ by train. 交通 單字
(A)comfortably (B)**fundamentally**[43] (C)mechanically (D)**permanently**[44]

[中譯] 有些人喜歡搭乘火車勝過於巴士，因為他們認為搭乘火車旅行更為舒適。
(A)舒適 (B)基本地 (C)機械的 (D)永久地 答 A

( ) 34. The agent in a car rental company _______ that he would reserve a car for Nancy if she could pay a deposit to confirm her reservation.
(A)declined (B)featured (C)guaranteed (D)**opposed**[45] 交通 單字

[中譯] 租車公司的仲介承諾，如果Nancy能支付訂金就能確認她的預訂，並會為她保留一輛車。
(A)拒絕 (B)功能 (C)保證 (D)反抗 答 C

( ) 35. Cindy: Would you like to go on a backpacking tour? Danial: _______
(A)Yes, the museum is worth visiting.
(B)Yes, I prefer other outdoors activities.
(C)No problem. I love staying indoors.
(D)Yes, I like going camping on the mountains. 生活 對話

[中譯] Cindy：你想要去背包客旅行嗎？ Danial：好，我喜歡去山上露營。
(A)好，博物館很值得去參觀 (B)好，我更喜歡其他戶外活動
(C)沒問題，我喜歡待在室內 (D)好，我喜歡去山上露營 答 D

( ) 36. I would like to have a freshly _______ orange juice and an order of pancakes.
(A)**squeezed**[46] (B)deserted (C)**scrambled**[47] (D)**poached**[48] 餐飲 單字

[中譯] 我想要一杯鮮榨橙汁和一份煎餅。
(A)壓榨的 (B)廢棄的 (C)翻攪的 (D)水煮的 答 A

( ) 37. Clerk: Do you know what a stored-value card is for? Traveler: _______
(A)Yes, you use a machine to add value to your card.
(B)Yes, you use it to pay for things instead of using cash.
(C)No, this isn't the right platform for you to board the train.
(D)No, I purchase single-journey tokens rather than a tourist pass. 購物 對話

[中譯] 店員：您知道儲值卡的用途嗎？ 旅客：是的，你使用它來付款而不是使用現金。
(A)是的，你使用機器來儲值你的卡片 (B)是的，你使用它來付款而不是使用現金
(C)不是，這不是您搭乘該火車的月台 (D)不是，我購買的是單程代幣不是旅遊通行證 答 B

情境篇 文法篇 片語篇 測驗篇 口試篇

( ) 38. In these rooms two twin-size beds can be _______ into a king-size bed.
(A)convertible (B)contrastable (C)considerable (D)consumable 住宿 單字

[中譯] 這些房間的兩張單人床可以換成一張特大號床。
(A)可轉換的 (B)可對比的 (C)大量的 (D)可消耗的 答 A

( ) 39. The child is _____ to seafood. We should order chicken nuggets instead of shrimps.
(A)sparkling (B)steamed (C)**allergic**[49] (D)available 餐飲 單字

[中譯] 這個孩子對海鮮過敏。我們應該點雞塊取代蝦。
(A)閃閃發光的 (B)蒸煮的 (C)對...過敏 (D)可得到的 答 C

( ) 40. Front desk clerk: What seems to be the problem with your invoice?
Hotel Guest: _______
(A)I don't think you offer excellent facilities.
(B)I need to reserve a room at the front desk.
(C)I don't need a **receipt**[50] of my bill.
(D)I think I have been **overcharged**[51]. 住宿 對話

[中譯] 櫃台職員：請問您的發票有什麼問題呢？ 飯店客人：我認為我被超收費用了。
(A)我不認為你們提供了良好的設施 (B)我需要在櫃台預訂一個房間
(C)我不需要收據 (D)我認為我被超收費用了 答 D

( ) 41. Official of the Immigration Area of the airport will stamp your passport once you are approved and **granted**[52] _______.
(A)admission (B)destination (C)carousal (D)**conductor**[53] 機場 單字

[中譯] 機場的移民官會在您的護照上蓋章，一旦您獲得許可並准予以入境。
(A)許可 (B)目的地 (C)狂歡 (D)列車長 答 A

( ) 42. The large area of _______ and redness is caused by insect bites. Urgent medical attention is necessary.
(A)**swamp**[54] (B)**swallow**[55] (C)**swarming**[56] (D)**swelling**[57] 生活 單字

[中譯] 大面積腫脹和發紅是昆蟲叮咬造成的。緊急醫療護理是必要的。
(A)沼澤 (B)吞下 (C)群聚；成群結隊 (D)腫脹 答 D

( ) 43. There is no hot water in my room; please contact _______ and ask them to send someone up.
(A)architecture (B)**maintenance**[58] (C)itinerary (D)sightseeing 住宿 單字

[中譯] 我的房間沒有熱水；請聯繫維修部門並要求他們派人來。
(A)建築 (B)維修 (C)行程 (D)觀光 答 B

( ) 44. Traveler: We're thinking of doing something cultural. Do you have any tour that we could join?

Clerk: _______
(A)I recommend the National Palace Museum with lots of artifacts.
(B)We offer other physical activities as well if you're interested in.
(C)Ecological tours are pretty dull and unexciting.
(D)There is no fast train going up to Alishan. 產業 對話

[中譯] 旅客：我們正在考慮從事一些有關文化藝術性的活動。你有什麼行程是我們可以參加的？
職員：我推薦故宮博物院，院內有很多的文物。
(A)我推薦故宮博物院，院內有很多的文物
(B)我們也有提供其他自然活動，如果您有興趣的話
(C)生態觀光非常地無聊並不讓人感到興奮
(D)這裡沒有高速火車可到達阿里山 答 A

( ) 45. It is always cheaper to travel at _______ peak train times that are less busy.
(A)down (B)with (C)off (D)on 交通 文法

[中譯] 在離峰時段搭乘火車總是比較便宜且較不繁忙。
(A)向下 (B)與.....一起 (C)非、(去)除 (D)在.....上 解 P2-52. 文法81 答 C
補 high peak 尖峰時段；off peak 離峰時段

( ) 46. Non-alcoholic beverages are _______ on all the flights. You don't have to pay for them. 交通 單字
(A)**compositional**[59] (B)**constitutional**[60] (C)contaminating (D)complimentary

[中譯] 不含酒精飲料在所有飛機上都是免費的，您不需要付錢。
(A)成分的 (B)本質的 (C)污染的 (D)免費的 答 D

( ) 47. The customer looking at the forks and spoons complained about the dirty and stained _______ to the waiter.
(A)**utensils**[61] (B)terraces (C)exhibitions (D)**boulevards**[62] 餐飲 單字

[中譯] 客人看著這些叉子和湯匙，對著服務員抱怨餐具上的髒污和污垢。
(A)餐具 (B)大陽台 (C)展覽 (D)林蔭大道 答 A

( ) 48. All the room guests are _______ to use the hotel facilities during their stay.
(A)absorbed (B)disputed (C)**entitled**[63] (D)**harbored**[64] 住宿 單字

[中譯] 在入住期間，所有房客都有權去使用飯店的設施。
(A)吸收 (B)有爭論的 (C)有權 (D)庇護 答 C

( ) 49. Nick: I'm hungry. Let's **grab**[65] some snacks to eat. Lisa: _______
(A)How do you want to shorten your pants?
(B)A new bookstore has just opened recently.
(C)All right. There's a sandwich shop on Main Street.
(D)There is hardly any expensive restaurant around. 餐飲 對話

[中譯] Nick：我餓了，我們找一些點心來吃吧。 Lisa：好啊，這裡有一間三明治店在大街上。
(A)你想要如何縮短你的褲子？ (B)一間新的書店最近剛開張
(C)好啊，這裡有一間三明治店在大街上 (D)幾乎沒有任何昂貴的餐廳在附近 答 C

( ) 50. On _______ airlines we pay less for our tickets, but have to pay for food, headsets, or drinks.
(A)budget (B)**margin**[66] (C)cabbage (D)**disclosed**[67] 交通 單字

[中譯] 搭乘廉價的航空我們可支付較少的機票費用，但必須支付食物、耳機及飲料的費用。
(A)廉價的 (B)邊沿、邊緣 (C)高麗菜 (D)揭露 答 A

( ) 51. Clerk: Are you looking for some souvenirs? Guest: _______
(A)Yes, where is the boarding gate for Flight 209?
(B)No, I've never visited any of the duty free shops.
(C)OK. I would like to buy a return ticket to Seoul.
(D)Yes, I need a jade necklace for my mother. 購物 對話

[中譯] 店員：您在尋找一些紀念品嗎？ 客人：是的，我需要一條玉質項鍊送給我的母親。
(A)是的，209號航班的登機口在哪裡？ (B)不是的，我從來沒有去過任何免稅商店
(C)好的，我想要買一張首爾的回程機票 (D)是的，我需要一條玉質項鍊送給我的母親 答 D

( ) 52. Clerk: Can I help you find anything? Customer: _______
(A)They have called for the police. (B)This is an **ethical**[68] issue.
(C)We have just moved in. (D)I'm just **browsing**[69]. 購物 對話

[中譯] 店員：有什麼我可以服務您？ 顧客：我就只是看看。
(A)他們已經通知警察 (B)這是一個道德問題
(C)我們剛剛搬進來 (D)我就只是看看 答 D

( ) 53. The plane is now _______ at 30,000 feet and the "fasten seat belts" sign has just been turned off.
(A)landing (B)switching (C)cruising (D)translating 交通 單字

[中譯] 飛機正航行在30,000英呎上，並且 "繫緊安全帶" 的指示燈剛熄滅。
(A)著陸 (B)切換 (C)航行 (D)翻譯 答 C

( ) 54. To ease the customer's anger, the manager offered her a free meal to _______ the problem. But she still felt displeased.
(A)add up to (B)get on with (C)keep up with (D)make up for 餐飲 片語

[中譯] 為了減輕客人的憤怒，經理提供她免費的餐食去補償這個問題，但她仍然感到非常不開心。
(A)總計 (B)與某人關係良好 (C)保持同一速度 (D)補償 答 D

( ) 55. While we're on board, we can get some great _______ of the waterfront. They will be wonderful pictures.
(A)traps (B)shots (C)muffs (D)**bracelets**[70] 交通 單字

[中譯] 當我們在船上時，我們可以拍攝一些不錯的沿岸景色，它們會成為很棒的照片。
(A)陷阱 (B)拍攝 (C)錯事、失去 (D)手鐲 答 B

( ) 56. Since most people now travel with cell phones, _______ calls are rarely used and have become almost **obsolete**[71].
(A)collect (B)**channel**[72] (C)proceed (D)**conditional**[73] 生活 單字

[中譯] 由於多數人現在旅行都攜帶著手機，受話人付費電話越來越少使用，且幾乎過時了。
(A)(打電話時)由受話人付費 (B)途徑、手段 (C)繼續進行 (D)有條件的 答 A

( ) 57. The _______ desk in large hotels is responsible for helping anything guests require such as buying tickets for theaters and arranging transport.
(A)**diagnosis**[74] (B)concierge (C)**binoculars**[75] (D)**entrepreneur**[76] 住宿 單字

[中譯] 大型飯店的禮賓服務櫃檯，負責協助任何客人需求，例如購買戲院門票和交通安排。
(A)診斷 (B)禮賓服務 (C)雙筒望遠鏡 (D)企業家 答 B

( ) 58. The original receipt is required to process a _______ to a customer who paid in cash.
(A)**rebel**[77] (B)recipe (C)remain (D)refund 購物 單字

[中譯] 使用現金支付的客人進行退款時，需要原始的收據。
(A)造反者 (B)處方、食譜 (C)剩下、餘留 (D)退款 答 D

( ) 59. Other _______ items include knives, sharp instruments, metal nail files, and ski poles.
(A)prohibited (B)**flammable**[78] (C)statement (D)receptionist 機場 單字

[中譯] 其他禁止物品包括刀具、鋒利的器具、金屬指甲銼刀和滑雪杖。
(A)禁止的 (B)易燃的、可燃的 (C)陳述、說明 (D)接待員 答 A

( ) 60. The tax is added to the total price at the cash _______, not included in the price.
(A)**route**[79] (B)register (C)**cottage**[80] (D)**campsite**[81] 購物 單字

[中譯] 稅金在結帳時才會加入總價，原價格是未稅價。
(A)路線 (B)收銀機 (C)農舍、小屋 (D)露營地 答 B

( ) 61. Clerk: Will a banqueting hall that holds 200 people be sufficient? Guest: _______
(A)Yes, a set meal for each one of them should be enough.
(B)No, we haven't settled on a date for our wedding.
(C)No, I need a large space for more than 250 people.
(D)Yes, 200 parking spaces are adequate for them. 生活 對話

[中譯] 店員：容納200人的宴會廳足夠嗎？ 客人：不，我需要一個能容納超過250人的寬敞空間。
(A)是的，一份套餐供給每一位是足夠的 (B)不，我們還沒有確定我們婚禮的檔期
(C)不，我需要一個能容納超過250人的寬敞空間 (D)是的，200個停車位對他們是夠的 答 C

(　) 62. We need to relax after our busy morning. Why don't we have a coffee break at a _______ to eleven?
(A)penny (B)quarter (C)bellhop (D)**descent**[82] 生活 單字

[中譯] 忙碌的早晨後我們需要放鬆一下，我們何不在10點45分的時候來個咖啡小憩時光？
(A)一分錢 (B)一刻鐘、四分之一 (C)(旅館)服務生 (D)下降 答 B

(　) 63. Passengers can stay connected with onboard WiFi or enjoy films, music, and other inflight _______ available during their flight.
(A)cloakroom (B)**quarantine**[83] (C)**merchandise**[84] (D)**entertainment**[85] 交通 單字

[中譯] 在飛行途中，乘客可以連接機上wifi或享受電影、音樂或其他機上的娛樂設施。
(A)衣帽間 (B)隔離區 (C)商品、貨物 (D)娛樂 答 D

(　) 64. Please keep your seat belt fastened at any time you are seated – in case your flight comes across unexpected _______.
(A)**turbulence**[86] (B)**occurrence**[87] (C)monument (D)**installment**[88] 交通 單字

[中譯] 任何時候當您就坐時，請繫緊您的安全帶 — 以防在飛行途中遇到不可預測的亂流。
(A)亂流 (B)發生、事件 (C)紀念碑 (D)安裝、分期付款 答 A

(　) 65. Linda: The tour we booked begins in ten minutes, but there's no way we'll get there in time with such heavy traffic. Steven: _______
(A)Let's wait for the bus to come here in ten minutes.
(B)If we run to the station now, maybe we can catch the plane.
(C)Let's take the metro instead. We can do our own city tour.
(D)No taxi is available to take us to the hospital. 交通 對話

[中譯] Linda：我們預定的行程將於十分鐘開始，但我們無法在如此擁擠的交通下及時抵達那裡。
Steven：我們改為搭乘捷運，可以來個專屬城市觀光。
(A)讓我們再等十分鐘讓公車抵達這裡 (B)如果我們現在趕到車站，我們也許可以趕上飛機
(C)我們改為搭乘捷運，可以來個專屬城市觀光 (D)沒有空的計程車可載我們去醫院 答 C

(　) 66. This is a city for bicycles and more tourists are ____ this way of exploring the city.
(A)grilling (B)**adopting**[89] (C)**scorching**[90] (D)**deceiving**[91] 產業 單字

[中譯] 這是一個自行車友善的城市，越來越多的遊客正在採用這個方式探索這座城市。
(A)盤問、審問 (B)採用 (C)灼熱的、(言語等)尖刻的 (D)欺騙的 答 B

(　) 67. If the customer is not satisfied with the item for any reason, the shop will offer a _______.
(A)requirement (B)**replacement**[92] (C)**retirement**[93] (D)**recruitment**[94] 購物 單字

[中譯] 如果消費者基於任何原因不滿意他們的物品，商店將會提供更換。
(A)需要 (B)更換 (C)退休、退職 (D)征募 答 B

( ) 68. This platform is for _______ trains. Uptown service is on the other side of the tracks.
(A)accessory (B)**escalator**[95] (C)**transparent**[96] (D)southbound 交通 單字

[中譯] 這個月台是用於南下的火車，北上服務在軌道的另一側。
(A)附件、配件 (B)電扶梯 (C)透明的 (D)南向的 答 D

( ) 69. Clerk: What currency would you like to have your money changed, sir?
Customer: _______
(A)I have been waiting in line for so long. (B)I need some Japanese yen, please.
(C)I haven't brought much money. (D)I have only a $100 note. 生活 對話

[中譯] 職員：您想要兌換哪一種貨幣呢，先生？ 客人：我需要一些日幣。
(A)我已經排隊等很久 (B)我需要一些日幣
(C)我沒有帶很多錢 (D)我只有一張100美金的紙鈔 答 B

( ) 70. Flight attendants can help senior citizens to lift and _______ their hand carry luggage to the overhead bins.
(A)**stow**[97] (B)**alter**[98] (C)refill (D)transit 交通 單字

[中譯] 空服員可以協助老年人抬起並放置他們的手提行李到上方的置物箱。
(A)裝載 (B)改變 (C)再裝滿 (D)運輸 答 A

閱讀測驗一

Creative Restaurant Review by Rebecca Wong

Like several restaurants that have recently opened in town, Creative Restaurant is different from a traditional one that provides a menu for customers to choose from. Instead, it is a new kind of restaurant that offers their dishes without a menu. Guests who are interested in trying their cuisine simply need to make a phone reservation, informing the staff in the restaurant of their budget for the meals. The restaurant will take care of the rest and there is no need for customers to worry about what they will eat. But booking well in advance is a must as the restaurant needs to prepare their food much earlier in order to meet customers' expectations. Since this kind of menuless restaurant affords high-quality food and service, guests need to be aware that they expect to pay more and the quality of the food provided by the restaurant varies according to the price they pay for. Yet, this type of restaurant strives for good reputation. The food and service they offer does reach a high standard. It is also a kind of featured restaurant whose offer of high-quality food is promised to fulfill customers' satisfaction.

My experience of eating in this kind of restaurant is superb. Once I went eat there with a couple of colleagues. We ordered a table and each one of us paid for our own share. Each dish they offered was like a piece of artwork that catered to our senses. Not only did it offer a mixture of local and exotic food, the cooking styles it afforded range from the East to the West.

They blended food from different countries and cultures so well that when you savor each dish, you never experience contradiction and even cultural shock. Further, each dish comes with artistic and colorful garnishes and decorations. Even the plates and bowls that go with the cuisine are well-designed and magnificent. It is truly a tantalizing experience. No wonder that this kind of restaurant is really popular among foodies and tourists. There is also no way that you can just pop into the restaurant and eat as all the tables are fully booked for months. But eating in this type of restaurant is certainly an experience you should have in a lifetime. Don't miss it and invite your friends to join you to enjoy your time together.

Rebecca Wong的創意餐廳評論

就像最近在鎮上開張的幾家餐廳一樣，創意餐廳不像傳統的餐廳提供菜單給顧客去選擇。取而代之的，是一種新型的餐廳，提供無菜單料理。顧客有興趣品嘗美食，只需要電話預約，告知餐廳的工作人員預算範圍，餐廳將會負責接下來的一切，顧客不需去擔心他們將要吃什麼。但是提前預訂是必須的，餐廳需要盡早的去準備餐點，才能滿足顧客的期望。類似這種無菜單式餐廳提供優質的餐點和服務，顧客需要意識到他們將要比預期支付的更多，並且餐廳根據他們支付的價格來提供餐點的質量。然而，這種類型的餐廳為了爭取好的聲譽，他們提供的食物和服務須達到一定的高標準，這也是一家特色餐廳承諾提供優質的食物以滿足顧客的期待。

我在這類餐廳用餐的經驗是非常好的。有一次我和幾個同事去那裡吃飯，我們預訂了一桌，並各自支付個人的餐點，他們提供的每一道料理都像是一個藝術品，迎合著我們的感官體驗。不僅提供混合當地和異國的料理，烹飪的風格更涵蓋東方到西方。當你品嘗每一道料理時，他們將不同國家和文化如此美好地融合，你並不會有違和感甚至是文化上的震撼。此外，每一道菜餚都帶有藝術性和多彩的配菜和裝飾。甚至連盤子和碗都伴隨著菜餚有著絕佳的設計及華麗感。這的確是一個很誘人的經驗，難怪此種類型的餐廳深受美食家及旅客的喜愛，你絕對無法不先預訂就入內用餐，因為未來幾個月的座位早已全部被預訂。但在這種類型的餐廳用餐絕對是你一生中值得的體驗。千萬不要錯過並且邀請你的朋友們加入，一起去享受美好的時光。

( ) 71. Where does this kind of review usually get published?
(A)in a referred journal (B)in a car magazine
(C)in a newspaper (D)in a science report

[中譯] 這種類型的評論通常在哪裡發表？
(A)在學術期刊中 (B)在汽車雜誌中 (C)在報紙中 (D)在科學報告中

答 C

( ) 72. Who are the most likely intended readers for this review?
(A)Children who are hungry without food.
(B)Gourmets with excellent taste buds.
(C)Tourists who go on adventure tours.
(D)Scientists who study animals' diseases.

[中譯] 誰最有可能成為這篇文章的讀者？
(A)很飢餓沒有食物的孩子 (B)有著極佳味蕾的美食品嘗家
(C)正在進行冒險旅行的旅客 (D)研究動物疾病的科學家

答 B

( ) 73. In which aspect can this type of restaurant be called creative?
(A)The dishes it makes contain a lot of creativity.
(B)They design the restaurant in an innovative way.
(C)The staff working in the restaurant is very smart.
(D)The guests are served in a comfortable manner.

[中譯] 根據哪個面向可以讓這類型的餐廳被稱之為創意餐廳？
(A)他們的菜餚包含許多的創意 (B)他們以一個創新的方式設計餐廳
(C)餐廳的員工非常聰明 (D)以舒適的方式服務客人
答 A

( ) 74. Why has this kind of restaurant become popular?
(A)Because people have no unique restaurant to go to.
(B)Because this restaurant offers expensive food.
(C)Because servers in this restaurant are friendly.
(D)Because it offers high-quality food with a difference.

[中譯] 這類型的餐廳為什麼會受到歡迎？
(A)因為人們沒有特別的餐廳可以去 (B)因為這家餐廳提供昂貴的食物
(C)因為這家餐廳的服務很友善 (D)因為它提供的優質食物與眾不同
答 D

( ) 75. Is this article a mixed review?
(A)Yes, it gets written from a personal opinion. (B)No, it only looks from the good side.
(C)Yes, there is a hint of confusion. (D)No, it doesn't offer figures.

[中譯] 這篇文章是混合型的評論嗎？
(A)是的，他以個人觀點寫的 (B)不是，他只有看好的一面
(C)是的，有一點混亂 (D)不是，他沒有提供數據
答 B

閱讀測驗二

Plastic pollution has become one of the most **pressing** environmental issues, as rapidly increasing production of disposable plastic products overwhelms the world's ability to deal with them. Plastic pollution is most visible in developing Asian and African nations, where garbage collection systems are often inefficient or nonexistent. But the developed world, especially in countries with low recycling rates, also has trouble properly collecting discarded plastics.

Plastics made from fossil fuels are just over a century old. Production and development of thousands of new plastic products accelerated after World War II, so transforming the modern age that life without plastics would be unrecognizable today. Plastics revolutionized medicine with life-saving devices, made space travel possible, lightened cars and jets—saving fuel and pollution — and saved lives with helmets, incubators, and equipment for clean drinking water. The conveniences plastics offer, however, led to a throw-away culture that reveals the material's dark side: today, single-use plastics account for 40 percent of the plastic produced every year. Many of these products, such as plastic bags and food wrappers, have a lifespan of mere minutes to hours, yet they may persist in the environment for hundreds of years.

Every year, about 8 million tons of plastic waste escapes into the oceans from coastal nations. That's the equivalent of setting five garbage bags full of trash on every foot of coastline around the world. Once at sea, sunlight, wind, and wave action break down plastic waste into small particles, often less than one-fifth of an inch across. These so-called microplastics are spread throughout the water column and have been found in every corner of the globe, from Mount Everest, the highest peak, to the Mariana Trench, the deepest trough. Microplastics are breaking down further into smaller and smaller pieces. Plastic microfibers, meanwhile, have been found in municipal drinking water systems and drifting through the air. Millions of animals are killed by plastics every year, from birds to fish to other marine organisms. Nearly 700 species, including endangered ones, are known to have been affected by plastics. Microplastics have been found in more than 100 **aquatic species**, including fish, shrimp, and mussels destined for our dinner plates.

Once in the ocean, it is difficult to retrieve plastic waste. Mechanical systems, such as **Mr. Trash Wheel**, a litter interceptor in Maryland's Baltimore Harbor, can be effective at picking up large pieces of plastic, such as foam cups and food containers, from inland waters. But once plastics break down into microplastics and drift throughout the water column in the open ocean, they are virtually impossible to recover. The solution is to prevent plastic waste from entering rivers and seas in the first place. This could be accomplished with improved waste management systems and recycling, better product design that takes into account the short life of disposable packaging, and reduction in manufacturing of unnecessary single-use plastics.

隨著免洗塑膠產品急遽增加，逐漸超過世界能夠處理的量，塑膠污染已成為**急迫**的環境問題之一。亞洲和非洲的開發中國家的塑膠污染是最常見的，其垃圾收集系統通常效率低或根本不存在。不過其實在已開發國家，特別是一些不注重回收的國家，也同時存在著無法有效集中處理廢棄塑膠的問題。

由化石燃料製成的塑膠已有一百多年歷史。二次大戰後，成千上萬種新塑膠產品被加速生產和開發，這樣的改變使得你根本無法想像當今生活若沒有塑膠製品將會變得如何。塑膠在醫學救護設備上帶來革命，使太空旅行成為可能，減輕了汽車和飛機的重量—節省了燃料也減少了污染，也被用來製造保護生命用的安全帽、保溫箱和淨水設備。然而便利的塑膠產品帶來一種隨用隨丟的文化，揭示了這種材料的黑暗面：如今，一次性塑膠製品佔全年塑膠品產量的40%。許多產品，例如塑膠袋和食品包裝紙，其生命週期只有幾分鐘到幾小時，但它們可能會在環境中存續數百年。

每年約有800萬噸的塑膠廢料從沿海國家外流到海洋。相當於每一英呎內放置五個裝滿垃圾的垃圾袋在世界各地的海岸線上。一到了海裡，陽光、風和海浪將塑膠廢料分解成直徑不到五分之一英吋的小顆粒。這些所謂的微塑膠分散在水體，且在全球各個角落，從最高的珠穆朗瑪峰到最深的馬里亞納海溝皆可發現。微塑膠進一步分解成越來越小的碎片。塑膠微纖維同時也在市區的飲用水系統中被發現，也有飄浮在空中的。每年有數以百萬計的動物死於塑膠，從鳥類到魚類到其他海洋生物。大概700種物種，包括瀕危物種，都受塑膠的影響。微塑膠在超過100多種**水生物種**中被發現，包括魚、蝦和蚌類，然後成為我們餐盤上的食物。

一旦進入海洋，將很難回收塑膠廢料。像是**垃圾輪先生**這樣在馬里蘭州巴爾海港的一個垃圾攔截器，可以有效地從內陸水域中撿起大塊塑膠，例如泡沫材質杯和食品容器。但是一旦塑膠分解成微塑膠並在開放性的海域中漂移，它們就幾乎不可能被回收了。解決方案便是從一開始就防止塑膠廢料進入河流和海洋，可達成的管道包含改善廢棄物的管理與回收系統、設計產品時考慮到使用拋棄式包裝的必要性，以及減少製造非必要的一次性塑膠品。

( ) 76. Which of the following is NOT considered to be making good use of plastics according to the passage?
(A)Equipment for clean water (B)Cars lightened for saving fuel
(C)Helmets made for saving lives (D)Food wrappers for conveniences

[中譯] 根據這篇文章，下列敘述何者不被認為適當地使用塑膠？
(A)淨水設備 (B)省油減重汽車
(C)保護生命的頭盔 (D)方便的食品包裝 答 D

( ) 77. Which of the following is closest in meaning to "pressing"?
(A)**drifting**[99] (B)urgent (C)destined (D)invisible

[中譯] "緊迫的"一詞的意思最接近何者？ (A)漂浮的 (B)緊急的 (C)命運的 (D)無形的 答 B

( ) 78. Which of the following statements is NOT true?
(A)Developed countries with low recycling rates have problem collecting throwaway plastics.
(B)Production of many different new plastic products sped up very fast after World War II.
(C)The largest quantity of plastic goods that are produced every year is for single-use.
(D)Microplastics can be found everywhere, from the highest mountain to the deepest trench.

[中譯] 下列敘述何者不正確？
(A)不注重回收的已開發國家，在收集廢棄塑膠方面還存在著問題。
(B)二次世界大戰後各種不同的新塑膠產品加速生產。
(C)每年製造出的塑膠產品，最大量的就是一次性用品。
(D)微塑膠可以在各個地方被發現，從最高的山脈到最深的海溝皆然。 答 C

( ) 79. What does the term "Mr. Trash Wheel" refer to?
(A)A device in a river to collect litter and debris
(B)A scientist studying how to remove microfibers
(C)An endangered species affected by microplastics
(D)An organization for waste management systems

[中譯] "垃圾輪先生" 一詞是什麼意思？
(A)一個在河流中收集垃圾和雜物的設備 (B)一個研究如何去除微纖維的科學家
(C)一個受微塑膠影響的瀕臨絕種的物種 (D)一個關於廢棄物管理系統的組織 答 A

( ) 80. Which of the following is similar in meaning to "aquatic species"?
(A)nonexistent animals (B)marine organisms
(C)litter interceptors (D)**disposal**[100] packaging

[中譯] 下列何者與"水生物種"的意思最接近？
(A)不存在的動物 (B)海洋生物 (C)垃圾攔截器 (D)包裝處理 答 B

Chapter. 06 | 測驗 | 110年度領隊試題

掌握關鍵單字，更快作答70%考題！

重要單字彙整

	單字	出現	音標	中文	詞性
1	**equipment**	7	[ɪ`kwɪpmənt]	設備; 器械; 配備; 才能 同義詞 apparatus, gear, contrivances	名詞
2	**manager**	19	[`mænɪdʒɚ]	經理; 負責人; 監督; 經理人 同義詞 administrator, executive	名詞
3	**agency**	10	[`edʒənsɪ]	經銷處; 代辦處; 動力	名詞
4	**reservation**	25	[ˌrɛzɚ`veʃən]	預訂; 保留; 自然保護區 同義詞 booking, engagement, retaining	名詞
5	**aboard**	1	[ə`bord]	登機, 上船, 上車; 並排在邊上	副詞
6	**abroad**	9	[ə`brɔd]	到國外; 在外面; 傳開; 離譜地 同義詞 overseas, away	副詞
7	**aspect**	7	[`æspɛkt]	方面, 觀點; 方位; 外觀	名詞
8	**reward**	10	[rɪ`wɔrd]	值得; 報答; 獎勵; 報應 同義詞 compensate, remunerate, award 反義詞 punishment 懲罰	動詞
9	**suggest**	28	[sə`dʒɛst]	建議; 暗示; 啟發; 使人想起 同義詞 propose	動詞
10	**customs**	1	[`kʌstəmz]	關稅; 海關; 報關手續; 海關出入境口	名詞
11	**charge**	26	[tʃɑrdʒ]	費用; 掌管; 責任; 指責; 控告	名詞
12	**allowance**	8	[ə`laʊəns]	津貼; 零用錢; 折價; 分配額 同義詞 allotment, portion, grant, budget	名詞
13	**expect**	19	[ɪk`spɛkt]	預期; 期待; 指望 同義詞 anticipate, suppose	動詞
14	**limit**	20	[`lɪmɪt]	限制; 界線; 極限; 範圍 同義詞 restriction, confine	名詞

	單字	出現	音標	中文	詞性
15	**confirm**	9	[kən`fɝm]	確認; 證實; 堅定; 加強	動詞
				同義詞 establish, settle	
16	**relocate**	3	[ri`loket]	搬遷; 重新安置; 調動	動詞
17	**spot**	10	[spɑt]	地點; 職位; 斑點; 汙點	名詞
18	**sightseeing**	15	[`saɪt͵siŋ]	觀光, 遊覽	名詞
19	**convention**	4	[kən`vɛnʃən]	會議; 集合; 公約; 習俗	名詞
				同義詞 meeting, gathering, congress	
20	**inhabitant**	2	[ɪn`hæbətənt]	居民; 住戶	名詞
21	**appointment**	3	[ə`pɔɪntmənt]	約會; 約定; 任命; 職位	名詞
				同義詞 assignment, nomination	
22	**facility**	25	[fə`sɪlətɪ]	設施; 技能; 簡易	名詞
23	**management**	18	[`mænɪdʒmənt]	管理; 經營; 技巧	名詞
24	**seminar**	2	[`sɛmə͵nɑr]	研討會; 研究班	名詞
				同義詞 discussion, symposium, meeting	
25	**policy**	19	[`pɑləsɪ]	政策; 策略, 手段	名詞
26	**scene**	17	[sin]	景象; 景色; 場面; 事件; (戲劇等的)背景	名詞
27	**remains**	12	[rɪ`menz]	遺跡; 廢墟; 遺體	名詞
28	**unspoiled**	1	[ʌn`spɔɪld]	未受破壞的; 未損壞的; 未寵壞的	形容詞
29	**domestic**	16	[də`mɛstɪk]	國內的; 國家的; 家庭的; 馴養的	形容詞
				同義詞 internal	
30	**release**	6	[rɪ`lis]	釋放; 放鬆; 免除; 發表	動詞
				同義詞 free, liberate	
				反義詞 capture 捕獲, arrest 逮捕, bind 綁	
31	**union**	8	[`junjən]	工會; 協會; 合併; 聯邦; 聯盟	名詞
				同義詞 association, guild	
32	**ingredient**	13	[ɪn`gridɪənt]	成分; (烹調的)原料; 要素	名詞
				同義詞 element, component	
33	**accompany**	1	[ə`kʌmpənɪ]	伴隨, 陪同; 伴奏, 伴唱	動詞
				同義詞 escort, chaperon, companion	

▸ 4-112

	單字	出現	音標	中文	詞性
34	**escort**	1	[`ɛskɔrt]	護送; 陪同 同義詞 accompany, squire, chaperon	動詞
35	**fever**	2	[`fivɚ]	發燒; 熱度; 熱病; 狂熱 同義詞 heat	名詞
36	**implement**	9	[`ɪmplə͵mɛnt]	實施; 履行; 執行; 手段	動詞
37	**implant**	1	[ɪm`plænt]	植入; 移植; 灌輸; 種植	動詞
38	**refund**	22	[rɪ`fʌnd]	退款; 退還; 償還 同義詞 repay, reimburse	名詞
39	**compliment**	6	[`kɑmpləmənt]	稱讚; 恭維; 問候; 致意 同義詞 commend, praise, congratulate 反義詞 insult 侮辱	動詞
40	**companion**	1	[kəm`pænjən]	同伴; 伴侶; 手冊	名詞
41	**compensation**	5	[͵kɑmpən`seʃən]	補償; 賠償; 賠償金; 報酬 同義詞 reimbursement, indemnity	名詞
42	**punishment**	4	[`pʌnɪʃmənt]	處罰, 懲罰; 刑罰; 虐待 同義詞 penalty, penalization, castigation	名詞
43	**authority**	4	[ə`θɔrətɪ]	管理機構; 權力; 職權; 官方; 權威 同義詞 government, legislature	名詞
44	**remind**	7	[rɪ`maɪnd]	提醒; 使想起, 使記起 同義詞 prompt	名詞
45	**reissue**	1	[ri`ɪʃʊ]	重新發行	動詞
46	**represent**	14	[͵rɛprɪ`zɛnt]	代表; 象徵; 提出抗議; 描繪	動詞
47	**reject**	9	[rɪ`dʒɛkt]	拒絕; 丟棄; 駁回; 排斥 同義詞 exclude, eliminate 反義詞 accept 接受	動詞
48	**decline**	6	[dɪ`klaɪn]	婉拒; 謝絕; 下降; 衰退 同義詞 refuse, reject 反義詞 accept 接受	動詞
49	**unexpired**	1	[͵ʌnɪk`spaɪrd]	未過期的	形容詞
50	**valued**	17	[`væljud]	貴重的; 寶貴的; 重要的	形容詞

	單字	出現	音標	中文	詞性
51	**resist**	3	[rɪˋzɪst]	抵抗; 抗拒; 忍耐 同義詞 oppose, withstand, counteract 反義詞 obey 服從, submit 屈從	動詞
52	**comprehensive**	5	[ˌkɑmprɪˋhɛnsɪv]	廣泛的; 全面的; 有充分理解力的 同義詞 extensive, broad, widespread 反義詞 incomprehensive 無包括性的	形容詞
53	**switch**	9	[swɪtʃ]	使轉換; 轉移; 打開(或關掉)......的開關 同義詞 shift	動詞
54	**replace**	12	[rɪˋples]	取代; 放回; 更換 同義詞 supplant, supercede	動詞
55	**substitute**	5	[ˋsʌbstəˌtjut]	代替; 替換 同義詞 replace	動詞
56	**retrieve**	12	[rɪˋtriv]	取回; 檢索; 挽回; 恢復 同義詞 recover, regain, recoup, repossess	動詞
57	**contract**	9	[kənˋtrækt]	訂契約; 承辦; 收縮 反義詞 annul 廢除	動詞
58	**separation**	1	[ˌsɛpəˋreʃən]	分離; 分開; 分居; 間隔 同義詞 divorcement, parting, disunion	名詞
59	**allergic**	3	[əˋlɝdʒɪk]	過敏的; 對...有過敏反應	形容詞
60	**private**	16	[ˋpraɪvɪt]	私人的; 祕密的; 非公開的; 私營的 同義詞 personal, individual, confidential 反義詞 public 公共的, 公用的	形容詞
61	**assessment**	1	[əˋsɛsmənt]	估價; 評價; 估計	名詞
62	**adjust**	10	[əˋdʒʌst]	調節; 校正; 解決; 適應 同義詞 adapt 反義詞 disturb 擾亂, 搞亂	名詞
63	**feature**	27	[fitʃɚ]	特色, 特徵; 面貌; 特寫 同義詞 characteristic, trait	名詞
64	**formality**	1	[fɔrˋmælətɪ]	禮節; 拘謹, 拘泥形式; 正式手續 同義詞 strictness, punctilio, precision	名詞
65	**overcharge**	3	[ˋovɚˋtʃɑrdʒ]	索價過高; 過度充電; 誇張	動詞

▶ 4-114

	單字	出現	音標	中文	詞性
66	**heritage**	15	[`hɛrətɪdʒ]	遺產; 遺留物; 傳統; 命運	名詞
67	**attraction**	18	[ə`trækʃən]	有吸引力的地方; 吸引力	名詞
68	**virtual**	12	[`vɝtʃʊəl]	虛擬的; 事實上的, 實際上的	形容詞
69	**adapt**	1	[ə`dæpt]	適應; 改編; 改造 同義詞 adjust 反義詞 unfit 使不相宜	動詞
70	**receipt**	10	[rɪ`sit]	收據; 收到; 收入 同義詞 voucher, quittance	名詞
71	**recipe**	15	[`rɛsəpɪ]	食譜; 處方; 烹飪法; 訣竅	名詞
72	**reception**	9	[rɪ`sɛpʃən]	接待; 歡迎; 宴會; 接受	名詞
73	**recommend**	13	[ˌrɛkə`mɛnd]	推薦, 介紹; 建議, 勸告 同義詞 advise, suggest	動詞
74	**secure**	4	[sɪ`kjʊr]	繫牢; 關緊; 保護; 獲得 同義詞 fasten, fix	動詞
75	**raise**	11	[rez]	抬起; 增加; 養育; 提出 同義詞 lift, elevate, boost 反義詞 lower 放下, 降下	動詞
76	**measure**	5	[`mɛʒɚ]	測量; 打量; 估量; 酌量 同義詞 appraise, estimate	動詞
77	**influence**	4	[`ɪnflʊəns]	影響, 作用; 權勢	名詞
78	**border**	3	[`bɔrdɚ]	邊界, 國界; 邊緣 同義詞 frontier, boundary, borderland	名詞
79	**exchange**	24	[ɪks`tʃendʒ]	匯率; 兌換; 交易; 交戰 同義詞 change, interchange, swap	名詞
80	**disturb**	2	[dɪs`tɝb]	打擾, 妨礙; 擾亂; 使心神不寧 同義詞 upset, perturb, disarrange, interfere	動詞
81	**direction**	7	[də`rɛkʃən]	指示; 方向; 領域; 指揮 同義詞 way, course, orientation	名詞
82	**prescription**	5	[prɪ`skrɪpʃən]	處方, 藥方; 指示; 慣例 同義詞 recipe	名詞

	單字	出現	音標	中文	詞性
83	**prediction**	5	[prɪ`dɪkʃən]	預測; 預言; 預報 同義詞 prophecy, forecast, vaticination	名詞
84	**resource**	21	[rɪ`sors]	資源; 財力; 對策; 機智 同義詞 property, wealth	名詞
85	**destroy**	4	[dɪ`strɔɪ]	破壞, 毀壞; 消滅; 打破(希望, 計畫)	動詞
86	**sustain**	2	[sə`sten]	維持; 支援; 支撐; 承受 同義詞 bear, support	動詞
87	**philosophy**	1	[fə`lɑsəfɪ]	哲理; 原理; 哲學; 人生觀	名詞
88	**consumption**	9	[kən`sʌmpʃən]	消費; 消耗; 用盡; 憔悴 同義詞 expenditure, depletion 反義詞 production 生產; 製作	
89	**cuisine**	28	[kwɪ`zin]	菜餚; 烹飪; 烹調法	名詞
90	**determinate**	1	[dɪ`tɝmənɪt]	確定的; 有限的; 決定的	形容詞
91	**renovation**	3	[ˌrɛnə`veʃən]	翻新; 更新; 修理; 恢復活力	名詞
92	**construct**	7	[kən`strʌkt]	建造; 創立; 製造; 構思	動詞
93	**decision**	4	[dɪ`sɪʒən]	決定; 判斷; 結論; 果斷 同義詞 resolution, determination 反義詞 hesitation 躊躇, 猶豫	名詞
94	**collection**	12	[kə`lɛkʃən]	收藏品; 收集; 募捐; 聚集	名詞
95	**propose**	10	[prə`poz]	提出, 提議; 推薦; 計畫; 求婚 同義詞 recommend, proffer	動詞
96	**function**	6	[`fʌŋkʃən]	功能; 職務, 職責; 盛大的集會	名詞
97	**negative**	7	[`nɛgətɪv]	負面的; 消極的; 否定的; 陰性的 反義詞 positive 積極的	形容詞
98	**competition**	9	[ˌkɑmpə`tɪʃən]	競爭; 比賽; 競爭者 同義詞 match, tournament	名詞
99	**compute**	1	[kəm`pjut]	計算; 估算; 推斷	名詞
100	**treasure**	6	[`trɛʒɚ]	珍藏, 財富; 貴重物品 同義詞 wealth, fortune, resources	名詞

110年領隊筆試測驗

●本書採用英語邏輯思維[中譯]
幫助更快看懂句子，拆解字義

題型	單字 53	片語 7	對話 7	情境	景物 3	餐飲 9	住宿 4	交通 3	機場 11
分析	文法 3	閱測 10		命題	生活 24	民俗 0	產業 4	職能 3	購物 9

單選題［共80題，每題1.25分］

( ) 1. Guest: My friend has just fallen over and cut his leg badly. It is Ms. Lin from room 510.
Clerk: ________
(A)That's right, ma'am. I hope you will have a good rest.
(B)I'm afraid we do not have any ambulance.
(C)Someone will get the first aid **equipment**[1] and come straight up immediately. Don't move him.
(D)Can you call a doctor? 生活 對話

[中譯] 客人：我的朋友剛剛摔倒並嚴重割傷了腿。是510房的林女士。
服務員：有人會拿急救設備並馬上來。不要移動他。
(A)是的，夫人。希望您休息愉快。 (B)我們恐怕沒有救護車。
(C)有人會拿急救設備並馬上來。不要移動他。 (D)你能叫醫生嗎？
答 C

( ) 2. Susan Lee is a sales **manager**[2] at a travel **agency**[3]. It specializes in selling flight tickets, hotel **reservation**[4], and tours ________.
(A)**aboard**[5] (B)**abroad**[6] (C)board (D)broad 產業 單字

[中譯] Susan Lee是一家旅行社的銷售經理。專門從事機票銷售、飯店預訂和國外旅遊。
(A)在(船、車、飛機)上 (B)在國外 (C) 搭乘(船、車、飛機) (D)寬廣的
答 B

( ) 3. Tom: Do not go into it for money. The most ________ **aspect**[7] of my job is that I go to different places and talk about my own travel experiences.
(A)anxious (B)incomplete (C)**rewarding**[8] (D)**suggestive**[9] 生活 單字

[中譯] Tom：不要為了錢而做。我工作中最有成就感的方面，就是到不同地方談論自己的旅遊經歷。
(A)焦慮的 (B)不完整的 (C)有成就的 (D)引起聯想的
答 C

( ) 4. If the tobacco products we bring exceed the travelers' ________, we may have to pay **customs**[10] duties and other **charges**[11].
(A)**allowance**[12] (B)budget (C)payment (D)**expectation**[13] 機場 單字

[中譯] 如果我們攜帶的煙草產品超過旅客限額，可能需要支付關稅和其他費用。
(A)限額 (B)預算 (C)支付全額 (D)預期
答 A

( ) 5. Clerk: Your suitcase is a bit heavy. You'll need to pay for an excess baggage fee.
Passenger: Oh. What's the weight ________ ?
(A)**limit**[14] (B)limitation (C)limited (D)limiting 機場 文法

[中譯] 服務員：您的手提箱有點重。您需要支付超重行李費。　乘客：哦。重量限制是多少？
(A)(B)(C)(D)限制　解 P2-24. 文法39　答 AB

(　　) 6. Clerk: Good afternoon, Miss. Your flight on next Monday has been ________.
You need to be at the airport by 10:00.
(A)repeated (B)**confirmed**[15] (C)**relocated**[16] (D)ordered　機場 單字

[中譯] 服務員：小姐，午安，您下週一的航班已經確認。您需要在10:00之前抵達機場。
(A)重複 (B)確認 (C)重新安置 (D)訂購　答 B

(　　) 7. Yosemite National Park, Yellowstone National Park, and Central Park all are on the top ________ **spots**[17] in USA.
(A)**sightseeing**[18] (B)**convention**[19] (C)gallery (D)**inhabitant**[20]　景物 單字

[中譯] 優勝美地國家公園、黃石國家公園和中央公園都是美國最熱門的觀光景點。
(A)觀光 (B)會議 (C)畫廊 (D)居民　答 A

(　　) 8. Our hotel is equipped with in-room ________, such as air-conditioning, hairdryer, Wi-Fi, iron and hypoallergenic bedding.
(A)**appointments**[21] (B)**facilities**[22] (C)entertainments (D)servants　住宿 單字

[中譯] 我們的飯店配備有室內設施，例如空調、吹風機、無線網絡、熨斗和低過敏原寢具。
(A)約會 (B)設施 (C)娛樂 (D)僕人　答 B

(　　) 9. Make the reservation early if you would like to attend next Tuesday's ________ on project **management**[23].
(A)**seminar**[24] (B)reason (C)**policy**[25] (D)**scene**[26]　生活 單字

[中譯] 如果您想參加下週二的方案管理研討會，請提前預約。
(A)研討會 (B)動機 (C)政策 (D)場面　答 A

(　　) 10. Ainokura cultural heritage largely **remains**[27] ________, creating an extraordinary atmosphere.
(A)unskilled (B)unrelated (C)**unspoiled**[28] (D)unspotted　景物 單字

[中譯] 相倉合掌村的文化遺產大體上未受破壞，營造出非凡的氛圍。
(A)不熟練的 (B)不相關的 (C)未受破壞的 (D)無瑕疵的　答 C

(　　) 11. Sharon: ________________
Front desk: Local calls and room to room calls are free of charge. **Domestic**[29] long distance calls are 3 dollars per minute. International calls are various depending on which country.　生活 對話
(A)How do you charge for each call? (B)Do you have Wi-Fi services?
(C)How can I pay for room services? (D)How can I get to the airport?

[中譯] Sharon：每次通話如何收費？
櫃台：撥打本地電話和客房間通話免費。國內長途電話每分鐘3美元。國際電話因國家而異。
(A)每次通話如何收費？(B)有Wi-Fi服務嗎？(C)如何支付客房服務費？(D)如何到機場？答 A

情境篇 文法篇 片語篇 測驗篇 口試篇

( ) 12. People often keep ______ animals as pets for fun. However, when pet owners **release**[30] these animals back into the wild, indigenous animals may be unable to compete.
(A)non-native (B)non-stop (C)non-stick (D)non-**union**[31] 生活 單字

[中譯] 人們經常把非原生動物當成寵物來娛樂。然而，當寵物主人將這些動物放回野外時，這些原生動物可能無法競爭。
(A)非原生 (B)直達的 (C)不粘的 (D)非工會的 答 A

( ) 13. Passenger: Could I have an aisle seat? I want to keep my guitar with me.
Check-in clerk: Oh, I'm sorry. The aisle should not be________ by any personal belonging.
(A)banned (B)blocked (C)backed (D)bridged 機場 單字

[中譯] 乘客：我可以坐靠走道的座位嗎？我想隨身帶著吉他。
櫃台專員：哦，很抱歉。走道不應被任何個人物品擋住。
(A)禁止 (B)阻擋 (C)支持 (D)橋接 答 B

( ) 14. Fresh herbs such as chives and parsley are essential **ingredients**[32] in the sauces that ________ most French savory dishes.
(A)**accompany**[33] (B)steam (C)**escort**[34] (D)follow 餐飲 單字

[中譯] 香蔥和歐芹等新鮮香草是大多數法式開胃菜醬汁中不可或缺的成分。
(A)伴隨 (B)蒸 (C)護送 (D)跟隨 答 A

( ) 15. To keep guests and employees safe, a hotel in Burbank ________ a thermal imaging and **fever**[35] detection system that can read body temperatures as guests and employees enter the hotel.
(A)**implemented**[36] (B)**implanted**[37] (C)lodged (D)planted 產業 單字

[中譯] 為確保客人和員工的安全，柏本克的一間飯店實施了一套紅外線熱影像和發燒檢測系統，它可以在客人和員工進入飯店時讀取體溫。
(A)實施 (B)植入 (C)嵌入 (D)栽種 答 A

( ) 16. Customer: I would like to return this shirt because it doesn't fit.
Clerk: I'm sorry. This shirt was on sale. We don't give a _____ if the item is on sale.
(A)**refund**[38] (B)reunion (C)request (D)reply 購物 單字

[中譯] 顧客：我想退回這件襯衫，因為它不合身。
服務員：很抱歉。這件襯衫是特價品。如果該商品正在特價，我們將不予退款。
(A)退款 (B)團聚 (C)要求 (D)回答 答 A

( ) 17. Traveler: I missed the connecting flight due to the weather. Can you rebook me on the next available flight? By the way, will the airline offer any ________ for meals or accommodations?
(A)**compliment**[39] (B)**companion**[40] (C)**compensation**[41] (D)**punishment**[42]

[中譯] 旅客：由於天氣因素，我錯過了轉機航班。您能為我重新預訂下一班有空位的航班嗎？順道一提，航空公司會提供餐食或住宿的任何補償嗎？
(A)稱讚 (B)同伴 (C)補償 (D)懲罰 機場 單字 答 C

( ) 18. A: Oh, my God! My passport is missing.
B: Calm down! Let us report it to the local police **authorities**[43] and contact the nearest Embassy. They can help us ________ your passport.
(A)**remind**[44] (B)**reissue**[45] (C)**represent**[46] (D)**reject**[47] 生活 單字

[中譯] A：哦，天哪！我的護照遺失了。
B：冷靜點！讓我們向當地警察機關報案並聯繫最近的大使館。他們可協助我們補發護照。
(A)提醒 (B)補發 (C)代表 (D)拒絕 答 B

( ) 19. Guest: I would like to check out, please.
Reception clerk: Sir, your credit card has been _____. Do you have another card?
(A)approved (B)**declined**[48] (C)**unexpired**[49] (D)**valued**[50] 住宿 單字

[中譯] 客人：我想退房。 接待員：先生，您的信用卡已被拒絕。您還有另一張卡嗎？
(A)批准 (B)拒絕 (C)未到期 (D)重視 答 B

( ) 20. ________ shopping is a kind of mental health disorder in which an individual cannot **resist**[51] the temptation to buy something, even if one does not need it.
(A)Comparable (B)Compatible (C)**Comprehensive**[52] (D)Compulsive

[中譯] 強迫性購物是一種精神健康障礙，是指一個人即使沒有需求，也無法抵抗購物的誘惑。
(A)可比較的 (B)相容的 (C)廣泛的 (D)強迫的 生活 單字 答 D

( ) 21. Angela: Don't I get a discount? That sign on the wall says 20 percent off on all purchases.
Clerk:________
(A)It is a good offer. (B)Yes, but the discount doesn't apply to sales items.
(C)Yes, buy one get one free. (D)They will go on sale soon. 購物 對話

[中譯] Angela：我沒有折扣嗎？牆上的標語顯示所有購買可享20%折扣。
服務員：是的，但折扣不適用於特價品。
(A)這是一個很好的折扣。 (B)是的，但折扣不適用於特價品。
(C)是的，買一送一。 (D)他們將很快就會開始特價。 答 B

( ) 22. Guest: I'd like to make an international call to Taiwan.
Operator: Certainly, sir. Is this a paid call?
Guest: ________
(A)It is a collect call.
(B)The phone number is 2-234-5678.
(C)It is a confirmation call.
(D)The country code is 886 plus area code is 2, and the number is 234-5678.

[中譯] 客人：我想打國際電話到台灣。　接線員：當然，先生。這是付費電話嗎？
客人：這是一個對方付費電話。
(A)這是一個對方付費電話。　(B)電話號碼是2-234-5678。　生活 對話
(C)這是一個確認電話。　(D)國家代碼為886，加區號2，電話號碼為234-5678。　答 A

( ) 23. Wearing seat belts is ________ in all vehicles for drivers globally.
(A)voluntary (B)mandatory (C)impermanent (D)momentary

[中譯] 全球所有車輛的駕駛員都強制佩戴安全帶。
(A)自願的 (B)強制的 (C)暫時的 (D)瞬間的　交通 單字　答 B

( ) 24. A: Excuse me. Can you tell me how to take the subway to the museum?
B: You can take the green line to Harrington stop and ________ to the orange line. Get out at Central Park and take the museum exit.
(A)**switch**[53] (B)**replace**[54] (C)**substitute**[55] (D)remove　交通 單字

[中譯] A：打擾一下。你能告訴我如何搭地鐵到博物館嗎？
B：你可搭乘綠線到哈靈頓站，換乘橙線。在中央公園站下車，然後從博物館的出口出來。
(A)轉移 (B)取代 (C)代替 (D)消除　答 A

( ) 25. It's pretty hot today. Would you mind ________ the air conditioning a little?
(A)turning down (B)turning in (C)turning off (D)turning up　生活 片語

[中譯] 今天很熱。你介意將空調開大一點嗎？
(A)調低 (B)遞交；就寢 (C)關掉 (D)開大　答 D

( ) 26. Guest: I would like to make a reservation for the bus tour tomorrow.
Travel agent: Oh, I'm sorry, sir. We just ________ the last seats on that one.
(A)booked (B)bought (C)**retrieved**[56] (D)**contracted**[57]　產業 單字

[中譯] 客人：我想預定明天的巴士觀光行程。
旅行社：哦，很抱歉，先生。我們剛剛已預訂了最後一個座位。
(A)預訂 (B)購買 (C)取回 (D)簽約　答 A

( ) 27. ABC Duty Free is the best place for duty free shopping. The prices are generally better than other duty free places, and it has got a big ________, too.
(A)entity (B)selection (C)**separation**[58] (D)unit　購物 單字

[中譯] ABC免稅店是免稅購物最好的地方。價格通常比其他免稅店好，選擇也很多。
(A)實體 (B)選擇 (C)分離 (D)單位　答 B

( ) 28. Guest: I will have a grilled chicken sandwich. Does that ________ with anything?
Waiter: Yes, it includes French fries and a soup.
(A)collect (B)come (C)compare (D)connect　餐飲 單字

[中譯] 客人：我要一個烤雞肉三明治。它有附餐嗎？　服務員：是的，它包含炸薯條和湯。
(A)收集 (B)產生 (C)比較 (D)連接　答 B

(　　) 29. I am **allergic**[59] to milk products. Would it be possible to request a ________ meal?
(A)meat (B)non-dairy (C)vegan (D)vegetarian 餐飲 單字

[中譯] 我對奶製品過敏。是否可以要求非乳製品/嚴格素食餐？
(A)葷食 (B)非乳製品 (C)嚴格素食 (D)素食的 答 B.C

(　　) 30. Singapore is well known for its strict laws. Graffiti on both public and **private**[60] properties can receive ________ ranging from fines, jail, to caning.
(A)**assessments**[61] (B)quotas (C)opportunities (D)punishments 生活 單字

[中譯] 新加坡以嚴格的法律聞名。在公共和私人財產上塗鴉都會受到從罰款、監禁到鞭刑的懲罰。
(A)估價 (B)配額 (C)機會 (D)懲罰 答 D

補 range from ... to ...　在從...到...的範圍內變化

(　　) 31. To provide a disabled-friendly lodging environment, the ________ of a guest room for people in a wheelchair include lower cloth rails, an **adjust**able[62] bed, a shower chair, and a raised toilet.
(A)signs (B)capacities (C)**features**[63] (D)**formalities**[64] 產業 單字

[中譯] 為提供無障礙住宿環境，提供輪椅客人入住的客房特色包含較低的掛衣桿、可調整的床、淋浴椅和可升高的馬桶座。
(A)標誌 (B)能力 (C)特色 (D)禮節；正式 答 C

(　　) 32. I would like a seafood fried rice. Please make it to ________.
(A)eat (B)get (C)take (D)take away 餐飲 片語

[中譯] 我要一份海鮮炒飯。請把它做成外帶。
(A)吃 (B)拿 (C)拿 (D)外帶 答 D

(　　) 33. Waitress: You order one Farmer's Breakfast. How would you like your eggs?
Guest: ________
(A)I like them very much. (B)Over-easy. (C)Not at all. (D)Medium. 餐飲 片語

[中譯] 服務員：您點了一份農夫早餐。您想要什麼樣的蛋作法？
客人：半熟荷包蛋。
(A)我非常喜歡他們 (B)半熟荷包蛋 (C)一點也不 (D)中等 答 B

(　　) 34. Guest: This is room 221. The air conditioning and recessed light are not working. They do not even turn on.
Clerk: Sir, to turn on the electricity in the room you need to place the key card in the ________ next to the door.
(A)hole (B)nook (C)switch (D)socket 住宿 單字

[中譯] 客人：這是221號房間。空調和嵌燈故障。它們甚至沒有啟動。
服務員：先生，要打開房間的電源，您需要將鑰匙卡放在門旁邊的插槽中。
(A)孔 (B)角落 (C)開關 (D)插座 答 C.D

( ) 35. Guest: We have waited over at least 30 minutes. Please tell the kitchen to speed it up.
....
Waitress: Here is your meal, sir. We are truly sorry for the delay. We would like to offer you a/an ________ drink.
(A)approving (B)apologetic (C)complimentary (D)friendly 餐飲 單字

[中譯] 客人：我們已經等了至少30分鐘。請告訴廚房加快速度。
服務員：先生，這是您的餐點。對於延遲我們深表歉意。我們為您提供一杯免費贈送的飲料。
(A)贊成的 (B)道歉的 (C)免費贈送的 (D)友好的 答 C

( ) 36. I only bought a pair of blue jeans at US$20, but here it says US$40. You seem to have ________ me.
(A)overburdened (B)**overcharged**[65] (C)overfilled (D)overloaded 購物 單字

[中譯] 我只花了20美元買一條藍色牛仔褲，但這裡顯示的是40美元。你似乎多收了我的錢。
(A)使裝載過多 (B)對...索價過高 (C)把...裝得太滿 (D)使超載 答 B

( ) 37. There are three flights available on August 10. Do you have a ________ for a particular airline?
(A)product (B)performance (C)problem (D)preference 機場 單字

[中譯] 8月10日有三個航班可訂位。您是否對特定航空公司有偏好？
(A)產品 (B)演出 (C)問題 (D)偏好 答 D

( ) 38. Technology allows people to go on ________ tours on their computers to see museums, world **heritage**[66] sites, and other **attractions**[67] before they plan a trip.
(A)various (B)vehicular (C)visionary (D)**virtual**[68] 生活 單字

[中譯] 科技允許人們在電腦上進行虛擬遊覽，在計劃旅行前先參觀博物館、世界遺產和其他景點。
(A)不同的 (B)汽車的 (C)幻覺的 (D)虛擬的 答 D

( ) 39. In the last decade, online shopping has experienced an explosive growth due to the fact it represents a more economic and convenient approach to purchasing in ________ to traditional shopping.
(A)**adaption**[69] (B)comparison (C)addition (D)communication 購物 片語

[中譯] 在過去的十年中，線上購物歷經了爆炸性的成長，這是因為與傳統購物相比，線上購物代表了一種更經濟、便捷的購物方式。
(A)適應 (B)比較 (C)附加 (D)交流 答 B
補 in comparison to 將...比喻為...；in comparison with 將...和...做比較

( ) 40. Emily: I would like to claim a tax refund.
Clerk: Sure, please have a seat. You need to fill in this application form and also provide me all ________ that you need to refund, and a 5% fee will be charged from the total amount.
(A)**receipts**[70] (B)**recipes**[71] (C)**reception**[72] (D)recreation 購物 單字

[中譯] Emily：我想申請退稅。

服務員：好的，請坐。您需要填寫此申請表，並提供給我您需要退稅的所有收據，5%的費用將會從退款總金額中收取。

(A)收據 (B)食譜 (C)接待 (D)娛樂 答 A

( ) 41. Lisa: ________

Hotel clerk: You can go to the 15th floor where our gym is and as long as you have running shoes with you, you can use all of our equipment with no extra charge.

(A)How would you like your room? (B)Do you want a non-smoking room?
(C)We offer various kinds of breakfast. (D)Do you have any exercise facilities?

[中譯] Lisa：你們有任何運動設施嗎？

職員：您可以去15樓是我們的健身房，只要您自備運動鞋，可以免費使用我們所有的設備。

(A)您想要什麼樣的房間？ (B)您要禁煙房嗎？
(C)我們提供各式早餐。 (D)您們有任何運動設施嗎？ 住宿 片語 答 D

( ) 42. Mary: I love seafood. What would you **recommend**[73] me to order?

Attendant: ________

(A)You will love to have an ice cream. (B)How about our signature house steak?
(C)Mojito. (D)Oyster Omelet. 餐飲 片語

[中譯] Mary：我喜歡海鮮。您會推薦我點什麼？ 服務員：蚵仔煎。

(A)你會喜歡吃冰淇淋的 (B)我們的招牌牛排如何？ (C)莫希托(雞尾酒) (D)蚵仔煎 答 D

( ) 43. Captain: Good afternoon, passengers. This is your captain speaking. First, I'd like to welcome everyone on Rightwing flight 86A. We are currently ________ at an altitude of 3,300 feet at an airspeed of 400 miles per hour.

(A)cruising (B)sailing (C)running (D)moving 交通 單字

[中譯] 機長：午安，乘客們。這是機長廣播。首先，歡迎大家搭乘Rightwing 86A班機。我們目前正巡航在3,300英尺的高度，以每小時400英哩速度前進。

(A)巡航 (B)航行(在海上) (C)行駛 (D)移動 答 A

( ) 44. Clerk: This is the final boarding call for John and Mary Smith booked on flight 321C to Salt Lake City. Please ________ to gate 3 immediately.

(A)sign (B)select (C)produce (D)proceed 機場 單字

[中譯] 服務員：這是最後登機廣播，預訂前往鹽湖城321C班機旅客John和Mary Smith，請立即前往3號登機口。

(A)簽名 (B)選擇 (C)生產 (D)前往 答 D

( ) 45. Captain: We are going to take off. Please fasten your seatbelt at this time and ________ all baggage underneath your seat or in the overhead compartment.

(A)take (B)replace (C)**secure**[74] (D)buy 職能 單字

[中譯] 機長：我們即將起飛。請即刻繫好您的安全帶，並將所有行李固定在您的座位下方或頭頂行李艙中。
(A)取走 (B)取代 (C)固定 (D)購買 答 C

( ) 46. Flight attendants can help travelers with young kids to ________ earlier for their convenience.
(A)board (B)leave (C)sleep (D)eat 職能 單字

[中譯] 空服員可以協助攜帶小孩的旅客提前登機，以方便他們。
(A)登(船、車、飛機) (B)離開 (C)睡覺 (D)吃 答 A

( ) 47. Traveler: May I pay by new Taiwan dollar here? Clerk: ________ 購物 對話
(A)Sorry, we only take US dollar. (B)How would you like the shirt?
(C)Would you like to try it on? (D)Hopefully, you would come again.

[中譯] 旅客：可以用新台幣支付嗎？ 服務員：很抱歉，我們只收美元。
(A)很抱歉，我們只收美元。 (B)您想要這件襯衫怎麼樣？
(C)您想試試嗎？ (D)希望您還會再來。 答 A

( ) 48. Traveler: Excuse me, I need some hot water to make the milk for my baby.
Flight attendant: ________ 職能 對話
(A)Yes, I can give you a blanket. (B)Sure, I can fill the bottle for you.
(C)Yes, I can take you to the toilet. (D)Sure, you can get off the plane.

[中譯] 旅客：打擾了，我需要一些熱水為寶寶泡牛奶。
空服員：當然，我可以為您裝滿瓶子。
(A)好的，我可以給您一條毯子。 (B)當然，我可以為您裝滿瓶子。
(C)好的，我可以帶您去廁所。 (D)當然，您可以下飛機了。 答 B

( ) 49. Traveler: May I have a local map? Receptionist: ________
(A)Sure, here is the menu. (B)Sure, here you go.
(C)Yes, here is a paper. (D)Yes, there is the cup. 生活 對話

[中譯] 旅客：可以給我一張當地地圖嗎？ 接待員：當然，給您。
(A)當然，這是菜單。 (B)當然，給您。 (C)是的，這兒有紙。 (D)是的，那兒有杯子。答 B

( ) 50. I am having a headache. Do you have any ________ to ease the uncomfortable feeling?
(A)painkiller (B)coke (C)hot soup (D)soy sauce 生活 單字

[中譯] 我頭疼。請問有沒有止痛藥可以緩解不適？
(A)止痛藥 (B)可樂 (C)熱湯 (D)醬油 答 A

( ) 51. Jean always puts ________ on to keep her hands away from water when she washes the dishes.
(A)jackets (B)rings (C)socks (D)gloves 生活 單字

[中譯] Jean在洗碗時總是戴上手套以防止雙手接觸水。
(A)外套 (B)戒指 (C)襪子 (D)手套 答 D

( ) 52. Can you ________ your feet a little off the floor? I want to clean the floor under the table.
(A)**raise**[75] (B)check (C)kick (D)show 生活 單字

[中譯] 你能把腳抬高稍微離地嗎？我想清潔桌子下面的地板。
(A)提高 (B)檢查 (C)踢 (D)露出 答 A

( ) 53. The beach near our hotel is a very ________ place. Every summer at least one kid is killed there in the water.
(A)popular (B)exciting (C)dangerous (D)happy 生活 單字

[中譯] 我們飯店附近的海灘是一個非常危險的地方。每年夏天至少有一個孩子在水中溺斃。
(A)受歡迎的 (B)令人興奮的 (C)危險的 (D)高興的 答 C

( ) 54. I just brought back some pineapple cakes from Taiwan. Do you want to try some? Please ________. 餐飲 片語
(A)behave yourself (B)help yourself (C)watch yourself (D)love yourself

[中譯] 我剛從台灣帶回來一些鳳梨酥。你想嚐嚐嗎？請自便。
(A)表現良好 (B)請自便；自取 (C)觀察自己 (D)愛自己 答 B

( ) 55. It's great that we can buy flight tickets via both phone and internet without calling the travel agents. It ________ us a lot of time.
(A)lends (B)prepares (C)saves (D)takes 購物 單字

[中譯] 很高興我們可以透過電話和網路購買機票，而無需致電旅行社。這為我們節省了很多時間。
(A)給予 (B)準備 (C)節省 (D)取走 答 C

( ) 56. Jonny has planned to make a trip to Houston and visits some popular ________ attractions.
(A)tourist (B)seeing (C)sight (D)park 景物 單字

[中譯] Jonny計劃去休斯頓旅行，並參觀一些受歡迎的觀光景點。
(A)觀光的 (B)看見的 (C)景象 (D)公園 答 A

( ) 57. For Jean, the price is ________ important thing when she shops for jeans. She cares even more about the shape and the size of pockets.
(A)the more (B)the most (C)the less (D)the least 購物 文法

[中譯] 對Jean來說，價格是她購買牛仔褲時最不重要的事。她更在乎牛仔褲的造型和口袋的大小。
(A)更加 (B)最多(最重要的) (C)較小 (D)最少(最不重要的) 解 P2-45. 文法74 答 D

( ) 58. Clerk: Your luggage seems ________. I will suggest you to find a scale to **measure**[76] its weight.
(A)overweight (B)overpriced (C)too colorful (D)too shiny 機場 單字

[中譯] 服務員：你的行李箱似乎超重了。我建議您找一個秤來測量它的重量。
(A)超重 (B)價格過高 (C)太繽紛了 (D)太閃亮了 答 A

( ) 59. Alice has learned from the news that ________ cannot enter Taiwan because of the COVID-19.
(A)foreigners (B)locals (C)idiots (D)humans 生活 單字

[中譯] Alice從新聞中獲悉，由於COVID-19，外國人無法進入台灣。
(A)外國人 (B)當地人 (C)極蠢的人 (D)人類 答 A

( ) 60. Due to the COVID-19, now everyone who takes the public transportation is required to wear a ________.
(A)hat (B)jacket (C)glove (D)mask 生活 單字

[中譯] 由於COVID-19，現在乘坐公共運輸的每個人都必須戴口罩。
(A)帽子 (B)外套 (C)手套 (D)口罩 答 D

( ) 61. Due to the **influences**[77] of the COVID-19, our ________ has been closed since last March.
(A)**border**[78] (B)boundary (C)bucket (D)budget 生活 單字

[中譯] 受到COVID-19的影響，自去年三月以來，我們的邊界已關閉。
(A)(政治或行政上)邊界 (B)一個地區(地理上)或區域的邊界 (C)水桶 (D)預算 答 A.B

( ) 62. Cathy: ________ your trip in Japan, Jerry? Jerry: I really enjoyed it.
(A)How's (B)What's (C)When is (D)Which is 生活 文法

[中譯] Cathy：Jerry，你的日本之旅如何？ Jerry：我真的很喜歡。
(A)如何 (B)什麼是 (C)什麼時候 (D)哪一個是 解 P2-39. 文法60 答 A

( ) 63. What's the ________ rate for US dollar? I have heard that it's a good time to buy US dollar.
(A)**exchange**[79] (B)buying (C)purchasing (D)change 生活 單字

[中譯] 美元的匯率是多少？我聽說現在是買入美元的好時機。
(A)匯率 (B)購買 (C)購買 (D)變更 答 A

( ) 64. Clerk: It's going to be a long flight. What is your preference for seat option?
Traveler: I don't like to be **disturbed**[80] so I prefer a/an ________ seat.
(A)aisle (B)window (C)middle (D)median 機場 單字

[中譯] 服務員：這將是一段長途飛行。您對於座位選擇的偏好是什麼？
旅客：我不喜歡被打擾，所以我更喜歡靠窗的座位。
(A)走道 (B)窗戶 (C)中間 (D)中央的 答 B

( ) 65. Passenger: I need to fly to the destination at the shortest time. Please help me find the best flight.
Clerk: Okay, I will arrange a ________ flight with no stop for you but it will cost more. Is that okay for you?
(A)connecting (B)indirect (C)direct (D)transfer 機場 單字

[中譯] 乘客：我需要在最短的時間內飛往目的地。請幫我找到最好的航班。
服務員：好的，我會為您安排直達的航班，中途沒有停靠，但費用會更高。這樣可以嗎?
(A)中轉的 (B)間接的 (C)直達的 (D)轉換 答 C

( ) 66. The medical service is very different from Taiwan to the US. In the US, you need a ________ to buy contact lenses.
(A)**direction**[81] (B)reception (C)**prescription**[82] (D)**prediction**[83] 生活 單字

[中譯] 台灣和美國的醫療服務有很大的不同。在美國，你需要處方才能購買隱形眼鏡。
(A)方向 (B)接待 (C)處方 (D)預測 答 C

( ) 67. When going through the security check, you need to ________ your water bottle.
(A)refill (B)empty (C)throw (D)give 機場 單字

[中譯] 通過安全檢查時，您需要倒空水瓶。
(A)再裝滿 (B)倒空 (C)扔 (D)給出 答 B

( ) 68. The weather is going to be really ________, so I don't think you should take a heavy coat on your trip.
(A)clear but windy (B)cold but dry (C)cool and wet (D)hot and sunny

[中譯] 天氣將會非常炎熱和晴朗，所以我不認為您在旅途中應該攜帶厚外套。
(A)晴朗但有風 (B)寒冷但乾燥 (C)涼爽和潮濕 (D)炎熱和晴朗 生活 單字 答 D

( ) 69. Waiter: Would you like a cup of coffee?
Customer: No, thanks. I ________ drink coffee. Coffee hurts my stomach.
(A)almost (B)already (C)seldom (D)still 餐飲 單字

[中譯] 服務員：您要來杯咖啡嗎？ 顧客：不，謝謝。 我很少喝咖啡。 咖啡傷胃。
(A)幾乎 (B)已經 (C)很少 (D)仍然 答 C

( ) 70. John: You really like the afternoon tea at Paul's, right?
Sharon: Sure, I love it. What are their afternoon tea hours in Taichung?
John: The afternoon tea hours run from 2 pm to 4 pm.
Sharon: Ok, I will call and make a reservation at ________ for next Monday.
(A)11 am (B)3 pm (C)5 pm (D)8 am 生活 單字

[中譯] John：您很喜歡Paul下午茶，對吧？ Sharon：當然，我很喜歡。它在台中的下午茶時間是？
John：下午茶時間從下午2點至下午4點。 Sharon：好的，我會打電話預定下週一下午3點。
(A)上午11點 (B)下午3點 (C)下午5點 (D)上午8點 答 B

閱讀測驗一

Tourism represents an important source of income. Most **resource**[84]-poor countries, therefore, cannot afford to neglect the economic opportunities tourism offers. However, tourism often ends up **destroying**[85] the landscape and culture that attracted visitors in the first place. Low-impact tourism is **sustainable**[86] travel and leisure activities that directly benefit local communities. The society and culture and environment of the people who live in the tourist destinations are not damaged or destroyed either.

Unfortunately, the environmental impacts of tourism can be **devastating** when profit takes precedence. As a result, it heavily depends on individuals travel responsibly as a "green tourist". Being a green tourist starts eating out on trips with a **philosophy**[87] of "buy local, eat and drink local." Tourism expenditure within the destination can create induced benefits. Try not to go for the international fast-food chains, because most of the money from tourism may undergo leakage. Furthermore, food is an important part of the culture of a region, through its **consumption**[88] gaining in-depth knowledge about the local **cuisine**[89] and of the destination's culture. Choosing locally made souvenirs and presents is another area where the tourist can be either a help or a hindrance, but never buy anything that's made from an endangered species. Never pick any plants or flowers either.

However, sometimes tourists behave very poorly while traveling. Therefore, the key factor in minimizing damage through tourism is to keep tourist groups to a management size and manage their movements and behavior. In fact, some popular attractions have tourist group size limit. For example, La Boqueria, the most famous market in Barcelona worldwide, banned tourist groups of more than 15 people in 2015.

觀光業是重要的收入來源。因此，大多數資源匱乏的國家不能忽視觀光業提供的經濟機會。然而，觀光業往往破壞了吸引遊客的景觀和文化。低衝擊旅遊是永續旅遊和休閒活動，並使當地社區直接受益。而在旅遊地區居民的社會、文化和環境也不會受到損害或破壞。

不幸的是，以盈利為優先時，觀光業對環境的衝擊可能是毀滅性的。因此，它在很大程度上取決於個人旅行者擔當起“綠色旅人”的責任。做為綠色旅人，開始以“在地購買，在地飲食”的理念在旅途中就餐。在當地的旅遊擴張可以創造出衍生利益。盡量不要去國際連鎖速食店，因為來自觀光業大部分的錢可能會就此流失。此外，食物是一個地區文化的重要組成部分，其透過消費獲得對當地美食和在地文化的深入了解。選擇當地製作的紀念品和禮物也是遊客是否能幫助或成為妨害的另一面向，但切勿購買任何由瀕臨滅絕的物種製成的東西，也不要採摘任何植物或花卉。

然而，有時候遊客在旅行時行為偏差。因此，最大限度地減少觀光損害的關鍵因素是保持觀光團的人數控管，並管理其活動和行為。實際上，一些熱門的景點有觀光團人數的限制。例如，全球著名的巴塞羅那的La Boqueria市場，2015年就禁止超過15人以上的觀光團。

( ) 71. Which of the following is closest in meaning to "devastating"?
(A)destined (B)destructive (C)**determinate**[90] (D)striking

[中譯] 下列何者與"毀滅性"的意思最接近？
(A)註定的 (B)破壞的 (C)確定的 (D)引人注目的 答 B

( ) 72. Which of the following best explains "… most of the money from tourism may undergo leakage" in the second paragraph?
(A)Most of the money from tourism may leave the destination.
(B)Most of the money from tourism may come from the destination.
(C)Most of the money from tourism may be repatriated to the destination.
(D)Most of the money from tourism may recover from the destination.

[中譯] 下列哪一項最能解釋第二段中"......來自觀光業大部分的錢可能會流失"？
(A)來自觀光業多數的錢可能會離開當地。(B)來自觀光業多數的錢可能來自當地。
(C)來自觀光業多數的錢可能會返回當地。(D)來自觀光業多數的錢可能會從當地收回。答 A

( ) 73. According to the passage, which of the following statements is NOT true?
(A)Businesses use the term of low-impact tourism to appeal to travelers without actually having any environmentally responsible policies.
(B)Travellers are recommended to make conscious, deliberate choices that increase the positive impact of travel.
(C)Sourcing locally-produced products for restaurants and gift shops should be encouraged.
(D)Low-impact tourism sustains the well-being of the local people.

[中譯] 根據這篇文章，下列敘述何者不正確？
(A)企業使用低衝擊旅遊一詞來吸引旅行者，而實際上沒有任何對環境負責的政策。
(B)建議旅客做出有意識、慎重的選擇，以增加旅行的正面影響。
(C)積極鼓勵採購當地餐館和禮品店生產的產品。
(D)低衝擊旅遊可維持當地人民的福祉。 答 A

( ) 74. Which of the following can be inferred from the second paragraph?
(A)Local food is the best way to taste the culinary culture of the destination.
(B)Food preparation and related services contribute substantially to tourism employment.
(C)Quality of taste is a primary motivational factor by visitors to consume local food during their trips.
(D)Local food could be a great medium for differentiating destinations and attract tightly scheduled travelers.

[中譯] 從第二段可以推斷出下列哪一項？
(A)當地美食是品嚐在地烹飪文化的最佳途徑。
(B)準備餐食和相關服務對觀光業的就業做出了重大貢獻。
(C)口味質量是遊客在旅途中消費當地食物的主要動機因素。
(D)當地美食可以成為在地鑑別度的絕佳媒介，並吸引時間緊迫的旅行者。 答 A

( ) 75. According to the passage, what "key factor" minimizes damage?
(A)Keeping tourists in one place as long as they can.
(B)Restricting access to sites of interest.
(C)Keeping groups to a manageable size and controlling their behavior.
(D)Making sure tourism does not impinge on local ways of life too much.

[中譯] 根據這篇文章，什麼"關鍵因素"可以最大程度地減少損害？
(A)盡可能將旅客留在一個地方。 (B)限制使用能引起興趣的網站。
(C)維持團體人數和活動行為管控。 (D)確保觀光業不會過多地影響當地的生活方式。 答 C

閱讀測驗二

The **renovation**[91] project of the Louvre signifies the possibility of harmony between modernity and history. Louvre, originally **constructed**[92] as a fortress, was the home of the kings of France until Louis XIV chose Versailles for his household, leaving the Louvre primarily as a home for artists and intellectuals. In the late 1800s, the Louvre was damaged in a fire. The fire entirely destroyed the interior of the palace, spreading to the museum next to it.

The **decision**[93] to turn the Louvre into a massive **repository** of the world's greatest fine art **collection**[94] was **proposed**[95] in 1981 by the French President François Mitterrand. However, the old royal palace was barely **functional**[96] as a museum. The challenge was in turning a historical building into a modern museum equipped to cater for a large ever-growing number of visitors. The architect Ieoh Ming Pei was named to design the Grand Louvre project. His proposal for a glass pyramid was extremely controversial. Many believed that this historic site was already "saturated with architectural styles…." Pei overcame the **negative**[97] response from officials and historians to his design.

Pei was convinced that, in addition to educating the public, with **competition**[98] from many other recreation businesses, museums needed to be attractive enough to make people want to spend the day there. The architecture must provide comfortable surroundings. Most importantly, a museum should not only be a place to see art but also should be an aesthetic experience in itself. Louvre's glass pyramid was once decried as an architectural "obscenity" but nowadays, it has become a cherished icon of the French capital, drawing over a million visitors every year.

羅浮宮的改造計畫意味著現代與歷史和諧並存的可能性。羅浮宮最初建造為一座堡壘，後來成為法國國王的住所，直到路易十四選擇凡爾賽宮作為居所後，將羅浮宮主要作為藝術家和知識分子之家。在1800年代後期，羅浮宮在一場大火中受損。大火完全摧毀了宮殿的內部，並波及旁邊的博物館。

法國總統弗朗索瓦•密特朗於1981年提議將羅浮宮變成世界上最大的藝術收藏品博物館。但是，古老的皇宮幾乎沒有能作為博物館的功用。所面臨的挑戰是將一座歷史建築變成一座現代化的博物館，以迎合不斷增長的大量遊客需求。建築師貝聿銘被任命設計羅浮宮這個大項目。他提出的玻璃金字塔提案極富爭議。許多人認為這個歷史遺跡已"充滿建築風格......"。貝聿銘克服了官員和歷史學家對他設計的負面回應。

貝聿銘深信，除了對大眾進行教育外，在與其他許多休閒活動競爭之下，博物館須要具備足夠的吸引力，以讓人們想在這裡度過一天。建築必須提供舒適的環境。最重要的是，博物館不應只是欣賞藝術的地方，更應是一種美感體驗。羅浮宮的玻璃金字塔曾被斥責為"建築上的巨大粗俗"，但如今，它已成為法國首都的珍愛標誌，每年吸引超過一百萬的遊客。

( ) 76. What is the passage mainly about?
(A)History of Louvre Museum.
(B)The most beautiful skyscrapers of the late 20th century.
(C)Modernity in harmony with a historical building.
(D)Failure of modernizing a historical setting.

[中譯] 這篇文章的主旨是什麼？
(A)羅浮宮博物館的歷史。 (B)20世紀後期最美麗的摩天大樓。
(C)現在性與歷史建築和諧並存。 (D)歷史性場景現代化的失敗。 答 C

( ) 77. What does the word "repository" mean?
(A)**computing**[99] (B)observatory (C)vessel (D)storehouse

[中譯] "儲藏室"一詞是什麼意思？
(A)計算 (B)天文台 (C)船隻 (D)倉庫 答 D

( ) 78. According to the passage, which of the following is NOT true about the Louvre?
(A)It is the world's largest museum.
(B)It was originally constructed as a fortress.
(C)The past Louvre as it used to be was successfully restored.
(D)The French people first opposed a change to the symbol of their national culture.

[中譯] 根據這篇文章，下列關於羅浮宮的敘述，何者不正確？
(A)它是世界上最大的博物館。 (B)它最初是被建造作為堡壘。
(C)昔日的羅浮宮曾經成功地修復。 (D)法國人民起初反對改變其民族文化的象徵。 答 A.C

( ) 79. What was the aim of the Grand Louvre project?
(A)To rediscover western art and Egyptian art.
(B)To safeguard the Louvre Museum and its collections.
(C)To use accessible digital tools to explore and reason about collection.
(D)To turn a historical building into a modern museum.

[中譯] 重大羅浮宮計畫的目標是什麼？
(A)重新發現西方藝術和埃及藝術。 (B)保護羅浮宮及其收藏品。
(C)使用有效的數據去探索和推理收藏品。 (D)將歷史建築變成現代化博物館。 答 D

( ) 80. What is the purpose of a museum according to I.M. Pei?
(A)To display its architectural style.
(B)To preserve and store national **treasures**[100].
(C)To entertain officials and historians.
(D)To educate the public and have aesthetic experiences.

[中譯] 在貝聿銘看來，博物館的目的是什麼？
(A)展示其建築風格。 (B)保存和收藏國寶。
(C)招待官員和歷史學家。 (D)教育大眾並獲得美感體驗。 答 D

Chapter. 07 | 測驗 | 111年度領隊試題

掌握關鍵單字，更快作答70%考題！

 重要單字彙整

	單字	出現	音標	中文	詞性
1	**shortcut**	1	[`ʃɔrt͵kʌt]	捷徑，近路	名詞
2	**proof**	2	[pruf]	證明；證據；物證 同義詞 evidence, verification	名詞
3	**verify**	4	[`vɛrə͵faɪ]	證實；核對，查實 同義詞 check, examine	動詞
4	**racial**	1	[`reʃəl]	種族的；種族之間的	形容詞
5	**ban**	8	[bæn]	禁止；禁令	名詞
6	**disable**	4	[dɪs`eb!]	失去能力；傷殘	動詞
7	**renew**	1	[rɪ`nju]	更新；恢復原狀；重新開始；繼續	動詞
8	**obstacle**	2	[`ɑbstək!]	障礙；妨礙 同義詞 obstruction, hitch, catch	名詞
9	**compete**	6	[kəm`pit]	競爭；比賽 同義詞 rival, contend, contest	動詞
10	**complement**	4	[`kɑmpləmənt]	互補；為...增色；補足	名詞
11	**compliment**	7	[`kɑmpləmənt]	讚美；致敬 同義詞 commend, praise 反義詞 insult 侮辱	名詞
12	**manners**	4	[`mænɚz]	禮儀；規矩；方式	名詞
13	**fare**	7	[fɛr]	票價，車費；乘客 同義詞 charge, toll, fee	名詞
14	**recommendation**	4	[͵rɛkəmɛn`deʃən]	推薦；介紹信 同義詞 reference, testimonial	名詞
15	**operation**	5	[͵ɑpə`reʃən]	運作，工作 同義詞 employment, utilization	名詞

	單字	出現	音標	中文	詞性
16	**transportation**	18	[ˌtrænspɚˋteʃən]	交通工具; 運送 同義詞 carrying, carriage	名詞
17	**accept**	19	[əkˋsɛpt]	接受; 同意; 認可 同義詞 adopt, believe, approve 反義詞 refuse 拒絕	動詞
18	**device**	12	[dɪˋvaɪs]	設備, 裝置; 手段 同義詞 machine, apparatus, tool	名詞
19	**pursue**	4	[pɚˋsu]	追求; 追趕; 追究 同義詞 chase, follow, seek	動詞
20	**issue**	15	[ˋɪʃʊ]	發行; 發表	動詞
21	**tag**	3	[tæg]	加上標籤; 標出	動詞
22	**redundant**	3	[rɪˋdʌndənt]	多餘的; 不需要的; 累贅的	形容詞
23	**dramatic**	3	[drəˋmætɪk]	戲劇性的; 充滿激情的 同義詞 theatrical, theatric, operatic	形容詞
24	**parallel**	2	[ˋpærəˌlɛl]	平行的; 相同的; 類似的 同義詞 coextensive, equidistant	形容詞
25	**public**	47	[ˋpʌblɪk]	公共的, 公用的; 公眾的 同義詞 people, populace, society 反義詞 private 私人的	形容詞
26	**decide**	13	[dɪˋsaɪd]	決定; 下決心 同義詞 settle, determine, resolve 反義詞 waver 猶豫不決	動詞
27	**describe**	8	[dɪˋskraɪb]	描述, 敘述; 形容 同義詞 define, characterize, portray	動詞
28	**deploy**	1	[dɪˋplɔɪ]	調動; 部署; 展開	動詞
29	**dispatch**	1	[dɪˋspætʃ]	派遣; 發送	動詞
30	**dismiss**	3	[dɪsˋmɪs]	解散; 解僱 同義詞 discharge, expel	動詞
31	**disconnect**	2	[ˌdɪskəˋnɛkt]	切斷; 斷開; 脫節 反義詞 connect 連接	動詞
32	**design**	17	[dɪˋzaɪn]	設計; 構思	動詞

▸ 4-134

	單字	出現	音標	中文	詞性
33	**disobey**	2	[ˌdɪsəˋbe]	不服從, 違抗; 違反 同義詞 defy, ignore, counter	動詞
34	**clarify**	1	[ˋklærəˌfaɪ]	澄清; 淨化 同義詞 explain, refine, simplify	動詞
35	**paralyze**	1	[ˋpærəˌlaɪz]	癱瘓; 麻痺; 喪失活動力 同義詞 deaden, numb, desensitize	動詞
36	**borrow**	2	[ˋbɑro]	借用, 借入 反義詞 loan 借出	動詞
37	**cost**	22	[kɔst]	付出; 代價; 損失 同義詞 loss, sacrifice, expense	名詞
38	**register**	5	[ˋrɛdʒɪstɚ]	註冊, 登記 同義詞 record, inscribe, enroll	名詞
39	**elect**	3	[ɪˋlɛkt]	選舉, 推選; 選擇 同義詞 choose, pick, appoint 反義詞 recall 罷免	動詞
40	**process**	20	[ˋprɑsɛs]	過程; 步驟 同義詞 operation, procedure, course	名詞
41	**species**	9	[ˋspiʃiz]	物種; 種類 同義詞 sort, type, variety	名詞
42	**designate**	5	[ˋdɛzɪgˌnet]	指定的, 選定的 同義詞 show, indicate, specify	形容詞
43	**diminish**	3	[dəˋmɪnɪʃ]	減少, 縮減; 削弱 同義詞 decrease, reduce, curtail 反義詞 increase 增大, raise 提升	形容詞
44	**book**	39	[bʊk]	預訂; 預約 同義詞 reserve	動詞
45	**bargain**	7	[ˋbɑrgɪn]	特價商品, 便宜貨	名詞
46	**express**	15	[ɪkˋsprɛs]	表達; 表示; 快遞	動詞
47	**explore**	14	[ɪkˋsplor]	調查; 探索; 探測 同義詞 search, research, examine	動詞
48	**exceed**	4	[ɪkˋsid]	超過; 超出 同義詞 better, excel, beat	動詞

	單字	出現	音標	中文	詞性
49	**extention**	2	[ɪks'tenʃn]	附名; 延伸	名詞
50	**transaction**	9	[træn`zækʃən]	交易; 買賣; 辦理	名詞
51	**declare**	3	[dɪ`klɛr]	申報; 宣告; 聲明 同義詞 state, assert, announce	動詞
52	**develop**	20	[dɪ`vɛləp]	發展; 展開; 成長 同義詞 grow, flourish, mature 反義詞 decay 衰敗	動詞
53	**procedure**	4	[prə`sidʒɚ]	程序; 手續; 常規 同義詞 process, course, measure	名詞
54	**validate**	11	[`vælə͵det]	使有效; 認可, 使生效 反義詞 invalidate 使無效	動詞
55	**decrease**	5	[dɪ`kris]	降低; 減少, 下降 同義詞 lessen, diminish, reduce 反義詞 increase 增加	動詞
56	**landing**	6	[`lændɪŋ]	登陸; 落地 同義詞 debarkation, disembarkation	名詞
57	**replacement**	3	[rɪ`plesmənt]	代替物; 代替者	名詞
58	**recipe**	16	[`rɛsəpɪ]	食譜; 烹飪法 同義詞 formula, instructions	名詞
59	**provide**	65	[prə`vaɪd]	提供; 供給 同義詞 supply, give, furnish 反義詞 consume 消耗	名詞
60	**landline**	1	[lænd.laɪn]	(電話的)固網; 地上通訊線	名詞
61	**transfer**	12	[træns`fɝ]	轉接; 轉換; 使換車	動詞
62	**transcend**	2	[træn`sɛnd]	超越; 優於	動詞
63	**transform**	13	[træns`fɔrm]	改變; 變換; 改造	動詞
64	**system**	23	[`sɪstəm]	系統; 制度, 體制	名詞
65	**symptom**	4	[`sɪmptəm]	症狀; 徵兆; 象徵 同義詞 indication, token, sign	名詞
66	**entry**	7	[`ɛntrɪ]	進入, 入場; 參加 同義詞 entrance, approach, access	名詞

	單字	出現	音標	中文	詞性
67	**expansion**	5	[ɪk`spænʃən]	擴大, 增加, 擴展 反義詞 contraction 收縮	名詞
68	**accommodation**	34	[ə͵kɑmə`deʃən]	住宿; 住處; 停留處	名詞
69	**safety**	11	[`seftɪ]	安全; 安全設施 同義詞 security, safeness 反義詞 unsafety 不安全	名詞
70	**brochure**	11	[bro`ʃʊr]	小冊子; 手冊 同義詞 booklet, leaflet, folder	名詞
71	**detection**	2	[dɪ`tɛkʃən]	偵查; 發現; 察覺 同義詞 discovery, find, perception	名詞
72	**detention**	2	[dɪ`tɛnʃən]	拘留; 滯留; 延遲	名詞
73	**relay**	1	[rɪ`le]	轉播; 傳達, 轉發 同義詞 carry, deliver, transfer	動詞
74	**restore**	4	[rɪ`stor]	恢復; 復原 同義詞 renovate, fix, repair	動詞
75	**shuttle**	8	[`ʃʌt!]	接駁車 同義詞 alternate, shuttlecock	名詞
76	**catalog**	4	[`kætələg]	目錄; 系列	名詞
77	**available**	28	[ə`veləb!]	可用的; 可獲得的; 可利用的 同義詞 handy, convenient 反義詞 unavailable 無法利用的	形容詞
78	**occupy**	2	[`ɑkjə͵paɪ]	佔用, 佔有, 佔據 同義詞 capture, seize, conquer	動詞
79	**insistent**	2	[ɪn`sɪstənt]	堅持的, 不屈服的 同義詞 persistent, pertinacious	形容詞
80	**authentic**	9	[ɔ`θɛntɪk]	正宗; 真正的; 可信的 反義詞 spurious, fictitious 偽造的	形容詞
81	**ethnic**	3	[`ɛθnɪk]	民族的; 種族的	形容詞
82	**temporary**	7	[`tɛmpə͵rɛrɪ]	臨時的; 短暫的 同義詞 passing, momentary 反義詞 permanent, eternal 永久的	形容詞

	單字	出現	音標	中文	詞性
83	**constant**	7	[`kɑnstənt]	經常發生的; 穩定的 同義詞 uniform, regular, even	形容詞
84	**promote**	21	[prə`mot]	促進; 推廣; 晉升 同義詞 encourage, inspirit, boost	動詞
85	**reward**	11	[rɪ`wɔrd]	獎賞; 報答 同義詞 compensate, remunerate	名詞
86	**independence**	16	[ˌɪndɪ`pɛndəns]	獨立, 自主, 自立	名詞
87	**deduction**	2	[dɪ`dʌkʃən]	扣除; 扣除額; 推論	名詞
88	**insurance**	8	[ɪn`ʃʊrəns]	保險; 保險契約; 保險業 同義詞 surety, security, indemnity	名詞
89	**immigration**	7	[ˌɪmə`greʃən]	移居; 移民 反義詞 emigration (向他國)移居	名詞
90	**guardian**	2	[`gɑrdɪən]	監護人; 保護者; 管理員	名詞
91	**emergency**	8	[ɪ`mɝdʒənsɪ]	緊急情況; 非常時刻 同義詞 crisis, pinch, exigency	名詞
92	**demand**	12	[dɪ`mænd]	需要, 要求, 請求 同義詞 require, need, want	名詞
93	**contribute**	8	[kən`trɪbjut]	導致; 歸因於; 貢獻 同義詞 give, donate, participate	動詞
94	**preservation**	5	[ˌprɛzə`veʃən]	保護; 維持; 保存, 保留	名詞
95	**reservation**	26	[ˌrɛzə`veʃən]	預訂; 預約; 保留(意見) 同義詞 retaining	名詞
96	**observation**	4	[ˌɑbzɝ`veʃən]	觀察; 監視; 評論	名詞
97	**vaccinate**	6	[`væksnˌet]	接種疫苗; 注射疫苗 同義詞 inoculate, immunize	動詞
98	**proficient**	1	[prə`fɪʃənt]	精通的, 熟練的 同義詞 skilled, adept, clever	形容詞
99	**ancient**	11	[`enʃənt]	古老的; 古代的; 舊的 同義詞 archaic, elderly	形容詞
100	**upgrade**	6	[`ʌp`gred]	升級; 提升	動詞

111年領隊筆試測驗

● 本書採用英語邏輯思維[中譯]
幫助更快看懂句子, 拆解字義

題型分析	單字 69	片語 0	對話 0	情境命題	景物 2	餐飲 6	住宿 6	交通 7	機場 13
	文法 1	閱測 10			生活 19	民俗 0	產業 3	職能 8	購物 6

單選題 [共80題, 每題1.25分]

( ) 1. If you take this ________, maybe you can get to the bus station in 15 minutes.
(A)**shortcut**[1] (B)sign (C)angle (D)landmark 生活 單字

[中譯] 如果你走這條捷徑，也許可以在15分鐘內抵達公車站。
(A)捷徑 (B)標誌 (C)角度 (D)地標 答 A

( ) 2. Do you have a(n)________ **proof**[2] to **verify**[3] that you have enough money to stay in this country?
(A)laborious (B)**racial**[4] (C)healthy (D)financial 生活 單字

[中譯] 你是否有財力證明來證實你有足夠的錢留在這個國家？
(A)耗時費力的 (B)種族的 (C)健康的 (D)財務的 答 D

( ) 3. Airline agent: Are there any ____ items in your luggage, such as hairspray or scissors?
Traveler: No, sir. There is none.
(A)**banned**[5] (B)**disabled**[6] (C)refreshed (D)**renewed**[7] 機場 單字

[中譯] 地勤人員：您的行李中是否有違禁物品，例如噴髮定型液或剪刀？
旅客：沒有，先生。一個也沒有。
(A)禁止 (B)喪失能力 (C)刷新 (D)更新 答 A

( ) 4. Guest: Could you please help me put my carry-on bag into the overhead _______.
Flight attendant: Yes, no problem.
(A)**obstacle**[8] (B)cabin (C)compartment (D)booth 交通 單字

[中譯] 客人：你能協助我把我的隨身行李放進頭頂上方的置物櫃嗎？
空服員：好的，沒問題。
(A)障礙 (B)座艙 (C)置物櫃 (D)攤位 答 C

( ) 5. The coach is leaving Taipei on Friday half an hour later, at a quarter ________ seven in the morning, not a quarter past six.
(A)on (B)off (C)to (D)in 交通 文法

[中譯] 長途巴士將於週五晚半小時離開臺北，也就是在早上6點45分，而非6點15分。
(A)開 (B)關 (C)到 (D)在 解 P2-53. 文法83 答 C

( ) 6. I prefer to pack ________. Does your hotel provide free toiletries?
(A)light (B)afield (C)atop (D)live 住宿 單字

[中譯] 我喜歡輕裝簡從。請問飯店是否有提供免費盥洗用品？
(A)輕便 (B)偏離著；離題 (C)頂上 (D)現場 答 A

( ) 7. Guest: Would the white wine go well with my meal?
Waiter: Yes, the wine should ________ it nicely.
(A)compile (B)**compete**[9] (C)**complement**[10] (D)**compliment**[11] 餐飲 單字

[中譯] 客人：白葡萄酒適合搭配我的餐點嗎？
服務員：是的，葡萄酒會是很好的搭配。
(A)編輯 (B)競爭 (C)搭配 (D)讚揚 答 C

( ) 8. Grandpa: Where are your table ___ ? Sit up straight and get your elbows off the table.
Grandson: Okay, my bad.
(A)**manners**[12] (B)matters (C)banners (D)trainers 餐飲 單字

[中譯] 爺爺：你的餐桌禮儀在哪裡？坐直並且將手肘從桌上移開。
孫子：好的，是我的錯。
(A)禮儀 (B)事項；事件 (C)橫幅 (D)教練 答 A

( ) 9. Ladies and gentlemen, please return to your seats and fasten your seatbelts. We will experience________ soon. Please remain seated for your own safety.
(A)turbo (B)trouble (C)turbulence (D)tremble 交通 單字

[中譯] 女士們，先生們，請回到座位上並且繫緊您的安全帶。我們將遇到亂流。為了您自身的安全，請留在座位上。
(A)渦輪 (B)麻煩 (C)不穩定氣流 (D)顫抖 答 C

( ) 10. How much is the taxi ________ from Kaohsiung to Taipei?
(A)route (B)room (C)fair (D)**fare**[13] 交通 單字

[中譯] 從高雄到台北的計程車費用是多少？
(A)路線 (B)空間 (C)公平的 (D)票價 答 D

( ) 11. Receptionist: Our one-day package tour includes a guided tour of the city and free ________.
Guest: That sounds perfect. 產業 單字
(A)**recommendation**[14] (B)**operation**[15] (C)**transportation**[16] (D)destination

[中譯] 接待員：我們的一日遊套裝行程包含城市導覽和免費交通。
客人：聽起來很完美。
(A)推薦 (B)行動；活動 (C)運輸 (D)目的地 答 C

( ) 12. Guest: I'd like to shop at the night market if they accept ________ payment such as Line Pay, Apple Pay, or Google Pay.
Tour guide: Some vendors even **accept**[17] Taiwan Pay or JKO Pay. Let's give it a try.
(A)**device**[18] (B)engine (C)mobile (D)media 購物 單字

情境篇 文法篇 片語篇 測驗篇 口試篇

[中譯] 客人：我會想去夜市購物，如果夜市接受Line Pay、Apple Pay或Google Pay等行動支付。
導遊：有些攤販甚至接受台灣 Pay 或街口支付。試一試吧。
(A)設備 (B)引擎 (C)行動電話 (D)媒體 答 C

( ) 13. Guest: Could I pay with traveler's checks?
Clerk: Sorry, Sir. Traveler's checks are no longer accepted. They can't be easily cashed, even at the banks that ________ them.
(A)**pursued**[19] (B)**issued**[20] (C)rocked (D)**tagged**[21] 購物 單字

[中譯] 客人：我可以用旅行支票付款嗎？
銷售員：很抱歉，先生。不再接受旅行支票。它不容易兌現，即使是到發行支票的銀行。
(A)追求 (B)發行 (C)震動 (D)標記 答 B

( ) 14. Foreign guest: How could I use this ________ phone to make a collect call?
Tour leader: Please dial 108.
(A)**redundant**[22] (B)**dramatic**[23] (C)**parallel**[24] (D)**public**[25] 生活 單字

[中譯] 外國遊客：我如何使用這個公共電話打付費電話？ 領隊：請撥108。
(A)多餘的 (B)表演的；戲劇性 (C)平行的 (D)公共的 答 D

( ) 15. Tourist: I'd like to report a theft case.
Police: Could you ________ the situation? I'll create a record for your case. You may need to stop by the police station.
(A)**decide**[26] (B)**describe**[27] (C)**deploy**[28] (D)decline 職能 單字

[中譯] 遊客：我想舉報一件竊盜案。
警察：您能描述一下情況嗎？我將為您的案件建立記錄。您可能需要到警察局一趟。
(A)決定 (B)描述 (C)調動 (D)拒絕 答 B

( ) 16. Tourist: Sir, a car accident just happened across the street.
Police: Do they need an ambulance?
Tourist: No, Sir. But I think they need help.
Police: OK, I'll ________ a police squad, and it will be there within five minutes.
(A)**dispatch**[29] (B)**dismiss**[30] (C)disclose (D)**disconnect**[31] 職能 單字

[中譯] 遊客：先生，對街剛剛發生車禍。
警察：他們需要救護車嗎？
遊客：沒有，先生。但我認為他們需要協助。
警察：好的，我將調度一組警察小隊，五分鐘之內就會抵達。
(A)調度 (B)解僱 (C)揭露 (D)中斷 答 A

( ) 17. In 1666, the Great Fire burnt for three days and destroyed most buildings in London. The famous architect, Christopher Wren, ________ many buildings after the Great Fire.

(A)**designed**[32] (B)**disobeyed**[33] (C)**clarified**[34] (D)**paralyzed**[35] 景物 單字

[中譯] 在1666 年，一場連續燃燒了三天的大火，摧毀了倫敦大部分的建築。著名建築師克里斯托弗．雷恩，在大火後設計了許多建築。
(A)設計的 (B)不服從的 (C)澄清的 (D)癱瘓的 答 A

( ) 18. Have you ________ the news report on the new variant of COVID-19?
(A)moved (B)read (C)thrown (D)slipped 生活 單字

[中譯] 您是否閱讀過有關新的COVID-19變種病毒的新聞報導？
(A)移動 (B)閱讀 (C)拋出 (D)滑走 答 B

( ) 19. Door man: Good day, Ma'am. You like watermelon, don't you?
Guest: Yes, I do. It tastes great and is inexpensive. This melon only ________ me $200 dollars.
(A)spends (B)**borrows**[36] (C)**costs**[37] (D)pays 購物 單字

[中譯] 門僮：早安，女士。您喜歡西瓜吧？
客人：是的，的確。它味道好極了，而且價格也不貴。我只花了200元買這個瓜。
(A)支出 (B)借款 (C)花費 (D)支付 答 C

( ) 20. International calls to mobile phones **registered**[38] in another country are ________ higher rates. The first zero of an international number must be deleted since it is a "trunk prefix" only for domestic calls within many countries.
(A)told (B)changed (C)**elected**[39] (D)charged 生活 單字

[中譯] 撥打國外註冊手機的國際電話費率較高。打國際電話撥號時，手機號碼的第一個零必須刪除，因為它是一個“長途冠碼”，僅適用於許多國家/地區的國內電話。
(A)告訴 (B)改變 (C)選舉 (D)收費 答 D

( ) 21. Traveler: I think my visa is no longer valid.
Border agent: Yes, you are right. Please ________ to the immigration service counter.
(A)plead (B)preach (C)proceed (D)**process**[40] 機場 單字

[中譯] 旅客：我想我的簽證已經失效了。 邊境人員：是的。請前往至指定的入境服務櫃檯。
(A)懇求 (B)鼓吹 (C)前進 (D)過程 答 C

( ) 22. Kaeng Krachan Forest Complex is ____ as a UNESCO World Heritage Site in 2021. This area is located between the Himalayan, Indochina, and Sumatran faunal with rich biodiversity and home to many endangered plants and wildlife **species**[41].
(A)**designated**[42] (B)**diminished**[43] (C)cemented (D)adjusted 景物 單字

[中譯] 崗卡章森林群於2021年被指定為聯合國教科文組織世界遺產。該地區位於喜馬拉雅、中南半島和蘇門答臘之間，擁有豐富的生物多樣性，是許多瀕危植物和野生動物物種的家園。
(A)指定的 (B)減少的 (C)固定的 (D)調整的 答 A

(　　) 23. Those who overstay their visa need to fill out an application form, provide a copy of passport, and ________ a ticket to leave the country in 7 days.
(A)push (B)loose (C)hang (D)**book**[44] 機場 單字

[中譯] 簽證逾期停留者需填寫申請表，提供護照影本，並預訂七天內出境的機票。
(A)推擠 (B)鬆開 (C)懸掛 (D)預訂 答 D

(　　) 24. Customer: Could you give me a 30% discount for this shirt?
Vendor: No. It is already a real ________. That's the best we can offer.
(A)**bargain**[45] (B)parade (C)circle (D)bill 購物 單字

[中譯] 顧客：能給我這件襯衫打七折嗎？ 販商：不。這已是特價品。這是我們能提供的最好價格。
(A)特價商品；便宜貨 (B)遊行 (C)圓形 (D)帳單 答 A

(　　) 25. Your suitcase ________ the weight limit by two kilograms. You might want to give up some items, or put them away in your carry-on bag.
(A)**expresses**[46] (B)excludes (C)**explores**[47] (D)**exceeds**[48] 機場 單字

[中譯] 您的行李箱超重兩公斤。您可能要放棄一些物品，或者將它們放在登機行李中。
(A)表達 (B)排除 (C)探索 (D)超過 答 D

(　　) 26. Guest: I ________ if I could have a straw for the juice.
Flight attendant: Sorry, Sir. Due to environmental concern, we do not provide straws to our customers.
(A)wander (B)wonder (C)cheat (D)shout 餐飲 單字

[中譯] 客人：我想知道我能不能有一根吸管來喝果汁。
空服員：很抱歉，先生。由於環保考量，我們不向客人提供吸管。
(A)徘徊 (B)想知道 (C)欺騙 (D)大聲說 答 B

(　　) 27. Guest: How much ________ do we need to wait in line before the take-off ?
Flight attendant: It depends on how many planes are ahead of us.
(A)greater (B)slower (C)lighter (D)longer 交通 單字

[中譯] 客人：在起飛前我們還需排隊多久？ 空服員：這取決於我們前面有多少架飛機。
(A)更大 (B)更慢 (C)更輕 (D)更長 答 D

(　　) 28. Reclaim on Demand is an automated system designed for the future of ________. It gives passengers visibility into when and where their bags will appear. Passengers will be contacted via an in-app message to collect their bags.
(A)air circulation (B)baggage claim
(C)air control (D)computer programming 機場 單字

[中譯] Reclaim on Demand 是未來為行李提取而設計的自動化系統。它讓乘客可以看到他們的行李何時何地會出現。乘客透過手機程式之通知即可領取行李。
(A)空氣循環 (B)行李領取 (C)空氣控制 (D)電腦程式設計 答 B

( ) 29. Guest: Do you charge handling fee for foreign exchange?
Cashier: Yes, we do. We charge NT$100 dollars per ________.
(A)sample (B)court (C)**extention**[49] (D)**transaction**[50] 生活 單字

[中譯] 客人：你們有收取國際匯兌手續費嗎？ 收銀員：是的。我們每筆交易收取新臺幣100元。
(A)樣本 (B)法院 (C)擴展 (D)交易 答 D

( ) 30. Customs officer: Do you have anything to ________ ?
Traveler: Yes, I have NT$100,000 dollars in cash with me.
(A)detect (B)depart (C)**declare**[51] (D)**develop**[52] 機場 單字

[中譯] 海關官員：您有什麼要申報嗎？ 旅客：是的，我有攜帶新臺幣10萬元現金。
(A)檢測 (B)出發 (C)申報 (D)發展 答 C

( ) 31. A cell phone parking lot is a parking lot where people wait for their friends to complete their ________ **procedures**[53].
(A)**validating**[54] (B)constructing (C)**decreasing**[55] (D)**landing**[56] 機場 單字

[中譯] 手機通知停車區是供接機者等候朋友完成飛機落地後程序期間之（暫時）停車處。
(A)驗證 (B)構建 (C)降低 (D)著陸；落地 答 D

( ) 32. Ground staff: You have been selected for a ________ luggage search. Please open your luggage.
Traveler: Sure, no problem.
(A)resourceful (B)spacious (C)random (D)competent 機場 單字

[中譯] 地勤人員：您被選中進行隨機行李檢查。請打開您的行李箱。 旅客：當然，沒問題。
(A)機敏的 (B)寬敞的 (C)隨機的 (D)有能力的 答 C

( ) 33. Tourist: I've lost my key and I need to get into my room. Can I get a ________ ?
(A)trolley (B)patent (C)**replacement**[57] (D)**recipe**[58] 住宿 單字

[中譯] 遊客：我弄丟了鑰匙，而我需要進入我的房間。我可以取得備用鑰匙嗎？
(A)手推車 (B)專利權 (C)替代品 (D)食譜 答 C

( ) 34. Hotel Customer: Do you **provide**[59] ________ for disabled people, such as adjustable beds, shower chairs, and barrier-free paths?
(A)premises (B)facilities (C)members (D)chains 住宿 單字

[中譯] 飯店顧客：是否有為殘障人士提供無障礙設施，例如可調節床、淋浴座椅和無障礙通道？
(A)生產場所 (B)設施 (C)成員 (D)鏈條 答 B

( ) 35. Guest: Excuse me. Where is the nearest drugstore?
Tour leader: Turn right when you leave the hotel. Keep walking for 5 minutes. The drugstore is three ________ away from the hotel.
(A)bricks (B)blocks (C)tiles (D)curbs 職能 單字

[中譯] 客人：不好意思。請問最近的藥局在哪裡？
領隊：離開飯店後右轉。繼續步行5分鐘。藥局距離飯店有3個街區。
(A)磚塊 (B)街區 (C)瓷磚 (D)路邊 答 B

( ) 36. Foreign guest: Where could I find a(n)________ phone? My cell phone doesn't work here.
Tour leader: You can probably find one at a gas station or a convenience store.
(A)direct (B)milky (C)milestone (D)pay 職能 單字

[中譯] 外國遊客：在哪裡可以找到付費電話？我的手機在這裡無法運作。
領隊：您也許可以在加油站或便利商店找到一個。
(A)直接的 (B)乳製的 (C)里程碑 (D)付費 答 D

( ) 37. If you are calling a(n)_____ from one city to another, you need to dial the area code.
(A)outline (B)headline (C)**landline**[60] (D)online 生活 單字

[中譯] 如果你從一個城市撥打有線電話到另一個城市，你需要撥打區域代碼。
(A)輪廓 (B)標題；頭條 (C)(電話的)固網 (D)線上 答 C

( ) 38. Receptionist: How may I direct your call?
Guest: Please ________ my call to an international operator.
Receptionist: I'll put you through. One moment, please.
(A)**transfer**[61] (B)**transcend**[62] (C)**transform**[63] (D)transcribe 生活 單字

[中譯] 接待員：我該如何轉接您的電話？ 客人：請把我的電話轉接給國際接線員。
接待員：我幫您轉接。請稍等。
(A)轉接 (B)超越 (C)轉換 (D)改編 答 A

( ) 39. Doctor: How long have you had these ________ ?
Patient: I was alright till this morning.
(A)**systems**[64] (B)syntheses (C)symbols (D)**symptoms**[65] 職能 單字

[中譯] 醫生：這些症狀出現多久了？ 病人：到今天早上都是好的。
(A)系統 (B)綜合 (C)象徵 (D)症狀 答 D

( ) 40. If your passport is lost or stolen abroad, and you need to return to Taiwan right away, you may apply for a(n)" ________ Certificate for the Republic of China Nationals."
(A)Critical (B)Joint (C)**Entry**[66] (D)Departure 生活 單字

[中譯] 如果你的護照在國外遺失或被竊，急需返台，你可以申請"中華民國入國證明書"。
(A)危急的 (B)聯合 (C)進入 (D)離開 答 C

( ) 41. ________ happens when there is not enough water and rainfall.
(A)Earthquake (B)Drought (C)Flood (D)Landslide 生活 單字

[中譯] 當沒有足夠的水和降雨時，就會發生乾旱。
(A)地震 (B)乾旱 (C)水災 (D)山崩 答 B

( ) 42. Customer: I would like to ________ my flight from Taipei to Los Angeles.
Airline agent: May I have your name and ticket number, please?
(A)target (B)confirm (C)require (D)construct 機場 單字

[中譯] 顧客：我想確認從台北到洛杉磯的航班。 地勤人員：請問您的姓名和機票號碼？
(A)目標 (B)確認 (C)要求 (D)構造 答 B

( ) 43. Flight attendant: I am sorry. Your bag is too large to take on board. Since we have a full flight today, we have to be strict about ________.
Passenger: But I never had any problem with this bag before.
Flight attendant: I am afraid we have to check in your suitcase at the boarding gate.
(A)**expansion**[67] (B)charge (C)commodity (D)allowance 機場 單字

[中譯] 空服員：我很抱歉。您的旅行包過大而無法帶上飛機。由於我們今天航班全滿，必須嚴格執行行李限額。
乘客：但我之前攜帶這個包沒有任何問題。
空服員：恐怕我們得在登機口託運您的行李。
(A)擴張 (B)收費 (C)商品 (D)限額；津貼 答 D

( ) 44. Flight attendant: Your flight has been cancelled due to a hurricane in Florida.
Passenger: Will the airline company arrange ________ for us?
(A)application (B)**accommodation**[68] (C)charity (D)schedule 機場 單字

[中譯] 空服員：您的航班已取消，由於佛羅里達州的颶風。
乘客：航空公司會為我們安排住宿嗎？
(A)申請 (B)住宿 (C)慈善 (D)時間表 答 B

( ) 45. Passenger: Could you show me how to operate the in-flight ________ ?
Flight attendant: You can start by touching the screen. It covers music, movies, news, information, video games, TV shows, and radio programs. You can also switch languages on the screen.
(A)**safety**[69] (B)newspaper (C)entertainment (D)**brochure**[70] 職能 單字

[中譯] 乘客：能告訴我如何操作機上娛樂嗎？
空服員：您可以按觸摸螢幕開始。它涵蓋音樂、電影、新聞、資訊、電玩遊戲、電視節目和廣播節目。您還可以在螢幕上切換語言。
(A)安全 (B)報紙 (C)娛樂 (D)小冊子；指南 答 C

( ) 46. Passenger: Excuse me, sir.
Flight attendant: How may I help you? Passenger: I feel like vomiting.
Flight attendant: Here is a _____ bag. Now, please cover your mouth and nose with it. Then, you could breathe slowly through your mouth till you feel much better.
(A)hand (B)post (C)goodie (D)sickness 職能 單字

[中譯] 乘客：不好意思，先生。　空服員：有什麼能為您服務的嗎？　乘客：我感覺想吐。
空服員：這是一個嘔吐袋。現在，請用它罩住您的嘴巴和鼻子。然後，您可以用嘴巴慢慢地呼吸，直到您感覺好些。
(A)手　(B)郵寄　(C)好東西　(D)嘔吐；疾病　答 D

( ) 47. I hereby certify that I have made a truthful ________. I understand that if I provide false information, I may be issued with a fixed penalty notice and/or a direction to return home.
(A)declaration (B)prescription (C)**detection**[71] (D)**detention**[72] 生活 單字

[中譯] 我在此保證我已如實申報。我明白，如果我提供不實資料，我可能會收到定額罰款通知和/或遣返指示。
(A)申報　(B)處方　(C)偵查　(D)拘留　答 A

( ) 48. Passenger: Excuse me. I would like to report a missing suitcase. I just arrived on flight 714 from Tokyo.
Airline representative: Please fill out this form. We'll ________ you for up to $100 so that you could buy the things you need. We will try our best to locate your suitcase as quickly as possible.
(A)relay (B)review (C)**issue**[73] (D)**restore**[74] 機場 單字

[中譯] 乘客：不好意思。我想通報行李箱遺失。我剛從東京搭乘714航班抵達。
航空公司代表：請填寫此表格。我們將向您發放最高100元的費用，以便您購買所需用品。我們將盡最大努力盡快找到您的行李箱。
(A)接替　(B)檢閱　(C)發放　(D)恢復　答 C

( ) 49. Many hotels in New York provide free airport ________ service. You could also take the subway if you are comfortable with public transportation.
(A)**shuttle**[75] (B)chanting (C)shopping (D)**catalog**[76] 交通 單字

[中譯] 紐約許多飯店皆提供免費機場接送服務。如您對於大眾交通不介意的話，也可以搭乘地鐵。
(A)接送　(B)吟誦　(C)購物　(D)目錄　答 A

( ) 50. Receptionist: The Sheraton Hotel. How can I help you?
Tourist: I would like to reserve a room for this weekend. Is there any suite ____ ?
(A)alone (B)**available**[77] (C)aloft (D)adrift 住宿 單字

[中譯] 接待員：喜來登酒店您好。有什麼能為您服務的嗎？
遊客：我想預訂這個週末的房間。目前有空的套房嗎？
(A)單獨　(B)可用　(C)高空　(D)漂流　答 B

( ) 51. Traveler: I would like to check out. My room number is 608 and here is the room key.
Receptionist: OK, sir. You pay a deposit in advance to ____ the reservation. In total, your bill is 800, including taxes and 15% service charge. How would you like to pay?
(A)commit (B)secure (C)slide (D)**occupy**[78] 住宿 單字

[中譯] 旅客：我想要退房。我的房間號碼是608，這是房間鑰匙。
接待員：好的，先生。您先前有支付押金以確保預訂。包含稅金和15%服務費，帳單總共是800。請問您要如何付款？
(A)承諾 (B)擔保 (C)滑動 (D)佔用 答 B

( ) 52. This particular restaurant in Marriott features and serves ________ Greek dishes.
(A)**insistent**[79] (B)tolerant (C)athletic (D)**authentic**[80] 餐飲 單字

[中譯] 這家萬豪酒店內的特色餐廳，提供正宗的希臘菜餚。
(A)堅持的 (B)寬容的 (C)強壯的 (D)真正的 答 D

( ) 53. Many immigrants live in Australia, so ________ food is very popular here.
(A)impractical (B)**ethnic**[81] (C)**temporary**[82] (D)**constant**[83] 生活 單字

[中譯] 許多移民居住在澳大利亞，因此各族群的食物很受歡迎。
(A)不切實際的 (B)種族的 (C)短暫的 (D)持續的 答 B

( ) 54. Visitor Information Center could ________ regional tourism since it provides free information and encourages tourists to participate in local events and visit local attractions.
(A)delay (B)juggle (C)retrieve (D)**promote**[84] 產業 單字

[中譯] 遊客詢問中心可推廣在地旅遊，提供免費資訊並鼓勵遊客參加當地活動及參觀當地名勝。
(A)延遲 (B)同時應付 (C)取回 (D)促進 答 D

( ) 55. Tourist: How much is this coat? Clerk: It’s 200 dollars.
Tourist: One hundred and fifty. This is my final ________.
(A)index (B)offer (C)**reward**[85] (D)comment 購物 單字

[中譯] 遊客：這件外套多少錢？ 店員：200元。 遊客：150。這是我最後的出價。
(A)指數 (B)報價 (C)獎勵 (D)評論 答 B

( ) 56. Visitors to the EU may buy goods free of VAT at the check-out. The clerk will ask you to show your passport and fill out a tax ________ form.
(A)**independence**[86] (B)conduct (C)**deduction**[87] (D)refund 購物 單字

[中譯] 到歐盟的遊客購買商品可以在結帳時退還消費稅。店員會要求您出示護照並填寫退稅單。
(A)獨立 (B)行為 (C)扣除 (D)退款 答 D

( ) 57. If you are sick when travelling, you could call the hospital and schedule an appointment. When you visit the hospital, you need to bring your health ________ policy documents.
(A)notation (B)**insurance**[88] (C)**immigration**[89] (D)annotation 生活 單字

[中譯] 如果你在旅行時生病了，你可以打電話到醫院並安排預約。當你前往醫院時，需要攜帶你的健康保險單文件。
(A)符號 (B)保險 (C)移民 (D)註釋 答 B

( ) 58. If a traveler loses his or her passport, he or she needs to find his or her country's ________ to apply for a temporary passport.
(A)terminal (B)code (C)embassy (D)**guardian**[90] 生活 單字

[中譯] 如果旅行者遺失護照，他或她需要找到其所在國家的大使館申請臨時護照。
(A)航站 (B)代碼 (C)大使館 (D)監護人 答 C

( ) 59. In a Japanese restaurant, your personal chef brings in the ________ and cooks the food in front of you. He then serves the steaming hot gourmet dish.
(A)purses (B)ingredients (C)recipients (D)feathers 餐飲 單字

[中譯] 在日本餐廳，您的私人廚師會帶著食材，並在您面前烹飪。然後端上熱騰騰的美食菜餚。
(A)錢包 (B)原料 (C)領受者 (D)羽毛 答 B

( ) 60. There are many kinds of short-term ________ jobs in the touring industry. People doing these jobs need to respond to different challenges every day.
(A)apparent (B)souvenir (C)seasonal (D)signal 產業 單字

[中譯] 旅行業有多種短期季節性的工作。從事這些工作的人們每天需要應對不同的挑戰。
(A)顯而易見的 (B)紀念品 (C)季節性的 (D)顯著的 答 C

( ) 61. Tourist: Hello, I would like to schedule an appointment to see a doctor. I have a high fever and feel terrible now.
Hospital staff: Please directly come to our ________ room now.
(A)veterinary (B)fatal (C)changing (D)**emergency**[91] 生活 單字

[中譯] 遊客：您好，我想預約看醫生。我發高燒，現在感覺很糟糕。
醫院人員：請現在直接到我們的急診室。
(A)獸醫 (B)致命的 (C)更衣室 (D)緊急情況 答 D

( ) 62. Most people were vaccinated last year, but Mary refused to get the vaccination because she had a ________ about needles.
(A)**demand**[92] (B)phobia (C)favor (D)fantasy 生活 單字

[中譯] 去年大多數人都接種了疫苗，但瑪麗拒絕，因為她患有針頭恐懼症。
(A)需求 (B)恐懼症 (C)好感 (D)幻想 答 B

( ) 63. Many factors ________ to increased level of toxic gases and one factor which is often ignored by people is the emissions of the public transportation.
(A)align (B)**contribute**[93] (C)happen (D)manage 交通 單字

[中譯] 許多因素導致有毒氣體層升高，其中一個常被人們忽視的是大眾交通的排放。
(A)對準 (B)提供；貢獻 (C)發生 (D)管理 答 B

( ) 64. At public places such as libraries, hotels, and airports, free Wi-Fi is very convenient but not secure. Travelers should avoid ______ into bank accounts and entering passwords at these public areas because someone else might see them.

(A)reading (B)writing (C)loading (D)logging 生活 單字

[中譯] 在圖書館、飯店、機場等公共場所，免費Wi-Fi很方便，但並不安全。旅行者應避免在這些公共區域登入銀行帳戶並輸入密碼，因為其他人可能會看到。

(A)讀取 (B)寫入 (C)下載 (D)登入 答 D

( ) 65. John: Some customers mentioned that the meals are good but they are a bit expensive.
Mary: We could provide them with some more _______ side dishes such as salad. Most customers feel like getting something free.

(A)empty (B)covert (C)complimentary (D)controversial 餐飲 單字

[中譯] John：有些顧客提到餐點不錯，但有點貴。
Mary：我們能為他們提供一些贈送配菜，例如沙拉。多數顧客都想得到一些免費的東西。

(A)空的 (B)隱蔽的 (C)贈送的 (D)有爭議的 答 C

( ) 66. Receptionist: Good afternoon. Welcome to the Sheraton hotel. How can I help you?
Tourist: Good afternoon. I have a ________ for two nights and here is my confirmation number. 住宿 單字

(A)conversation (B)**preservation**[94] (C)**reservation**[95] (D)**observation**[96]

[中譯] 接待員：午安。歡迎來到喜來登飯店。有什麼能為您服務的嗎？
遊客：午安。我有預訂兩個晚上，這是我的確認號碼。

(A)談話 (B)保存 (C)預訂 (D)觀察 答 C

( ) 67. The _______ rate between New Taiwan Dollars and the Euros has not changed much recently.

(A)option (B)interchange (C)failure (D)exchange 生活 單字

[中譯] 新台幣與歐元之間的匯率近期變化不大。

(A)選項 (B)交替 (C)失敗 (D)交換 答 D

( ) 68. Travelers selecting Program C (7+7+7 days) are required to be fully ________ against COVID-19 for 14 days if they would like to enter Taiwan, as stipulated by the Lunar New Year quarantine program.

(A)**vaccinated**[97] (B)accused (C)charged (D)inflicted 生活 單字

[中譯] 按照農曆新年隔離計劃的規定，選擇計劃 C（7+7+7 天）的旅客如要進入台灣，在14天前須全面接種 COVID-19疫苗。

(A)接種 (B)被告 (C)指控 (D)施加 答 A

( ) 69. Pilots and air traffic controllers are all ________ in aviation English as well as everyday English.

(A)adaptive (B)productive (C)**proficient**[98] (D)**ancient**[99] 職能 單字

[中譯] 飛行員和空中交通管制員皆需精通航空英語以及日常英語。

(A)適應的 (B)生產的 (C)精通的 (D)古老的 答 C

(　　) 70. Passenger: Is there any chance for a(n)________ to the business class?
Check-in clerk: Let me check if there are any business class seats available.
(A)dismay (B)installment (C)**upgrade**[100] (D)coverage 機場 單字

[中譯] 乘客：有升等商務艙的機會嗎？
報到櫃台人員：讓我看看有沒有空的商務艙座位。
(A)沮喪 (B)分期付款 (C)升級 (D)覆蓋範圍 答 C

閱讀測驗一

It's noon. You're starving, and you need some food now—right now. Back in the old days, if you ordered some delivery, that food might come from a driver or bicycle delivery person. But this is the age of the **drone**. Therefore, your takeaway might not come with a knock at the door, but with a drone **hovering** outside your window.

Drone delivery hasn't advanced to the point that it will fly up to your 14th floor office window, but in Shanghai's Jinshan Industrial Park, drone delivery has already started. There, online retail giant Alibaba directs the service through its Ele.me food delivery brand. Drones fly along 17 specific routes. Customers can order from any one of 100 restaurants operating in the park. After the order is received and made, a member of the restaurant staff places the meal in the drone. It then flies to a delivery point nearest the customer. It is then picked up by an Alibaba employee and carried the rest of the way.

All of this takes just 20 minutes. Ele.me says the drone delivery method greatly reduces operating costs. If it's faster and cheaper, what's not to love about flying food?

現在是中午。你快餓死了，此時你需要一些食物—就是現在。在過去，如果你點了一些外賣，食物可能來自司機或自行車送貨員。但這是無人機的時代。因此，您的外賣抵達時伴隨著可能不是敲門聲，而是無人機懸停在你的窗外。

無人機送貨還沒有發展到可以飛到你14樓辦公室窗外的地步，但在上海的金山工業園區，無人機送貨已經開始了。在那裡，線上零售巨頭阿里巴巴通過其Ele.me餓了麼外賣品牌指導這項服務。無人機沿著 17 條特定路線飛行。顧客可以向園區內的 100 家餐廳中的任何一家訂購。收到訂單並備餐後，餐廳工作人員將餐點放入無人機中。然後它會飛到離客戶最近的交貨點。接著由阿里巴巴員工領取並完成剩下的運送。

所有這些只需 20 分鐘。Ele.me餓了麼表示，無人機送貨方式大大降低了運營成本。如果它更快更便宜，那麼飛行食品有什麼不喜歡的呢？

(　　) 71. What is the passage mainly about?
(A)fried food (B)new way to deliver food
(C)new food sold in an amusing park (D)machine-made food

[中譯] 這篇文章的主旨是什麼？
(A)油炸食品 (B)新的送餐方式 (C)在遊樂園出售的新食品 (D)機制食品 答 B

(　　) 72. What is "**drone**"?
(A)dolphin cruise (B)camera eye (C)monitor system (D)unmanned plane

[中譯] 何謂"無人機"？
(A)賞海豚船 (B)攝像頭 (C)監控系統 (D)無人駕駛飛機 答 D

( ) 73. Which word is closest in meaning to the word "**hovering**" in the passage?
(A)circling (B)hugging (C)hoping (D)waiting

[中譯] 哪一詞與文章中"懸停"一詞的意思最接近？
(A)盤旋 (B)擁抱 (C)希望 (D)等待 答 A

( ) 74. Which is true according to the passage?
(A)Technology has made big progress to deliver food up to the 14th floor.
(B)Drones of Ele.me fly fixed paths only.
(C)Ele.me cooks all the food.
(D)Drone delivery doesn't need a human to complete the delivery job.

[中譯] 根據文章，下列敘述何者正確？
(A)技術進步很大，可以將食物送到 14 樓。 (B)Ele.me餓了麼無人機隻飛固定路徑。
(C)Ele.me餓了嗎煮所有的食物。 (D)無人機送貨不需要人來完成送貨工作。 答 B

( ) 75. According to the passage, what may not be the incentive for people to use the service of Ele.me food delivery?
(A)lower cost (B)faster delivery
(C)better packaging (D)more innovative delivery method

[中譯] 根據文章，何者可能不是人們使用Ele.me餓了麼外賣品牌服務的動機？
(A)更低的成本 (B)更快的交付 (C)更好的包裝 (D)更創新的交付方式 答 C

閱讀測驗二

The best title: ________

Safety & hygiene tourism trends

Whether it is airlines, cruises, hotels, restaurants or bars, since the outbreak of COVID-19, safety and hygiene standards have been absolutely **paramount**. With this in mind, there are a number of tourism trends that are related to this, such as increased cleaning, socially distanced seating, providing hand gel and enforcing masks in some settings.

This is also now a vital part of tourism marketing, with companies needing to make clear what their hygiene and safety policies are and what measures they are taking to keep customers safe. The threat of COVID-19 has meant people are more reluctant to travel and visit tourism hot spots, so they will need to be persuaded that it is safe.

Shift from international to local

The various travel restrictions and the reluctance of many people to travel abroad has meant many in the tourism industry are having to focus on local customers, rather than international ones. This does not mean giving up on international travelers entirely, but it is likely to require a change in your core marketing strategies.

With hotels, it could be best to highlight the kinds of facilities that may appeal to the local market, such as your restaurant, your gym facilities, your Wi-Fi and even the fact that your hotel rooms are ideal for remote work. Airlines and tourism management companies may also need to shift gears to domestic tourists.

It is worth remembering that local customers are less likely to cancel too, as they will only have to pay attention to local restrictions and are not as likely to have to **quarantine** after their visit.

Virtual reality tourism trends

Virtual reality is another of the major tourism trends disrupting the industry and capitalizing on the technology can give you an edge over rivals who have not yet adopted it. Through online VR tours, customers can experience hotel interiors, restaurant interiors, outdoor tourist attractions and more, all from their home.

Importantly, they are able to do this at the decision-making phase of the customer journey. This can then be the difference between customers completing a booking or backing out, and VR is especially useful within the context of COVID-19, where customers may have second thoughts and may need extra encouragement to press ahead with their plans.

安全衛生旅遊趨勢

無論是航空公司、郵輪、飯店、餐館還是酒吧，自 COVID-19 爆發以來，安全和衛生標準絕對是**最重要的**。考慮到這一點，有許多與此相關的旅遊趨勢，例如增加清潔程度、保持社交距離的座位安排、提供手凝膠和在某些環境中強制佩戴口罩。

這現在也是旅遊營銷的重要組成部分，公司需要明確知道他們的衛生和安全政策是什麼，以及他們正在採取哪些措施來保證客戶的安全。 COVID-19 的威脅意味著人們更不願意旅行和參觀旅遊熱點，因此需要說服他們相信這裡是安全的。

從國際轉向本地

各種旅行限制以及許多人不願出國旅行，這意味著旅遊業中的許多人不得不關注本地客戶，而不是國際客戶。這並不意味著完全放棄國際旅行者，但可能需要改變您的核心營銷策略。

對於飯店，最好突出可能吸引當地市場的設施種類，例如餐廳、健身設施、Wi-Fi，甚至飯店房間是遠端工作的理想選擇。航空公司和旅遊管理公司也可能需要轉向國內游客。

值得一提的是，本地客戶也不太可能取消，因為他們只需要注意當地的限制，而且到訪後不太可能需要**隔離**。

虛擬現實旅遊趨勢

虛擬現實是另一種顛覆產業的主要旅遊趨勢，利用該技術可以讓您比尚未採用它的競爭對手更具優勢。通過線上虛擬實境導覽，客戶可以在家中體驗飯店內的裝飾、餐廳擺飾、戶外旅遊景點等。

重要的是，他們能夠在客戶旅程的決策階段做到這一點。這可能是客戶完成預訂或退出之間的區別，VR 在 COVID-19 的背景下特別有用，在這種情況下，客戶可能會重新考慮並特別鼓勵來推進他們的計劃。

( ) 76. Which is the best title of the whole passage?
(A)The Security Guidelines for the Local Tourism Industry
(B)The Latest Trends in the Tourism Industry
(C)Promoting Tourism Industry through Virtual Reality
(D)Increasing Contactless Payment during the Pandemic

[中譯] 整篇文章的最佳標題為何？
(A)本地旅遊業保安指引 (B)旅遊業的最新動向
(C)以虛擬現實促進旅遊業 (D)大流行期間增加非接觸式支付 答 B

( ) 77. What does the word, "**paramount**," in the first paragraph mean?
(A)crucial (B)mentioned (C)total (D)evaluated

[中譯] 第一段中"**最重要的**"一詞是什麼意思？
(A)關鍵 (B)提到 (C)總 (D)評估 答 A

( ) 78. In paragraph 5, which of the following words is closest in meaning to "**quarantine**"?
(A)promise (B)qualification (C)separation (D)property

[中譯] 第五段中，下列哪一詞與"**隔離**"的意思最接近？
(A)承諾 (B)資格 (C)分離 (D)財產 答 C

( ) 79. What does the author mean "Virtual reality can give you an edge over rivals who have not yet adopted it"?
(A)Virtual reality pushes tourism industry to the corner.
(B)Virtual reality makes tourism industry recognize the reality.
(C)Virtual reality is a good means to increase competitiveness.
(D)Virtual reality benefits enemies.

[中譯] 如何解讀作者說的"虛擬實境可以讓您比尚未採用它的競爭對手更具優勢"？
(A)虛擬實境將旅遊業推向絕境。 (B)虛擬實境使旅遊業認識現實。
(C)虛擬實境是提高競爭力的好手段。 (D)虛擬實境使敵人受益。 答 C

( ) 80. If a similar section is going to be added to this passage, which is a possible section to fit in?
(A)Growth of Contactless Payments
(B)Knowing Various Pandemic Prevention Policies
(C)Taking Action to Keep Customers Safe
(D)Closing Business to Avoid Financial Loss

[中譯] 如果要在這篇文章中增加一段相似的內容，何者可能適合？
(A)非接觸式支付的增長 (B)了解各種防疫政策
(C)採取行動保障客戶安全 (D)關閉業務以避免財務損失 答 A

Chapter. 08 | 測驗 | 112年度領隊試題

掌握關鍵單字，更快作答70%考題！

重要單字彙整

	單字	出現	音標	中文	詞性
1	**pressure**	3	[`prɛʃɚ]	壓力；壓迫；催促 同義詞 force, burden, influence	名詞
2	**cabin**	6	[`kæbɪn]	客艙；駕駛艙；小屋	名詞
3	**oxygen mask**	1	[`ɑksədʒən mæsk]	氧氣面罩	名詞
4	**life jacket**	1	[laɪf `dʒækɪt]	救生衣	名詞
5	**departure**	17	[dɪ`pɑrtʃɚ]	出發，起程；離開 同義詞 leaving, exit 反義詞 arrival 到達	名詞
6	**deliver**	13	[dɪ`lɪvɚ]	傳送；運送；投遞 同義詞 pass, transfer, consign 反義詞 collect 收集，withdraw 移開	動詞
7	**priority**	2	[praɪ`ɔrətɪ]	優先，重點；優先權 同義詞 anteriority, precedence	名詞
8	**position**	6	[pə`zɪʃən]	位置，地點，方位 同義詞 place, location, situation 反義詞 displace 移開，remove 搬開	名詞
9	**carousel**	6	[͵kærʊ`zɛl]	行李傳送帶；旋轉木馬	名詞
10	**formula**	2	[`fɔrmjələ]	配方；慣例；準則	名詞
11	**absorption**	2	[əb`sɔrpʃən]	吸收；全神貫注；專心致志	名詞
12	**intolerant**	1	[ɪn`tɑlərənt]	難耐的；偏執的；不寬容的 同義詞 impatient, bigoted	形容詞
13	**disregard**	2	[͵dɪsrɪ`gɑrd]	忽視；漠視；不尊重 同義詞 omission, neglect, indifference 反義詞 regard 注重	名詞
14	**negligence**	2	[`nɛglɪdʒəns]	疏忽，粗心；不修邊幅	名詞

	單字	出現	音標	中文	詞性
15	**elite**	3	[e`lit ɪ`lit]	上等的；高層次的；精銳的	形容詞
16	**downgrade**	1	[`daʊn͵gred]	使降級；使降職；降低	動詞
17	**reduce**	13	[rɪ`djus]	減少；縮小；降低 同義詞 lessen, lower, decrease 反義詞 increase 增加	動詞
18	**conserve**	6	[kən`sɝv]	保存；保護；節省 同義詞 guard, maintain, save	動詞
19	**preserve**	15	[prɪ`zɝv]	保護；保藏；維護 同義詞 defend, shield, retain 反義詞 abandon 丟棄	動詞
20	**reserve**	12	[rɪ`zɝv]	預約，預訂；保留；儲備，保存 同義詞 keep, store, hold	動詞
21	**courtesy**	3	[`kɝtəsɪ]	禮貌；殷勤，好意 同義詞 politeness, greeting 反義詞 discourtesy 無禮	名詞
22	**mileage**	1	[`maɪlɪdʒ]	行駛哩數；總英里數	名詞
23	**access**	12	[`æksɛs]	接近，進入；通道 同義詞 entry 反義詞 retirement 退去, retreat 撤退	名詞
24	**barrier**	5	[`bærɪr]	障礙；路障；剪票口；海關關卡 同義詞 barricade, obstruction	名詞
25	**prevalent**	2	[`prɛvələnt]	流行的，盛行的；普遍的 同義詞 widespread, fashionable	形容詞
26	**illegal**	4	[ɪ`lig!]	不合法的，非法的；違反規則的 同義詞 unlawful, criminal, illegitimate 反義詞 legal 合法的	形容詞
27	**lawful**	1	[`lɔfəl]	合法的；法定的，法律認可的 反義詞 unlawful 不合法的	形容詞
28	**legitimate**	1	[lɪ`dʒɪtəmɪt]	合法的；正統的；正當的 同義詞 rightful, allowed, authorized	形容詞
29	**absorbing**	1	[əb`sɔrbɪŋ]	引人入勝的；極有趣的 同義詞 fascinating, charming	形容詞

▶ 4-156

	單字	出現	音標	中文	詞性
30	**announce**	6	[ə`naʊns]	宣布; 聲稱; 顯示 同義詞 proclaim, broadcast, report	動詞
31	**valid**	4	[`vælɪd]	有效的; 有根據的; 合法的 同義詞 effective, established, cogent 反義詞 invalid 無效的, fallacious 騙人	形容詞
32	**instrument**	7	[`ɪnstrəmənt]	儀器; 器具, 器械 同義詞 device, implement, appliance	名詞
33	**consist**	9	[kən`sɪst]	組成, 構成; 存在於 同義詞 comprise	動詞
34	**dispose**	2	[dɪ`spoz]	處置, 處理; 配置 同義詞 arrange, categorize	動詞
35	**fusion**	1	[`fjuʒən]	融合; 聯合; 熔化 同義詞 combination, merger	名詞
36	**structure**	2	[`strʌktʃɚ]	結構; 構造; 建築物 同義詞 building, construction, form	名詞
37	**courier**	1	[`kʊrɪɚ]	快遞員; 導遊, 嚮導	名詞
38	**dimension**	1	[dɪ`mɛnʃən]	尺寸; 面積; 規模 同義詞 measurement, extent	名詞
39	**advantage**	15	[əd`væntɪdʒ]	優勢; 利益, 好處 同義詞 benefit, vantage, gain 反義詞 disadvantage 不利條件	名詞
40	**itinerary**	16	[aɪ`tɪnə,rɛrɪ]	預定行程; 旅程; 路線	名詞
41	**necessary**	9	[`nɛsə,sɛrɪ]	必要的, 必需的; 必然的 同義詞 required, essential, imperative 反義詞 unnecessary, needless 不需要	形容詞
42	**virus**	1	[`vaɪrəs]	病毒; 有害影響	名詞
43	**vaccination**	4	[,væksn`eʃən]	疫苗接種; 牛痘疤	名詞
44	**surface**	10	[`sɝfɪs]	表面; 水面 同義詞 outside, exterior 反義詞 interior 內部	名詞
45	**display**	16	[dɪ`sple]	陳列; 展出; 表現 同義詞 exhibit, illustrate	動詞

	單字	出現	音標	中文	詞性
46	**terminal**	8	[ˋtɝmən!]	航廈；總站；終點	名詞
47	**carry-on bag**	1	[ˋkærɪ ɑn bæg]	隨身行李	名詞
48	**prohibit**	11	[prəˋhɪbɪt]	禁止；妨礙，阻止 同義詞 forbid, prevent, veto 反義詞 permit 允許, admit 准許進入	動詞
49	**airsickness**	1	[ˋɛr͵sɪknɪs]	暈機	名詞
50	**confiscate**	1	[ˋkɑnfɪs͵ket]	沒收；徵收	動詞
51	**residence**	4	[ˋrɛzədəns]	住所；住宅；居住 同義詞 lodging, accommodation	名詞
52	**currency**	22	[ˋkɝənsɪ]	貨幣；通用，流通	名詞
53	**personal check**	1	[ˋpɝsn! tʃɛk]	個人支票	名詞
54	**passport**	22	[ˋpæs͵port]	護照；通行證；執照 同義詞 admission, permission	名詞
55	**fingerprint**	1	[ˋfɪŋgɚ͵prɪnt]	指紋，指印；特徵	名詞
56	**registration**	5	[͵rɛdʒɪˋstreʃən]	登記，註冊；掛號	名詞
57	**vacancy**	5	[ˋvekənsɪ]	空房；空白；空地 同義詞 emptiness, vacuity, space	名詞
58	**housekeeping**	1	[ˋhaus͵kipɪŋ]	家務，家政；總務	名詞
59	**postal**	1	[ˋpost!]	郵政的；郵局的；郵件的	名詞
60	**concierge**	8	[͵kɑnsɪˋɛrʒ]	門房；旅館服務臺職員	名詞
61	**laundry**	5	[ˋlɔndrɪ]	洗衣店，洗衣房；送洗的衣服	名詞
62	**parlor**	2	[ˋpɑrlɚ]	客廳；起居室；接待室	名詞
63	**upload**	4	[ʌpˋlod]	上載，上傳	動詞
64	**update**	5	[ʌpˋdet]	使現代化；更新；最新的情況	動詞
65	**upscale**	3	[ˋʌp͵skel]	高檔的，高端的；高收入的	形容詞
66	**appearance**	6	[əˋpɪrəns]	外觀；出現；演出 同義詞 exterior, semblance, advent	名詞
67	**satisfying**	1	[ˋsætɪs͵faɪɪŋ]	滿意的；充分的；確信的 反義詞 unsatisfying 無法令人滿足的	形容詞

▶ 4-158

	單字	出現	音標	中文	詞性
68	**bill**	13	[bɪl]	帳單; 目錄, 清單 同義詞 invoice, account, fee	名詞
69	**napkin**	1	[`næpkɪn]	餐巾; 小毛巾	名詞
70	**detour**	6	[`ditʊr]	繞道; 繞行的路	名詞
71	**take a selfie**	1	[tek ə `sɛlfi]	自拍	名詞
72	**manual**	3	[`mænjʊəl]	手冊, 簡介 同義詞 directory, handbook	名詞
73	**staycation**	1	[ste`keʃən]	居家度假; 留守假期	名詞
74	**remittance**	1	[rɪ`mɪtns]	匯款; 匯款額	名詞
75	**monument**	12	[`mɑnjəmənt]	紀念碑, 紀念館; 歷史遺跡 同義詞 memorial, tower, shrine	名詞
76	**refreshment**	2	[rɪ`frɛʃmənt]	茶點; 飲料; 精力恢復 同義詞 snack, renewal, nutriment	名詞
77	**stock**	6	[stɑk]	存貨, 進貨; 積蓄 同義詞 accumulate, amass, gather	名詞
78	**revenue**	7	[`rɛvə͵nju]	收入, 收益; 稅收 同義詞 income, earning, profit 反義詞 expenditure 支出	名詞
79	**tight**	7	[taɪt]	緊的; 繃緊的; 牢固的 同義詞 firm, taut, compact 反義詞 loose, slack, lax 鬆弛的	形容詞
80	**previous**	4	[`priviəs]	在前, 在先, 在以前 同義詞 earlier, former, preceding 反義詞 following 順次的	副詞
81	**toll-free**	1	[͵tol`fri]	免費撥打的	形容詞
82	**itchy**	1	[`ɪtʃɪ]	發癢的; 渴望的	形容詞
83	**wheelchair**	6	[`hwil`tʃɛr]	輪椅	名詞
84	**assistance**	4	[ə`sɪstəns]	援助, 幫助 同義詞 avail, support, succour	名詞
85	**side effect**	1	[saɪd ɪ`fɛkt]	副作用	名詞

	單字	出現	音標	中文	詞性
86	**over-the-counter**	1	[`ovɚ ðə `kaʊntɚ]	免處方籤, 非處方藥	名詞
87	**drought**	5	[draʊt]	乾旱; 旱災, 長期乾旱 同義詞 aridity, dehydration 反義詞 wet 多雨的	名詞
88	**reassure**	2	[ˌriə`ʃʊr]	使放心, 使消除疑慮	動詞
89	**resign**	4	[rɪ`zaɪn]	放棄, 辭去; 委託 同義詞 relinquish, abandon	動詞
90	**receive**	13	[rɪ`siv]	收到, 接到; 得到 同義詞 obtain, accept, gain	動詞
91	**responsibility**	2	[rɪˌspɑnsə`bɪlətɪ]	責任; 責任感 同義詞 duty, obligation, burden	名詞
92	**consumer**	10	[kən`sjumɚ]	消費者; 消耗者 同義詞 purchaser, client, patron 反義詞 producer 生產者	名詞
93	**environment**	25	[ɪn`vaɪrənmənt]	環境; 四周狀況; 自然環境 同義詞 surrounding, setting, vicinity	名詞
94	**volunteer**	5	[ˌvɑlən`tɪr]	志願者, 義工; 志願兵 同義詞 offer, come forward	名詞
95	**protection**	7	[prə`tɛkʃən]	保護, 防護; 警戒 同義詞 defence, guard, shield	名詞
96	**decoration**	12	[ˌdɛkə`reʃən]	裝飾, 裝潢; 裝飾品 同義詞 adornment, ornament	名詞
97	**observe**	5	[əb`zɝv]	看到, 注意到; 觀察 同義詞 perceive, review	動詞
98	**patrol**	3	[pə`trol]	巡邏, 偵察; 巡邏兵 同義詞 guard, protect, police	名詞
99	**pollution**	12	[pə`luʃən]	汙染; 汙染物; 汙染地區	名詞
100	**disturbance**	1	[dɪs`tɝbəns]	擾亂; 打擾; 混亂 同義詞 disorder, confusion	名詞

112年領隊筆試測驗

● 本書採用英語邏輯思維[中譯]
幫助更快看懂句子，拆解字義

題型分析	單字 59	片語 3	對話 4	情境命題	景物 3	餐飲 11	住宿 7	交通 10	機場 15
	文法 4	閱測 10			生活 18	民俗 1	產業 1	職能 0	購物 4

單選題 [共80題，每題1.25分]

( ) 1. Flight attendant: Sir, please switch off your mobile phone as we are about to ______.
(A)get rid of (B)put off (C)remove (D)take off 交通 片語

[中譯] 空服員：先生，我們即將起飛，請關閉您的手機。
(A)擺脫 (B)熄滅 (C)移除 (D)起飛 答 D

( ) 2. When the **pressure**[1] drops in the **cabin**[2], ________ **masks** will fall.
(A)helium (B)hydrogen (C)nitrogen (D)**oxygen**[3] 交通 單字

[中譯] 當機艙內的艙壓下降時，氧氣面罩會掉落。
(A)氦氣 (B)氫氣 (C)氮氣 (D)氧氣 答 D

( ) 3. Flight attendant: Don't inflate your **life** ________ until you've left the plane in case of emergency.
(A)cufflinks (B)**jacket**[4] (C)pajama (D)socks 交通 單字

[中譯] 空服員：在緊急情況下，請勿在離開飛機前充氣你的救生衣。
(A)袖扣 (B)夾克 (C)睡衣 (D)襪子 解 P2-53. 文法83 答 B

( ) 4. Please remain ________ until the "fasten seat belt" sign is switched off and the aircraft has come to a complete stop.
(A)sat (B)seat (C)seated (D)seats 交通 文法

[中譯] 請保持坐姿直到「繫上安全帶」燈號熄滅且飛機完全停止前。
(A)坐 (B)座位 (C)坐著 (D)座位 解 P2-11. 文法13 答 C

解 seat 是及物動詞，表示「就座」的意思，常見用法為 be seated。

( ) 5. Could you please tell me where ________?
(A)has the **departure**[5] gate (B)is the departure gate
(C)the departure gate has (D)the departure gate is 機場 文法

[中譯] 請告訴我登機門在哪裡？ 答 D

解 句子的主語是「departure gate」，請求對方告訴自己這個地點在哪裡，需要一個表示「位置」的連繫動詞。本題應選(D) the departure gate is，其中 is 是一個連繫動詞，用來描述主語的狀態或特性。

( ) 6. A: Excuse me, I can't find my baggage. B: Do you have your ________ tag?
(A)claim (B)hash (C)page (D)price 機場 單字

[中譯] A：不好意思，我找不到我的行李。 B：請問您有行李領取憑證嗎？
(A)領取 (B)雜亂信號 (C)頁面 (D)價格 答 A

( ) 7. A: ________. B: By credit card.
(A)Could I have a receipt? (B)How would you like to pay?
(C)Is that before or after tax? (D)Where's the cashier? 購物 對話

[中譯] A：您想用什麼方式支付？ B：用信用卡支付。
(A)我能要一張收據嗎？ (B)您想用什麼方式支付？
(C)是含稅前還是含稅後？ (D)收銀台在哪裡？ 答 B

( ) 8. Normally, checked baggage will be **delivered**[6] to the ________ after the flight arrives depending on the **priority**[7] and the **position**[8] of baggage.
(A)**carousel**[9] (B)ferris wheel (C)pirate ship (D)roller coaster 機場 單字

[中譯] 正常情況下，託運行李將根據艙等的高低和位置，在航班抵達後送至行李輸送帶。
(A)行李輸送帶 (B)摩天輪 (C)海盜船 (D)過山車 答 A

( ) 9. A: Do you have any dress ________?
B: T-shirts, shorts and slippers are strictly prohibited.
(A)circle (B)code (C)crypt (D)cypher 生活 單字

[中譯] A：你們有任何著裝規定嗎？ B：嚴格禁止穿著 T 恤、短褲和拖鞋。
(A)圓形 (B)規則；代碼 (C)密室 (D)密碼 答 B

( ) 10. Flight attendant: You seem to have some airsickness. B: ________
(A)Yes, airborne diseases are difficult to prevent.
(B)Yes, do you have medicine for that?
(C)Yes, effervescent **formula**[10] offers fast-acting **absorption**[11].
(D)Yes, today's air quality is poor. 交通 對話

[中譯] 空服員：你似乎有點暈機的症狀。 B：是的，你有治療這種症狀的藥嗎？
(A)是的，空氣中的傳染病很難預防 (B)是的，你有治療這種症狀的藥嗎？
(C)是的，泡腳式配方有快速吸收效果 (D)是的，今天的空氣品質很差 答 B

( ) 11. Gluten ________ meal does not contain any gluten-based product.
(A)accepting (B)indulgent (C)**intolerant**[12] (D)rich 餐飲 單字

[中譯] 不耐麩質的餐點不含任何有麩質的產品。
(A)接受的 (B)放縱的 (C)不耐受的 (D)豐富的 答 C

( ) 12. To maintain your rights, please arrive at the airport three hours prior to your departure time for tax refund ________.
(A)application (B)**disregard**[13] (C)inactivity (D)**negligence**[14] 機場 單字

[中譯] 為維護您的權益，請在您的出發時間前三小時抵達機場，以進行退稅申請。
(A)申請 (B)忽視 (C)停滯 (D)疏忽 答 A

情境篇 文法篇 片語篇 測驗篇 口試篇

( ) 13. Some hotel loyalty programs award **elite**[15] members ________ benefits after staying a certain number of nights.
(A)degrade (B)**downgrade**[16] (C)**reduce**[17] (D)upgrade 住宿 單字

[中譯] 有些飯店的忠誠計劃會在會員住滿一定天數後，提供會員升等福利。
(A)降低 (B)降級 (C)減少 (D)升級 答 D

( ) 14. Waiter: Good evening, Grand Restaurant, may I help you?
Customer: I would like to ________ a table for tonight.
(A)**conserve**[18] (B)**preserve**[19] (C)**reserve**[20] (D)serve 餐飲 單字

[中譯] 服務生：晚上好，歡迎光臨大飯店，請問需要什麼協助？ 顧客：我想預訂今晚的桌位。
(A)保存 (B)保護 (C)預訂 (D)提供服務 答 C

( ) 15. Ladies and gentlemen, please ________ your seat belts for landing.
(A)detach (B)fasten (C)lose (D)unseal 交通 單字

[中譯] 女士們和先生們，請繫好您的安全帶，準備降落。
(A)分離 (B)繫上 (C)鬆開 (D)解封 答 B

( ) 16. Some pet-friendly hotels offer ________ bags for walking your dog.
(A)aloofness (B)**courtesy**[21] (C)disregard (D)disfavor 住宿 單字

[中譯] 有些寵物友善的旅館提供禮貌袋，供您遛狗使用。
(A)冷漠 (B)禮貌 (C)忽視 (D)厭惡 答 B

補 courtesy bags指提供遛狗時使用的一種禮貌性質塑膠袋，用於清理寵物排泄物。

( ) 17. Airline ________ programs are designed to encourage customers to collect points which may then be exchanged for air travel rewards.
(A)faithlessness (B)**mileage**[22] (C)scholarship (D)treachery 交通 單字

[中譯] 航空公司的里程計畫旨在鼓勵顧客累積里程點數，可用來換取航空旅行獎勵。
(A)不忠 (B)里程數 (C)獎學金 (D)背叛 答 B

( ) 18. Passengers arriving in Taiwan must fill out a health ________ form.
(A)concealed (B)cyphered (C)declaration (D)encrypted 機場 單字

[中譯] 抵達台灣的旅客必須填寫健康聲明書。
(A)隱藏 (B)密碼 (C)聲明 (D)加密 答 C

( ) 19. The hotel offers easy ________ to the National Palace Museum.
(A)**access**[23] (B)bail (C)ban (D)**barrier**[24] 住宿 單字

[中譯] 這間旅館提供前往國立故宮博物院的交通。
(A)進入 (B)保釋 (C)禁止 (D)障礙 答 A

( ) 20. We missed the warning ________ and that's why the car accident happened.
(A)autographs (B)flaws (C)signs (D)stigmas 交通 單字

[中譯] 我們沒有注意到警告標誌，這就是車禍發生的原因。
(A)親筆簽名 (B)瑕疵 (C)警示標誌 (D)污名 答 C

( ) 21. ________ Wi-Fi is available throughout the five-star hotel.
(A)Complimentary (B)Derogatory (C)Inconvenient (D)Unfavora 住宿 單字

[中譯] 五星級飯店提供免費的Wi-Fi服務。
(A)贈送的 (B)貶低的 (C)不方便的 (D)反對的 答 A

( ) 22. Tipping is ________ across most of North America, with 15%-20% being seen as a reasonable amount.
(A)**prevalent**[25] (B)rare (C)uncommon (D)unusual 生活 單字

[中譯] 在北美地區給小費是普遍的，15%到20%被視為合理的金額。
(A)普遍的 (B)稀有的 (C)不常見的 (D)不尋常的 答 A

( ) 23. Some prescription medications are ________ in Taiwan. Authorities may jail or fine you if you have them.
(A)**illegal**[26] (B)**lawful**[27] (C)**legitimate**[28] (D)permitted 生活 單字

[中譯] 在台灣的一些處方藥物是非法的。如果你擁有這些藥物，當局可能會對你進行拘留或罰款。
(A)非法的 (B)合法的 (C)正當的 (D)許可的 答 A

( ) 24. The water in Sun Moon Lake is green and clear, ________ the images of surrounding mountains and serene landscape.
(A)**absorbing**[29] (B)devouring (C)reflecting (D)sucking 景物 單字

[中譯] 日月潭的水是綠色而清澈的，能映射出周圍山脈和寧靜的景觀。
(A)引人入勝的 (B)貪婪的 (C)反映的 (D)吸吮的 答 C

( ) 25. Effective from October 13, 2022, Taiwan has _______ the quarantine requirement for all arrivals, so arriving travelers will no longer be required to quarantine.
(A)**announced**[30] (B)declared (C)implemented (D)lifted 機場 單字

[中譯] 自2022年10月13日起，台灣已取消對所有入境者的檢疫要求，因此抵達的旅客不需再檢疫。
(A)宣布的 (B)聲明的 (C)實施的 (D)取消的 答 D

( ) 26. The night market was ________ with many people during holidays.
(A)boxed (B)herded (C)packed (D)schooled 生活 片語

[中譯] 假日時夜市擠滿了許多人。
(A)裝箱 (B)集中（人群或動物） (C)擁擠的；打包的 (D)接受教育 答 C

解 was packed with 常用來描述人潮、物品等過多，空間有限的情況。

( ) 27. Foreigners with a ________ passport/travel document and whose stay in R.O.C does not exceed a period of 183 days are eligible to apply for a tax refund.
(A)null (B)revoked (C)**valid**[31] (D)void 機場 單字

[中譯] 持有效護照/旅行文件，且在中華民國停留不超過183天的外籍人士，有資格申請退稅。
(A)無效的 (B)被撤銷的 (C)有效的 (D)無效的 答 C

( ) 28. Muslim visitors to Taiwan will also find many restaurants and other ________ available to cater to their dietary and religious needs.
(A)facilities (B)**instruments**[32] (C)theme parks (D)tools 民俗 單字

[中譯] 來台灣的穆斯林遊客也會發現有許多餐廳和其他設施，能滿足他們的飲食和宗教需求。
(A)設施 (B)儀器 (C)主題公園 (D)工具 答 A

( ) 29. A: Shall we order a bottle of the house red? B: ________
(A)Yes, sausage is my favorite main course.
(B)Yes, that's my favorite side dish.
(C)Yes, the house is painted in red.
(D)Yes, today's Pinot Noir goes well with steaks. 餐飲 對話

[中譯] A：我們要點一瓶紅酒嗎？ B：是的，今天的黑皮諾紅酒很適合搭配牛排。
(A)是的，香腸是我最喜歡的主菜 (B)是的，那是我最喜歡的配菜
(C)是的，這棟房子是紅色的 (D)是的，今天的黑皮諾紅酒很適合搭配牛排 答 D

( ) 30. Bubble tea most commonly **consists**[33] of tea accompanied by chewy ________ balls ("boba" or "pearls").
(A)foot (B)soccer (C)tapioca (D)tennis 餐飲 單字

[中譯] 珍珠奶茶最常見的成分是茶搭配有嚼勁的木薯粉圓（又稱為 "波霸" 或 "珍珠"）。
(A)腳 (B)足球 (C)木薯澱粉 (D)網球 答 C

( ) 31. You can go to the Lost and Found Service Center for your ________ items.
(A)**disposed**[34] (B)donated (C)missing (D)winning 生活 單字

[中譯] 您可以前往失物招領服務中心尋找你遺失的物品。
(A)丟棄的 (B)捐贈的 (C)遺失的 (D)中獎的 答 C

( ) 32. Police: How may I help you? Ann: I want to ________ a crime.
(A)refuse (B)report (C)speak (D)talk 生活 單字

[中譯] 警察：我能為您效勞嗎？ Ann：我想要報案。
(A)拒絕 (B)報告 (C)說話 (D)談話 答 B

( ) 33. Many Taipei's patisseries offer ________ dessert options designed to intrigue both Eastern and Western palates.
(A)stale (B)fiasco (C)frustrated (D)**fusion**[35] 餐飲 單字

[中譯] 許多台北的糕點店提供多口味的甜點選擇，旨在迎合東方和西方口味的喜好。
(A)不新鮮的 (B)慘敗 (C)感到挫敗的 (D)融合的 答 D

( ) 34. The online food delivery industry has a special relationship with users in a three-way **structure**[36] that includes consumers, restaurants, and ________.
(A)clerks (B)conductors (C)**couriers**[37] (D)curators 產業 單字

[中譯] 線上美食外賣產業與使用者間存在一種特殊的三方結構關係，包括消費者、餐廳和外送員。
(A)職員 (B)指揮者 (C)快遞員 (D)管理者；館長；策展人 答 C

( ) 35. Waiter: What would you like to have for your side dish? John: ________.
(A)I'll have French fries (B)Medium-rare please
(C)Pecan pie please (D)Yes, please put it by my side 餐飲 對話

[中譯] 服務生：您的配餐想要點什麼？ John：我要炸薯條。
(A)我要炸薯條 (B)五分熟 (C)胡桃派 (D)是的，請放在我旁邊 答 A

( ) 36. Hand luggage carried aboard aircraft by passengers must be within the following ________ : length 56 cm, width 36 cm, height 23 cm.
(A)costs (B)**dimensions**[38] (C)**advantages**[39] (D)weights 機場 單字

[中譯] 乘客攜帶的手提行李須符合以下尺寸限制：長度56公分，寬度36公分，高度23公分。
(A)費用 (B)尺寸 (C)優勢 (D)重量 答 B

( ) 37. Taipei 101 is one of the top tourist ________ in Taipei.
(A)annex (B)attractions (C)authorities (D)cathedrals 景物 單字

[中譯] 台北101是台北熱門的旅遊景點之一。
(A)附屬物 (B)景點 (C)官方機構 (D)大教堂 答 B

( ) 38. Here is the ________ for my trip to Europe this coming summer. Do you have any suggestions?
(A)primary (B)**itinerary**[40] (C)**necessary**[41] (D)victory 生活 單字

[中譯] 這是我這個夏天歐洲之旅的行程表。你有任何建議嗎？
(A)首要的 (B)行程表 (C)必要的 (D)獲勝 答 B

( ) 39. I locked my key in the room, and fortunately, I have a ______ set in the office to use.
(A)space (B)main (C)pair (D)spare 生活 單字

[中譯] 我把鑰匙鎖在房間裡了，幸好我有一套備用的鑰匙在辦公室。
(A)空間 (B)主要的 (C)成對 (D)備用的 答 D

( ) 40. Taiwan has become more and more popular among foreign tourists because it is quite ________ and friendly.
(A)affordable (B)costly (C)expensive (D)unreasonable 生活 單字

[中譯] 台灣越來越受外國遊客歡迎，因為來台旅遊的價格相對實惠和友善。
(A)負擔得起的 (B)昂貴的 (C)高昂的 (D)不合理的 答 A

( ) 41. Besides your passport, the ground staff also needs to check your COVID-19 ________ card during the check-in.
(A)variety (B)**virus**[42] (C)vacuum (D)**vaccination**[43] 機場 單字

[中譯] 除了您的護照，地勤人員在辦理登機手續時還需查驗您的 COVID-19 疫苗接種證明卡。
(A)多樣化 (B)病毒 (C)吸塵器 (D)疫苗接種 答 D

( ) 42. Excuse me, which ________ should I go to for the connecting flight to Chicago?
(A)**surface**[44] (B)**display**[45] (C)temple (D)**terminal**[46] 機場 單字

[中譯] 不好意思，我應該去哪個航廈轉搭飛往芝加哥的班機？
(A)表面 (B)展示 (C)寺廟 (D)航廈 答 D

( ) 43. Each passenger can have two pieces of checked baggage allowance and one ________ **bag**.
(A)hardy (B)**carry-on**[47] (C)sit-in (D)brown 機場 單字

[中譯] 每位旅客可以攜帶兩件託運行李和一件隨身行李。
(A)強健的 (B)隨身行李 (C)參與的 (D)棕色的 答 B

( ) 44. This is a non-smoking flight. Please be aware that smoking is ________ on the entire aircraft.
(A)tolerant (B)tolerated (C)**prohibited**[48] (D)prohibiting 機場 文法

[中譯] 本航班禁止吸煙。請注意，在飛機上吸菸是被禁止的。
(A)寬容的 (B)被允許的 (C)被禁止的 (D)禁止 解 P2-11. 文法13 答 C

解 依題意在飛機上吸菸是被禁止的，其文型為被動式 be + P.P.。

( ) 45. A: I feel dizzy and I am about to vomit.
B: Are you OK? Here is the ________ bag, right in front of your seat pocket.
(A)doggie (B)**airsickness**[49] (C)lunch (D)sleeping 交通 單字

[中譯] A：我覺得暈眩，快要嘔吐了。 B：你還好嗎？這是嘔吐袋，就在你的座椅口袋前面。
(A)小狗 (B)暈機 (C)午餐 (D)睡覺 答 B

( ) 46. If you carry more than the duty-free allowance, including a bottle of alcohol, the items will be ________.
(A)**confiscate**[50] (B)confiscating (C)confiscated (D)confiscation 機場 文法

[中譯] 如果您攜帶的物品超過免稅限額，包括一瓶酒，這些物品將被沒收。
(A)沒收 (B)正在沒收 (C)被沒收 (D)沒收行為 解 P2-11. 文法13 答 C

解 本題中的物品將被沒收，其文型為被動式 be + P.P.。

( ) 47. Changing money at the airport is convenient to get local ________ , but you may be charged some service fees.
(A)**residence**[51] (B)**currency**[52] (C)exchange (D)**personal check**[53] 機場 單字

[中譯] 在機場兌換貨幣是方便取得當地貨幣，但可能會被收取一些服務費。
(A)住所 (B)貨幣 (C)兌換 (D)支票 答 B

( ) 48. The immigration officers will ask you to look at the camera. Also, you have to press the buttons to leave your ________.
(A)message (B)numbers (C)**passport**[54] (D)**fingerprints**[55] 機場 單字

[中譯] 移民官會要求您看著攝影鏡頭，同時，您需要按下按鈕以留下您的指紋。
(A)信息 (B)數字 (C)護照 (D)指紋 答 D

( ) 49. A: Hello. I would like to stay for two nights. Is there any ________ today?
B: Yes, we have a standard twin room available.
(A)**registration**[56] (B)brochure (C)kettle (D)**vacancy**[57] 住宿 單字

[中譯] A：你好。我想住兩個晚上。今天有空房嗎？ B：是的，我們有一間標準雙人房可供入住。
(A)登記 (B)小冊子；指南 (C)水壺 (D)空房 答 D

( ) 50. A: Is it possible to book an opera ticket and a local tour for me?
B: Sure. The ________ service in our hotel can help.
(A)**housekeeping**[58] (B)**postal**[59] (C)**concierge**[60] (D)**laundry**[61] 住宿 單字

[中譯] A：我能預訂歌劇票和當地旅遊嗎？ B：當然可以。我們飯店的禮賓服務可以協助。
(A)客房服務 (B)郵政 (C)禮賓服務 (D)洗衣服務 答 C

( ) 51. A: The lamp in my room does not work. It is quite dark.
B: Sorry about that. I will send a ________ staff up right away.
(A)facilities (B)**parlor**[62] (C)maintenance (D)polish 住宿 單字

[中譯] A：我房間的燈不亮了，非常暗。 B：很抱歉，我會立即派遣維修人員上來。
(A)設施 (B)客廳 (C)維護 (D)擦亮 答 C

( ) 52. If you plan to go to this _____ restaurant, men and women are required to dress up.
(A)upright (B)**upload**[63] (C)**update**[64] (D)**upscale**[65] 餐飲 單字

[中譯] 如果你計畫去這家高檔的餐廳，男士和女士都需要穿著正式的服裝。
(A)正直的 (B)上傳 (C)更新 (D)高檔的 答 D

( ) 53. A: Would you like a glass of wine to go with your meal?
B: Sure. How about a soft bouquet with a sweet ________?
(A)**appearance**[66] (B)aftertaste (C)stopper (D)decanter 餐飲 單字

[中譯] A：你想來杯葡萄酒搭配您的餐點？ B：當然。來一杯溫和香氣且帶有甜味餘韻的如何？
(A)外觀 (B)餘韻 (C)瓶塞 (D)醒酒瓶 答 B

( ) 54. It is relaxing to sit in this café and hang ________ with my friends a bit. We can enjoy the riverside view and have a chat.
(A)in (B)out (C)up (D)over 餐飲 片語

[中譯] 坐在這家咖啡館裡和朋友一邊聊天，一邊享受著河畔的美景，非常放鬆。
(A)裡面 (B)外面 (C)升起 (D)在上面 答 B

補 hang out 表示在一起消磨時間、聊天

( ) 55. A: The meal is so **satisfying**[67].
B: I think so. Let me get the ______. It is on me today. You always help me a lot.
A: Thanks.
(A)**bill**[68] (B)menu (C)**napkin**[69] (D)roll 餐飲 單字

[中譯] A：這一餐真是令人滿足。
B：我也這麼認為。讓我付帳。今天我請客，你總是幫我很多忙。
A：謝謝。
(A)帳單 (B)菜單 (C)餐巾 (D)滾動 答 A

( ) 56. I am afraid that part of the highway to the airport is under construction, so you may need to take a ______.
(A)look (B)glance (C)nap (D)**detour**[70] 交通 單字

[中譯] 很抱歉，通往機場的高速公路部分路段正在施工中，所以您可能需要繞道。
(A)看 (B)瞥見 (C)小睡 (D)繞路 答 D

( ) 57. Everyone can come to this corner. Based on my experience, it is the best view to **take a** ________ or a group photo.
(A)castle (B)**selfie**[71] (C)**manual**[72] (D)route 生活 單字

[中譯] 每個人都可以來到這個角落。根據我的經驗，這裡是自拍或團體照的最佳視角。
(A)城堡 (B)自拍 (C)手冊 (D)路線 答 B

( ) 58. Instead of driving a long way for vacation, we had a ________ , visiting the local museums and staying in a hotel nearby.
(A)pullover (B)protection (C)**staycation**[73] (D)**remittance**[74] 生活 單字

[中譯] 我們選擇了留在當地度假，而不是長途開車。參觀了當地的博物館，住在附近的旅館。
(A)罩衫 (B)保護 (C)留在當地度假 (D)匯款 答 C

( ) 59. Look at the map. We can take the subway to the ________ . It is easy to find this popular historical site.
(A)**monument**[75] (B)entertainment (C)**refreshment**[76] (D)appointment 景物 單字

[中譯] 看地圖，我們可以搭乘地鐵到紀念碑。這個受歡迎的歷史遺跡很容易找到。
(A)紀念碑 (B)娛樂 (C)點心 (D)約定 答 A

( ) 60. I highly recommend this blue tote bag because of its high quality. It is very ________ and water- resistant.
(A)edible (B)incapable (C)fable (D)durable 購物 單字

[中譯] 我強烈推薦這款藍色手提袋，因為它的品質非常好。非常耐用且防水。
(A)食用的 (B)無能力的 (C)寓言 (D)耐用的 答 D

( ) 61. A: This red blouse is too ________ . Do you have a smaller one to try?
B: Yes. Here you are. The fitting room is right there.
(A)**stock**[77] (B)loose (C)**tight**[78] (D)silky 購物 單字

[中譯] A：這件紅色的襯衫太寬鬆了，你有比較小的尺寸可以試穿嗎？ B：有的，試衣間在那裡。
(A)存貨 (B)寬鬆的 (C)緊身的 (D)絲綢般的 答 B

( ) 62. A: Besides the discount, we can also keep the ________ to get a VAT (value-added tax) refund at the airport.
B: So great!
(A)recipes (B)receipts (C)renovation (D)**revenues**[79] 購物 單字

[中譯] A：除了享受折扣外，我們還可以保留收據，到機場時申請退稅。 B：太棒了！
(A)食譜 (B)收據 (C)裝修 (D)收入 答 B

( ) 63. Excuse me, could you show me how to make a ________ long-distance call from San Diego to New York?
(A)state (B)domestic (C)**previous**[80] (D)calling 生活 單字

[中譯] 不好意思，請問能告訴我如何從聖地牙哥打一通國內長途電話到紐約嗎？
(A)州 (B)國內的 (C)先前的 (D)撥打 答 B

( ) 64. A: I am hungry and want to grab some food.
B: Try this ________ number 1-800-522-5942 for Burger Hot to order a meal.
(A)personal (B)public (C)extension (D)**toll-free**[81] 餐飲 單字

[中譯] A：我餓了，想買些東西吃。
B：試試撥打這個免費的電話號碼 1-800-522-5942，可以向Burger Hot點餐。
(A)個人的 (B)公共的 (C)分機 (D)免費的 答 D

( ) 65. 「#」is called the ________ key, and is a button on a telephone or keyboard labeled.
(A)star (B)well (C)pound (D)mill 生活 單字

[中譯] 「#」被稱為「井字鍵」，它是電話或鍵盤上標有該符號的一個按鈕。
(A)星號 (B)安好的 (C)井號 (D)磨坊 答 C

( ) 66. A: What happened?
B: Doctor, it seems I am allergic to seafood. I have rashes and feel ________ all over my arms.
(A)**itchy**[82] (B)stuffy (C)catchy (D)gassy 生活 單字

情境篇 文法篇 片語篇 測驗篇 口試篇

[中譯] A：發生了什麼事？ B：醫生，我好像對海鮮過敏。我的手臂長了紅疹，感到很癢。
(A)發癢的 (B)悶熱的 (C)容易記住 (D)氣體的 答 A

( ) 67. My ________ was sprained, so walking was quite hard. I think I may need a **wheelchair**[83] for **assistance**[84] at the airport.
(A)stomach (B)ankle (C)forehead (D)elbow 生活 單字

[中譯] 我的腳踝扭傷了，走路相當困難。在機場可能需要輪椅協助。
(A)胃 (B)腳踝 (C)額頭 (D)手肘 答 B

( ) 68. A: I need to buy medicine for my splitting headache.
B: Here is the one you can take. It is ________, no prescription needed.
(A)clinic (B)**side effect**[85] (C)**over-the-counter**[86] (D)symptom 生活 單字

[中譯] A：我需要買藥來治療我劇烈的頭痛。 B：這是一款非處方的藥物，無需處方。
(A)診所 (B)副作用 (C)(指藥品)非處方 (D)症狀 答 C

( ) 69. A: I would like to report a ________ . My wallet was gone.
B: I see. Please calm down and tell me what happened.
(A)rob (B)theft (C)**drought**[87] (D)tsunami 生活 單字

[中譯] A：我想報案竊盜，我的錢包不見了。 B：了解。請冷靜下來，告訴我發生了什麼事。
(A)搶奪 (B)偷竊 (C)乾旱 (D)海嘯 答 B

( ) 70. A: What can I do if I lose my passport during the trip?
B: You have to go to the embassy to have a new one________ .
(A)**reassured**[88] (B)**resigned**[89] (C)**received**[90] (D)reissued 生活 單字

[中譯] A：如果在旅行中遺失了護照，我該怎麼辦？ B：你必須去大使館重新辦一本新的護照。
(A)放心的 (B)放棄的 (C)收到的 (D)重新發行的 答 D

閱讀測驗一

Global warming and environmental problems raise people's environmental concerns and increase their environmental **responsibility**[91] in their buying. Countries all over the world are increasingly emphasizing environmental conservation matters. Green **consumers**[92] are those who are aware of and interested in environmental issues. They support businesses that run in environmentally friendly ways. In addition, green consumers are also concerned about how green the products they bought are. Green products are products that are non-toxic, made from recycled materials, or minimally packaged. In general, green products are known as ecological products or environmentally friendly products that impact less on the **environment**[93]. The goal of green marketing is bringing environment issue into marketing. If we can make consumers consider that information of environmental protection during their decision process, we can push companies to produce more environmentally friendly products.

Although the tourism and hospitality industry is also referred to as the non-factory-made industry, companies are still trying hard toward the goal of sustainable development. In Taiwan, the government took several ways to encourage sustainability development in the industry. For example, the Environmental Protection Administration (EPA) held a reward program that customers could earn "green points" after dinning at environmentally friendly restaurants.

全球暖化和環境問題引起人們對環境的關注，也增加了他們在購物中的環保責任感。世界各國越來越重視環保問題。綠色消費者是那些意識到並關注環境問題的人。他們支持以環保方式經營的企業。此外，綠色消費者還關心他們所購買的產品有多環保。綠色產品是指無毒、由回收材料製成或包裝極簡的產品。一般而言，綠色產品也被稱為生態產品或環保產品，對環境影響較小。綠色行銷的目標是將環境問題納入市場營銷中。如果我們可以讓消費者在決策過程中考慮到環保訊息，就可以推動企業生產更多環保產品。

雖然旅遊和餐飲業被稱為非工廠製造業，但企業仍在努力實現可持續發展的目標。在台灣，政府採取了多種方式鼓勵該行業實現可持續發展。例如，環境保護署舉辦了一個獎勵計劃，顧客在環保餐廳用餐後可以獲得"綠色積分"。

( ) 71. Which of the following statements is true?
(A)Countries all over the world are ignoring environmental conservation issues.
(B)Green products are made of plastic.
(C)The Taiwan government took actions to promote green dining.
(D)The goal of green marketing makes no difference from marketing in general.

[中譯] 下列哪一項敘述正確？
(A)世界各國都忽視環境保護問題。 (B)綠色產品是由塑料製成的。
(C)台灣政府採取措施推廣綠色用餐。 (D)綠色行銷的目標與一般行銷沒有差異。 答 C

( ) 72. Which of the following is not a possible characteristic of green products?
(A)Made from recycled materials. (B)Minimally packaged.
(C)Non-toxic. (D)Packaged in many layers and boxes.

[中譯] 下列哪一項不是綠色產品可能的特點？
(A)由回收材料製成。 (B)包裝極簡。 (C)無毒。 (D)多層次和多個盒子包裝。 答 D

( ) 73. Which of the following is true about green consumers?
(A)They are aware of environmental issues.
(B)They are enthusiastic about death penalty issues.
(C)They are enthusiastic about human rights.
(D)They are interested in racial rights issues.

[中譯] 下列哪一項是關於綠色消費者的正確說法？
(A)他們意識到環保問題 (B)他們熱衷於死刑問題
(C)他們熱衷於人權問題 (D)他們對種族權利問題感興趣 答 A

( ) 74. Which feature are green products known for?
(A)Cheap. (B)Ecological. (C)Planetary. (D)Mechanical.

[中譯] 綠色產品因為哪個特點而聞名？
(A)便宜 (B)生態 (C)行星的 (D)機械的 答 B

( ) 75. What is one of the causes that raise people's environmental concerns?
(A)Gender inequality. (B)Global poverty.
(C)Global warming. (D)Regional war.

[中譯] 什麼是引起人們環保意識提高的原因之一？
(A)性別不平等 (B)全球貧困 (C)全球暖化 (D)區域戰爭 答 C

閱讀測驗二

The sea turtle has been a species at high risk of extinction for many years. In Taiwan, Xiaoliuqiu (also called Little Liuqiu or Liuqiu), an island belonging to Pingtung County in Taiwan has a high number of sea turtles, and the majority of the residents there have been aware of the importance of protecting sea turtles.

However, the island has so many tourist attractions that many visitors come to the island on weekends and holidays. They come for scuba diving, SUP (stand-up paddling), snorkeling, and so on. Although these activities promote local economic growth, it leads to some influences on marine life and the environment.

To decrease the burden on the environment, a team of **volunteers**[94], consisting of university students in Taiwan, non-profit organizations, and residents have started to conduct a project about environmental **protection**[95], including sea turtle conservation and marine-debris **decoration**[96]. The team **observes**[97] the life of sea turtles, keeping records of their migration behaviors. The team also has a sea turtle **patrol**[98] at night from 7:00 p.m. to 5:00 a.m., learning about how sea turtles lay their eggs. On the other hand, the team conducts beach clean-ups every day. The volunteers collect marine debris to create an art wall near the beach. This decoration wall aims to remind visitors that they should reduce **pollution**[99] and **disturbance**[100]. The head of the team says the volunteers will take more actions to keep the island green.

海龜是多年來面臨高度瀕臨絕種的物種。在台灣，屏東縣的小琉球（又稱琉球或小琉球）是一個擁有大量海龜的島嶼，而島上大部分居民已經意識到保護海龜的重要性。

然而，這個島上有許多旅遊景點，以至於許多遊客在週末和假期前來島上進行深潛、直立式划槳(SUP)、浮潛等活動。雖然這些活動促進當地經濟增長，但也對海洋生物和環境造成了一些影響。

為了減少對環境的負擔，一支由台灣大學生、非營利組織和居民組成的志願者團隊開始進行環境保護項目，其中包括海龜保育和海洋垃圾裝飾。團隊觀察海龜的生活，記錄它們的遷徙行為。團隊還在晚上7:00至早上5:00進行海龜巡邏，了解海龜產卵的情況。另外，團隊每天進行海灘清潔行動，志願者們收集海洋垃圾，用它們在海灘附近創造一道藝術牆。這道裝飾牆的目的在提醒遊客應該減少污染和干擾。團隊負責人表示，志願者們將採取更多行動，保持島嶼的綠化。

( ) 76. What is the passage mainly about?
(A)A beautiful country. (B)Environmental protection.
(C)Wild animals. (D)Hardworking residents.

[中譯] 這篇文章的主旨是什麼？
(A)一個美麗的國家。 (B)環境保護。 (C)野生動物。 (D)勤勞的居民。 答 B

( ) 77. Why do visitors come to this island?
(A)To join beach clean-ups. (B)To observe the economic growth.
(C)To paint the houses. (D)To enjoy water activities.

[中譯] 為什麼遊客會來這個島嶼？
(A)參加海灘淨灘。 (B)觀察經濟成長。
(C)為了粉刷房子。 (D)享受水上活動。 答 D

( ) 78. According to the passage, who is NOT likely involved in the volunteer team?
(A)University students.
(B)Teachers at Liuqiu Junior High School.
(C)Staff from a non-profit organization.
(D)Tour managers from other countries.

[中譯] 根據文章，誰不太可能參與志工團隊？
(A)大學生。 (B)六龜國中的老師。
(C)非營利組織的工作人員。 (D)其他國家的旅遊經理人。 答 D

( ) 79. According to the passage, when do sea turtles likely lay eggs?
(A)At noon. (B)In the early afternoon.
(C)At midnight. (D)At 10 in the morning.

[中譯] 根據文章，海龜可能在什麼時間產卵？
(A)中午。 (B)下午早些時候。 (C)半夜。 (D)上午10點。 答 C

( ) 80. According to the passage, how to keep the island green effectively?
(A)Promote ecotourism.
(B)Produce more debris to create the art wall.
(C)Introduce more friends to visit this island.
(D)Make food to feed sea turtles.

[中譯] 根據文章，如何有效地讓這個島嶼保持綠化？
(A)推廣生態旅遊。
(B)產生更多垃圾來製作藝術牆。
(C)向更多朋友介紹來這個島嶼旅遊。
(D)準備食物餵海龜。 答 A

歷年重要單字彙整

單字	出現	音標	中文	詞性
abolition	6	[ˌæbəˋlɪʃən]	廢除，消滅，黑奴制度的廢除	名詞
abundance	5	[əˋbʌndəns]	大量；充足；多	名詞
abundant	3	[əˋbʌndənt]	豐富的；大量的；充足的	形容詞
accelerate	3	[ækˋsɛləˌret]	使加速；促進；增加	動詞
accessible	4	[ækˋsɛsəb!]	可進入的；可接近的；易受影響的	形容詞
accessory	3	[ækˋsɛsərɪ]	配件；婦女飾品；附加物件	名詞
acclaim	4	[əˋklem]	稱讚；歡呼；宣布；擁立	動詞
accommodate	3	[əˋkɑməˌdet]	能容納；通融；考慮到	動詞
accuse	1	[əˋkjuz]	指責；把...歸咎；控告	動詞
acquire	5	[əˋkwaɪr]	取得，獲得；學到；養成	動詞
administer	3	[ədˋmɪnəstɚ]	管理，經營，實施	動詞
admire	5	[ədˋmaɪr]	欣賞；稱讚；欽佩；誇獎	動詞
advantage	14	[ədˋvæntɪdʒ]	優勢；有利條件；利益	名詞
adventure	3	[ədˋvɛntʃɚ]	冒險，冒險精神；冒險活動	名詞
advertise	3	[ˋædvɚˌtaɪz]	為...做廣告，為...宣傳，公佈	動詞
advice	4	[ədˋvaɪs]	勸告；消息，報告	名詞
advocacy	2	[ˋædvəkəsɪ]	擁護，提倡	名詞
affirmation	5	[ˌæfɚˋmeʃən]	證實；批准；斷言	名詞
against	16	[əˋgɛnst]	違反；反對；對比	介係詞
aggressive	5	[əˋgrɛsɪv]	侵略的；好鬥的，挑釁的	形容詞
allegation	6	[ˌæləˋgeʃən]	斷言，申述，辯解	名詞
allowance	6	[əˋlaʊəns]	限額；津貼；零用錢	名詞
alternate	13	[ˋɔltɚnɪt]	交替的，輪流的；供選擇的	形容詞
altitude	5	[ˋæltəˌtjud]	高度；海拔；高處	名詞
ambition	5	[æmˋbɪʃən]	雄心，抱負，追求的目標	名詞

單字	出現	音標	中文	詞性
amenity	4	[ə`minətɪ]	便利設施；舒適；禮儀	名詞
ancillary	3	[`ænsə͵lɛrɪ]	補助的，從屬的，有關的	形容詞
annotate	4	[`æno͵tet]	註解，給...作註解	動詞
anticipation	2	[æn͵tɪsə`peʃən]	預期，預料	名詞
anticipative	2	[æn`tɪsə͵petɪv]	預期的；充滿期望的；先發制人的	形容詞
antique	3	[æn`tik]	古董；古玩；古物	名詞
appetizer	2	[`æpə͵taɪzə-]	開胃的食物，開胃小吃	名詞
application	10	[͵æplə`keʃən]	應用；申請；申請書	名詞
approval	4	[ə`pruv!]	批准，認可；贊成，同意	名詞
architecture	9	[`ɑrkə͵tɛktʃə-]	建築風格；結構；建築學	名詞
artificial	5	[͵ɑrtə`fɪʃəl]	人工的；假的；不自然的	形容詞
ascend	1	[ə`sɛnd]	上升；登高；追溯	動詞
assign	3	[ə`saɪn]	分配，指定；把...歸於	動詞
assignment	3	[ə`saɪnmənt]	任務；工作；功課	名詞
associate	4	[ə`soʃɪɪt]	使結合；聯想；使有聯繫	動詞
assume	3	[ə`sjum]	承擔；多管閒事；裝腔作勢	動詞
atmosphere	10	[`ætməs͵fɪr]	大氣；空氣	名詞
attendant	8	[ə`tɛndənt]	參加者；服務員；侍者	名詞
attitude	3	[`ætətjud]	態度，姿勢；敵視態度	名詞
avalanche	2	[`æv!͵æntʃ]	雪崩；山崩；突然來到的大量事物	名詞
award	5	[ə`wɔrd]	授予，給予；判給	動詞
bankruptcy	2	[`bæŋkrəptsɪ]	破產，倒閉；(名譽) 完全喪失	名詞
banquet	5	[`bæŋkwɪt]	宴會，盛宴；款待	名詞
beat	5	[bit]	敲；衝擊；跳動	動詞
belongings	7	[bə`lɔŋɪŋz]	攜帶物品；財產；家眷；親戚	名詞
benefit	8	[`bɛnəfɪt]	利益；優勢；津貼	名詞
benevolence	1	[bə`nɛvələns]	仁慈，恩惠，捐贈	名詞

▶ 4-176

單字	出現	音標	中文	詞性
betray	2	[bɪ`tre]	背叛，出賣，對 ... 不忠；洩漏	動詞
boutique	4	[bu`tik]	精品店；流行女裝商店	名詞
breathtaking	2	[`brɛθ͵tekɪŋ]	驚人的；令人屏息的；極其美麗的	形容詞
cabinet	2	[`kæbənɪt]	櫃，櫥；內閣；全體閣員；密室	名詞
calligraphy	3	[kə`lɪgrəfɪ]	書法；筆跡	名詞
capability	5	[͵kepə`bɪlətɪ]	能力，才能，功能，耐受力；潛力	名詞
capable	1	[`kepəb!]	有能力的，能幹的；能夠...的	形容詞
censure	2	[`sɛnʃɚ]	責備，譴責	動詞
ceremony	5	[`sɛrə͵monɪ]	儀式；形式；典禮；禮儀	名詞
certificate	3	[sɚ`tɪfəkɪt]	證明書；單據；執照；憑證	名詞
charity	2	[`tʃærətɪ]	慈善；博愛；慈悲，仁愛；施捨；善舉	名詞
chronic	3	[`krɑnɪk]	長期的；習慣性的；久病的	形容詞
citizen	4	[`sɪtəzn]	市民，居民；公民；平民	名詞
civil	4	[`sɪv!]	市民的，公民的；民間的	形容詞
client	12	[`klaɪənt]	客戶；委託人，當事人	名詞
collaborate	4	[kə`læbə͵ret]	共同工作，合作；勾結	動詞
colleague	3	[`kɑlig]	同事，同僚	名詞
comment	4	[`kɑmɛnt]	評論；註釋，解釋；發表意見	動詞
commodity	2	[kə`mɑdətɪ]	商品；日用品	名詞
communication	8	[kə͵mjunə`keʃən]	交流；溝通；傳達；傳染；訊息；情報	名詞
commute	6	[kə`mjut]	通勤；減輕；替代；代償；交換；改變	動詞
compare	9	[kəm`pɛr]	比較；比喻為；對照；(可與...) 相比	動詞
compensative	2	[kəm`pɛnsətɪv]	償還的，補充的	形容詞
competitive	10	[kəm`pɛtətɪv]	競爭的，經由競爭的，競爭性的	形容詞
compile	1	[kəm`paɪl]	編輯；匯編；收集 (資料等)	動詞
complicate	1	[`kɑmplə͵ket]	使複雜化；使惡化；使難對付；併發	動詞

單字	出現	音標	中文	詞性
compliment	5	[ˋkɑmpləmənt]	讚美的話；問候；致意	名詞
concern	18	[kənˋsɝn]	關心的事；擔心；利害關係；企業	名詞
concert	1	[ˋkɑnsɚt]	音樂會，和諧，一致行動	名詞
condition	19	[kənˋdɪʃən]	情況；狀態；條件	名詞
condolence	2	[kənˋdoləns]	慰問，弔辭，弔唁	名詞
confidential	2	[ˌkɑnfəˋdɛnʃəl]	機密的；祕密的；表示信任的	形容詞
confrontation	3	[ˌkɑnfrʌnˋteʃən]	對質；比較；對抗	名詞
congest	3	[kənˋdʒɛst]	充塞，充滿；使充血	動詞
congestion	3	[kənˋdʒɛstʃən]	擁塞；擠滿；充血	名詞
conjunction	1	[kənˋdʒʌŋkʃən]	連接；結合；關聯；同時發生	名詞
connection	6	[kəˋnɛkʃən]	連接；聯絡；關聯	名詞
consent	3	[kənˋsɛnt]	同意，贊成，答應	名詞
consequence	3	[ˋkɑnsəˌkwɛns]	結果；重要性；重大	名詞
consist	7	[kənˋsɪst]	組成；一致；存在於	動詞
console	1	[ˋkɑnsol]	安慰，撫慰，慰問	動詞
constituent	3	[kənˋstɪtʃʊənt]	成分，組成的要素；選舉人	名詞
construct	13	[kənˋstrʌkt]	建造；創立；構成；製造	動詞
consumption	8	[kənˋsʌmpʃən]	消耗；用盡；消費量	名詞
contaminate	1	[kənˋtæməˌnet]	汙染；毒害；使受毒氣影響；使受放射汙染	動詞
contemplate	2	[ˋkɑntɛmˌplet]	仔細考慮；凝視；計議	動詞
contemporary	5	[kənˋtɛmpəˌrɛrɪ]	當代的；同時代的；同年齡的	形容詞
contingency	2	[kənˋtɪndʒənsɪ]	意外事故，偶然事件；可能性	名詞
contract	8	[ˋkɑntrækt]	合約書；合同；契約書	名詞
contribute	7	[kənˋtrɪbjut]	貢獻，提供；捐助	動詞
conventional	1	[kənˋvɛnʃən!]	慣例的；習慣的；傳統的	形容詞
convict	2	[kənˋvɪkt]	證明有罪，判決；使深感有錯	動詞

4-178

單字	出現	音標	中文	詞性
cooperate	4	[ko`ɑpə͵ret]	合作，協作；配合	動詞
costume	6	[`kɑstjum]	服裝；戲裝；裝束	名詞
counselor	3	[`kaʊnslɚ]	顧問；指導老師；律師	名詞
courtesy	2	[`kɝtəsɪ]	禮貌；好意；殷勤；謙恭有禮的言辭	名詞
crisis	2	[`kraɪsɪs]	危機，緊急關頭，轉折點；病情危險期	名詞
criticize	1	[`krɪtɪ͵saɪz]	批評；批判；苛求；非難；評論；評價	動詞
crucial	3	[`kruʃəl]	重要的；艱難的；決定性的；嚴酷的	形容詞
cultivate	3	[`kʌltə͵vet]	耕種；栽培；建立；養殖；培養	動詞
decisive	1	[dɪ`saɪsɪv]	決定性的；確定的；決定的；堅決的	形容詞
decorate	3	[`dɛkə͵ret]	裝飾，布置，修飾；粉刷	動詞
dedicate	11	[`dɛdə͵ket]	致力於；奉獻，獻身於；題獻給	動詞
defend	4	[dɪ`fɛnd]	防禦，保衛，保護	動詞
deliberate	2	[dɪ`lɪbərɪt]	深思熟慮的，謹慎的，故意的	形容詞
delicate	2	[`dɛləkət]	易碎的；精緻的，雅緻的；嬌貴的；纖弱的	形容詞
delightful	1	[dɪ`laɪtfəl]	令人愉快的，令人高興的；可愛的	形容詞
deliver	10	[dɪ`lɪvɚ]	給予；傳送；投遞；運送；發動；實現	動詞
demolish	2	[dɪ`mɑlɪʃ]	毀壞，拆除，推翻，打敗，廢除，撤銷	動詞
demote	2	[dɪ`mot]	降級	動詞
depletion	1	[dɪ`pliʃən]	用盡；消耗	名詞
depress	6	[dɪ`prɛs]	使沮喪；使消沉；壓低；壓下；削弱	動詞
descend	3	[dɪ`sɛnd]	下來，下降，下傾，來自於	動詞
desert	2	[`dɛzɚt]	沙漠；荒野	名詞
deserve	2	[dɪ`zɝv]	應受，該得	動詞
despite	10	[dɪ`spaɪt]	儘管，任憑，不管	介係詞
destiny	2	[`dɛstənɪ]	命運；天數，天命，神意	名詞
determine	6	[dɪ`tɝmɪn]	決定；終止；確定；判決；影響	動詞
detour	5	[`ditʊr]	繞道；繞行的路	名詞

單字	出現	音標	中文	詞性
devote	5	[dɪ`vot]	將...奉獻；把...專用於	動詞
devotion	2	[dɪ`voʃən]	奉獻；忠誠；祈禱	名詞
digest	1	[daɪ`dʒɛst]	消化；領悟，整理	動詞
disaster	4	[dɪ`zæstɚ]	災害，災難；徹底的失敗	名詞
discussion	2	[dɪ`skʌʃən]	討論，商討；談論	名詞
disorder	2	[dɪs`ɔrdɚ]	混亂，無秩序；騷亂，動亂	名詞
dispensable	3	[dɪ`spɛnsəb!]	非必要的，可分配的；可寬恕的	形容詞
displace	2	[dɪs`ples]	移開，取代；替代	動詞
display	14	[dɪ`sple]	表現；陳列；展出	動詞
disposable	4	[dɪ`spozəb!]	用完即丟棄的，一次性使用的	形容詞
distinction	2	[dɪ`stɪŋkʃən]	區別；對比；特徵	名詞
distribution	2	[ˌdɪstrə`bjuʃən]	分配，配給物；銷售 (量)	名詞
district	9	[`dɪstrɪkt]	地區；行政區；區域	名詞
diversity	2	[daɪ`vɝsətɪ]	差異，不同點；多樣性	名詞
dummy	1	[`dʌmɪ]	服裝人體模型；仿製品；樣品	名詞
duplicate	2	[`djupləkɪt]	複製的，副本的，影印	形容詞
eligible	2	[`ɛlɪdʒəb!]	有資格當選的，法律上合格的；合適的	形容詞
emphasize	6	[`ɛmfəˌsaɪz]	著重；強調；使顯得突出	動詞
engagement	2	[ɪn`gedʒmənt]	訂婚，婚約；銜接	名詞
enhancement	2	[in`hænsmənt]	增加，提高	名詞
enormous	3	[ɪ`nɔrməs]	巨大的，龐大的	形容詞
entertainment	6	[ˌɛntɚ`tenmənt]	款待；演藝；娛樂	名詞
enthusiasm	2	[n`θjuzɪˌæzəm]	熱心，熱情，熱忱	名詞
envelope	3	[`ɛnvəˌlop]	信封；封套；外殼	名詞
escape	3	[ə`skep]	逃跑，漏出，流出	動詞
esteem	2	[ɪs`tim]	尊重；評價；珍重；認為	動詞
evacuation	2	[ɪˌvækjʊ`eʃən]	疏散；撤退；排泄物	名詞

▶ 4-180

單字	出現	音標	中文	詞性
evidence	5	[`ɛvədəns]	證據；證詞；證人；物證；跡象	名詞
evolution	3	[ˌɛvə`luʃən]	發展，進展；演化，進化論	名詞
excess	3	[ɪk`sɛs]	超越；過剩；無節制；暴行	名詞
exchange	23	[ɪks`tʃendʒ]	匯率；交流；交易	名詞
excursion	2	[ɪk`skɝʒən]	短途旅行；遊覽團；離題	名詞
excuse	15	[ɪk`skjuz]	原諒，辯解，試圖開脫，免除	動詞
exhibition	23	[ˌɛksə`bɪʃən]	展覽；展示會；展覽品，陳列品	名詞
exotic	3	[ɛg`zɑtɪk]	異國情調的；奇特的；外來的	形容詞
expert	5	[`ɛkspɚt]	專家；能手；熟練者	名詞
expiration	3	[ˌɛkspə`reʃən]	期滿；吐氣；終結	名詞
explode	2	[ɪk`splod]	爆發；爆炸；爆破	動詞
expression	3	[ɪk`sprɛʃən]	表情；表達；措辭	名詞
extend	3	[ɪk`stɛnd]	擴展，擴大；延長；伸展	動詞
extinct	3	[ɪk`stɪŋkt]	絕種的，破滅的；廢除的	形容詞
extinction	2	[ɪk`stɪŋkʃən]	滅絕；消滅；破滅	名詞
facilitate	3	[fə`sɪləˌtet]	促進，幫助；使容易	動詞
faculty	4	[`fæk!tɪ]	機能，官能，能力，技能	名詞
fasten	12	[`fæsn]	扣緊；繫緊；集中注意力；抓住	動詞
feature	18	[fitʃɚ]	特徵，特色；臉的一部分	名詞
ferry	5	[`fɛrɪ]	渡輪，擺渡船；經營擺渡的特許權	名詞
flu	3	[flu]	流行性感冒	名詞
fluctuation	3	[ˌflʌktʃʊ`eʃən]	波動；變動；動搖	名詞
folk	4	[fok]	民間的，通俗的，民眾的	形容詞
formula	1	[`fɔrmjələ]	慣例；配方；準則；客套話	名詞
fragile	9	[`frædʒəl]	脆弱的；易碎的；易損壞的；精細的	形容詞
furnish	4	[`fɝnɪʃ]	給 (房間) 配置 (傢俱等), 裝備	動詞
gourmet	4	[`gʊrme]	美味的；菜餚精美的	形容詞

單字	出現	音標	中文	詞性
grocery	4	[`grosərɪ]	食品雜貨，南北貨；食品雜貨店	名詞
guarantee	8	[ˌgærən`ti]	保證；抵押品；保證人；被保證人	名詞
heritage	13	[`hɛrətɪdʒ]	遺產；繼承物；傳統	名詞
hesitate	3	[`hɛzəˌtet]	猶豫，躊躇；有疑慮	動詞
hospitality	8	[ˌhɑspɪ`tælətɪ]	殷勤招待；好客；理解力	名詞
hostility	2	[hɑs`tɪlətɪ]	敵意，敵視，戰鬥	名詞
identify	9	[aɪ`dɛntəˌfaɪ]	識別；鑑定；使參與	動詞
impact	16	[ɪm`pækt]	衝擊；壓緊；擠滿	動詞
impressive	2	[ɪm`prɛsɪv]	令人深刻印象的；感人的；令人欽佩的	形容詞
improve	10	[ɪm`pruv]	改善；增進；變得更好	動詞
inbound	1	[`ɪnˈbaʊnd]	回內地的；歸本國的	形容詞
indigenous	7	[ɪn`dɪdʒɪnəs]	當地的；內在的；本地的	形容詞
infrequently	5	[ɪn`frikwəntlɪ]	稀少地，珍貴地	副詞
initiate	3	[ɪ`nɪʃɪɪt]	啟動的；接受初步知識的；新加入的	形容詞
innovation	5	[ˌɪnə`veʃən]	革新，改革	名詞
institute	2	[`ɪnstətjut]	協會；研究所；大學；摘要	名詞
instruction	5	[ɪn`strʌkʃən]	教學，命令，指示	名詞
interact	8	[ˌɪntə`rækt]	互動；互相影響；互相作用	動詞
interpreter	2	[ɪn`tɝprɪtɚ]	口譯員，通譯員；解釋者	名詞
intersection	3	[ˌɪntɚ`sɛkʃən]	交叉，橫斷；十字路口	名詞
intervention	1	[ˌɪntɚ`vɛnʃən]	干預；介入；調停，斡旋	名詞
invasive	2	[ɪn`vesɪv]	侵入的；侵略性的	形容詞
invent	5	[ɪn`vɛnt]	發明，創造，捏造	動詞
investigate	1	[ɪn`vɛstəˌget]	調查，研究	動詞
investment	2	[ɪn`vɛstmənt]	投資；投資物；授權	名詞
irrelevance	1	[ɪ`rɛləvəns]	無關係；不恰當；不對題	名詞
isolate	4	[`aɪslˌet]	孤立；隔離；脫離	動詞

單字	出現	音標	中文	詞性
itinerary	15	[aɪˋtɪnəˏrɛrɪ]	旅行計畫；旅程	名詞
lack	2	[læk]	欠缺；不足	名詞
legislate	4	[ˋlɛdʒɪsˏlet]	立法，制定法律；用立法規定	動詞
leisure	10	[ˋliʒɚ]	悠閒；閒暇，空暇時間	名詞
longitude	1	[ˋlɑndʒəˋtjud]	經度	名詞
luxury	16	[ˋlʌkʃərɪ]	奢侈品；奢侈，奢華	名詞
magnificent	3	[mægˋnɪfəsənt]	華麗的；很動人的；豪華的；壯麗的	形容詞
magnitude	3	[ˋmægnəˏtjud]	震級，巨大，重要	名詞
management	14	[ˋmænɪdʒmənt]	管理；經營；處理	名詞
mandatory	2	[ˋmændəˏtorɪ]	強制的；義務的；命令的；指令的	形容詞
manufacture	1	[ˏmænjəˋfæktʃərɚ]	製造業者，廠商，廠主；製造公司	名詞
marble	2	[ˋmɑrb!]	大理石，大理石雕刻品，彈珠遊戲	名詞
masterpiece	3	[ˋmæstɚˏpis]	傑作；最傑出的作品；名作	名詞
material	10	[məˋtɪrɪəl]	資料；原料；素材；工具	名詞
memorial	12	[məˋmorɪəl]	紀念物；紀念碑；紀念館	名詞
merge	2	[mɝdʒ]	合併；融合；同化	動詞
mineral	3	[ˋmɪnərəl]	礦物；礦泉水；無機物；蘇打水	名詞
moderate	5	[ˋmɑdəˏret]	使和緩，減輕，節制；主持	動詞
monument	11	[ˋmɑnjəmənt]	紀念碑，紀念塔，紀念館	名詞
multiple	5	[ˋmʌltəp!]	多樣的；多人共享的；複合的	形容詞
mutual	2	[ˋmjutʃʊəl]	共同的；相互的，彼此的；共有的	形容詞
narrow	6	[ˋnæro]	狹窄的；勉強的；精細的	形容詞
navigate	2	[ˋnævəˏget]	航行於；駕駛，操縱，導航	動詞
necessary	8	[ˋnɛsəˏsɛrɪ]	必要的；無法避免的，必然的	形容詞
nutrition	1	[njuˋtrɪʃən]	營養；食物；滋養；營養物	名詞
object	9	[ˋɑbdʒɪkt]	物體；目標；對象；目的	名詞
observatory	2	[əbˋzɝvəˏtorɪ]	瞭望台；天文台；氣象台；觀測所	名詞

單字	出現	音標	中文	詞性
obstacle	2	[`ɑbstək!]	障礙，阻礙，妨礙	名詞
obtain	10	[əb`ten]	獲得；通用；流行；存在	動詞
obvious	2	[`ɑbvɪəs]	明顯的；顯著的；平淡無奇的	形容詞
occupancy	2	[`ɑkjəpənsɪ]	入住率；佔有；居住	名詞
offend	4	[ə`fɛnd]	冒犯，觸怒，傷害 ... 的感情	動詞
omit	2	[o`mɪt]	遺漏；省略；刪去；忘記	動詞
organization	12	[͵ɔrgənə`zeʃən]	組織；系統；機構，團體	名詞
outfit	2	[`aʊt͵fɪt]	全套裝備；全套工具，全套用品	名詞
participate	7	[pɑr`tɪsə͵pet]	參加，參與	動詞
passionate	2	[`pæʃənɪt]	熱情的；激昂的；易怒的	形容詞
passive	3	[`pæsɪv]	被動的，消極的；順從的	形容詞
pedestrian	4	[pə`dɛstrɪən]	徒步的；行人的；平淡的	形容詞
penalty	6	[`pɛn!tɪ]	罰款；處罰，刑罰	名詞
perform	8	[pɚ`fɔrm]	表演；執行；完成；表現	動詞
perspective	7	[pɚ`spɛktɪv]	觀點；洞察力；遠景	名詞
persuade	2	[pɚ`swed]	說服，勸服，使某人相信	動詞
petition	4	[pə`tɪʃən]	請願；請求，申請；祈求	名詞
plentiful	3	[`plɛntɪfəl]	豐富的，充足的；多的	形容詞
population	16	[͵pɑpjə`leʃən]	人口；(某地區) 全部居民；族群；總體	名詞
postpone	3	[post`pon]	延遲；使延期，把...放在次要地位	動詞
poverty	5	[`pɑvɚtɪ]	貧窮，貧困；缺少；虛弱	名詞
prescription	5	[prɪ`skrɪpʃən]	處方；指示；慣例；法定期限	名詞
presentation	4	[͵prizɛn`teʃən]	介紹；顯示；演出；表現	名詞
preserve	15	[prɪ`zɝv]	保存；防腐；維持	動詞
prestige	3	[prɛs`tiʒ]	聲望，名望，威望	名詞
presume	2	[prɪ`zum]	推定；擅自；假設	動詞

單字	出現	音標	中文	詞性
production	2	[prə`dʌkʃən]	生產；製作；產量；作品	名詞
project	11	[prə`dʒɛkt]	計畫；投射；闡述；預計	動詞
promote	14	[prə`mot]	促進；發起，創立	動詞
property	3	[`prapɚtɪ]	財產，資產，財產權	名詞
proposal	4	[prə`poz!]	提案；求婚；建議；計畫	名詞
prosperous	1	[`prasperəs]	興旺的，繁榮的	形容詞
protest	5	[prə`tɛst]	抗議，異議，反對；斷言，聲明	名詞
publication	3	[͵pʌblɪ`keʃən]	出版物；公布；刊物； 發行	名詞
puppetry	4	[`pʌpɪtrɪ]	木偶；傀儡；木偶製作	名詞
purpose	11	[`pɝpəs]	目的，意圖；效果；決心	名詞
radical	1	[`rædɪk!]	基本的；徹底的；極端的	形容詞
rank	5	[ræŋk]	地位；等級；身分；隊伍	名詞
rate	12	[ret]	等級；比率；速度，速率	名詞
reaction	1	[rɪ`ækʃən]	反應，反作用；復古；倒退	名詞
receive	20	[rɪ`siv]	得到；接受；承認；容納	動詞
recognition	5	[͵rɛkəg`nɪʃən]	識別；認可；報償；認出	名詞
recommend	11	[͵rɛkə`mɛnd]	推薦，介紹；託付	動詞
recruit	5	[rɪ`krut]	招募；吸收 (新成員)；僱用；補充	動詞
reduce	9	[rɪ`djus]	減少；迫使；降服；縮小	動詞
refrain	3	[rɪ`fren]	忍住，抑制，節制，戒除	動詞
refuge	5	[`rɛfjudʒ]	避難所；躲避；藏身處；收容	名詞
regard	1	[rɪ`gard]	注重；考慮；關心；尊敬	名詞
region	10	[`ridʒən]	地區，地帶；領域，範圍	名詞
rehearsal	1	[rɪ`hɝs!]	排練；練習；敘述	名詞
reimburse	5	[͵riɪm`bɝs]	付還；償還；歸還	動詞
request	12	[rɪ`kwɛst]	要求，請求；需求	名詞
resignation	3	[͵rɛzɪg`neʃən]	辭職，放棄；辭職書，辭呈	名詞

單字	出現	音標	中文	詞性
respectful	1	[rɪ`spɛktfəl]	尊敬人的；恭敬的；尊重人的	形容詞
respective	2	[rɪ`spɛktɪv]	各自的；分別的	形容詞
resume	3	[rɪ`zjum]	重新開始，繼續；重返	動詞
reveal	2	[rɪ`vil]	展現，揭露，洩露	動詞
revise	2	[rɪ`vaɪz]	修訂，校訂	動詞
revolution	6	[ˌrɛvə`luʃən]	革命，革命運動，公轉	名詞
reward	8	[rɪ`wɔrd]	報答；獎勵；報應	動詞
rustic	2	[`rʌstɪk]	鄉下的，農村的，質樸的	形容詞
salvation	2	[sæl`veʃən]	拯救，救星，救世	名詞
scenery	12	[`sinərɪ]	風景，景色；舞台布景	名詞
sensitive	8	[`sɛnsətɪv]	敏感的；易受傷害的；易怒的	形容詞
separate	5	[`sɛpəˌret]	分隔；區分，識別	動詞
significance	6	[sɪg`nɪfəkəns]	重要性，意義，意思	名詞
specific	9	[spɪ`sɪfɪk]	具體的；明確的；特殊的；獨特的	形容詞
spectacular	5	[spɛk`tækjələ]	壯觀的，引人注目的；輝煌的	形容詞
state	16	[stet]	狀況，形勢，國家	名詞
statue	15	[`stætʃʊ]	雕像，塑像	名詞
stature	3	[`stætʃɚ]	身材，高度水準，身高	名詞
status	5	[`stetəs]	地位，身分，重要地位，狀況	名詞
stimulate	2	[`stɪmjəˌlet]	刺激，使興奮，促進...的功能	動詞
straight	5	[stret]	筆直的；正確的；循規蹈矩的	形容詞
stroll	4	[strol]	散步，流浪，巡迴演出	動詞
subscribe	7	[səb`skraɪb]	訂閱；同意；捐助；簽(名)	動詞
suffer	6	[`sʌfɚ]	遭受；經歷；忍受	動詞
summon	1	[`sʌmən]	鼓起；召喚；請求	動詞
superstition	4	[ˌsupɚ`stɪʃən]	迷信，盲目崇拜，盲目恐懼	名詞
supervise	2	[`supɚvaɪz]	監督；管理；指導	動詞

▸ 4-186

單字	出現	音標	中文	詞性
supplement	5	[`sʌpləmənt]	補充，附錄；補給品	名詞
suspect	4	[sə`spɛkt]	懷疑；不信任；猜疑；察覺	動詞
sustainability	6	[sə͵stenə`bɪlɪtɪ]	永續性；持續性	名詞
symbolize	2	[`sɪmbl͵aɪz]	象徵，標誌；用符號表示；採用象徵	動詞
technique	17	[tɛk`nik]	技術；技巧；技法	名詞
tenant	1	[`tɛnənt]	房客；承租人；居住者；佃戶	名詞
terminate	2	[`tɝmə͵net]	使停止，使結束，使結尾	動詞
threat	8	[θrɛt]	威脅，恐嚇；凶兆	名詞
tie	4	[taɪ]	繫；被繫住；拴，捆，紮；打結	動詞
trade	5	[tred]	交易；營業額；同業者	名詞
translate	3	[træns`let]	翻譯；說明，表達	動詞
transportation	22	[͵trænspɚ`teʃən]	運輸；運輸工具；運費	名詞
trespass	1	[`trɛspəs]	擅自進入；侵犯；侵佔	動詞
tribe	11	[traɪb]	族；部落；種族；群；一夥	名詞
unconscious	5	[ʌn`kɑnʃəs]	無意識的，失去知覺的；不知道的	形容詞
underestimate	2	[`ʌndɚ`ɛstə͵met]	低估；對...估計不足	動詞
unique	9	[ju`nik]	獨特的；珍奇的；罕有的	形容詞
vacant	2	[`vekənt]	空白的；空缺的；空著的	形容詞
validity	2	[və`lɪdətɪ]	有效性；合法性；效力	名詞
value	14	[`vælju]	重視，價值，價格	名詞
venue	6	[`vɛnju]	發生地；犯罪地點；審判地	名詞
village	8	[`vɪlɪdʒ]	村莊，村民；聚居處	名詞
violator	1	[`vaɪə͵letɚ]	違背者；侵犯者；褻瀆者	名詞
vote	6	[vot]	投票；選舉；表決	動詞
warranty	3	[`wɔrəntɪ]	保證書；擔保；授權	名詞
worship	4	[`wɝʃɪp]	敬仰；聲望	名詞

Unit .

05.

口試篇

報考外語導遊的考生，
除通過筆試外，還須再參加口試。
許多考生對於口試的準備內容，
抓不著頭緒，也不知從何準備起，
本單元特別收錄歷年口試題型及文章範例，
幫助輕鬆準備，提升口說自信！

Chapter. 01 | 口試 | 外語導遊第二試

試前充分準備，臨場口試不慌亂！

考試分析

依目前評量測驗規定，外語導遊類組分為二階段測驗，第一試【筆試】於每年三月舉行，平均60分及格，並且外語單科分數須至少50分以上，即符合參加第二試【口試】資格。同樣地，口試須達60分以上合格(如口試未達60分，則須重新參加第一試)。

口試測驗每人10~12分鐘，採現場抽號碼方式決定題目，每道題目約有3小題，以「自我介紹」、「本國文化與國情」、「風景節慶與美食」三大部分為命題範圍。當考生進入試場後，須先對著攝影機報上准考證號碼及抽到的題目編號，接著口試官會依考生所抽到的題目依序發問，通常第一題為自我介紹，建議考生務必提前準備，即能輕鬆得分。

本單元特別彙整重要專有名詞及口說文章範例供參考練習，有助於掌握範圍及提升準備效率。

準備指標　交通部觀光局網站 www.taiwan.net.tw　　馬跡祝您　金榜題名

112 年度口試題目 (以號碼抽題方式，考生從10 道題目中，抽 1 題回答)

題目	內容	題目	內容
題目一	❶ 自我介紹 ❷ 介紹台灣原住民 ❸ 介紹咖啡文化	題目六	❶ 自我介紹 ❷ 介紹臺灣的跳島旅遊 ❸ 介紹元宵節的習俗
題目二	❶ 自我介紹 ❷ 介紹台灣節日的送禮文化 ❸ 介紹士林官邸公園	題目七	❶ 自我介紹 ❷ 介紹臺灣的排隊文化 ❸ 介紹屏東黑鮪魚
題目三	❶ 自我介紹 ❷ 介紹臺灣的自行車旅遊 ❸ 向外國人介紹珍珠奶茶	題目八	❶ 自我介紹 ❷ 請說明臺灣節能減碳的作法 ❸ 介紹台灣的美食 - 粽子
題目四	❶ 自我介紹 ❷ 介紹臺灣的棒球運動 ❸ 介紹馬祖	題目九	❶ 自我介紹 ❷ 介紹台南安平 ❸ 介紹放風箏的活動文化
題目五	❶ 自我介紹 ❷ 介紹溫泉旅遊 ❸ 向外國人介紹台灣的刈包	題目十	❶ 自我介紹 ❷ 臺灣的「美甲」產業與看法 ❸ 介紹端午節文化

★「自我介紹」包含報考動機、經歷嗜好、旅遊經驗及理想抱負

111 年度口試題目 （以號碼抽題方式，考生從10 道題目中，抽 1 題回答）

題目	內容	題目	內容
題目一	❶ 自我介紹 ❷ 介紹臺灣七夕習俗 ❸ 向外國人介紹臺灣烏龍茶	題目六	❶ 自我介紹 ❷ 介紹臺灣的全民健保制度 ❸ 介紹澎湖花火節
題目二	❶ 自我介紹 ❷ 介紹清明節 ❸ 介紹臺灣牛肉麵	題目七	❶ 自我介紹 ❷ 介紹臺灣村里長制度及工作內容 ❸ 介紹日月潭
題目三	❶ 自我介紹 ❷ 介紹祭孔大典的意義與儀式 ❸ 介紹客家美食	題目八	❶ 自我介紹 ❷ 臺灣少子化現象及影響 ❸ 介紹淡水紅毛城
題目四	❶ 自我介紹 ❷ 介紹媽祖遶境文化 ❸ 介紹蚵仔煎	題目九	❶ 自我介紹 ❷ 介紹臺灣的科學園區 ❸ 介紹澎湖雙心石滬
題目五	❶ 自我介紹 ❷ 介紹東京奧運以及臺灣獲得哪些獎牌 ❸ 介紹內門宋江陣	題目十	❶ 自我介紹 ❷ 介紹臺灣不同的族群 ❸ 介紹馬祖八八坑道

110 年度口試題目 （以號碼抽題方式，考生從10 道題目中，抽 1 題回答）

題目	內容	題目	內容
題目一	❶ 自我介紹 ❷ 向登山客介紹臺灣國情與文化 ❸ 介紹臺灣風景、人情、飲食	題目六	❶ 自我介紹 ❷ 介紹臺灣現行的消費付款方式 ❸ 介紹臺灣有名的茶飲品
題目二	❶ 自我介紹 ❷ 介紹臺灣新年習俗 ❸ 介紹臺灣中部櫻花景點	題目七	❶ 自我介紹 ❷ 介紹臺灣的觀光工廠 ❸ 介紹臺南擔仔麵特色
題目三	❶ 自我介紹 ❷ 介紹端午節划龍舟習俗 ❸ 介紹阿里山遊樂區	題目八	❶ 自我介紹 ❷ 介紹臺灣的眷村文化 ❸ 介紹蔬食餐廳特色
題目四	❶ 自我介紹 ❷ 介紹台北大眾捷運交通系統 ❸ 介紹綠島	題目九	❶ 自我介紹 ❷ 介紹中秋節的由來 ❸ 介紹臺灣小籠包有名的原因
題目五	❶ 自我介紹 ❷ 介紹臺灣四季氣候 ❸ 介紹臺中高美濕地	題目十	❶ 自我介紹 ❷ 介紹媽祖繞境文化 ❸ 介紹臺灣芒果冰受歡迎的原因

▸ 5-4

109 年度口試題目（以號碼抽題方式，考生從10 道題目中，抽 1 題回答）

題目	內容	題目	內容
題目一	❶ 自我介紹 ❷ 面對COVID19，臺灣政府和觀光業如何因應 ❸ 向外國人介紹松菸文創園區	題目六	❶ 自我介紹 ❷ 棒球為什麼是臺灣的國球 ❸ 介紹清境農場
題目二	❶ 自我介紹 ❷ 介紹臺灣的大學和專科制度 ❸ 介紹臺灣的滷肉飯	題目七	❶ 自我介紹 ❷ 介紹臺灣的建築結構和居住習慣 ❸ 介紹嘉義奮起湖特色和當地美食
題目三	❶ 自我介紹 ❷ 介紹臺灣的KTV文化 ❸ 介紹八里十三行博物館	題目八	❶ 自我介紹 ❷ 介紹行天宮收驚的宗教文化 ❸ 介紹臺南小吃
題目四	❶ 自我介紹 ❷ 介紹臺灣的麻將 ❸ 介紹西門町	題目九	❶ 自我介紹 ❷ 介紹原住民豐年祭 ❸ 向外國人介紹鐵道旅遊
題目五	❶ 自我介紹 ❷ 介紹臺灣婚喪喜慶文化 ❸ 介紹烏來風景區	題目十	❶ 自我介紹 ❷ 介紹臺灣的臭豆腐 ❸ 介紹炸寒單活動

108 年度口試題目（以號碼抽題方式，考生從10 道題目中，抽 1 題回答）

題目	內容	題目	內容
題目一	❶ 自我介紹 ❷ 臺灣的地震 ❸ 東北角暨宜蘭海岸國家風景區	題目六	❶ 自我介紹 ❷ 臺灣檳榔文化 ❸ 臺灣端午節
題目二	❶ 自我介紹 ❷ 臺灣佛教文化 ❸ 臺江國家公園	題目七	❶ 自我介紹 ❷ 臺灣傳統美食文化 ❸ 東港燒王船祭典
題目三	❶ 自我介紹 ❷ 介紹臺灣水果王國 ❸ 日月潭國家風景區	題目八	❶ 自我介紹 ❷ 客家特色美食 ❸ 臺灣元宵節
題目四	❶ 自我介紹 ❷ 三月媽祖遶境文化 ❸ 介紹三種臺灣小吃	題目九	❶ 自我介紹 ❷ 客家民俗信仰 ❸ 澎湖玄武岩自然保留區
題目五	❶ 自我介紹 ❷ 臺灣溫泉 ❸ 介紹三道雞肉料理	題目十	❶ 自我介紹 ❷ 宜蘭搶孤活動與習俗 ❸ 介紹福爾摩沙—臺灣

107 年度口試題目（以號碼抽題方式，考生從10 道題目中，抽 1 題回答）

題目	內容	題目	內容
題目一	❶ 自我介紹 ❷ 外籍旅客購物退稅 ❸ 臺灣鐵路便當	題目六	❶ 自我介紹 ❷ 臺灣高科技產業 ❸ 日月潭環潭自行車道
題目二	❶ 自我介紹 ❷ 臺灣觀光老街 ❸ 臺灣麵食文化	題目七	❶ 自我介紹 ❷ 臺灣季風氣候與颱風 ❸ 臺灣候鳥生態
題目三	❶ 自我介紹 ❷ 臺灣宗教現況 ❸ 臺灣知名夜市與文化	題目八	❶ 自我介紹 ❷ 臺灣知名伴手禮 ❸ 介紹921地震園區
題目四	❶ 自我介紹 ❷ 臺灣知名高山 ❸ 臺灣中秋節	題目九	❶ 自我介紹 ❷ 如何向外國觀光客介紹布袋戲 ❸ 介紹臺東熱氣球嘉年華
題目五	❶ 自我介紹 ❷ 臺灣高速鐵路 ❸ 臺灣地質公園	題目十	❶ 自我介紹 ❷ 臺灣原住民祭典 ❸ 介紹臺灣小籠包

106 年度口試題目（以號碼抽題方式，考生從10 道題目中，抽 1 題回答）

題目	內容	題目	內容
題目一	❶ 自我介紹 ❷ 最受歡迎的臺灣運動 ❸ 向外國人介紹迪化街	題目六	❶ 自我介紹 ❷ 客家文化和擂茶 ❸ 介紹鹿港
題目二	❶ 自我介紹 ❷ 臺灣飲酒文化、對酒駕的看法 ❸ 阿里山小火車	題目七	❶ 自我介紹 ❷ 臺灣北部溫泉 ❸ 介紹新竹市區的特色
題目三	❶ 自我介紹 ❷ 臺灣人的養生方式 ❸ 介紹花蓮	題目八	❶ 自我介紹 ❷ 臺灣糖業發展史 ❸ 行銷太陽餅
題目四	❶ 自我介紹 ❷ 介紹便利商店的關東煮 ❸ 介紹飲料店泡沫紅茶	題目九	❶ 自我介紹 ❷ 介紹藍白拖 ❸ 介紹一個宜蘭的國際觀光活動
題目五	❶ 自我介紹 ❷ 臺灣人與外國人休閒活動的差異 ❸ 介紹苗栗觀光	題目十	❶ 自我介紹 ❷ 介紹臺灣生態年 ❸ 介紹清明節

105 年度口試題目 (以號碼抽題方式，考生從10 道題目中，抽 1 題回答)

題目	內容	題目	內容
題目一	❶ 自我介紹 ❷ 臺灣辦桌文化 ❸ 澎湖特色美食	題目六	❶ 自我介紹 ❷ 貓空/九份特色茶屋和臺灣茶文化 ❸ 陽明山國家公園半日遊介紹
題目二	❶ 自我介紹 ❷ 月老由來與臺灣月老廟 ❸ 臺灣四季介紹與對應四季的旅遊	題目七	❶ 自我介紹 ❷ 介紹臺灣紙鈔 ❸ 你最喜歡的臺灣節慶介紹
題目三	❶ 自我介紹 ❷ 推薦一款臺灣紅茶 ❸ 創意行銷臺灣鳳梨酥	題目八	❶ 自我介紹 ❷ 介紹臺灣水果王國 ❸ 推薦高雄地區的特色美食
題目四	❶ 自我介紹 ❷ 臺灣特色食材與水果 ❸ 大鵬灣國家風景區	題目九	❶ 自我介紹 ❷ 臺灣的便利商店 ❸ 大甲媽祖文化節
題目五	❶ 自我介紹 ❷ 介紹臺灣主要花卉 ❸ 臺北101的介紹以及和其他國外高樓差異	題目十	❶ 自我介紹 ❷ 臺灣早餐店文化 ❸ 向外國人推薦臺東的兩項休閒活動

104 年度口試題目 (以號碼抽題方式，考生從10 道題目中，抽 1 題回答)

題目	內容	題目	內容
題目一	❶ 自我介紹 ❷ 臺灣的族群 ❸ 阿里山櫻花季	題目六	❶ 自我介紹 ❷ 人情味小故事 ❸ 國家公園
題目二	❶ 自我介紹 ❷ 臺灣黑熊 ❸ 臺北著名景點	題目七	❶ 自我介紹 ❷ 臺灣養生樂活 ❸ 除夕農曆年習俗
題目三	❶ 自我介紹 ❷ 介紹傳統中醫 ❸ 臺灣的國家公園、遊客預約分流	題目八	❶ 自我介紹 ❷ 介紹電音三太子、宋江陣 ❸ 臺灣特色小吃與由來
題目四	❶ 自我介紹 ❷ 布袋戲 ❸ 介紹金門或馬祖	題目九	❶ 自我介紹 ❷ 臺灣特色餐廳 ❸ 休閒農場
題目五	❶ 自我介紹 ❷ 廟宇文化藝術 ❸ 日月潭紅茶	題目十	❶ 自我介紹 ❷ 茶對臺灣文化的影響 ❸ 原住民節慶和飲食

103 年度口試題目 （以號碼抽題方式，考生從10 道題目中，抽 1 題回答）

題目	內容	題目	內容
題目一	❶ 自我介紹 ❷ 臺灣的旅外棒球選手 ❸ 臺南安平	題目六	❶ 自我介紹 ❷ 臺灣氣候概況 ❸ 宜蘭童玩節
題目二	❶ 自我介紹 ❷ 臺北市垃圾不落地政策 ❸ 花東地區	題目七	❶ 自我介紹 ❷ 臺灣職棒 ❸ 墾丁
題目三	❶ 自我介紹 ❷ 日月潭自行車道 ❸ 說明北天燈南蜂炮	題目八	❶ 自我介紹 ❷ 臺北捷運發展概況 ❸ 澎湖
題目四	❶ 自我介紹 ❷ 臺灣檳榔西施 ❸ 介紹臺中	題目九	❶ 自我介紹 ❷ 臺灣夜市文化 ❸ 馬祖
題目五	❶ 自我介紹 ❷ 介紹臺灣知名國際品牌 ❸ 北海岸野柳公園	題目十	❶ 自我介紹 ❷ 介紹觀光工廠 ❸ 綠島

102 年度口試題目 （以號碼抽題方式，考生從10 道題目中，抽 1 題回答）

題目	內容	題目	內容
題目一	❶ 自我介紹 ❷ 臺灣知名運動選手 ❸ 高雄佛陀紀念館	題目六	❶ 自我介紹 ❷ 離島特色發展潛力 ❸ 臺南鹽水烽炮
題目二	❶ 自我介紹 ❷ 上午公園跳舞意義 ❸ 打狗領事館	題目七	❶ 自我介紹 ❷ 民族文化融合 ❸ 介紹總統府
題目三	❶ 自我介紹 ❷ 臺灣環島鐵公路 ❸ 金門特產	題目八	❶ 自我介紹 ❷ 外勞來臺工作適應 ❸ 達悟族飛魚祭
題目四	❶ 自我介紹 ❷ 國內宗教文化 ❸ 雪霸國家公園	題目九	❶ 自我介紹 ❷ 替代能源 ❸ 澎湖花火祭
題目五	❶ 自我介紹 ❷ 金馬戰略地位差異 ❸ 賽夏族矮靈祭	題目十	❶ 自我介紹 ❷ 國家公園收費看法 ❸ 阿美族豐年祭

專有名詞 — 發現臺灣 DISCOVER TAIWAN

分類	專有名詞	中文
語言 Language	Mandarin	國語
	Taiwanese	閩南語
	Hakka	客家語
	Formosan	臺灣原住民語
宗教 Religion	Buddhism	佛教
	Taoism	道教
	Christianity	基督教
	Islam	伊斯蘭教
地形 Topography	High mountain	高山
	Peaks	山峰
	Hills	丘陵
	Plains	平原
	Basins	盆地
	Coastlines	海岸線
	Offshore Island	離島
	Natural Landscapes	自然景觀
氣候 Climate	Tropical	熱帶
	Subtropical	亞熱帶
	Temperate	溫帶
特有物種 Endemic species	Land-locked Salmon	櫻花鉤吻鮭(國寶魚)
	Formosan Rock Monkey	臺灣獼猴
	Formosan Black Bear	臺灣黑熊
	Blue Magpie	藍鵲
	Mikado Pheasant	帝雉
	Gray-faced Buzzard	灰面鷲(國慶鳥)

宗教慶典活動 RELIGIOUS ACTIVITIES

專有名詞		系列活動	
Chinese New Year	農曆春節	New Year's Eve Dinner	年夜飯
		Visiting the wife's family	回娘家
		The spring cleaning	春節大掃除
Lantern Festival	元宵節	Pingxi (Pingsi) Sky Lantern Festival	平溪放天燈
		Yenshui Fireworks Festival	鹽水蜂炮
		Bombing of Master Han Dan	炸寒單
		Taiwan Lantern Festival	臺灣燈會
Dragon Boat Festival	端午節	Dragon boat races	賽龍舟
		Eating glutinous rice dumplings/zongzi	吃粽子
Zhongyuan Festival	中元節	Zhongyuan Universal Salvation Ceremonies	中元普渡
		Launching of the Water Lanterns	放水燈
		Grappling with the Ghosts	搶孤
Mid-Autumn Festival	中秋節	Eating pomelos	吃柚子
		Eating moon cakes	吃月餅
其他傳統慶典		Dajia Mazu Pilgrimage	大甲媽祖遶境進香
		Burning of the Plague God Boat in Donggang	東港燒王船祭
		Neimen Song Jiang Battle Array	內門宋江陣

特色產業活動 SPECIALLY INDUSTRY ACTIVITIES

專有名詞	中文
Hsinchu International Glass Art Festival	新竹國際玻璃藝術節
Sanyi Wood-Carving Festival	三義木雕節

示意圖／ 搶孤活動

原住民活動 INDIGENOUS CEREMONIES

專有名詞	中文	祭典	中文	祭典(族語)
Amis	阿美族	Harvest Festival	豐年祭	Malaikid / Malikoda / Ilisin / Kiloma'an
Atayal	泰雅族	Ancestral Spirit Ritual	祖靈祭	Maho
Paiwan	排灣族	Human-Deity Alliance Ritual / Five-Year Ritual	五年祭	Maleveq
Bunun	布農族	Ear Shooting Festival	射耳祭	Malahodaigian
Pinuyumayan	卑南族	Monkey Hunting Ritual	猴祭(少年年祭)	Vasivas
Rukai	魯凱族	Millet Harvest Festival / Millet Ritual	小米收穫祭	Kalalisine / Kalabecengane
Tsou / Cou	鄒族	Millet Harvest Festival	小米收穫祭	Homeyaya
		Triumph Festival	戰祭 (凱旋祭)	Mayasvi
		Sowing Ritual / Festival	播種祭	Miyapo
Saisiyat	賽夏族	Ritual of worshipping the little black spirits	矮靈祭	Pas-taai / paSta'ay
Tao (Yami)	達悟族 (雅美)	Flying Fish Festival	飛魚祭	AliBangBang
			招魚祭	Meyvanwa
			飛魚收藏祭	Mamoka
			飛魚終食祭	Manoyotoyon
Thao	邵族	Lus'an	播種祭	Mulalu piskanar
Kavalan	噶瑪蘭族	Ancestral Spirit Ritual	歲末祭祖	Palilin
Truku	太魯閣族	Ancestral Spirit Ritual	祖靈祭	Mgay Bari
Sakizaya	撒奇萊雅族	Harvest Ritual	豐年祭	Malaliki
		Sowing Ritual / Festival	播種祭	Mitiway A Lisin
Hla'alua	拉阿魯哇族	Holy Shell Ritual	聖貝祭	Miatungusu
Kanakanavu	卡那卡那富族	Millet Ritual	米貢祭	Mikongu
Sediq	賽德克族	Sowing Ritual / Festival	播種祭	Smratuc

臺灣美食 TASTES OF TAIWAN

分類	專有名詞	中文
小吃 Snacks	Steamed Sandwich	刈包
	Salty Rice Pudding	碗粿
	Taiwanese Meatballs	肉圓
	Steamed Dumplings	小籠包
	Pan-fried Bun	生煎包
	Wheel Pie	車輪餅
夜市小吃 Night Market Snacks	Pearl Milk Tea/Bubble Tea	珍珠奶茶
	Pig's Blood Cake	豬血糕
	Stinky Tofu	臭豆腐
	Coffin Board	棺材板
	Veggie and Meat Wrap	潤餅捲
	Fried Chicken Fillet	炸雞排
	Small Sausage in Glutinous Rice	大腸包小腸
	Intestine Vermicelli	大腸麵線
	Oyster Vermicelli	蚵仔麵線
	Oyster Omelet	蚵仔煎
	Spring Roll	春捲
	Angelica Duck	當歸鴨
	Tempura	天婦羅
	Pot-side Scrapings Soup	鼎邊銼
	Spicy Hot Bean Curd	麻辣豆腐
甜食 Desserts	Bean Curd Pudding	豆花
	Candied Fruits	蜜餞
	Candied Haws	糖葫蘆
	Twisted Rolls	麻花捲
	Glutinous Rice Sesame Balls	芝麻球

▸ 5-12

分類	專有名詞	中文
甜食 Desserts	Nougat	牛軋糖
	Pineapple Cake	鳳梨酥
	Glutinous Rice Ball	湯圓
飲品 Drinks	Winter Melon Tea	冬瓜茶
	Sour Plum Drink	酸梅汁
	Sugar Cane Juice	甘蔗汁
	Herb Tea	青草茶
中式早餐 Chinese-styled Breakfast	Clay Oven Rolls	燒餅
	Fried Bread Stick	油條
	Fried Leek Dumplings	韭菜盒
	Boiled Dumplings	水餃
	Steamed Buns	饅頭
	Rice Ball	飯糰
	Chinese Omelet	蛋餅
	Turnip Cake	蘿蔔糕
	Century Egg	皮蛋
	Salted Duck Egg	鹹鴨蛋
	Soy Milk	豆漿
	Rice & Peanut Milk	米漿
飯類 Rice	Taiwanese Porridge	稀飯
	Taiwanese Sticky Rice	油飯
	Braised Pork Rice	滷肉飯
	Bamboo Rice Cake	筒仔米糕
	Meat Rice Dumplings	肉粽
	Fried Rice with Eggs	蛋炒飯
	Seafood Congee	海產粥

分類	專有名詞	中文
麵類 Noodles	Danzai Noodles	擔仔麵
	Wonton Noodles	餛飩麵
	Sliced Noodles	刀削麵
	Sesame Paste Noodles	麻醬麵
	Flat Noodles	粄條
	Fried Rice Noodles	炒米粉
	Mung Bean Noodles	冬粉
	Pork, pickled mustard green noodles	榨菜肉絲麵
湯類 Soup	Egg Drop Soup	蛋花湯
	Fish Ball Soup	魚丸湯
	Fish Skin Soup	魚皮湯
	Clams Soup	蛤蜊湯
	Oyster Soup	蚵仔湯
	Seaweed Soup	紫菜湯
	Squid Thick Soup	花枝羹
	Pork Thick Soup	肉羹湯
	Fried-Spanish Mackerel Thick Soup	土魠魚羹
	Shrimp Thick Soup	蝦仁羹
	Sailfish Thick Soup	旗魚羹
	Duck Thick Soup	鴨肉羹
	Milkfish Ball	虱目魚丸
其它 Others	Betel nut	檳榔
	Pyramid Dumplings	水晶餃
	Pig Knuckle	豬腳

交通資訊 TRAFFIC INFORMATION

專有名詞	中文
Airlines	航空公司
Railway	鐵路
Taiwan High Speed Rail	臺灣高鐵
MRT	捷運
Intercity Buses	客運
Taxi	計程車
Car Rental	租車
Marine Transport	海運

購物萬象 SHOPPING

分類	專有名詞	中文
都會商圈 Metropolitan Business Circles	Ximending	(臺北)西門町
	Jingming 1st Street	(臺中)精明一街
	Donghai Art Street	(臺中)東海藝術街
	New Juejiang Commercial Area	(高雄)新崛江
	Sanduo Shopping District	(高雄)三多商圈
特色產業街 Feature Markets	Jianguo Holiday Flower Market	(臺北)建國假日花市
	Guanghua Market	(臺北)光華商場
	Dihua Street	(臺北)迪化街

觀光景點 TOURIST ATTRACTIONS

分類	專有名詞	中文
國家公園 National Parks	Yangmingshan National Park	陽明山國家公園

分類	專有名詞	中文
國家公園 National Parks	Yushan National Park	玉山國家公園
	Shei-Pa National Park	雪霸國家公園
	Kenting National Park	墾丁國家公園
	Taroko National Park	太魯閣國家公園
	Kinmen National Park	金門國家公園
	Taijiang National Park	台江國家公園
	Dongsha Marine National Park	東沙環礁國家公園
	South Penghu Marine National Park	澎湖南方四島國家公園
國家風景區 National Scenic Areas	North Coast & Guanyinshan National Scenic Area	北海岸及觀音山國家風景區
	Northeast and Yilan Coast National Scenic Area	東北角暨宜蘭海岸國家風景區
	East Coast National Scenic Area	東海岸國家風景區
	East Rift Valley National Scenic Area	花東縱谷國家風景區
國家森林遊樂區	National Forest Recreation Areas	
休閒農場	Leisure Farms	
觀光工廠	Tourism Factory	
旅遊小鎮	Tourism Town	

熱門景點 HOT SPOT

分類	專有名詞	中文
基隆市 Keelung City	Heping Island Park	和平島公園
	Keelung Temple Mouth (Miaokou)	基隆廟口
	Keelung Harbor	基隆港
臺北市 Taipei City	Presidential Office Building	總統府
	Maokong Gondola	貓空纜車
	Dadaocheng Wharf	大稻埕碼頭
	Taipei Arena	臺北小巨蛋

▶ 5-16

分類	專有名詞	中文
臺北市 Taipei City	Taipei Flora Expo Park	臺北國際花卉博覽會園區
	Taipei Botanical Garden	臺北植物園
	Shilin Night Market	士林夜市
	National Palace Museum	國立故宮博物院
	Taipei Martyrs' Shrine	臺北忠烈祠
	National Chiang Kai-Shek Memorial Hall	中正紀念堂
	National Theater & Concert Hall	國家兩廳院
	National Concert Hall	國家音樂廳
	National Theater	國家戲劇院
	National Dr. Sun Yat-sen Memorial Hall	國父紀念館
	Taipei Fine Arts Museum	臺北市立美術館
	Taipei Astronomical Museum	臺北市立天文科學教育館
	Shilin Official Residence	士林官邸
	Taipei Confucius Temple	臺北孔廟
	Dihua Street	迪化街
新北市 New Taipei City	Tamsui River Mangrove Conservation Area	淡水河紅樹林保護區
	Bitan Scenic Area	碧潭風景區
	Yingge Ceramics Museum	鶯歌陶瓷博物館
	The Lin Family Mansion and Garden	林家花園
	Yeliu Geopark	野柳地質公園
	Shisanhang Museum of Archaeology	十三行博物館
	Wulai Atayal Museum	烏來泰雅博物館
宜蘭縣 Yilan County	Su'ao Cold Springs	蘇澳冷泉
	Jiaoxi Hot Springs	礁溪溫泉
	Lanyang Museum	蘭陽博物館
	National Center for Traditional Arts	國立傳統藝術中心

分類	專有名詞	中文
桃園市 Taoyuan City	Cihu Memorial Sculpture Park	慈湖紀念雕塑公園
	Shimen Reservoir	石門水庫
	Daxi Township (Presidential Town)	大溪鎮(總統鎮)
	Taimall Shopping Mall	臺茂購物中心
新竹縣 Hsinchu County	Neiwan Township	內灣
	Hsinchu Science Park	新竹科學工業園區
	Glass Museum of Hsinchu City	新竹市玻璃博物館
苗栗縣 Miaoli County	Remains of Longteng Bridge in Sanyi	三義龍騰橋遺跡
	Shengxing Train Station	盛興火車站
	Huoyanshan Nature Reserve	火焰山山自然保護區
	Sanyi Wood Sculpture Museum	三義木雕博物館
臺中市 Taichung City	Taichung Metropolitan Park	臺中都會公園
	Taichung Folklore Park	臺中民俗公園
	921 Earthquake Museum of Taiwan	臺灣921地震博物館
彰化縣 Changhua County	Lukang Tianhou Temple	鹿港天后宮
	Wanggong Fishing Port	王功漁港
南投縣 Nantou County	Xitou Nature Education Area	溪頭自然教育園區
	The Stele of Taiwan's Geographical Center	臺灣地理中心碑
	Sun Moon Lake Lalu Island	日月潭拉魯島
	Sun Moon Lake Ita Thao	日月潭伊達邵
	Huisun Forest Area	惠蓀林場
	Chung Tai Chan Monastery	中臺禪寺
	Qingjing Farm	清境農場
雲林縣 Yunlin County	Xiluo Bridge	西螺大橋
嘉義縣 Chiayi County	Alishan Forest Railway	阿里山森林鐵路
	Budai Salt Flats	布袋鹽田

▸ 5-18

分類	專有名詞	中文
嘉義市 Chiayi City	Landmark of Tropic of Cancer	北迴歸線紀念碑
	Koji Pottery Museum	交趾陶博物館
臺南市 Tainan City	Baihe Lotus	白河蓮花
	Qigu Lagoon	七股潟湖
	Koxinga Shrine	延平郡王祠
	Anping Old Fort	安平古堡
	Chikanlou (Fort Provintia)	赤崁樓(普羅明遮城)
	Eternal Golden Castle	億載金城
高雄市 Kaohsiung City	Fo Guang Mountain (Guang Shan) Monastery	佛光山
	Love River Sightseeing Boat	愛河觀光船
	Lianchihtan / Lotus Pond	蓮池潭
	Spring and Autumn Pavilions	春秋閣
	Dragon and Tiger Pagodasr	龍虎塔
	Xizi Bay	西子灣
	Former British Consulate	前英國領事館
屏東縣 Pingtung County	Old Hengchun City Wall	恆春古城門
臺東縣 Taitung County	Stone Umbrella/Shiyusan	石雨傘
	Sanxiantai/Terrace of the Three Immortals	三仙臺
	Zhaori Hot Springs	朝日溫泉
花蓮縣 Hualien County	Tunnel of Nine Turns	九曲洞
	Qingshui Cliff	清水斷崖
	Swallow Grotto/Yanzikou	燕子口
	Tzu Chi Headquarters	慈濟
澎湖縣 Penghu County	Penghu Great Bridge/Trans-Ocean Bridge	澎湖跨海大橋

分類	專有名詞	中文
金門縣 Kinmen County	Guningtou Battle Museum	古寧頭戰史館
	Qiu Lianggong's Mother Chastity Arch	邱良功母節孝坊
連江縣(馬祖) Lienchiang County (Matsu)	88 Tunnel	八八坑道
	Matsu Folklore Culture Museum	馬祖民俗文物館

傳統文藝 LITERATURE AND ART

專有名詞	中文
Glove Puppetry	布袋戲 (雲林-布袋戲的故鄉)
Oil Paper Umbrellas	油紙傘 (美濃-油紙傘的故鄉)
Spinning Tops	陀螺 (大溪-陀螺的故鄉)
Dough Figures	捏麵人
Blowing Sugar Figurines	吹糖
Chinese Knots	中國結
Scented Sachets	香包
Kites	風箏
Diabolos	扯鈴
Calligraphy	書法

| Closet 的由來 |

Closet又稱為**water closet**，縮寫為**W.C.**，為廁所或盥洗室的意思。詞來源於拉丁詞**clausum**，意思是「**closed place**」。**Closet**原意為私室、不公開的場所，例如國王的議事室、密室等，至今仍有「**to be closeted with sb.**」的說法，意為「與某人在密室中商談」。

Chapter. 02 | 口試 | 文章範例

試前充分準備，臨場口試不慌亂！

口說示範

Self-introduction 自我介紹範本

Good morning, first of all, I'd like to introduce myself. My name is ***Paula Hsieh*** and I come from ***Taipei***. I graduated from ***Tamkang University*** and majored in ***German***. (In the past 20 years I worked in ***Pharmaceutical*** related industry as ***Product Manager***.) The reason why I took the examination and hope to become a tour guide is ***because that, I used to tour the foreign customers around Taiwan when they visited on behalf of our company, and I enjoyed it so much! Also I've discovered many beautiful places here in Taiwan that are worth recommending to the tourists.***

※文字斜線部分，建議考生依個人實際情況填寫！

To be honest, being a tour guide is a true challenge for me. I surely am willing to learn from the good experienced tour guides with sincere attitude and pick up as much skills as I can. From my past travelling experiences, I think the tour guide is the key man of the quality of the tour. A good tour guide can make the trip much fun and bring everyone enjoyment! And foreign tourists' first impression on Taiwan often come from the behaviors of the tour guide. Therefore, the mission of the tour guide is very important. I think a tour guide is supposed to be responsible and patient, and is able to get along with people very well and love helping others. Meanwhile, a tour guide should be knowledgeable and neutral when making statements. I will spare no effort to fulfill those points I mentioned above, and make myself become a professional tour guide.

As far as I know, some people have negative comments on tour guides. I think this is caused by some tour guides who didn't do their jobs well. So I set up disciplines and expect myself to change the bad images about the tour guides. Also, I anticipate making the contribution to the industry of tourism and doing my best to devote myself to the sightseeing industry in Taiwan.

早安(午安)，首先，我做個自我介紹。我的名字是 Paula Hsieh ，我來自於 臺北 。我畢業於 淡江大學 ，主修 德語 。(過去的 20 年，我從事與 藥廠 領域相關的工作並擔任 產品經理 職務。) 我參加考試，想成為導遊的原因是因為 在我過去的工作經驗中，經常有許多廠商到臺灣參觀，我常常代表公司擔任招待，接待貴賓在臺灣旅遊。因而，我發現我非常享受扮演引導者的角色；並且，也發掘臺灣有這麼多美麗的地方值得推薦給觀光客。

目前，導遊這個角色對我來說是一個很大的挑戰，但我願意以虛心的態度向資深的前輩學習，並盡快培養需具備的技能。從我過去的旅遊經驗，我發現導遊是一個關鍵人物，決定旅遊的品質。在一個高水準的導游領導下，這個旅程將會是一個高品質的旅遊，讓每個人都能夠融入並享樂其中！同時，對於那些初次來到臺灣的旅客，對臺灣的第一印象常來自於導遊展現的形象。因此，導遊的工作其實是非常重要的。我認為導遊的特性需要具備責任感、耐心，和每一位團員相處融洽且樂意去協助他人。同時，導遊也應增廣見聞，以中立的立場來導覽解說。以上對於我提到的這幾個要點，我會盡力的去達成這些目標，讓自己成為一位專業的導遊。

就我所知，有些人對於導遊有負面的評價，我想這樣的印象是由於有些導遊沒有做好他(她)的職責工作。根據以上，我為自己建立一個紀律當我成為一位導遊後，我希望能提升導遊的形象。並且，我期許自己能有所貢獻於觀光產業，盡所能地投入臺灣觀光產業的發展。

Introduction on Taiwan 介紹臺灣

Natural Environment 自然環境

Welcome to Taiwan, a land of breathtaking natural diversity! Nestled off the southeastern coast of Asia, Taiwan is a blend of lush landscapes, dramatic mountains, beautiful beaches, and forests. The island's heart is adorned with majestic peaks, most notably the renowned Jade Mountain, standing as East Asia's highest summit. Cascading waterfalls, such as Shifen and Wufengqi (五峰旗), add a touch of enchantment to the scenery.

Venture along Taiwan's coastline to discover captivating beaches, from the golden sands of Kenting to the volcanic black sands of Northeast Coast. Taroko Gorge, a masterpiece of nature, showcases stunning marble cliffs, serene rivers, and lush vegetation. For a touch of tranquility, the Sun Moon Lake reflects the sky in its crystal-clear waters, surrounded by emerald forests and hills.

Taiwan's diverse ecosystems harbor unique flora and fauna, including the elusive Formosa black bear and Formosa rock monkey. Orchid enthusiasts will find themselves in awe of the island's vast collection of orchid species.

Whether you're hiking the trails of Alishan, soaking in natural hot springs, exploring the vibrant flora of Yangmingshan National Park, or marveling at the ecological wonders of Kenting National Park, Taiwan's natural environment promises an unforgettable adventure for every nature lover.

歡迎來到台灣，一個擁有令人驚嘆的自然多樣性國度！台灣坐落在亞洲東南沿海，融匯了鬱鬱蔥蔥的風景、壯麗的山脈、美麗的海灘和森林。島嶼的中心地帶點綴著雄偉的山峰，其中最著名的就是玉山，為東亞地區最高的山峰。瀑布飛瀑如仙，諸如十分瀑布和五峰旗瀑布，為風景增添了一抹迷人的色彩。

沿著台灣的海岸線探險，你將發現迷人的海灘，從墾丁的金色沙灘到東北海岸的火山黑沙灘。太魯閣峽谷是大自然的傑作，展示了美麗的大理石峭壁、寧靜的河流和茂盛的植被。為了體現一絲寧靜，日月潭在晶瑩剔透的湖水中倒映著天空，被翠綠的森林和山丘環繞。

台灣的多樣生態系統孕育著獨特的植物和動物，包括台灣黑熊和台灣獼猴。尤其蘭花愛好者將對台灣擁有眾多的蘭花品種感到驚嘆不已。

無論您是徒步在阿里山的小徑、浸泡天然溫泉中、探索在陽明山國家公園充滿活力的植物群，還是驚嘆於墾丁國家公園的生態奇觀，台灣的自然環境都為每位熱愛大自然的人帶來難忘的冒險。

Literature and Art 文學與藝術

★ Glove puppetry 布袋戲

Glove puppetry stands as a cornerstone of Taiwan's cherished traditional performing arts. This captivating art form incorporeally blends literary themes, music, and voice acting.

The puppets themselves are masterfully sculpted, featuring intricately carved wooden heads and exquisite costumes that transform them into artistic marvels. Their faces bear subtle expressions, brought to life through the puppeteer's skillful manipulation. The intricate carvings and paintings of the puppet stage add an extra layer of enchantment to the performance.

布袋戲是台灣珍貴傳統表演藝術中的重要基石。這個引人入勝的藝術形式，巧妙地融合了文學主題、音樂和聲音表演。戲偶本身經由高超的雕刻技藝塑造而成，以精緻木雕的頭像和精美的服飾，變成藝術般的奇蹟，透過操偶師熟練的操縱技巧，使它們臉部具有微妙神情、栩栩如生。布袋戲的戲台上也以細膩的雕刻和繪畫，為表演增添了魅力色彩。

★ Oil Paper Umbrella 油紙傘

Oil paper umbrellas hold significance in the lives of the Hakka community. Beyond offering protection from sun and rain, they also carry the symbolism of prosperity. The town of Meinong in southern Taiwan stands out for its exceptional oil paper umbrellas. Among the locals, gifting these umbrellas signifies bestowing good luck. On rainy days, it's a common sight to witness people in Meinong strolling through the streets, clutching their oil paper umbrellas. These umbrellas embody not just a deep affection for their hometown, but also a sense of pride in their craftsmanship and artistic heritage.

油紙傘在客家社區的生活中具有重要的意義。除了提供遮陽和避雨的功能外，它們還象徵著繁榮與吉祥。台灣南部的美濃鎮就因油紙傘而聞名。在當地人看來，贈送這些雨傘代表著帶來好運。遇到雨天，人們撐著油紙傘在美濃街頭漫步的景象屢見不鮮。這些雨傘不僅體現了對家鄉的情感，還表現了他們在工藝和藝術傳承上的自豪感。

★ Calligraphy 書法

Calligraphy stands as the most revered expression among all Chinese arts, often seen as a distillation of Chinese culture's essence.This art form presents itself in diverse styles. Characters may be meticulously and tidily written, or penned with graceful flourishes. Alternately, characters can be highlighted to accentuate their meanings. Each beholder interprets calligraphy in a distinct manner, as it elicits unique responses. Calligraphy is believed to cultivate a sense of serenity and inner calm, elevate one's spiritual essence, and enhance the capacities for observation and judgment. It is also thought to foster persistence and strengthen determination.

書法是所有中國藝術中最受讚賞的藝術，有人說它蘊藏著中國文化的文字精髓。文字有多種風格。文字可以仔細地書寫，也可以華麗的裝飾。每個人對書法作品的反應也不同。據稱書法能帶來心靈的平靜與內在的平靜，提升一個人的精神境界，並促進觀察和判斷的能力。更有人說書法能增強毅力和意志力。

Religion 宗教

Taiwan boasts diverse religious beliefs that shape its people's lives. With a harmonious coexistence of faiths, the island's history and society are mirrored in its religion.

For instance, Taoism thrives, entwined with folklore, through rituals and festivals, honoring deities like Mazu for protection; Buddhism, seen in vibrant temples like Fo Guang Shan and Longshan, offers solace and guidance; Christianity has gained followers since colonial times, enriching Taiwan's religious landscape; Indigenous cultures celebrate harvest festivals, honoring nature and ancestors, enriching the nation's spiritual fabric.

Mutual respect and tolerance shine in Taiwan's religious tapestry, showcasing its commitment to diversity. Religion here isn't just personal; it's a thread weaving the island's past, present, and future in a vibrant mosaic of beliefs.

台灣擁有多元的宗教信仰，塑造出人們的生活型態。在各種信仰和諧共存的背景下，島嶼的歷史和社會在宗教中得以反映。

例如道教在台灣繁榮發展，與民間傳說緊密交織，透過儀式和節日，向神明表示敬意以獲得保護，就像每年三月的大甲媽祖繞境活動；佛教如佛光山和龍山寺，提供信徒心靈上的安慰和指引；自殖民時代以來基督教就贏得追隨者，豐富了台灣的宗教景觀；另一方面原住民文化的各種慶典，向大自然和祖先表示敬意，豐富了國家的精神面貌。

台灣宗教中閃耀著相互尊重和寬容，展示了其對多樣性的承諾。這裡的宗教不僅僅是個人的信仰，更是將島嶼的過去、現在和未來編織成一個充滿活力的信仰多彩鑲嵌的紐帶。

National Park 國家公園

Taiwan features 9 captivating National Parks, each with its own unique charm. Yangmingshan's volcanic landscapes near Taipei, Taroko's grand canyons, and Yushan's sunny expanses in central Taiwan showcase natural wonders. Kenting, in the south, provides a taste of Southeast Asia. Kinmen preserves wartime history, while Dongsha Atoll's coral-crafted white sands stand out. Taijiang national park safeguards culture, history, and environment. Lastly, South Penghu Marine National Park unites ecology, geology, culture, and history. These parks form a vibrant tapestry reflecting Taiwan's diverse beauty and heritage.

台灣擁有九座迷人的國家公園，每座都擁有獨特的魅力。台北附近的陽明山火山景觀、太魯閣的雄偉大峽谷，以及陽光灑滿於廣闊地區的玉山位在台灣中部，顯現了自然的奇蹟。位於南部的墾丁則提供一種南洋風味。金門保留著戰爭歷史，而東沙環礁國家公園的珊瑚白沙更加引人注目。台江國家公園保護著文化、歷史和環境。最後，澎湖南方四島國家公園融合了生態、地質、文化和歷史。這些公園構成了一個充滿活力的圖景，反映了台灣多樣化的美麗和遺產。

★ Yushan National Park 玉山國家公園

Yushan National Park is the largest national park on the island, across 4 counties including Chiayi, Kaohsiung, Nantou, and Hualien. Yushan, or Jade Mountain, located in the center of the national park, is the highest mountain in Taiwan. The higher the height, the lower the temperate. Basically the climate can be classified into temperate and frigid zone. Entering the park, you can see high mountain sceneries everywhere. Seasonal changes bring a rich variety of plant life. Animals, birds, butterflies and fishes in the river valleys are all abundant in this national park. In the past, many of these species are almost endangered, but with the establishment of the national park, they are gradually saved, such as Formosa black bear. You might hear it roaring while visiting Yushan National Park.

玉山國家公園是最大的國家公園，涵蓋嘉義、高雄、南投及花蓮4縣。玉山位於這座國家公園的中心，為臺灣最高的山峰。溫度隨著高度的上升而下降，基本上氣候可分為溫帶和寒帶。走進公園，高山風景無處不在。季節變化帶來豐富多樣的生物之美，動物、鳥類、蝴蝶和河谷中的魚都蘊藏在這個國家公園裡。在過去，許多物種幾乎瀕臨絕種，但隨著國家公園的建立，牠們漸漸被挽救回來，例如臺灣黑熊。當你拜訪玉山國家公園時，你可能聽到牠的咆哮。

★ **Taijiang National Park** 台江國家公園

Taijiang national park is located in the southwest coast of Taiwan. It was established in 2009, and it covers the land and the sea. The newest national park of all. The range is covering the land and the sea. The tidal land is one of the most valuable treasure of the park's coastal landscape. Besides, the park has four main wetland areas including Zengwen River mouth wetlands, Sicao wetlands, Qigu Salt fields wetlands and Yanshui River wetlands as well as the mangrove forest. In addition, the black-faced spoonbill refuge and sailing routes used by early Han Chinese immigrants can also be found in the park. The park has both abundant ecological environment and historical culture that worth visiting.

台江國家公園位於臺灣西南沿岸地區。它成立於2009年，是最新的國家公園。範圍涵蓋陸地和海洋區域。潮間帶是公園濱海景觀最寶貴的財富之一。此外，這個公園有四個主要的濕地，包括曾文溪口濕地、四草濕地、七股鹽田濕地和鹽水溪口濕地以及紅樹林景觀。此外，黑面琵鷺棲息和中國漢族早期從中國沿海移民使用的航道也可以在這個公園中發現。這個公園擁有豐富的生態環境及歷史文化，非常值得一去。

★ **Taroko National Park** 太魯閣國家公園

Taroko National Park was established in 1986. The range covers the counties of Taichung, Nantou and Hualien. It is famous for its spectacular mountains and marble canyons. Canyons and cliffs stretch along Li Wu River. Through millions years of wind erosion, the marble rocks were exposed and cut by Li Wu River, and impressive grand canyons were created. The most impressive natural scenery of Taroko are Yen Tze Kou (Swallow Grotto) and Chiu Chu Tung (Tunnel of Nine Turns), and they are also the narrowest part of the canyon. Tourists can view the natural beauty along the path and find swallows nests in the cliff. Additionally, there is a central cross-island highway to pass through this national park. Eternal Spring Shrine is built to memorize those people who sacrificed their lives in building the highway.

太魯閣國家公園成立於1986年，範圍涵蓋臺中、南投及花蓮縣。這裡有最著名的壯麗山脈和大理石峽谷，峽谷和懸崖沿著立霧溪伸展。經過萬年的風蝕，大理石岩石被立霧溪切穿蝕刻，創造出令人印象深刻的宏偉峽谷。太魯閣最令人印象深刻的自然景觀是燕子口及九曲洞，這裡是峽谷最窄的地方。遊客可以沿著遊覽小徑欣賞自然美景，同時可以在峭壁上找到燕子的巢。此外，中橫公路穿過這個國家公園，而太魯閣紀念碑的建立就是為了紀念這些犧牲自己的生命來建設這條中橫公路的人。

★ Kinmen National Park 金門國家公園

Kinmen National Park is located off the coast of Mainland China. Because of the military location, this island did not open to the public before. However, the island has attracted a great number of visitors every year as soon as it was established as national park. As there were wars between Communist and Nationalist, Kinmen is known for the battlefield monuments. In the meantime, most of the earliest residents are from Zhanghou and Quangzhou of Fujian provinces and they still follow the old tradition. Hence, the original style of architecture and the customs can still be seen in this island. Besides, Kinmen mainly consists of hills formed with granite. It is always regarded as a marine park thanks to the government's effort and the greater eco-awareness from the residents. It is a perfect spot for birds watching too because the population of rare species of birds have gradually grown in recent years.

金門國家公園位於中國大陸海岸外，因軍事位置，這個島以前沒有開放觀光。但自從成立了國家公園以來，每年都吸引大量遊客前來。 由於共產黨和國民黨曾經在這個島上發生戰爭，金門有著名的戰爭紀念碑。同時，金門最早的居民大多來自福建的漳州與泉州，他們仍然遵循古老的傳統。因此，建築和文化習俗的原有風貌迄今仍可以在這個島上看到。此外，這個島主要是由花崗岩構成，且一直被認為是海洋公園，感謝政府的努力和居民強大的環保意識。這個小島也是賞鳥的絕佳場所，因為近幾年珍稀物種的鳥類數量已逐漸成長。

Hot Spots 觀光景點

Taipei 101 臺北101

Situated in one of Taipei's premier districts, TAIPEI 101 stands as the most extensive engineering project in Taiwan's construction history. Benefiting from the collaboration of numerous local businesses, TFC Corp. was fortunate to lead this project under the guidance of both domestic and international experts. The architectural prowess of world-renowned designer C.Y. Lee brought the project's blueprint to life. Departing from the conventional uni-body concept, the design draws inspiration from the auspicious Chinese numeral 8, symbolizing good luck. The structure assembles eight-floor units, stacked rhythmically atop one another, creating a novel aesthetic for skyscrapers. Taipei 101 introduces patrons to a staggering variety of global fashion and culinary options, ensuring 101% fresh choices.

The 89th-floor observation deck, situated at an elevation of 382 meters, offers tourists an exceptional panoramic view and a glimpse of the world's largest wind damper, weighing 660 metric tons. The two dedicated high-speed elevators at Taipei 101 Observatory, reaching a speed of 1010 meters per minute, broke the Guinness World Record for the fastest pressurized elevator in 2004. It takes only 37 seconds to reach the 89th-floor observation deck.

坐落於台灣最重要的地區，101是台灣建築業歷史上最為龐大的工程項目。該專案是由國內十四家企業共同組成的台灣金融大樓股份有限公司。與國內外專業團隊聯手規劃，並由世界著名建築設計師李祖原（C.Y. Lee）的建築才華將此藍圖轉化為現實。在設計上，摒棄了傳統一體式概念，汲取中國數字"8"的靈感，象徵著好運。這座建築以每八層樓為一個結構單元，為摩天大樓帶來了新穎的美學。台北101向遊客提供多種全球時尚和美食選擇，確保提供101%國際級的時尚美饌選擇。

標高382公尺的89樓觀景台，提供觀光客絕佳的觀景視野，並可一覽全世界最大的風阻尼器，重達660公噸。臺北101觀景台兩部專用最快速電梯，以每分鐘1010公尺的速度，打破了2004年最快速恆壓電梯的金氏世界紀錄，僅需37秒即可達89樓觀景台。

National Palace Museum 故宮博物院

The National Palace Museum was established in 1965 and is one of the largest museums in the world. Its origins can be traced back to the Nationalist Communist Civil War, during which the Nationalist Party (Kuomintang) lost and retreated to Taiwan, bringing along a vast collection of priceless treasures. The museum houses nearly 620,000 artworks, encompassing nearly 5,000 years of Chinese history. The majority of these art pieces were originally part of the imperial collections from the Song, Yuan, Ming, and Qing dynasties. The collection includes paintings, calligraphy, rare books, documents, ceramics, bronzes, jade artifacts, and antiques. Every year, millions of people are drawn to visit this museum. Among its collection, there are three artworks known as the "Three Treasures of the National Palace Museum": the Jadeite Cabbage, the Meat-shaped Stone, and the Mao Kung Ting.

故宮建於1965年，是世界上最大的博物館之一。背景可以追溯至日本投降後緊接著發生的國共內戰，結果國民黨在這場戰鬥中失敗，一大批價值連城的珍藏寶物與國民政府一起被撤退到臺灣。這博物館收藏了接近620,000件藝術品，這些無價珍寶跨越近5000年的中國歷史。大多數藝術品都是從宋、元、明、清時期的中國皇室收藏。收藏品包括繪畫、書法、珍本書籍、文件、陶瓷、青銅器、玉器和古玩。每年總是吸引著數以百萬計的人參觀這個博物館。其中有3件藝術品被稱為故宮3寶，它們是翠玉白菜、肉形石和毛公鼎。

★ Jadeite Cabbage with Insects 翠玉白菜

The Jadeite Cabbage closely resembles an actual cabbage, as it is a single piece of jade carved into the shape of a Chinese cabbage. The rich, vibrant green leaves contrast with the pure white body to create a stunning work of art. Upon closer inspection, two insects are visible on the leaves – a locust and a katydid – symbolizing numerous offspring. Originally displayed in the Imperial Palace's Yonghe Palace, it might have been part of the dowry when the Empress Dowager Jin married the Emperor Guangxu. One of the most significant treasures in the National Palace Museum's collection is the Jadeite Cabbage, and many souvenirs produced by the museum feature designs inspired by the Jadeite Cabbage.

翠玉白菜的樣子幾乎等同於真實白菜，它是一整塊翡翠雕刻成中國白菜的形狀。那色度飽和的白色的身體與燦爛的綠色葉子創造出完美的藝術品，並且，近看還可以看到飛落在菜葉上的兩隻昆蟲。他們是蝗蟲和螽斯，代表有眾多的孩子。這件作品原本是放在紫禁城永和宮，光緒皇帝瑾妃的住處，這可能是她嫁給光緒皇帝時，作為她的嫁妝之一。在國立故宮博物院中最重要的珍藏品之一是翠玉白菜，許多由博物館製作的紀念品其設計是以翡翠白菜為主題。

★ Meat-shaped Stone 肉形石

The Meat-shaped Stone is an antique from the Qing Dynasty and is one of the most beloved artworks in the collection, with popularity comparable to that of the Jadeite Cabbage. Crafted from agate, the Meat-shaped Stone is a product of natural formation over many years. The stone layers contain various impurities, creating distinct layers of color. The surface of the Meat-shaped Stone resembles a piece of real "Tong-po" pork. At the first glance, it can evoke a mouthwatering sensation.

肉形石是清朝宮廷的一種古玩，是展示藏品中最受喜愛的藝術品之一，人氣與翠玉白菜相當。肉形石是由瑪腦製成，經過多年自然生成，石層中含有不同的雜質，堆積成不同的色層。肉形石的表面看起來像塊真實的“東坡”肉。乍看之下，它會令人產生垂涎的感覺。

★ Mao-Kung Ting 毛公鼎

The Mao Gong Ding is also one of the precious cultural relics in the collection of the National Palace Museum. Its appearance resembles a large cauldron with a wide mouth, two vertical handles, and three hoof-like feet. Dating back to around 800 BC, it is a bronze artifact with the longest inscription among Chinese bronzes, consisting of approximately 500 characters.

This historical account originates from the reign of King Husan of the Zhou Dynasty. After his ascension, he entrusted his uncle, the Duke of Mao, with governing domestic and foreign affairs. To commemorate this honor, the Duke of Mao cast this vessel and inscribed the story upon it, hoping it would be passed down to his descendants.

毛公鼎也是國立故宮博物院中珍貴文物之一，它的外觀看起來像個大鍋，有一個廣口和兩個垂直耳朵、三足蹄。它是約公元前800年的青銅製品，刻有至今中國銘文之中最長的青銅器，大約500字。

這段歷史起源於周宣王繼位後，他吩咐他的叔叔毛公爵執政掌管國內及對外事務。為記錄這項榮譽，毛公爵鑄造這個容器並刻上這個故事，希望能被他的後裔永久保存。

Yehliu 野柳

Yehliu is a cape of about 1,700 meters long formed by Datun Mountain reaching into the sea. When overlooked from above, the place is like a giant turtle submerging into the sea. Thus, it is also called "Yehliu Turtle". Because the rock layer of seashore contains sandstone of limestone texture and it is subject to sea erosion, weathering and earth movements, there is particular scenery consisting of sea trenches/holes, candle shaped rocks, and pot shaped rocks.

The place is divided into three sections. The first section has rocks like Queen's Head. The second section has rocks like Bean Curd. The third section has sea-eroded caves. The place is suitable for geological study and field research. In addition, there is a statue of Lin Tien Jane in commemoration of the person's bravery of scarifying own live for saving others.

野柳地質公園，長約1700公尺，是大屯山餘脈伸出於東海中的岬角。從金山遠眺，猶如潛入海中的巨龜，故又名為「野柳龜」。其因波浪侵蝕、岩石風化及地殼運動等作用，造就了海蝕洞溝、燭狀石、壺穴等各種奇特景觀。

野柳的岩層主要分為三層，第一層以女王頭為代表，第二層以豆腐岩聞名，第三層以海蝕洞著名，具有教育解說與學術研究的價值。此外，區內的林添楨塑像是紀念其當年捨身救人的英勇事蹟。

Sun Yat-sen Memorial Hall 國父紀念館

The Sun Yat-sen Memorial Hall was established in 1972 and is located in the eastern district of Taipei, near Taipei City Hall. It was built to commemorate the centenary of the birth of Dr. Sun Yat-sen, the founding father of the Republic of China. The architectural design of the building imitates the structure of Chinese palaces, standing grand and solemn. Inside the hall, there is a bronze statue of Dr. Sun Yat-sen for people from both home and abroad to admire. Additionally, the exhibition hall displays historical materials related to the establishment of the Republic of China.

The memorial hall boasts the renowned National Theater, which can accommodate over 3,000 people. Equipped with top-notch facilities and hardware, it has become an important venue for performances. The building also offers ample outdoor space, where one can often see people flying kites or roller skating together. The Sun Yat-sen Memorial Hall not only serves as a monument for commemoration but also functions as a park for outdoor, leisure, and artistic activities.

國父紀念館建於1972年，座落於臺北東區，近臺北市政府，是為紀念中華民國國父 孫中山先生百年誕辰而興建。建築外型模仿中國宮殿的結構，巍峨而莊嚴。館中有國父的銅像，供海內外人士瞻仰。此外，展覽館也陳列了關於創建中華民國的歷史資料。

紀念館擁有知名的國家演藝廳，可容納3000餘人，配備一流的設施和硬體設備，已成為重要的表演場所。建築物外還有很大的戶外空間，通常可以看到很多人在來放風箏或一起玩輪式溜冰。國父紀念館不只為發揚紀念，也是一個供戶外、休閒和藝術活動的公園。

Chiang Kai-shek Memorial Hall 中正紀念堂

Chiang Kai-shek Memorial Hall is located in the heart of Taipei City. The area is 250,000 square meters and it is the attraction most visited by foreign tourists. The architecture of Chiang Kai-shek Memorial Hall is inspired by Tiantan in Beijing. The four sides of the structure are similar to those of the pyramids in Egypt. The material is white marble. The roofs are decorated with deep-blue glass as part of the reflection of blue sky and bright sun. The garden is planted with red flowers. As a whole, the colors of blue, white and red express the National Flag and the spirit of freedom, equality and brotherhood.

The great building has become a landmark of Taipei City. There are also places for international art performances. They are National Theater and National Concert Hall. World famous musicians and renowned playgroups have conducted performance here. The park has not only provided a relaxing space for local residents but also an ideal place for art performance.

中正紀念堂位於臺北市的心臟地帶，占地25公頃，為國外旅客必訪之地。中正紀念堂的建築，造型仿北平天壇之頂，四邊的主體結構與埃及金字塔之體相仿，材質為白色大理石，而屋頂上裝飾著深藍色的玻璃瓦，象徵青天白日。花園則種植著紅色的花。整體說來，藍、白、紅三色代表著國旗顏色，象徵自由、平等和博愛的精神。

這座紀念建築物目前已經成為臺北市的地標，許多國內外的文化藝術表演也在此進行。紀念堂左右分列戲劇院與音樂廳，許多國際級知名的音樂家及表演團體都在這裡舉辦表演。這個公園不僅提供當地居民一個放鬆活動的去處，也是藝術演出的地方。

Shilin Night Market 士林夜市

Shilin Night Market is one of the largest night markets in Taipei City. Centered around the Yangming Theater and the Cicheng Temple, it is formed by bustling streets and includes areas like Wenlin Road, Dadong Road, and Danan Road. Shilin Market itself was built as early as two years before the Republic of China and is renowned for its various traditional snacks. It attracts many tourists who come to taste the famous treats, such as large pancake enfolding small pancake, hot pot on stone, and Shilin sausages. These have become well-known culinary landmarks that almost everyone recognizes.

As the night market is close to several educational districts, students form a significant portion of its main consumer base. The prices are also much more affordable compared to regular stores, offering items such as furniture, clothing, photo printing shops, and pet supplies.

士林夜市為臺北市最具規模的夜市之一，以陽明戲院及慈誠宮為中心，由熱鬧街市集結而成，包含文林路、大東路、大南路等。其中，士林市場早在民國前二年即已興建，以各種傳統小吃聞名，吸引許多觀光客慕名而來品嘗，像是大餅包小餅、石頭火鍋或是士林大香腸等，已成為無人不曉的美食地標。

由於夜市鄰近許多學區，以學生為主要的消費族群，價格也比一般商店便宜許多，例如家具、衣飾、相片沖印店或寵物用品等。

Sun Moon Lake National Scenic Area 日月潭國家風景區

Sun Moon Lake is situated in the central part of Taiwan, with its surface at an elevation of 748 meters. It is divided by Lalu island into the eastern and western parts, which are named after their resemblance to the "sun" and "crescent moon," respectively. Renowned as one of Taiwan's eight scenic spots, it also holds the distinction of being a significant hydroelectric power generation site in Taiwan. The scenic area is characterized by features like "mountainous lakes," "indigenous culture," and "natural ecology," attracting over 6 million visitors from both domestic and international origins annually. Among Sun Moon Lake's most famous attractions are Itashao, Lalu Island, Xuanzang Temple, Ci'en Pagoda, and Wenwu Temple. The natural forest paths in the area are also great spots for birdwatching.

The Thao tribe was the earliest indigenous community to inhabit the Sun Moon Lake region. They hold annual harvest festivals, planting rituals, and showcase their unique artistic culture, contributing to the preservation of the distinctive cultural heritage of the Sun Moon Lake area.

日月潭座落於臺灣的中心位置，湖面海拔748公尺，以拉魯島為界，東、西兩側因形似「日輪」和「月鉤」因而得名，享有臺灣八景的美譽，也是臺灣地區最負盛名水力發電重地；風景區以「高山湖泊」、「原住民文化」、「自然生態」等觀光遊憩特色，每年吸引超過6百萬中外遊客到訪。而日月潭最有名的觀光景點，包含伊達邵、拉魯島、玄奘寺、慈恩塔及文武廟等，而天然林道相間更是觀賞鳥的好地方。

邵族是最早居住在日月潭的原住民，每年在此舉行豐年祭、播種祭及其特有的工藝文化，有助於保存日月潭地區的特殊文化。

Alishan National Scenic Area 阿里山國家風景區

Alishan is blessed with rich natural resources, such as sun rise, cloud sea and old forests. No matter in spring, summer, autumn or winter, visitors can expect to appreciate some of its beauty. For years, Alishan has been famous for its historical forest railway and indigenous tribes, too.

The Alishan National Scenic Area Administration was established in 2001. It serves the four townships of Meishan, Zhuqi, Fanlu and Alishan which cover 41,520 hectares of land. Alishan is very famous for the sunrise view and the cloud ocean. The best time to watch the cloud season is autumn. In addition, the Alishan Forest Railway is also very famous.

阿里山擁有豐富的自然資源，像是日出、雲海和森林，無論春、夏、秋、冬，四季皆能體驗其中之美。近年來，森林鐵道及原住民文化更是受到觀光客的喜愛。

阿里山國家風景區管理處成立於2001年，轄區範圍包含嘉義縣梅山鄉、竹崎鄉、番路鄉及阿里山鄉等4個鄉，面積合計41,520公頃。阿里山以日出及雲海聞名，欣賞雲海最佳季節是在秋季，此外，阿里山森林鐵路也是非常知名。

Anping Fort 安平古堡

In 1624, Dutch built the first fort in Anping, Taiwan, called "Fort Zeelandia", now known as Anping Fort, where has been the administrative center of the Dutch regime, and the hub for trading. The building was originally constructed in square inner fortress and rectangle outer walls. In 1661, the fort was renamed as Anping to commemorate his home town when Cheng Cheng-Kung has driven the Dutch out of Taiwan. Therefore, Fort Zeelandia was also known as "King's Fort" or "Taiwan Fort", nicknamed Anping Fort.

In Kangxi Emperor's regime of Qing Dynasty, Taiwan was included in the empire that the political center was transferred to Tainan City, causing the decline of the Fort. The red bricks of the Fort have been taken for construction of Eternal Fortress. During the Japanese occupation, the Dutch style buildings in inner fortress were completely destroyed. A square red-bricked step platform was constructed with a western style house on the platform, being served as dormitory for Customs officials, where the memorial hall now is located.

It was named Anping Fort after Restoration of Taiwan and become an attraction for tourists. The remaining more than 70 meters long south walls of the outer fort with worn-out red bricks, accompanied by the old banyan roots, chanted its odyssey. The fort is the very historical replica over three hundred years.

1624年，荷蘭人佔領臺灣南部並在臺南安平設立基地，最初被命名為"熱蘭遮城"，即今日的安平古堡，為荷蘭人統治的中樞，更是對外貿易的總樞紐。原建築格局分為方形內城與長方形外城。1661年，在荷蘭人被鄭成功趕出臺灣後，這個堡壘在鄭成功政權下改名為安平。因此，熱蘭遮城也稱為「王城」或「臺灣城」，俗稱安平古堡。

到了清朝康熙年間，隨著臺灣的政治重心移至臺南市，安平古堡的重要性也隨之降低。之後曾破壞城壁紅磚挪為建造億載金城之用。甚至在日軍佔領期間，堡壘內部荷式建築被徹底摧毀。四周以紅磚砌成方形階臺，臺上建造西式平房作為海關宿舍，而成為今日的紀念館風貌。

光復後改名為安平古堡，並成為觀光勝地，目前紀念館邊殘存七十多公尺長的外城南牆殘壁依然屹立，紅磚斑駁，老榕攀爬，訴說著曾經過往的滄桑，是 300 餘年來僅存的歷史遺跡。

Former British Consulate 打狗英國領事館

The consulate was built in 1865 with more than a hundred years of history. It is now the most antique western building preserved in Taiwan. It was the western building designed by a British engineer and built by Chinese craftsmen, and it is the most meaningful ancient building of Chinese modern history. Semicircle arches are rhythmically arranged in order with considerably rhyming. At the corner, the circle arch is smaller and the wall pillar is bigger, which has reinforced function in dynamics. It is the Baroque typed building of the Renaissance era.

Among the existing western style buildings in Taiwan, it provides an excellent example of technique and style and that possesses the value of historical architecture study and conservation value. It is the building that has double function, administrative and residential function, and also the first formal consulate built by foreigners in Taiwan.

前英國領事館始建於1865年，已有百年的歷史，至今為臺灣保存之最古老洋樓。該建築是由英國工程師設計，中國建築師建造，是最具意義代表的中國近代古建築。整體外觀為連續的半圓栱，使造型非常富有節奏感，轉角處的栱較小而牆柱較大，是力學上的強固作用，屬於後文藝復興時代巴洛克式建築風格。

在臺灣現有的西式建築中，它展現卓越的技術及風格，擁有歷史建築研究和保存的價值，並具有行政和住所雙重功能，也是外國人在臺建立的第一個領事館。

Fo Gunag Mountain (Fo Gunag Shan) Monastery 佛光山佛陀紀念館

At the north-east of Dashu Township in Kaohsiung city on the left bank of the Kaoping river, a famous tourist destination is located. Here you will find the Buddhist center of South Taiwan, established by Master Hsing Yun and his disciples.

The architecture of the temples is very characteristic, and at the southeastern side of Fo Gunag Mountain (Gunag Shan) Monastery the most prominent landmark of the region is found: a huge golden statue of Buddha Amitabha which measures some 120 meters. The main square is surrounded by 480 standing Buddha's, while water and mountains form the magnificent scenery. The main structures consist of four temples. The main god of worship here is Sakyamuni.

位於高雄市東北方大樹區面對高屏溪左岸，有一個著名的旅遊勝地。在這裡有臺灣最大的佛教中心，由星雲大師及其弟子創辦。這個寺廟的建築風格非常具有特色，在寺廟東南邊可以看到一個很顯眼的地標 – 一個巨大的金色阿彌陀佛雕像，高約120公尺。主廣場被480尊立佛的雕像包圍，與山水連成壯麗的景色。其建築結構是由四個寺廟組成，主要祭拜釋迦牟尼。

Sanxiantai (Terrace of the Three Immortals) 三仙臺

Sanxiantai is situated at the coastal highway of eastern Taiwan. It is composed of highland and small islands. The island used to connect to the highland by a neck of land. But because of the evasion of wind and sea, the island is separated from the land and is now connected to a long footbridge. Sanxiantai then becomes a popular attraction for its rocky view as well as the footbridge. Sanxiantai is surrounded by coral reef and the sea is full of tropical fish. It is also an ideal spot for diving.

三仙台位於臺灣東部的沿海高速公路，由高地和小島所組成。它原是由一岬角頸部連接到高地的島嶼。後來因為風和海的侵蝕，使該島上從土地分離，而現在是由一座天橋所連接。三仙臺被珊瑚礁所環繞，大海充滿了熱帶魚而成了潛水的旅遊勝地。

Penghu (Two Heart Fish Trap) – The tide of rising and reducing
澎湖 (雙心石滬) – 潮起潮落

The Penghu archipelago is Taiwan's offshore island group, situated in the straits that separate Taiwan from China. Penghu is made up of 90 small islands with a combined coastline that stretches more than 320 kilometers. Each season brings its own particular scenery, and rich natural and cultural resources can be found here. The landscape here is characterized by basaltic rocks, coral reefs, sea-eroded formations, and beaches, while the fishing culture and migratory birds add extra dimensions to the picture.

澎湖列島是臺灣的島縣，位於中國大陸與臺灣之間，由約90餘座島嶼所組成，海岸線長達320多公里，每個季節都有其獨特的風光和豐富的自然生態及文化資源。這裡的景觀特點是玄武岩、珊瑚礁、沙灘、漁村文化與候鳥棲地，而漁村文化及候鳥更是為澎湖的景色更添風采。

Matzu 馬祖

Situated in the northeast corner of the Taiwan Straits and separated from China by only a narrow strip of water, Matsu, like Kinmen to the south, is also made up largely of granite. Its scenery consists of sea-eroded terrain, natural sand and pebble beaches, sand dunes, precipitous cliffs, and other scenic features. In addition to its beautiful jagged coastline and the migratory birds that pass through Matsu also offers traditional eastern Fujian villages built on mountainsides as well as defensive fortifications built by the military.

馬祖位於臺灣海峽的東北角和僅靠著一狹小海域與中國分離，像金門的南方一樣，也是由大量的花崗岩所組成。它的風景包含了海侵蝕地形、天然砂、卵石海灘、沙丘、懸崖陡峭及其它風景秀麗的面貌。除了其美麗的海岸線和候鳥會經過之外，馬祖還有著建立在山坡上做為軍事上防禦的傳統閩東式建築。

Distinctive Townships 觀光小城

Lugang Township, Changhua County: Craftsmanship, Cuisine, and Historic Sites 鹿港鎮工藝、美食、古蹟

Lukang was the economic and transport hub of central Taiwan in earlier times. The saying "first Tainan, second Lukang and third Mengjia," illustrates the high position of the town in its glory days.

In addition to being the early cultural capital of Taiwan, Lukang was also a commercially prosperous area. During the Qing period, the town was an important trading port, bringing all types of products to the town and fueling Lukang's economic rise. Lukang was also unrivaled for its high cuisine and a diversity of local snack foods reflecting its broad immigrant mix. Delicious seafood, baked goods, and distinctive street food are part of Lukang's signature appeal. This diverse food culture, along with historic sites, scenic attractions, beautiful craftsmanship, make Lukang a destination as rewarding to the eyes and mind as it is to the palate.

Visit Lukang and discover why it shares a spot with Taichung City and Nantou County among Taiwan's must-see "Golden Triangle" tourism destinations.

由於鹿港是座文化的古都，人文薈萃，商業繁盛，清朝時期更因為貿易港口具通商之便，百貨充盈，經濟繁榮，飲食之美自然高人一籌，且因匯聚各地移民，也帶來許多不同口味的鄉土小吃。除味美的海鮮外，更有各式的糕餅與風味獨特的鄉土小吃，拜訪鹿港，除參觀古蹟、景點，領略工藝之美外，品嚐各式美食更是不容錯過，一次鹿港之旅，達到精美、知識與口腹多重的滿足，滿載而歸。

鹿港與臺中市、南投縣成為中臺灣觀光「金三角」，更是觀光客旅遊中臺灣的必訪景點。

Anping District, Tainan City: Namesake of Taiwan

安平－臺灣之名源自安平

Anping abounds with historic sites—Anping Fort, the Eternal Golden Castle, and Anping Tree House are a few of its major attractions. Other points of interest include the Old Julius Mannich Merchant House, Haishan Hostel, Tait & Co. Merchant House and Anping Minor Artillery Fort. These historical sites reflect the history and architectural styles of the Dutch occupation, Cheng Cheng-kung (Koxinga) period, Qing administration, and Japanese colonial era, embodying more than 300 years of quintessential history in Taiwan.

No visit to Anping is complete without trying the amazing array of delicious local foods—shrimp cakes, bean curd pudding, candied fruit, shrimp rolls, oyster rolls, fish ball soup, and oyster pancakes, for a start. The shops around Yanping Old Street are good places to find distinctive mementos and gifts—no one leaves Yanping empty-handed!

安平知名古蹟眾多，安平古堡、億載金城、安平樹屋早已是知名景點，來此非得前往一遊不可，其他如東興洋行、海山館、德記洋行、安平小砲台等，也都有豐富的歷史背景及各具特色的建築風貌，分別呈現荷據、明鄭、清朝、日治等不同時期所遺留下來的歷史足跡。臺灣三百多年來最精彩的歷史，皆化作優美的古蹟，留存在安平的結構之中。

品嚐安平小吃，更是遊客到安平不容錯過的節目，蝦餅、豆花、蜜餞、蝦捲、蚵捲、魚丸湯、蚵仔煎等美食，多得令人目不暇給。延平老街附近也變身為觀光特產區，可以滿足遊客血拼的慾望，總而言之，來一趟安平，一定讓你滿載而歸。

Ruifang District, New Taipei City: Gold Mines of Discovery in Shuinandong, Jinguashi, and Jiufen 瑞芳區水金九地區礦山秘境

Shuinandong, Jinguashi, and Jiufen are former mining towns in Ruifang District, New Taipei City. The three towns present living records of the history and culture of Taiwan's mining industry, each one distinguished by the different mining methods they adopted: the simple charm of Shuinandong; the tranquility of Jinguashi; and the traces of the miners' nightlife in Jiufen. Though the gold mines are now closed, these towns continue to exert an allure that attracts visitors to visit and dream.

In Shuinandong, the abandoned "13-Level Smelter" evokes the image of Pompeii. The Yin Yang Sea, with its yellow and blue waters, and the beautiful Golden Waterfall are other attractions here. Jinguashi is a quiet hillside town. And along the old lanes of bustling Jiufen, one can find gold mines of history and culture. Together, these areas offer welcome comfort to the road-weary traveler and provide plenty of food for thought.

水金九二個字串起了新北市瑞芳區三個美麗的小城鎮「水湳洞」、「金瓜石」與「九份」。水金九就像是臺灣礦業的縮影般，充滿了歷史與人文風情；因採金而繁榮，也因採礦方式的不同，呈現不同的面貌；純樸可愛的水湳洞、高貴幽靜的金瓜石、礦工夜夜笙歌的九份，即使在金礦停採後，亦呈現不同風貌，吸引人們探訪、逐夢。

其中水湳洞擁有媲美「龐貝古城」的十三層選礦場、交疊著金黃與湛藍的陰陽海以及展現大自然鬼斧神工的「黃金瀑布」；金瓜石獨有的清幽、純樸的小鎮景緻，訴說著對山城無盡的眷戀；而繁華熱鬧的九份老街則蘊藏豐富的人文故事與藝術文化，給予疲憊的旅人無盡的慰藉與癒療，提供一種簡單卻回味無窮的心靈體驗。

Beitou District, Taipei City: Small Town Elegance 北投風華小鎮

Featured in the Travel section of the The New York Times online edition, Beitou a hot spring escape with abundant natural, cultural and historical attractions, as well as convenient rapid transit access, making it one of Taipei's premier tourism destinations.

Beitou District encompasses the Beitou Hot Springs, Yangmingshan National Park, and the Guandu scenic area. The Beitou Hot Spring Museum, Taiwan Folk

Arts Museum, and Plum Garden are a few of the many points cultural and historic interest here. Distinctive hot spring hotels, Taiwan's first green library building, and the hot-spring themed MRT train art are other attractions here. In 2011, Beitou was ranked as a three-star tourist attraction in the Michelin Green Guide. Fox News also gave a thumbs-up to this very special tourism district.

被美國紐約時報旅遊版網站推崇是臺灣溫泉天堂的「北投」，擁有豐富的自然資源、濃厚的歷史文化，是臺北市著名的旅遊勝地，其幅員涵蓋北投溫泉、陽明山國家公園、關渡風景區等。

北投得天獨厚的環境，在時代潮流的需求與思古溯源的探尋下，發展為觀光休閒的熱門景點，除了北投溫泉博物館、北投文物館、梅庭等豐富的古蹟人文景點，還有林立的溫泉特色旅館，加上直達的捷運系統、全臺第一座綠建築圖書館及獨一無二的溫泉彩繪捷運列車等加持下，於2011年相繼獲得米其林綠色三星城鎮及美國福斯新聞網的推薦，讓北投成為臺灣最具特色的觀光地區。

Events 民俗節慶活動

Toucheng "Qianggu" -Grappling with the Ghost pole-climbing competition 頭城搶孤－攀爬搶孤棚柱

Starting in the Qing dynasty, there has been a custom of people seizing sacrificial goods after the Ghost Festival is over. Some say this is to scare away lingering spirits, and is known as "Qianggu" . The Qianggu competition held in Toucheng is Taiwan's largest and one of Yilan's important traditional events during the seventh lunar month. The tower consists of pillars made of China fir, 11 meters tall and 8 meters wide, with 7 or 8 meter bamboo trestlework on top. Squid, rice dumplings, rice noodles, meat, fish, and other foods are tied to the trestlework.

Team members must climb on top of each other to reach the top of the trestlework and pillars, which are covered in oil. Reaching the top, they cut down the food and throw it to the frame below, where it is taken by spectators. Whoever claims the wind banner at the top is declared the winner. There are a variety of other events, including the water lantern old street tour, releasing water lanterns into Zhu'an River a day before the ghost gates close, and Beiguan Battle. There is a period of one month between the first day when the ghost gates open and the last day when Qianggu is held. In addition to remembering the ancestors and their pioneering efforts, the month includes a variety of religious traditional and folk culture events.

源自於清代，在中元節的普渡後，會將祭祀的供品提供民眾搶奪，或有一說是為了嚇退流連忘返的鬼魂，稱為「搶孤」。頭城搶孤是臺灣規模最大的搶孤活動，也為宜蘭縣傳統農曆七月之民間重要活動之一。高聳参天的搶孤棚，是以福杉製成的棚柱，高約十一公尺，寬約八公尺；其上再以約七、八丈高的青竹編紮成為孤棧；棧上綁繫包含魷魚、肉粽、米粉、肉、魚等多樣食品。

参賽隊伍必須以疊羅漢方式，才能攀上塗滿牛油的棚柱及孤棧，在攀登過程中所割下的食品則丟下棚架供棚下觀眾撿拾，取下棧尾的順風旗才算奪標。另外還有水燈遊街之老街巡禮、鬼門關閉前一天之竹安河口放水燈、北管鬥陣...等活動，內容包羅萬象。從七月一日中元鬼門開的第一天，至七月底鬼門關閉的搶孤，為期一個月，除了紀念篳路藍縷的開蘭先賢，更結合豐富的宗教傳統與民俗文化活動等。

Pingxi Lantern Festival 平溪天燈節

The Pingxi Sky Lantern Festival is one of the most colorful activities of the Lantern Festival. Pingxi is a remote hillside town. In the past, those who worked or farmed in the mountains faced the risk of being robbed or killed, and they used lanterns to inform their families they were safe. The lanterns do not function as signals anymore, but are now used as symbols of peace and good fortune.

平溪放天燈是元宵節當晚另一項精彩的活動。追溯平溪天燈的由來，主要因新北市平溪區地處偏遠山區，早年入山開拓者常遭殺害搶劫，為便於通信，乃以放天燈的方式來互報平安。流傳至今，平溪放天燈已不再具有互通信息的功能，而演變成元宵夜的一項觀光活動，成為遊人許願祈福的象徵物。

Bombing Master Han Dan – Taitung county 炸寒單 – 臺東

The Lantern Festival is celebrated on the 15th day of the first month of the Chinese lunar calendar with a series of activities throughout Taiwan. Among the highlight events at this time is the inspection tour of the deity Master Han Dan in Taitung City. As guardian of the celestial treasury, Master Han Dan is revered today as a God of wealth, but people believe that he was once a real person named Zhao Gong-ming. When the Master Han Dan makes his annual inspection tour of the earthly world, crowds turn out to pray for his blessing and for good fortune. On the day of the festival, Master Han Dan is joined on his tour of the community by gods from, other temples in Taitung and surrounding townships.

Households along the route of the divine procession prepare offerings of fresh flowers and fruit, and light strings of firecrackers to welcome the Master Han Dan. The person representing the Master Han Dan on the tour wears only a headscarf, mask and pair of red short. He stands courageously amid the fusillade of firecrackers, protected only by a tree branch.

每年農曆元月十五日鬧元宵的時候，臺東市主要活動是「寒單爺出巡」。對民眾來說，便是接財神爺。因為相傳寒單爺，是封神榜中，管天庫、善聚財的武財神趙公明，所以一出巡，大家爭相迎接，在一年之始討個吉利。祂生性怕冷，所以又稱寒單爺。當天，各鄉鎮廟宇和臺東市各寺廟一樣，眾神齊聚繞境。家家戶戶不只準備香案，供上鮮花水果，而一串串鞭炮，更是迎寒單爺所不可少的。扮這位財神爺的人，頭上紮著頭巾並蒙著臉，身上僅穿件紅色短褲，赤裸上身，接受民眾鞭炮轟擊。他手上雖拿著小樹枝，但只稍作撥弄掩護，表現其勇武不懼的精神。

Religious Activities 宗教慶典活動

Dajia Mazu Pilgrimage 大甲馬祖遶境

Mazu, the Goddess of the Sea, migrated to Taiwan with the people of Fujian Province in the 17th century to become one of the most revered deities on the island, where today about 870 temples are dedicated to her worship. Mazu's birthday falls in the third month of the Chinese lunar calendar, and at that time temples all over the island hold birthday activities including the burning of incense and tours of the deities around their domains. Some of the largest of the celebrations take place at Dajia's Zhenlan Temple in Taichung City, Lugang's Tianhou Temple in Changhua County, Chaotian Temple in Yunlin County, Datianhou Temple in Tainan City, and Fengtian Temple in Chiayi County. Zhenlan Temple's is the largest celebration of all, and also has the longest history.

十七世紀以來，媽祖隨著閩南一帶的移民信眾分靈來臺奉祀後，即成為臺灣民間百姓普遍的信仰。臺灣各地共有870餘間媽祖廟，每逢農曆3月媽祖誕辰，全臺各地如臺中市大甲鎮瀾宮、彰化縣鹿港天后宮、雲林縣北港朝天宮、嘉義縣新港奉天宮、臺南市大天后宮等廟宇都會擴大舉辦祭祀、進香、遶境等活動，其中尤以臺中市大甲鎮瀾宮的媽祖遶境，歷史最久且規模最盛大。

Burning of the Plague God Boat in Donggang 東港燒王船

The burning of the plague god boat is a folk ritual practiced by fishermen in southwestern Taiwan. The original purpose of this ritual was to send the Plague God out to the sea, taking disease and pestilence along with him. Today, it has become an activity whose purpose is to solicit peace and good fortune. In Donggang, Pingtung County, the festival is held once every three years, around the ninth month of the Chinese lunar calendar, at Donglong Temple. There is also another festival, held in the middle of the fourth month, at Qing'an Temple in Xigang, Tainan County. Generally, the Donggang event is larger. These celebrations include large-scale temple activities which climax with the burning of the plague god boat on the last day.

The Donggang boat-burning celebration runs for eight days and seven nights. According to custom, first the boat is set on fire by devotees as other participants prepare goods for the symbolic trip. Then a big fire is made--(to force any bad spirits and the Plague God to go aboard)--and the boat is finally burned as the devotees pray for peace.

「東港迎王平安祭」為臺灣西南沿海著名的民俗祭典之一，原始用意為送瘟神出海，如今已演變成祈安降福的活動。每三年舉行一次的「東港迎王平安祭」約在農曆9月份於屏東縣東港鎮東隆宮舉行，西港燒王船在農曆4月中旬於臺南市西港區慶安宮舉行，其中「東港迎王平安祭」場面最為熱鬧盛大，聞名全臺，除廟會活動外，最後一天的燒王船儀式更是整個祭典的高潮。

整個祭典為期8天7夜，包含請王、過火、遶境、宴王、送王等諸多儀式。整艘王船仿古戰船而建，以紙和木材搭建，造價數百萬，雕工精細華美。在燒王船之前，東隆宮會為王爺及部屬們添配許多航行中的必備品，如梳洗、衣服、食物、神轎、桌椅等，並且舉行盛大的「宴王」儀式，以突顯祭典之隆重；「送王」儀式選在凌晨吉時開始伴隨著一連串鞭炮聲，王船緩緩起航，接著引燃熊熊大火(寓意將不好的瘟神邪神押解上船)，連同代天巡狩的王爺一起離開，祈求平安降福。

Indigenous Ceremonies 原住民慶典活動

Mayasvi Ceremony for the Tsou tribe 鄒族－戰祭

The Mayasvi is the holiest of all the religious ceremonies of the Tsou tribe. In the early years, it was held before a battle or hunt; today, it is held annually in February and is alternately organized by the communities of Dabang and Tefuye in Chiayi County. The ceremony is held at the tribal gathering house for men (Kupah).

The tribe's war ceremony includes the rites of triumph, rites for the heads of the enemies, and welcoming rites for the gods.

戰祭(Mayasvi)是鄒族部落中最神聖的祭典，早年依征戰及狩獵的情況擇期舉行，如今則於每年國曆2月份左右，由達邦及特富野二社輪流舉辦，固定於男子聚集會所(庫巴)舉行。

鄒族的戰祭又有「凱旋祭」、「人頭祭」等說法，其主要供奉征戰之神，除向其祈求戰力外，也藉此求得神靈的庇祐，並含有激勵族人士氣的功用。

The Ear-Shooting Festive for the Bunun tribe 布農族－打耳祭

The Ear-shooting Festival is the most important celebration of the Bunun people. Held at from the end of the April and to the beginning of the May, the celebration is divided into sowing rites, hunting rites, and ear-shooting rites; pig roasting, apportioning the meat, and storing the meat; work celebrations, witch inductions, and other major activities.

The traditional ear-shooting ceremony starts well before the celebration itself when the young men of the tribe go into the mountains and hunt. Then they cut off the ears of their kills, sticking the ears on a pole or a tree branch for the village men to shoot with arrows. Little children, accompanied by their fathers and older brothers, also practice shooting arrows, hoping that this will enable them to become good hunters.

打耳祭是布農族一年中最重要的祭典，約在每年4月下旬至5月初舉行；祭典主要分成狩獵、射耳、烤豬肉、分豬肉、獵槍祭、誇功慶、成巫祭等主要活動。

傳統的「打耳祭」，在祭典舉行前成年男子都必須上山打獵，將獵物的耳朵割下掛在木架或樹枝上，讓全村的男子輪流用弓箭射擊；而年幼的孩子則由父兄陪伴，到場中練習射擊，如此可訓練他們日後成為狩獵的高手。

Flying Fish Festival of the 達悟族－飛魚祭

The lives of the Yami people are closely intertwined with the Flying Fish Festival. Each year the flying fish come with the Kuroshio Current from January to June, and this brings a rich harvest of fish for the Yami living on Orchid Island. That is why the tribe's people believe that these fish are gifts from the gods, and why they treasure this natural resource. Some of the tribe's social customs and taboos are also closely associated with the coming and going of the flying fish.

達悟族和飛魚有著密不可分的關係，每年1~6月間飛魚會隨著黑潮而來，帶給蘭嶼達悟族人莫大的豐收。因此，達悟族人相信飛魚是神的賜予，格外珍惜這項天然資源，甚至一些日常生活中的規律和禁忌，也隨著飛魚洄游的生態來明訂。

The Flying Fish Festival consists of ceremonies that begin in the second or third month of the lunar calendar and run for approximately four months. The festival is divided into different parts, including the blessing of the boats, praying for a bountiful catch, summoning the fish, first-fishing night ceremony, fish storing ceremony, and fishing cessation ceremony. The men of the tribe wear loincloths, silver helmets, and gold strips, and face the sea to pray for a bountiful catch. Participation is restricted to men.

「飛魚祭」是一種獵魚的儀式，約在每年農曆2、3月間舉行，為期近4個月。整個活動分為祈豐魚祭、招魚祭、飛魚收藏祭等階段。祭典時，達悟族男子會穿著丁字褲、頭戴銀盔及金片，面向大海祈求飛魚豐收。而此項活動僅限於男性參加。

Harvest Festival of the Amis tribe 阿美族－豐年祭

The Harvest Festival is the largest festival of the Amis tribe. Different villages hold separate festivals during July and August; the festival has three stages, including welcoming the spirits, feasting the spirits, and sending the spirits off. In modern times, the ceremony has been shortened and the religious ceremonies simplified. Several activities have been added, including a race, tug-of-war, and arrow shooting competition. The festivities, once limited to tribal participation, are now open to the general public.

「豐年祭」是阿美族人最盛大的活動，不同的部落於每年7、8月間分別舉辦。整個過程包含「迎靈」、「宴靈」和「送靈」三階段。現今，除了祭典天數縮短、宗教儀式簡化外，亦在活動中加入賽跑、拔河、射箭等競技活動助興，一般遊客也可加入同歡。

Public Holidays in Taiwan 臺灣的節慶

Taiwan hosts four major festivals: Chinese New Year, Lantern Festival, Dragon Boat Festival, and Mid-Autumn Festival. Among them, Chinese New Year, or Spring Festival, is the most significant. It's called "passing the year," marked by house cleaning to sweep away the previous year's misfortune. "Gathering around the stove" is vital for family reunions, and red envelopes with cash are given to children for future peace and fortune.

Lantern Festival, known as "Little New Year," involves god worship, lantern riddles, rice-flour dumplings, and releasing lanterns in New Taipei City's Pingxi Township.

Dragon Boat Festival on the 5th day of the lunar calendar's 5th month honors poet-patriot Qu Yuan. Dragon boat races and glutinous rice dumplings (zongzi) are highlights. It's believed to ward off evil, leading to customs like hanging calamus and wearing fragrant sachets.

Mid-Autumn Festival, known as "Moon Day," exudes romance. Activities revolve around the moon, with moon cakes and pomelos symbolizing unity. Strolling under the full moon is common, and recently, barbecues while enjoying the moon's radiance with family and friends have gained popularity.

台灣有四個重要的節日：春節、元宵節、端午節和中秋節。其中最重要的是新年又稱為“春節”，也被稱為“過年”，以清掃房屋來掃除前一年的不幸。對於家庭團聚至關重要的是圍爐，同時也會發紅包給孩子，以期未來和平與幸運；元宵節，又稱為“小新年”，包括神靈祭祀、猜燈謎、糯米粉糰和在新北市平溪區放天燈；端午節在農曆五月五日，以紀念詩人兼愛國者屈原。龍舟比賽和粽子是亮點。而也有掛菖蒲和佩戴香囊被認為能驅邪的習俗。中秋節，又稱為“月節”，充滿浪漫氣息。活動圍繞月亮展開，月餅和柚子象徵團結。在明亮的月光下漫步很常見，現今則是與家人朋友一起賞月的同時一邊烤肉變得越來越受歡迎。

International Spotlight 國際光點

The "Nationwide International Spotlight" project aims to uncover Taiwan's unique and appealing destinations, utilizing technology and regional development. By merging, activating, and elevating these areas into the "GIFT Cluster" (Good Inspiration From Taiwan), the project seeks to enhance Taiwan's global tourism competitiveness and boost tourist revisit rates.

This initiative encompasses several clusters: Nanao's natural farm cluster in Yilan, the Fu-Hsing Aboriginal fruit orchard cluster in Taoyuan, the Puli landscape and paper craft cluster in Nantou, the Dongding tea agronomy cluster in Lugu, Nantou, and the Hakka arts and design cluster in Meinong, Kaohsiung. These clusters will be developed and promoted in different phases.

The project's standout feature lies in aligning tourism with technology, empowering cluster operators to effectively manage local resources. This allows international tourists to independently arrange flexible itineraries using convenient information, offering immersive experiences close to nature through hands-on learning. This model encourages visitors to become friendly patrons of Taiwan, using concepts such as working holidays or custom farming tourism.

"國際光點計畫" 致力於利用技術以及區域發展，發掘出台灣獨特而吸引人的景點。通過將這些地區整合再造並提升為 "GIFT Cluster" （Good Inspiration From Taiwan，台灣的焦點），該項目旨在提升台灣的全球旅遊吸引力，增加遊客的回流率。

該計劃涵蓋了幾個地點：宜蘭南澳的自然農場、桃園復興的原住民果園、南投埔里的風景與工藝紙、南投鹿谷的凍頂茶農業，以及高雄美濃的客家藝術與設計。這些資源將分成不同階段進行開發和推廣。

該計劃的顯著特點在於將旅遊與技術相互結合，賦予經營者有效管理資源的能力。這使得國際遊客能夠利用便利取得的資訊，獨立自主安排行程，透過實作學習所提供的沉浸式體驗去貼近自然。這個模式鼓勵遊客成為台灣友客，運用工作假期或定制農業旅遊等概念。

資料參考：交通部觀光局 www.taiwan.net.tw

Note

| Apple of one's eye 珍愛的人 |

無論在東方還是西方，人們一直將蘋果視為一種吉祥的水果。「**Apple of one's eye**」用來表示珍貴的東西，常被形容「真愛的人或物」。此說法最早出現於聖經，詩篇**17:8**：**Keep me as the apple of the eye, hide me under the shadow of thy wings.**

在**2011**年，臺灣發行的青春愛情片電影《那些年，我們一起追的女孩》，英文片名正是 **"You're The Apple Of My Eye"**！當中的**apple**是指人的瞳孔，形容你倒映在我的瞳孔內，即「我的眼裡只有你」的意思。

參考資料

- 考選部
- 柯旗化 新英文法 第一出版社
- 仲華美語
- 劉毅 文法寶典 學習出版社
- 林語堂
- 陳思 新英文法
- 維基百科

絕對考上導遊+領隊. 英語篇 = Tour leader & tour guide : for English license / 陳安琪總編輯. -- 十一版. - 臺北市 : 馬跡庫比有限公司, 馬跡領隊導遊訓練中心, 2023.09　面；　公分

ISBN 978-626-97748-0-7 (平裝)

1.CST: 英語 2.CST: 導遊 3.CST: 領隊 4.CST: 讀本

805.18　　112014287

絕對考上 導遊＋領隊 TOUR GUIDE & TOUR LEADER【英語篇】

出　　版　馬跡庫比有限公司 / 馬跡領隊導遊訓練中心

總 編 輯　陳安琪

製作團隊　馬崇淵 楊惠萍 羅永青等暨馬跡中心講師 編製

單字導讀　王翊玟

內容增修　劉志鴻 陳燕亭

地　　址　臺北市大安區復興南路二段 268 號 5 樓

電　　話　(02) 2733-8118

傳　　真　(02) 2733-8033

馬跡官網　https://www.magee.tw

匯款帳號　台北富邦銀行 (012) - 和平分行 ｜ 帳號 : 4801-027-027-88

戶名 : 馬跡庫比有限公司

E-MAIL　magee@magee.tw

出版日期
2012 年 10 月 初版一刷
2013 年 09 月 二版一刷
2014 年 08 月 三版一刷
2015 年 08 月 四版一刷
2016 年 09 月 五版一刷
2017 年 08 月 六版一刷
2018 年 08 月 七版一刷
2019 年 08 月 八版一刷
2020 年 09 月 九版一刷
2022 年 09 月 十版一刷
2023 年 09 月 十一版一刷

定　　價　480 元